"Chris Kuzneski . . . completely understands what makes for a good story: action, sex, suspense, humor, and great characters."
—Nelson DeMille

PRAISE FOR

THE PROPHECY

"Kuzneski has hit his stride. He's writing at full throttle, with unparalleled acceleration and expert control. Hop aboard for a great ride."
—Steve Berry, *New York Times* bestselling author of *The Emperor's Tomb*

"A page-turner extraordinaire, rippling with dark legends, violence, and pulse-pounding excitement. Payne and Jones are fabulous!"
—Douglas Preston, *New York Times* bestselling coauthor of *Fever Dream*

"*The Prophecy* takes a sharp look at the enduring mystery of Nostradamus in a fresh, exciting way. Reminiscent of Dan Brown, only better!"
—David Hagberg, *New York Times* bestselling author of *The Cabal*

"Kuzneski has the Da Vinci Code formula down pat: cool, collected heroes who know a lot about a lot; short, action-filled chapters; a riddle wrapped in a mystery inside an enigma . . . Those who enjoy the books of Dan Brown and Steve Berry, among others, should have fun as Kuzneski skips across continents, moving from clue to clue."
—*Booklist*

"Once you start *The Prophecy*, don't plan on sleeping. Chris Kuzneski really knows how to tell a story. Action, adventure, humor, *The Prophecy* has it all. Find someplace comfortable and settle in for a great time!"
—Brett Battles, Barry Award–winning author of *Shadow of Betrayal*

"Chris Kuzneski knows what thriller readers crave—nonstop action, ancient mysteries, twisted villains, and memorable heroes. Kuzneski's books have got it all!"
—Boyd Morrison, author of *The Ark*

continued . . .

THE LOST THRONE

"A reader's delight from beginning to end. Tautly written, expertly told, smart, and exhilarating."

—Steve Berry, *New York Times* bestselling author of *The Emperor's Tomb*

"A gripping, fantastic read that guarantees chills, laughs, and pulse-pounding action!"

—David Morrell, *New York Times* bestselling author of *First Blood*

"One hell of a thrill ride, mixing the intensity of *300* and the adventure of *Raiders of the Lost Ark*."

—Vince Flynn, *New York Times* bestselling author of *American Assassin*

"A fast and furious thrill ride with the perfect amount of history and humor blended in."

—Raymond Khoury, *New York Times* bestselling author of *The Templar Salvation*

"A lightning-paced tale that seamlessly stitches threads from the past into the fabric of the present. Genre giants Steve Berry, James Rollins, and Brad Thor may soon find themselves looking over their shoulders . . . A smoothly layered, serpentine, and scintillating thriller."

—Jon Land, national bestselling author of *Strong Justice*

"A fresh new voice that you won't forget."

—W.E.B. Griffin, *New York Times* bestselling author of *The Vigilantes*

"Kept me turning pages all night long. Kuzneski has written a superb thriller that you won't be able to put down."

—James Swain, *New York Times* bestselling author of *The Night Monster*

SWORD OF GOD

"Kuzneski is a master in the making . . . A nonstop locomotive of a thriller that had me burning the midnight oil 'til breakfast."

—Vince Flynn, *New York Times* bestselling author of *American Assassin*

TITLES BY CHRIS KUZNESKI

The Plantation

Sign of the Cross

Sword of God

The Lost Throne

The Prophecy

THE PROPHECY

CHRIS KUZNESKI

BERKLEY BOOKS
New York

THE BERKLEY PUBLISHING GROUP
Published by the Penguin Group
Penguin Group (USA) Inc.
375 Hudson Street, New York, New York 10014, USA

Penguin Group (Canada), 90 Eglinton Avenue East, Suite 700, Toronto, Ontario M4P 2Y3, Canada
(a division of Pearson Penguin Canada Inc.)
Penguin Books Ltd., 80 Strand, London WC2R 0RL, England
Penguin Group Ireland, 25 St. Stephen's Green, Dublin 2, Ireland (a division of Penguin Books Ltd.)
Penguin Group (Australia), 250 Camberwell Road, Camberwell, Victoria 3124, Australia
(a division of Pearson Australia Group Pty. Ltd.)
Penguin Books India Pvt. Ltd., 11 Community Centre, Panchsheel Park, New Delhi—110 017, India
Penguin Group (NZ), 67 Apollo Drive, Rosedale, Auckland 0632, New Zealand
(a division of Pearson New Zealand Ltd.)
Penguin Books (South Africa) (Pty.) Ltd., 24 Sturdee Avenue, Rosebank, Johannesburg 2196,
South Africa

Penguin Books Ltd., Registered Offices: 80 Strand, London WC2R 0RL, England

This is a work of fiction. Names, characters, places, and incidents either are the product of the author's imagination or are used fictitiously, and any resemblance to actual persons, living or dead, business establishments, events, or locales is entirely coincidental. The publisher does not have any control over and does not assume any responsibility for author or third-party websites or their content.

THE PROPHECY

A Berkley Book / published by arrangement with the author

PRINTING HISTORY
G. P. Putnam's Sons hardcover edition / July 2010
Berkley premium edition / July 2011

ISBN: 978-0-425-24205-6

BERKLEY®
Berkley Books are published by The Berkley Publishing Group,
a division of Penguin Group (USA) Inc.,
375 Hudson Street, New York, New York 10014.
BERKLEY® is a registered trademark of Penguin Group (USA) Inc.
The "B" design is a trademark of Penguin Group (USA) Inc.

PRINTED IN THE UNITED STATES OF AMERICA

10 9 8 7 6 5 4 3 2 1

ACKNOWLEDGMENTS

As always, I'd like to start off by thanking my family. Without their love and support, I wouldn't be the writer (or the person) that I am today. Thanks for putting up with me!

Professionally, I want to thank my agent, Scott Miller. Before we teamed up, I was a lowly, self-published author. Now my books are available in more than twenty languages around the world. How he pulled off that miracle, I'll never know—but I'm guessing incriminating photos and blackmail were involved. While I'm at it, I want to thank Claire Roberts and everyone else at Trident Media who has helped my career during the past few years.

Although there are dozens of people to thank at Penguin, I'd like to single out my editor, Natalee Rosenstein, and her amazing assistant, Michelle Vega. Working with them has been wonderful. I'd also like to thank

Ivan Held and the publishing and marketing wizards at Putnam.

Next up is my good friend Ian Harper, who gets to read my work before anyone else. Even though he's strong enough to kill a rhinoceros with his bare hands, his suggestions and advice are surgically precise. If anyone's looking for a freelance editor (or is having problems with large horned mammals), please let me know. I'd be happy to put you in touch with him.

Finally, I'd like to thank all the readers, librarians, booksellers, and critics who have read my thrillers and have recommended them to others. At this stage of my career, I need all the help I can get, so I would appreciate your continued support.

Okay, I think that just about covers it. It's finally time to get to the good stuff. Without further delay, please sit back, relax, and let me tell you a story . . .

PROLOGUE

JUNE 17, 1566

Salon-de-Provence, France

The letter was written by an apothecary who had gained his notoriety in another field. Knowing the uproar it would cause, Michel sealed it and several documents inside a wooden box. He gave the box to his lawyer on the same day he signed his last will and testament.

The year was 1566. He was sixty-two years old.

He died fifteen days later.

When his possessions were divided among his heirs, the box was not mentioned. If it had been, the rest of his estate would have seemed inconsequential, for the contents of the box were far more valuable than gold or jewels or anything else he owned. Knowing this, he added a secret codicil to his will that only his lawyer knew about. The four-page appendix described in very specific terms what was to be done with the mysterious box and, more important, *when*.

To ensure that his wishes were followed, Michel established a trust fund that compensated the guardians of his secret from one generation to the next. None of these men knew who their benefactor was—otherwise curiosity would have overwhelmed them, tempting them to open the box. Instead, all they were given was a date and a simple set of instructions.

If they completed their task, they would be paid handsomely for their efforts.

If they didn't, they wouldn't see a cent.

Amazingly, the chain remained unbroken for more than four hundred years. Decade after decade, century after century, they followed their orders like scripture and were rewarded as promised. Wars raged throughout Europe, but somehow the box survived. Cities burned to the ground, but somehow the box survived. No matter what happened, no matter where it was stored, the box *always* survived—as if it had a guardian angel. Or was protected by magic.

Those familiar with Michel might have suspected the latter, since he had been publicly accused of practicing "the dark arts" on more than one occasion. But those charges never stuck. Partially because of his connection to the queen of France, a loyal patron who believed in his special powers, and partially because of his cunning. Nearly everything he had written was hidden in plain sight, published for the world to see, but purposely ambiguous. This was his way of avoiding prosecution. Authorities couldn't convict him of witchcraft or wizardry because his writings could be interpreted in a variety of ways, most of which were benign.

Yet most scholars knew his work was anything but innocuous. They realized it was complex, and layered, and intentionally cryptic. A riddle, wrapped in a mystery, inside an enigma. Just like the man himself. Of course, Michel knew how he was perceived, which was why he penned his final letter in straightforward language and sealed it inside the box.

This was his last chance to explain himself to the world.

His last chance to warn the human race.

1

Louis Keller had been waiting for this moment for more than thirty years, ever since his dying father had explained what must be done in the distant future. For five generations, their family had been in charge of a mysterious trust fund at Credit Suisse, the second-largest bank in Switzerland, and now, after three decades of waiting, the big day was finally here.

Keller would soon be free.

In the beginning, he had viewed his duties with frustration, nothing more than a silly game that his father had forced him to play. But as the years went on, his viewpoint had started to change. What had once been a mild annoyance was now a burden he was forced to bear, a yoke he couldn't shake. Although he was a healthy man, he'd had trouble sleeping in recent months, afraid he would pass away before he completed his final task, worried he would let down his ancestors. He realized it was a foolish thought, completely irrational, yet he knew the weight wouldn't be lifted until he had fulfilled his obligation.

Then, and only then, could he sleep in peace.

Wearing a dark suit and overcoat, Keller entered the bank as soon as it opened on the first morning of December. He nodded to the elderly guard who had unlocked the door, removed his fedora in the warmth of the foyer, then climbed the stairs to the main lobby.

Although he had visited this building on many occasions, he was always reassured by its architecture. In his opinion, every bank should be built this way: marble floors, stone pillars, and vaulted ceilings. Everything about the place felt solid, as a proper bank should. Like a medieval fortress or a modern museum. Over the years he had spent some time in the United States and was amazed at the inferiority of its banks. Oftentimes they were wedged into local shopping malls or grocery stores, nothing more than plastic countertops and fake wood paneling squeezed into cheap retail space. Nothing about them seemed safe or secure, which probably explained why the wealthiest Americans deposited their fortunes in Swiss banks.

For peace of mind. And to hide it from Uncle Sam.

Keller smiled at the thought as he strode past the bank tellers, all of whom were locked behind sturdy iron bars, and made his way toward the safe-deposit vault. It was downstairs, nestled underneath the lobby floor. To gain access to the facility, customers were required to pass through security. Ten years earlier, everything had been done with picture IDs and signature cards. Now the system was high-tech, like something out of a Hollywood movie.

As he approached the first checkpoint, Keller removed his leather gloves and tucked them into the pockets of his overcoat. Still stiff from the morning cold, he cracked his knuckles, then typed his ten-digit alphanumeric code into the computer. The hard drive whirred for several seconds before his password was accepted and additional instructions filled the screen.

Knowing the procedure by heart, Keller ignored the monitor and placed his hand on the scanner, making sure his fingers were positioned in the proper slots. Instantly, a beam of green light, which resembled the lamp inside a copy machine, moved under the surface of his hand. Starting at the tips of his fingers, it slowly made its way toward the base of his palm, analyzing the ridge structures of his skin and the nuances of his hand. In a flash, millions of computations were made, and his identity was verified: Louis Keller, age fifty-two.

A split second later, the electronic lock buzzed in front of him.

Keller opened the door, glanced over his shoulder to make sure no one was behind him, then walked inside and pulled the door shut. After double-checking the lock, he turned and faced the marble staircase that led to the vault below. A uniformed guard waited for his arrival.

"Bonjour, monsieur."

"Bonjour," Keller said as he pulled out his passport.

The guard inspected the document, compared the

name and photo to the information on his computer monitor, then asked Keller to sign the electronic tablet on the security desk. Once his signature was verified, he was finally granted access to the floor.

"Merci."

Keller nodded politely, tucked his passport into his jacket pocket, and headed toward the massive vault. Made with steel-reinforced concrete, its walls were three feet thick and virtually indestructible. Over the years he had been tempted to move the contents of his safe-deposit box to a newer bank down the street, which always bragged about its sleek, modern vault. However, after consulting with a structural engineer, he learned that the older vaults were actually harder to break into—unless their locks had never been upgraded. But Credit Suisse had spared no expense installing a dual-control combination lock that worked in conjunction with a separate time lock designed to deny any access during nonbusiness hours.

Since the bank had just opened, Keller was the first visitor of the morning. A citrus scent lingered in the air, as if the floor had been waxed the night before. Hundreds of brass locks lined the left and right walls. Several of the boxes were as wide as a brick; others were much larger. The biggest boxes filled the far wall. A few of them were so massive they looked like they could hold caskets. Keller had always wondered what treasures were hidden within: gold, jewels, stacks of foreign currency. Whatever it was, he knew it had to be valuable because a box of that size cost thousands of dollars to rent.

By comparison, his box was a bargain. It measured two feet by two feet and never cost him anything since it was financed by the mysterious trust fund. A long time ago, he had tried to track down the original source of the revenue, but the paper trail stopped cold the same year that his family had taken ownership of the box, way back in the 1800s.

Keller stared at the box wistfully, reflecting on his visits over the years. Then, with a lump in his throat, he entered his combination with the brass dial for the final time.

Seven . . . two . . . fifteen.

As the tumblers fell into place, he pulled his safe-deposit key from his pocket and shoved it into the lock. As the key twisted to the right, the metal door popped open with a *click*.

Keller smiled at the sound; a mixture of joy and relief filled his face.

The big moment was finally here.

After three decades of waiting, thirty-plus years of stress and anxiety and sleepless nights, he was about to fulfill the promise that he had made to his dying father.

After all that time, Keller could *finally* breathe a sigh of relief.

But not until he followed the instructions within.

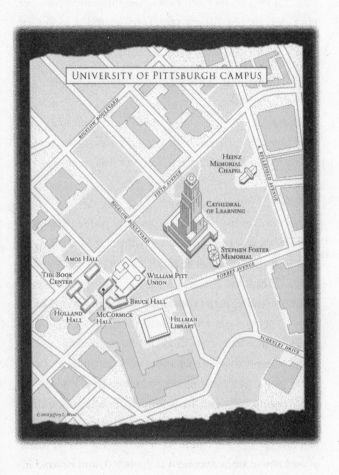

2

University of Pittsburgh
Pittsburgh, Pennsylvania

Dressed in black, the shadowy figure trudged through the blizzard on the nearly deserted campus. Six inches of snow had already fallen, and three more were expected by midnight, thanks to a storm that blanketed the region. Although the evening's temperature was in the upper twenties, it felt much colder as a result of the harsh winds that whipped down the empty streets, pelting everything with ice.

Lowering his head, he continued onward, unwilling to stop despite the tiny crystals that had formed on his hair and clothes. He had lived in the city for several years, so he knew Forbes Avenue was up ahead, and beyond it, his final destination.

Dedicated in 1937, the Cathedral of Learning towers above the University of Pittsburgh (Pitt) campus. The sand-colored skyscraper stands forty-two stories high and contains more than two thousand rooms. Its steel frame, overlaid with Indiana limestone, is Gothic Revival in design, similar in style to the Palace of Westminster in London and St. Patrick's Cathedral in New York.

Simply put, it is one of the most breathtaking buildings in the world.

On most nights, the golden lights on top of the Cathedral can be seen for miles, but because of the snow, he could barely see the building from across Bigelow Boulevard.

Five minutes later, he tramped up the stone stairs behind the panther-head fountain, then stomped his feet outside the main entrance of the Cathedral, trying to clean his dress shoes the best he could. After brushing the ice from his clothes and hair, he straightened his bow tie and pushed his way through the giant revolving door. A surge of warm air greeted him inside the building, as did two female students, a blonde and a redhead, who were manning the registration table.

"Good evening, sir," said the blonde. "May I take your coat?"

The black man nodded as he took off his overcoat, revealing a tuxedo underneath. He wasn't used to fancy clothes. In fact, the last time he had worn a tux was at his senior prom, nearly twenty years before. But because of the formality of the event, he had promised to wear one. Not that he was happy about it. If he'd had his way, he would have been on the other side of campus—near the building where Dr. Jonas Salk developed the polio vaccine—settling into his seat at the sold-out Petersen Events Center, watching the Pitt basketball team beat

Duke University in front of a raucous college crowd. Instead, his evening would consist of boring speeches, watered-down drinks, and cheese cubes on toothpicks. Or so he thought.

The redhead looked at the guest list. "And you are?"

A voice from the side answered for him. "That's the infamous David Jones."

Jones turned and snarled at Jonathon Payne. Not only was Payne his best friend, he was the only reason that Jones was there. "Don't start with me, Jon. I'm not in the mood."

Also dressed in a tux, Payne put his massive hand on his friend's shoulder and squeezed. "What's wrong, princess? Still pissed about the game?"

"Of course I'm pissed. We're playing *Duke*."

Payne shrugged. He wasn't happy about it, either. Even though he had played football and basketball at the U.S. Naval Academy, he had been a Pitt fan since birth. "Like I told you, the event was planned before the game was scheduled. There was nothing I could do."

"But it's *your* event," Jones complained. "You should've canceled it."

Payne laughed at the thought. Five hundred of the area's wealthiest people were gathered inside for a black-tie gala. The goal was to raise money for local charities and the continued renovation of the Cathedral of Learning. "This isn't the type of event that you can cancel."

"Well, the least you could've done was ask for better weather. I froze my ass off outside."

"I find that hard to believe."

"I'm telling you, I had to walk a mile from my parking spot."

"Why in the world did you do that?"

"Because the street outside was blocked off."

"Yeah, blocked off for valet parking."

"Seriously?" Jones demanded.

"Seriously," Payne said, laughing. "Come on, you should know better than that. Rich people don't walk anywhere. Especially not in a foot of snow."

Jones glanced at the two female students, who were nodding their heads in total agreement. As if only a moron would think otherwise.

"Son of a bitch," he mumbled to Payne. "I'm so cold I can't feel my nuggets."

"Well, don't look at me. I'm not going to feel them for you."

"That's not what I meant."

"I should hope not," Payne teased. "Heck, you'd have to donate a hell of a lot of money for me to even consider something like that."

"Knock it off, Jon. I simply meant—" He paused in mid-sentence, realizing there was no reason to explain himself. "Which way to the bar?"

Payne pointed to the right. "It's over there."

"Thank God. Me and my boys need a drink. Wake me when your speech is over."

JONATHON PAYNE was the CEO of Payne Industries, a multinational corporation founded by his grandfather, a self-made millionaire who went from mill worker to mill owner in less than thirty years. Payne had shunned the family business as a youngster—opting instead for a decorated career as a Special Forces officer—but returned home when his grandfather passed away and left him controlling interest in the company.

Although he willingly took over for his grandfather, the man who had raised him after Payne's parents were killed in a car accident, he wasn't thrilled about his career change. In private he often joked that business meetings were held in the "bored room," yet he never publicly complained about his obligations, not only to avoid sounding like an ingrate but because he realized his current position had certain advantages. Like the ability to help others. It was something he had always been passionate about. Even in his former life.

In the past, he had used blades and guns to get the job done.

Now he used his quick wit and killer smile.

As host of the charity event, Payne took the stage in the center of the Commons Room, a four-story Gothic hall in the belly of the tallest academic building in the Western hemisphere.

"Ladies and gentlemen," he said as he adjusted the microphone to accommodate his height, "my name is Jonathon Payne. Thank you for braving the cold and coming out tonight."

Dressed in tuxedos and formal gowns, his guests turned toward the podium where Payne waited to kick off his fund-raiser. At six foot four and two hundred and forty pounds, he had the ability to control a room with his physical presence alone. Throw in his charisma and his boyish good looks, and the crowd didn't stand a chance.

"I realize most of you are here for the free cocktails, so I promise I'll be brief."

Payne smiled as he gazed at the sea of faces in front of him. Normally, the great hall was filled with Pitt students doing homework or studying for exams. However, since this was the last day of classes for the fall semester, Pitt's Chancellor Nordenberg had given Payne permission to hold his event where it would have the most success— right across the hall from the Nationality Rooms, one of the main beneficiaries of that evening's fund-raiser.

"We are standing in the Commons Room, which is a true example of Gothic architecture. The stone ceiling is fifty-two feet high and all the arches are self-supporting. How they built them without steel beams is beyond me." Payne paused and looked skyward. No matter how many times he had been inside the Cathedral, he always left impressed. "Amazingly, this entire room was a gift from one man, Pittsburgh native Andrew Mellon."

Applause filled the room, even though Mellon died in 1937, the same year the Cathedral had officially opened. Then again, in the history of Pittsburgh, certain names stood above all others when it came to philanthropy: Andrew Mellon, Andrew Carnegie, and H. J. Heinz.

"As you know, one of the best things about Pittsburgh is the ethnic diversity of our population. Thanks to the steel industry, immigrants from every corner of the world came to our city, looking for jobs. And if you've ever glanced at a local phone book, you know a lot of them stayed." The crowd laughed at the joke. "One of those immigrants was my great-grandfather, who came here from a small town in Poland and actually worked on this building. I never met the man, but according to my grandfather, he had a favorite expression. He used to say, 'If America is the original melting pot, the blast furnaces of Pittsburgh provided the heat.'"

Once again, applause echoed throughout the great hall.

"For those of you who are new to the Cathedral, we are currently surrounded by one of its unique features: the Nationality Rooms. Scattered throughout the first three floors are a collection of twenty-seven classrooms that were donated by many of the ethnic groups that helped to build our wonderful city. By simply walking down one of the corridors, you can visit a Greek classroom from the Age of Pericles, a palace hall from China's Forbidden City, or a room from London's House of Commons. All of these rooms are decorated with authentic artifacts that are meant to enrich the learning experiences of Pitt students and the thousands of visitors who come to the Cathedral every year to learn more about our city's past."

Payne stared into the crowd, making eye contact with as many people as possible.

"One of our main goals tonight is to raise money for these rooms. Not only to aid the preservation of the current classrooms, but hopefully to build several more. This is our way of honoring the ethnic groups that helped shape our city and make it the special place that it is today. With that in mind, we have representatives of more than forty countries here to answer your questions about the Nationality Rooms and to discuss our amazing plans for the future. Who knows? With a little help from you, that future might begin tonight."

Amid loud applause, Payne glanced at the crowd one last time before he left the main stage. As he did, his eyes focused on a solitary figure in the back of the Commons Room. She was standing alone, partially hidden behind a stone column and obscured by shadows. Although he could barely see her, years of training told him that something was wrong.

Somehow he knew she didn't belong.

3

By the time Payne made his way to the back of the room, she was no longer there. He glanced up and down the corridor, hoping to catch a glimpse of her, but a sea of people blocked his view.

"What's wrong?" Jones asked as he approached from behind. He had spent too many years in the trenches with Payne not to recognize his moods. Even from afar.

They used to lead the MANIACs, an elite Special Forces unit composed of the top soldiers from the Marines, Army, Navy, Intelligence, Air Force, and Coast Guard. Whether it was personnel recovery, unconventional warfare, or counterguerrilla sabotage, the MANIACs were considered the best of the best. The boogeymen that no one talked about. The government's secret weapon. And even though they had retired a few years before, the duo was still deadly.

"Nothing," Payne said. "Just looking for someone."

"Does this someone have a name?"

Payne flashed a smile and shrugged, as if to say he didn't know it.

"Let me guess," Jones said. "The woman behind the pillar."

"You spotted her?"

"Of course I spotted her. I had nothing better to do during your speech. Pretty boring stuff, if you ask me. I'll be damned if I'm giving you a cent."

"Did you see what she looked like?"

Jones shrugged. "Couldn't really tell. She stayed in the shadows the entire time, which is why I noticed her. For a minute there, I thought I might have to take her out."

"Please tell me you're not armed."

"Of course I'm armed. I feel naked without my gun."

Payne shook his head. "You brought your gun to a charity event?"

"In my defense, you told me to wear a tux. You said nothing about being unarmed. Oh, and for the record, you also said nothing about valet parking. Or was that for white guests only?"

Payne laughed at the comment. For as long as they had known each other, race had never been an issue, which was why Jones felt comfortable teasing him. Both of them knew it was a joke. Nothing more, nothing less. "Damn! Are you going to be this pissy all night?"

"Probably not," Jones admitted. "Once I thaw out, I'll cheer up."

"You know, I actually thought you might enjoy yourself tonight. You're always talking about history and foreign cultures. Yet here you are, bitching to me instead of mingling with the assembled experts. What's wrong? Are you afraid they might be smarter than you?"

Jones rolled his eyes at the statement. "Come on, you know I'm the smartest person here. And to prove it, I'm going to pester your *experts* until they cry." He emphasized the word *experts* by making air quotes with his fingers. "Oh, yeah, one more thing: If any of your guests asks me where the African Room is, I swear to God I'm gonna shoot 'em."

HER INITIAL goal had been to blend in with her surroundings. She had wanted to get a feel for the room before she finally made her move. But her plan wasn't to be.

They had noticed her immediately, spotting her in the large crowd even though she had stayed in the back shadows of the Cathedral. Less than five minutes later, they had converged on her position, swooping in like predators from both sides of the room. If not for all the people in the hallway, they would have cornered her for sure. The mere thought of it made her heart beat faster. Somehow it gave her hope.

Perhaps, she thought, her long journey had been worthwhile.

Perhaps these guys were as good as she'd heard.

———

PAYNE MADE his way to the registration table, where he talked to the two female students.

"Great speech, Mr. Payne," gushed the blonde. "We were impressed."

"Thank you, ladies. But please, call me Jon."

"Okay, Jon," said the redhead, giggling.

Payne smiled at them. If he had been several years younger, this conversation would have gone in a much different direction, but he decided to focus on the business at hand. "Out of curiosity, did any more guests arrive while I was onstage?"

The blonde shook her head. "Nope, Mr. Jones was the last one here."

The redhead corrected her, "You mean the *infamous* Mr. Jones."

The blonde frowned. "Wait, why is he infamous?"

Payne leaned closer and whispered something. A few seconds later, the blonde burst out laughing. The redhead giggled and blushed.

"Are you serious?" she demanded.

Payne nodded. "Completely. If you don't believe me, ask him yourself."

"No way," said the redhead. "I could never ask him *that*."

The blonde grinned naughtily. "But I could."

Payne laughed for a few seconds before he got the conversation back on track. "So, you're sure no one came in after him."

The redhead furrowed her brow. "Wait! Do you mean guests, or *anyone*?"

"Anyone."

"Oh, in that case, some lady came in. She wasn't a guest, though."

"What was she?" Payne wondered.

"A brunette."

"No, that's not what I meant. Was she a student? A professor? Something else?"

"She was thin," the blonde offered. "Does that help?"

Payne nodded. "At this point, everything helps. Did she leave her name?"

The blonde shook her head. "She didn't leave her coat, either. But it was really cute. It was green and had big buttons."

"Did you talk to her?"

"No," the redhead replied. "She walked right past us and stood over there in the back of the room. I lost sight of her after that. I was watching your speech."

The blonde looked concerned. "Did we do something wrong?"

"Not at all," Payne assured them. "You two are doing a great job. I'll make sure someone brings you some soft drinks and appetizers."

"Thanks," they said in unison.

"Do me a favor, though. When Mr. Jones comes back for his coat, make sure you ask him about what I said." Payne grinned mischievously. "I bet he denies everything."

4

Although he would have preferred the basketball game, this type of event was a great consolation prize for Jones. A voracious reader with a thirst for knowledge, he had always been a fan of history and world culture. Throw in his incredible memory, and he had the ability to spout random facts about every subject imaginable, often to Payne's amazement.

As he roamed the crowded halls of the Cathedral, Jones ducked into a few of his favorite rooms, starting with the German Classroom. Designed to reflect the sixteenth-century German Renaissance, it was based on the Great Hall at the University of Heidelberg. Walnut paneling framed the blackboards. The intarsia doors of the corner cabinets featured images from German folklore, including Lorelei, the beautiful maiden who lured sailors onto the rocks of the Rhine River with her enchanting songs. Wrought-iron chandeliers hung from the extravagant wood ceilings, and rows of walnut arm-chairs graced the floor.

Jones had seen the German Room several times before, but he had never noticed the whimsical details of the stained-glass windows until he overheard one of the tour guides discussing them. The images depicted several characters from the Grimm Brothers' fairy tales, including Hansel and Gretel, Snow White and the Seven Dwarfs, Cinderella, and Little Red Riding Hood.

"I wonder," said the tour guide, "if Walt Disney visited the Cathedral of Learning prior to making his animated classics. If so, this room might have been his inspiration."

A few minutes later, Jones decided to journey across Europe. He bypassed the crowded Italian and Czechoslovak Rooms and headed toward the Syria-Lebanon Room. Because of the extravagance of its furnishings, it was one of two display rooms where no classes were taught. Originally a library and prayer room in a wealthy merchant's home in Damascus, it was moved intact to its current location.

The linden-paneled walls and ceilings were decorated with gesso, a mixture of chalk and glue applied by brush, then painted and overlaid with silver and gold leaf. The room featured a *mihrab*, a decorative niche that indicated the direction of Mecca, and a marble ledge for the placement of the Koran during daily prayers. An old mosque oil lamp made of perforated copper and hand-blown glass wells illuminated the room. The sofas were covered in satin and rested on a dark red and white marble floor that sloped down at the entrance, where visitors were asked to remove their shoes before entering. In 1997, a glass-paneled door was added that allowed the opulent decor to be seen even when the room was closed.

But on this night, the room was open for guided tours. Inside, a Lebanese professor was commenting on the room's furniture. "Very few Americans know this," he said in heavily accented English, "but the word *sofa* comes from the Arabic word *suffa*. According to tradition, it was a reclining piece of wood or stone that was often covered in cushions."

Not surprisingly, Jones already knew that fact and many others about the Arab world. He had acquired most of his knowledge years ago, when his unit was stationed in the Middle East. However, he had recently added to his collection during a classified mission to Mecca, a journey that he and Payne weren't allowed to discuss outside the confines of the Pentagon.

After listening for a moment, Jones walked down the corridor and visited the English Classroom. It was the largest of the Nationality Rooms and was designed in the sixteenth-century Tudor Gothic style of the House of Commons, which was destroyed by Luftwaffe bombing in 1941. The British government rescued several original relics—a stone fireplace, hearth tiles, oak paneling, the entrance door frame, lintels—and donated them to the Cathedral of Learning.

Under the ceiling trusses were four limestone corbels from the House of Commons, carved with a Tudor rose. Stained-glass window medallions depicted the coats of arms of several English towns and cities, literary figures, scholars from Cambridge and Oxford, and the Houses of Lords and Commons. Portraits of Andrew Mellon, former ambassador to the Court of St. James, and William Pitt, the former Earl of Chatham after whom Pittsburgh was named, flanked the stained-glass windows in the rear bay. And a brick from 10 Downing Street, the residence and office of the prime minister of the United Kingdom, served as the room's cornerstone.

As Jones crouched to admire it, he sensed someone staring at him from the entrance to the classroom. Always attentive, he glanced over his shoulder and caught a glimpse of a woman a split second before she hustled into the hallway. Her face was obscured by her shoulder-length brown hair and the collar of her green coat. Long legs and a slender frame were showcased in a snug pair of faded jeans that were tucked into stylish black boots.

Jones stood at once, realizing that this was the same brunette he had seen in the shadows of the Commons Room during Payne's speech. Now she was watching him, too. He didn't feel threatened—his gun and his training put his mind at ease—but he was intrigued.

Who was this woman, and what did she want?

Suddenly, his evening had become a lot more exciting.

PAYNE'S CELL PHONE vibrated in his jacket pocket. He looked at his screen and shook his head before he answered. "Don't tell me you're lost."

"Where are you?" Jones demanded.

"Why?"

"I just spotted your stalker. Now she's following me."

"Where are you?"

"Didn't I just ask you that?"

Payne growled in frustration. "I'm in the Polish Room."

"Of course you are."

"It's near the registration table."

"Then you better hustle. You're on the wrong side of the building. She just left the English Room, number 144. It's in the far corner. I'm not sure where she went, though. She blended in with all the white people."

Payne walked into the corridor, trying to picture the layout of the Cathedral and the nearby streets. Fifth Avenue was to his left, Forbes Avenue to his right. Bigelow Boulevard was behind him, and S. Bellefield Avenue was on the far side of the building, much closer to Jones.

"Take the hallway that runs parallel to Bellefield. I'll take the one along Fifth. Those are the only two routes from your current position."

"Unless you count all the rooms and stairs."

"Worry about them later. For now, concentrate on the hallways."

"Just so you know, she's wearing jeans and a green coat. She should stand out."

Payne nodded in agreement as he passed several older couples who were dressed in formal attire. "Remember, this is a charity event, and she's done nothing wrong. Try not to shoot her."

Jones grinned. "No promises."

"And no running. I don't want anyone else to worry."

"I know, and no sweets between meals. I got it, Mom."

Payne smirked and hung up the phone, which was one of the only ways to stop Jones's yapping. Some of the others included duct tape and medical-grade pharmaceuticals, neither of which Payne had in his tuxedo.

JONES SMILED in triumph when he heard the click of his phone. That meant Payne was unable to think of a suitable retort and had hung up instead.

Keeping his phone in his hand, Jones shifted his attention to his surroundings. This was the same corridor he had strolled down minutes before, so its layout was fresh in his head. The French Classroom was on his immediate left, followed by the Norwegian Classroom, then the Russian Classroom. Up ahead on his right was the Syria-Lebanon Room that he had viewed earlier. After that, the hallway split: stairs to the left, elevators to the right, and several regular classrooms in the distance. Rooms on the first floor were rarely locked, giving students a quiet place to study. Unfortunately, it also gave the woman plenty of places to hide.

At this point, Jones viewed her more as a curiosity than a threat. He had jokingly referred to her as a stalker because she had acted like one when he had spotted her—quickly retreating into the hallway—but he knew her reaction could be explained in several innocent ways. His best guess was she didn't belong at the event. It was invitation-only, and she was obviously underdressed. Perhaps she had hustled away to avoid an embarrassing confrontation.

On the other hand, her behavior had raised a red flag.

And for that reason alone, they were determined to find her.

5

Bruges, Belgium
(60 miles northwest of Brussels)

François Dubois was a very bad man who had impeccable taste.

Although he had been born into an upper-class family, his life of crime had started at an early age on the streets of Paris. During the week, Dubois had attended Lycée Louis-le-Grand (LLG), one of the best secondary schools in the city, known for such alumni as Victor Hugo, Jean-Paul Sartre, and Voltaire. On the weekend, he had run a gang that specialized in robbing tourists near the city's biggest attractions. By the age of sixteen, Dubois had already killed three people.

Worst of all, he had enjoyed it.

Thirty years later, Dubois still had a taste for blood but preferred for his minions to do the dirty work. That way, there was less of a chance of staining one of his custom-made suits. It also helped to insulate him from possible arrest, which was an important benefit for one of the most notorious businessmen in all of Europe. Most law-enforcement personnel considered him a crime lord, but he didn't have a record—other than a few juvenile offenses that were later expunged.

However, Dubois had been detained and questioned more times than he could remember, especially in the early days when he was still laying the groundwork for his criminal empire. His interview sessions with the French authorities had happened so frequently he actually penciled them into his weekly schedule. Of course, it helped that Dubois had many cops on his payroll, who tipped him off ahead of time about impending interrogations.

That was one of the most important things he had learned early on.

No matter how expensive, inside information was always priceless.

Over the years, Dubois had slowly realized something else about the criminal career he had chosen for himself. Even though he loved the culture and excitement of his hometown, he knew his life would be cut short if he remained in Paris. Most of the cops recognized him, and so did many of the crooks. He knew he would eventually agitate the wrong person and find himself in jail, or dead, or both. And since none of those options appealed to Dubois, he decided to move his operation to one of the least likely places in Europe: Bruges, Belgium.

As a schoolboy at LLG, Dubois had watched a slide-show presentation on Bruges, the self-proclaimed "Venice of the North," and had been captivated by its medieval charm. Later, when he finally had an opportunity to explore its scenic canals and historic Grand Square, he fell in love with the city. Although the pace was *much* slower than in Paris, he felt at ease while walking the streets, something he was no longer able to do in France. Nevertheless, Dubois wasn't reckless during his evening strolls. Bodyguards accompanied him wherever he went.

After making a financial killing on several arms deals in the mid-1990s, he bought a castle on the outskirts of Bruges, which he named Château Dubois. Then he traveled around Europe in search of the perfect furnishings to adorn his home. Most men in his position would have hired a decorator to take care of such trivial tasks, but Dubois considered himself a new breed of criminal— classically educated, exquisitely dressed, and, above all else, culturally superior to all those around him. Sure, he had dabbled with street gangs in his youth, but he had done that strictly for research purposes. His intent hadn't been to befriend the dregs of society or to make a fortune with his escapades; instead, his goal had been to understand the criminal mind so he could always be several steps ahead of his rivals. Sort of like a grandmaster playing chess.

Once again, it always came back to inside information for Dubois.

The more he acquired, the better off he would be.

DRESSED IN SLACKS and a cashmere sweater, Dubois read his notebook near a roaring fire in his study. A snifter of Armagnac and an encrypted phone sat next to him on a hand-carved table he had acquired at an auction house in Malta.

Much like his furniture, he was solidly built and well maintained. Neither short nor tall, he exercised just enough for his clothes to fit him properly. Broad shoulders and a thick chest showcased his tailored suits. His shoes were always polished, and his pants were always cuffed. His chestnut hair, tinged with a hint of gray near the ears, was always slicked back with an all-natural gel that he imported from the Orient. Last but not least, his scent had been custom-designed at a small boutique in Paris. A single bottle cost more than some cars.

Despite all this pampering, which might suggest he was a little too familiar with his feminine side, Dubois was a raging heterosexual. To help quench his libido, he flew in female courtesans from all around the globe, sometimes partaking in several at once. Although he had a few personal favorites who were flown in monthly, that was as close as he came to having an actual relationship. For him, women were disposable, meant to be used and discarded like toothpicks.

Usually, at this hour, some exotic beauty would be writhing on top of him in his bedroom, but due to a business concern in America, the fire and the alcohol were the only things keeping him warm. All told, there were twelve fireplaces in his château, which had seemed like overkill until he moved in and realized how drafty a fourteenth-century castle could be. The temperature outside was in the low thirties—pretty typical for a December night in Belgium—but would warm up to the fifties during the day. Normally, Dubois spent this time of year in his exquisite vacation homes, particularly the ones he owned near tropical beaches.

Otherwise, his suntan faded and his mood soured.

As an antiquarian book collector, Dubois possessed one of the finest rare-book collections in all of Europe. Recently, thanks to a very expensive bribe or two, he had been given new information about the mythical manuscript he had dreamed about since he was a little boy. Although many historians doubted the book ever existed—most of them claimed it was a figment of someone's overactive imagination—Dubois was confident it was real. In fact, he was so convinced, he had learned several ancient languages just so he could read firsthand accounts of all the people who had searched for the book before him.

By learning about their failed attempts, he hoped to achieve success.

Thumbing through his notes on *The First Face of the French Janus* by Jean-Aimé de Chavigny, a sixteenth-century writer who had guided his search on multiple occasions, Dubois heard the phone ring. Glancing at his watch, he noted the time and approved. The call had been placed within the time frame they had discussed.

Apparently, everything had gone as planned.

"Hello," he said in Dutch. "Do you have news?"

"Yes, sir, the leak has been found. It will be plugged shortly."

Dubois shook his head, irritated. "You consider that news? *That* is not news. *That* is a waste of my time. I already knew about the leak. *That's* why you were sent there in the first place. Call me back when the leak has been eliminated!"

6

Payne was known for his gut feelings. Sometimes they went against empirical evidence, and often they defied common sense. But he had learned long ago to trust his instincts, even if he couldn't rationally explain them. Sometimes he just knew when something was wrong.

And this was one of those times.

From the moment he had spotted her in the back of the crowd, Payne knew she was there for him. For what purpose, he didn't know. But he planned to find out as soon as they found her.

Trying not to draw attention, he walked calmly but quickly down the long corridor. He passed the Irish, Lithuanian, and Romanian Rooms, nodding to several guests along the way, then made a sharp right. The English Classroom, the last place the woman had been seen, was at the far end of the hallway. In between were dozens of people, multiple classrooms, and plenty of places to hide.

This would be harder than he had thought.

In a hostile situation, Payne would have had a weapon in his hand and would have been ordering everyone out of the corridor, possibly firing a warning shot to stress the urgency of his directive. He had a lot of experience with urban warfare, and the minimization of civilian casualties was priority number one. His current objective was a lot less dramatic, yet challenging nonetheless. The woman wasn't a criminal, a suspect, or a terrorist. So far, her only transgression was wearing jeans to a formal gala. Outside of Muslim countries, dress code violations were rarely a punishable offense.

Payne continued to move forward, his eyes scanning everything in the corridor, looking for the slightest hint of green or blue—the colors of her coat and jeans—in the black-and-white world of men's formalwear. Some of the women wore colorful gowns, often complemented by lavish jewels and designer accessories, but none of them fit the criteria he was searching for.

"Shit," he mumbled to himself, realizing she had probably left the hallway for the sanctuary of a classroom or the freedom of nearby stairs. But first things first. Before he concerned himself with other floors, he knew he had to search the nearby rooms, starting with the one on his left.

The door to the Swedish Room was wide open, and several guests were standing inside. The walls were built with two-hundred-year-old handmade bricks that were coated with multiple layers of whitewash. The sloped ceiling and back wall were covered in murals, many of which showcased the subtle humor that Sweden was known for. A fresco depicted the Three Wise Men, dressed as cavaliers, riding to Bethlehem in opposite directions. In another image, Lady Justice used her blindfold to hold a scale that appeared to be balanced but actually had an off-center fulcrum.

Ignoring the scenery, Payne focused on the people instead. A quick scan of the room proved that the mystery woman was not there.

A few seconds later he stepped next door and visited China.

Inspired by a reception hall in the Forbidden City, the Chinese Room was dedicated to the memory of Confucius and his democratic model of education. Teachers and students sat at the same level around a moon-shaped teakwood table. Above it, the ceiling contained a golden five-clawed imperial dragon, the symbol of nature's energy. Surrounding squares portrayed the dragon as a guardian of the pearl of wisdom and the phoenix as a symbol of cultural wealth. All of the walls were painted red, which reminded Payne of his last trip to the Far East, a gruesome mission where he and Jones had been asked to investigate a cave bathed in blood on the tiny island of Jeju, South Korea. During his military career, he had witnessed and inflicted his fair share of carnage, but something about that cave still haunted his dreams.

Thankfully, the room was small and practically empty, allowing him to move onward.

The Greek Room represented classical architecture from the fifth century B.C. The marble columns and pilasters were made at a stone quarry near Mount Penteli, the same quarry used to build the Parthenon. They were transported on the last ship to sail to America prior to the occupation of Greece in World War II. Two Greek artists came from Athens to paint the marble, the doorway, and the coffered ceiling. Instead of using stencils, they drew each line by hand. To highlight the colors, they applied beeswax and 24-carat gold leaf, rubbing it in with a polishing bone. The entire process took them more than seven months to complete.

A half dozen people sat in the white-oak chairs that lined the table. The backs of student chairs were carved with the names of Greek islands and towns. Meanwhile, the guest professor sat in a chair bearing the name of Socrates. In front of him were a number of books written in English and Greek. He pointed to them often as he told a story about John Travlos, the architect who had designed the room. Because of World War II, Travlos was unable to leave occupied Greece. However, hidden under a blanket in his closet, he listened to a banned BBC broadcast in which the citizens of Pittsburgh dedicated the Greek Room to his native country.

During the anecdote, Payne walked around the perimeter of the room, casually studying all the faces that surrounded the center table. The windows were flanked with gold-colored curtains that hung from sturdy wooden rods. Payne ran his hand over the coarse material, making sure no one was hidden behind them, before heading back to the door.

JONES WAS HAVING similar luck on his side of the Cathedral. He walked the entire length of the hallway, then turned around and started searching rooms. The Russian Classroom was first, followed by the Norwegian one. Although both were impressive in design, neither contained the woman he was searching for.

Getting more frustrated by the minute, Jones ducked into the final room in his corner of the building. The French Classroom, which sat next to the English Room, was designed in the French Empire style, inspired by the ancient worlds that had been rediscovered during the Napoleonic campaigns in Egypt, Greece, and Italy. The walls were lined with classic wood paneling. Carved ornaments of Egyptian griffins and rosettes accentuated the panel divisions. Crystal and metal chandeliers, simplified versions of those found in the Palace of Versailles, hung from a gray plaster ceiling. A mahogany professor's chair and table included bronze ornaments that were replicas of the originals from the Louvre, and the student armchairs were mahogany and upholstered in royal blue.

Nearly all of the chairs were empty, as was most of the room. A few people were hanging out by the side chalkboard, discussing an upcoming trip to France, but all of them were older men, including a French tour guide who blabbed on and on about wine and cheese. Jones did his best to ignore the rambling as he searched for his prey in the back of the room.

Gold damask drapery, bearing the Empire wreath-and-lyre design, framed the windows and the splendid view of Heinz Memorial Chapel, which sat on the far side of the spacious Cathedral lawn. An example of French Gothic architecture, the chapel seemed to be an extension of the French Room itself, albeit an elaborate one. It was patterned after the Sainte-Chapelle in Paris; its steeple stood two hundred and fifty-three feet above the ground. Similar to the Cathedral, its exterior walls were made out of Indiana limestone. Four thousand square feet of stained-glass windows lined the building, including a seventy-three-foot-tall transept window that was among the tallest in the world.

As snow continued to fall, coating the chapel's façade in the steady glow of its spotlights, Jones shifted his gaze to a solitary figure who was trudging across the icy sidewalk. At first he thought he was imagining things, his mind playing tricks on him, but after wiping the frost from the classroom window and taking a closer look, he smiled in victory.

Only one person was out there, braving the ice and cold.

And she was wearing a green coat.

7

Jones rushed into the hallway, where he spotted Payne leaving the Scottish Classroom.

"Jon," he called as he jogged toward him. "She's outside."

"Where?"

"Heading toward Heinz Chapel."

Payne paused in thought. "What do you think?"

"I say we go after her."

"Are you gonna bitch about the cold?"

Jones grinned. "Not if you don't."

"Then let's go."

Ignoring the nearest exit, they hustled to the back of the Cathedral, where a pair of revolving doors opened onto a large stone patio. They pushed their way outside and instantly felt the sting of the arctic air on their hands and faces. Rock salt, recently scattered to break up the ice, crunched under their dress shoes and provided them with enough traction to quicken their pace.

"Which way?" Payne demanded as he shielded his eyes from the wind.

Jones motioned toward the ground, where a single set of footprints could be seen in the freshly fallen snow. It led them down two steps and onto a long path known as the Varsity Walk, a place where the names of former Pitt athletes, like Mike Ditka and Tony Dorsett, had been carved in stone. Trees and benches lined the path, as did a series of black lampposts that gave them just enough light to follow her tracks to the other side of the spacious east lawn, one of the largest patches of grass on a mostly urban campus.

Payne led the way, walking briskly despite the unsteady footing. Never slipping or sliding, he continued forward until he reached a fork in the sidewalk. Heinz Chapel sat off to the left, but the footprints continued straight ahead toward S. Bellefield Avenue.

He glanced back at Jones. "Are you sure it was her?"

"Positive."

Payne nodded. That was good enough for him. Without saying another word, he started walking again through the swirling wind. Although it hindered his vision and coated his clothes with snow, he blocked the elements out of his mind. He had survived much worse as the leader of the MANIACs, places so harsh that wildlife couldn't survive—the type of locales that made hell look like Hawaii. Unlike some soldiers who were trained for specific types of warfare, his squad was known for its flexibility. Hot, cold, wet, dry—it didn't matter. They were equal-opportunity warriors, willing to kick ass in the jungle, on a glacier, or anywhere in between.

One hundred feet ahead, the stone path ended in an icy set of steps that led down to the road. Payne grasped the handrail for support but didn't slow his pace until he reached the bottom. Suddenly, the footprints he had been following were no longer distinct, thanks to a group of Pitt students who had recently trudged by. Payne looked to his left and studied the sidewalks that lined both sides of the street. No people, no movement, no signs of life—except for the occasional car that trickled past on Fifth Avenue, about a half block away.

"Over there," Jones said from his perch on the steps.

Payne glanced in that direction and smiled at the sight. Across the slush-filled street, roughly fifty feet to their right, the woman in the green coat was scraping snow and ice from her windshield. It was a winter ritual in the Northeast.

"Stay here," Payne ordered, realizing she would feel less threatened if only one of them approached, and since she had listened to his speech, he knew he was the best candidate.

Before Jones could argue, Payne carefully made his way across S. Bellefield Avenue. Even though it was a one-way road, he had learned long ago to always look both ways when crossing streets on the Pitt campus. For some strange reason, the city of Pittsburgh had designed its bus-only lanes to go in the opposite direction of car traffic on a few of its streets. Vehicles rarely collided with buses—all they had to do was stay out of each other's designated lanes—but pedestrians weren't always as fortunate. Nearly every year some visitor or clueless freshman who wasn't familiar with the setup stepped off the sidewalk and got flattened by a bus heading in the "wrong" direction. It happened so often that local police called it *death by bus*.

"Can I give you a hand?" Payne called from a distance.

The woman stopped scraping her passenger-side window and searched for the source of the sound. When she realized it was Payne, she became noticeably flustered.

"I'm sorry," she yelled to him while hustling around the front of her Ford Taurus. Her headlights were off, but her car's engine and heater were running.

"For what?"

"For showing up like that. I shouldn't have done it."

"Don't worry about it. I'm not here to yell at you."

"Then why are you here?" she asked as she opened her door.

When the interior light popped on, Payne could finally see the woman they had been following. Until that point, she had been nothing more than a ghost moving in the shadows of the Cathedral, a green coat trekking through the snow. Now he could put a face on their subject. She was an attractive woman in her early thirties. Brown hair, brown eyes, and very little makeup. Not the least bit glamorous, but sexy nonetheless. The type of woman who used to be a cheerleader but now spent her days at work and her nights with her kids.

Payne answered, "I'm here to help."

"To help with what? You don't even know why I'm here."

"I will if you tell me."

"Listen," she said as she climbed into her car, "I appreciate you coming outside to talk to me. But like I mentioned, I shouldn't have shown up unannounced."

He shrugged. "Trust me, it's not a problem. I made my speech and welcomed my guests. As far as I'm concerned, I've earned myself a coffee break. Why don't we go back inside and get ourselves something to drink? I don't know about you, but I'm freezing my ass off."

For the first time that night, she smiled. "It *is* kind of cold."

Payne theatrically rubbed his arms. "Brrrrrrrrrrrr."

She smiled again, this time even wider. "Fine, we can go somewhere and talk, but not inside the Cathedral. I'm severely underdressed."

Payne glanced at his watch. "How about Heinz Chapel? I bet it's still open."

She considered his suggestion, then nodded.

"Do you mind if my friend joins us?" He pointed back at Jones, who was keeping an eye on things from the nearby steps. "I swear, he's harmless."

"No, he's not," she replied. It wasn't an accusation, more like a statement of fact. "Then again, neither are you. If you guys were harmless, I wouldn't have come so far to talk."

He raised an eyebrow. "Where did you come from?"

"Philadelphia."

"In this weather? What's that, a seven-hour drive?"

"Closer to ten. Lots of accidents on the turnpike."

Payne nodded in understanding. This time of year, Pennsylvania highways were an adventure—especially in the central part of the state, where the roads were so mountainous it was like riding a roller coaster. "What time did you leave?"

She turned off her car. "Early."

"And you came all this way to talk to me?"

"To both of you."

"Both of us?"

She closed her door and nodded.

"About what?"

"If you don't mind, I'd rather tell you together. It'll be easier that way."

"Not a problem," he said. "No pressure from me."

"Thanks. I appreciate that."

"However," he said as they walked across the road, "since you crashed my party, I feel like I'm entitled to one piece of information that you still haven't told me."

"Oh, yeah? What's that?"

Payne looked at her. "What's your name?"

She glanced at him and smiled. "Ashley. My name is Ashley."

8

After shaking Ashley's hand, Jones led the way to the front entrance of Heinz Chapel. The massive front doors, each weighing over eight hundred pounds, were made of oak and attached with wrought-iron fixtures. As the three of them approached, one of the doors inched open as an elderly black janitor tried to push his way outside. He was wearing a gray hooded sweatshirt underneath a khaki work jacket stitched with his name: Sam. In his left hand, he had a metal snow shovel. In his right, a bucket filled with rock salt.

Jones saw him struggling and rushed forward to help. "Let me get that for you, sir."

"Thank you. Thank you indeed. Awfully nice of you."

"Not a problem."

Sam hobbled outside and set down his bucket with a clang. "Can I help you guys?"

Jones nodded. "We were wondering if the chapel was open."

Sam studied Jones in his tuxedo, then noticed Payne in his. "Sorry, fellas, you'll have to go somewhere else. Gay marriage ain't legal in Pennsylvania."

Sam instantly burst out laughing, a loud mix between a cackle and a wheezing cough. The type of sound someone makes after fifty years of smoking. "I'm sorry, I'm sorry. I'm just playin' with you. I hope you ain't offended."

"Not at all."

"You see," Sam explained, "I don't got much time left, so I like to joke around."

"Don't worry about it, sir. I'm not the least bit offended."

"Good!" he said, patting Jones on his shoulder. "You're proud of your gayness. That's good to hear. Ain't nothing to be ashamed about."

"No, sir, that's not what I meant. I'm *not* gay."

Sam shook his head. "I guess you ain't black, neither."

Once again, Sam burst out laughing—even louder than before. Jones humored him with a smile, but realized their conversation was going to be pretty one-sided.

"Anyway," Jones said, "it was nice talking to you. The three of us are pretty cold, so we're heading inside. Make sure you stay warm out here."

"Oh, I will," the janitor said as he grabbed a handful of salt and scattered it on the stone steps. "Don't worry about me none. The cold ain't gonna kill ol' Sam. I can promise you that!"

"Nice meeting you," said Payne as he followed the others inside.

The lobby, known as the narthex, was surprisingly dark. What little light there was came from deeper inside the chapel. The middle section, known as the nave, extended from the edge of the entryway to the railing in front of the altar and was filled with several rows of oak pews. Wrought-iron lanterns, dangling on chains from the arches above, scattered soft beams of light in every direction, but they went virtually unnoticed because of the transept windows on the left side of the nave. Four vertical rows of stained glass, each seventy-three feet tall, showcased important figures from secular history, representing politics, science, music, and literature. People like George Washington, Leonardo da Vinci, Ludwig van Beethoven, and Edgar Allan Poe.

"Wow," Ashley whispered as she stared at the rainbow of colors that were projected inside the chapel by its exterior spotlights. "The windows are beautiful."

"If you look closely," Jones explained, "there's an equal number of men and women. For every Shakespeare, there's a Pocahontas. That level of equality is pretty rare in older art."

Ashley scanned the stained glass, searching for examples of famous women. In a matter of seconds, she spotted Emily Dickinson, Florence Nightingale, and several others. "Thanks for pointing that out. I definitely would have missed that."

"Glad I could be of service."

"Speaking of which," Payne said as he settled into a

nearby pew, "I get the sense that you were looking for our help."

Ashley turned toward him and nodded. But before she was willing to sit down and explain, she glanced up and down the rows, making sure they were alone. Once she was satisfied, she took off her coat and sat to Payne's left, one row behind Jones.

"First of all," she said, "I'd like to apologize to both of you. I really shouldn't have ambushed you like this. Earlier today, it seemed like a great idea. You know, bumping into you in a public forum. But once I got to your party, I realized I was out of my element."

"Hardly," Payne said with a reassuring smile. "Your appearance brought some excitement to an otherwise boring night. Feel free to crash all my parties."

"No," she said, "this will be my last. I've embarrassed myself enough."

"Seriously, don't worry about it. We're not the least bit mad."

"Curious," Jones interjected, "but not mad."

"Exactly."

"So," she wondered, "where should I start?"

Payne shrugged. "The floor is all yours. Start wherever you'd like."

Ashley paused for a moment, trying to remember what she had rehearsed on her journey to the Pitt campus. Without practicing it first, she knew she might get flustered and screw up her explanation, which was something she couldn't afford to do. With men like Payne and

Jones, it was a one-shot deal. If she didn't pique their interest now, there wouldn't be a second chance.

"I'm a nobody," she assured them. "I'm a grade-school teacher from a nice suburb in Philadelphia. I was raised by a single mom, who died of cancer a few years back. I have no siblings, I've never been married, and despite today's events, I normally try to avoid drama. My idea of a good day is sleeping late, walking my dog in the park, and renting a romantic comedy."

"Hold up. I think I saw your ad on a dating site," Jones joked.

Payne rolled his eyes. "Just ignore him. He's been drinking."

"Actually," she admitted, "I'm not offended. He managed to sum up my life in a single punch line. I know I'm a walking stereotype, and I'm not the least bit embarrassed. The truth is, I like my life. It's a good, solid life. And other than my mom's passing, I wouldn't change a thing about it."

"So," Payne wondered, "what happened?"

She looked at him, confused. "Why would you ask me that?"

"Why? Because *something* compelled you to abandon your life, hop in your car, and drive across the state to talk to two strangers."

"Don't forget the snow," Jones added.

"Excuse me?" Payne asked.

"She drove through a blizzard to meet us. To me, that screams of desperation."

"Good point. Something compelled you to wake up early on your day off and drive through a major snow-storm. Therefore, it must be something big. Or, at the very least, pressing."

"Actually," she said, "the word I would use is *puzzling*."

"Puzzling?"

She nodded. "Puzzling."

"Go on."

"On Monday, I came home from school and grabbed my mail, as I always do. Inside my mailbox, there was a stack of letters, mostly bills. The lone exception was a cream-colored envelope. My name and address were written on it, but no return address. In the right cor-ner, there were several foreign stamps and a strange postmark."

"What do you mean by strange?" Jones wondered.

"Asian, I think. I simply couldn't read it."

"Go on."

"I've been a teacher for ten years now, so I've had plenty of students. Sometimes one of them goes on a trip and sends me a postcard. You know, *I'm seeing the sights and having fun*. Nothing more complex than that. But this thing? It was completely different."

"How so?" Payne wondered.

"First of all, it was written in calligraphy on real fancy paper. You know, the kind that feels old and expensive but isn't brittle."

"Parchment?" Jones guessed.

"Yeah, *parchment*. Like an old Bible or something. Definitely not normal paper."

"That's because parchment is made out of animal skin, not trees."

"Really?"

Jones nodded. "Depending on its age and country of origin, it could be goatskin, calfskin, or even human."

"What?" she blurted.

Payne shook his head. That wasn't the type of thing she needed to hear. "Don't worry, he's kidding. Sometimes he likes to joke around in serious situations. Just ignore him and continue."

Jones stared at him and mouthed: *I wasn't joking.*

Thankfully, Ashley was looking at Payne when that occurred.

"Wait," she said, trying to recall her place in the story, "where was I?"

"You were telling us about the letter."

She nodded slowly, as if remembering. "That's right, the letter. Not only was the paper different, but so was the language."

"In what way?"

"The letter *wasn't* written in English. It was written in French."

"French?" Jones asked, getting more intrigued. "The postmark was Asian, but the letter was French. I have to admit, that's a weird combination."

"Trust me," she said, "it gets even weirder."

9

Ashley reached into her coat and pulled out a single sheet of paper. It had been folded in half, then folded again, and tucked into one of her pockets. "I didn't want to damage the original, so I made a photocopy at my school. I hope that's all right."

"A copy is fine," Jones said. "May I see it?"

"Of course you may. That's partly why I'm here. To show you the letter."

"Really? It must be one hell of a letter."

She smiled as she unfolded it. "Let's just say it's puzzling."

"There's that word again. That's the third time you've used it."

"I know, but it's the only word that fits."

Payne reentered the conversation. "Speaking of puzzling, why us?"

"What do you mean?"

"Obviously, the letter confused you, but why come to us?"

"Why?" She blushed slightly. "Because of the newspaper."

"What newspaper?"

"The *Philadelphia Inquirer*."

Payne furrowed his brow. "I'm afraid you just lost me."

"Me, too," Jones seconded.

"Sorry," she apologized. "I better explain. I rarely read the newspaper—it's just too depressing to me—but yesterday at lunch I was glancing through the *Philadelphia Inquirer*. In the weekend section, they had an article about your recent adventures in Greece. It also mentioned your annual fund-raiser. As soon as I read that, I figured this had to be fate. I honestly didn't know where to turn, but the story gave me your names—two of the biggest experts in the field of archaeology—and where you were going to be today. I figured I couldn't pass that up."

"We're hardly experts in archaeology," Payne said. "We got lucky and stumbled onto something big. Nothing more, nothing less."

"Speak for yourself," Jones argued. "We flew halfway around the world and found one of the largest treasures in the history of mankind. How in the hell is that stumbling? It's not like we tripped over a pot o' gold in my backyard. I mean, *that* would be stumbling. What we did required a certain level of expertise, and, if I may be so bold, a dash of panache."

Payne rolled his eyes at Jones's comment. Not because

it was inaccurate—their discovery of an ancient Greek treasure had rocked the archaeological world and had filled their bank accounts with unbelievable wealth—but because Payne didn't like to boast about his accomplishments. It didn't matter that they had risked their lives to find an artifact that had been dubbed "the lost throne" by the media, or that they had appeared on magazine covers around the globe. His grandfather had taught him about humility at a very early age, and it had left a lasting impression. About the only time he ever bragged was when he was talking trash with Jones, and that was done out of self-defense.

"Although we possess expertise in some areas," Payne said, "I think it would be misleading to claim that we're experts in archaeology. And even if we were, how does that relate to your letter? We're certainly not experts in French."

"That's okay," Ashley said. "The letter wasn't written in French."

"Hold up," Jones blurted. "You just told us it was written in French."

"Well, I *thought* it was written in French. I even took it to a French teacher in my school, hoping he could translate it for me, but the best he could do was help me with a few words. Even then, it was still a struggle."

"Why? Is he a shitty teacher?"

"No, the letter was written in Middle French, not modern French."

Payne grimaced. "What's the difference?"

Jones answered for her. "Middle French is an early form of the language, one that hasn't been used in over four hundred years. As you know, all languages evolve. During the past millennium, French has undergone some radical changes. Although it's still considered a Romance language—like Latin, Spanish, and Italian—its basic syntax has been drastically altered over the years. Word order and sentence structure are much more important than they were in the past. In addition, thousands of foreign words have entered the French lexicon, replacing older terms that were used during the Middle Ages but are now extinct."

"No wonder your friend couldn't understand it," Payne said.

Jones stared at him. "By the way, what were you saying about my expertise in French?"

Payne shook his head. "D.J., let me ask you a question. Can you *speak* French?"

"Not really, but—"

"Then you're *not* an expert in French."

Jones was tempted to defend himself, then decided against it. Instead, he turned toward Ashley and changed the subject. "So, the entire letter was written in Middle French?"

"Not all of it," she said as she handed the copy to Jones. "That's the weird part. As far as my friend could tell, it's a mixture of several languages. And none of them are modern."

Intrigued, Jones glanced at the document and tried to read it, but quickly realized it was beyond his comprehension. "Damn, this thing is confusing." He ran his finger over the handwritten text, searching for clues of any kind. "I recognize a few prefixes here and there, but other than that, this letter is, well, puzzling."

"See," she said, laughing, "I told you so."

"And you're sure you don't know who sent it to you?"

"I'm positive."

Jones paused in thought. "Would it bother you if we showed it to some linguists?"

"Not at all. In fact, I was hoping . . ."

"You were hoping what?"

"Well," she said tentatively, "I was hoping maybe we could ask your friends."

Payne grimaced. "Our friends?"

She nodded. "Right now your party is filled with experts from around the world. I thought maybe you could ask some of them to help us translate the letter."

"Wait," Payne said. "How long have you been thinking that?"

She smiled. "Honestly? Ever since I read the article."

"If that's the case, why didn't you approach us inside the Cathedral?"

"I told you, I got flustered. I wasn't expecting everything to be so formal. I mean, you guys are in tuxedos, and I'm wearing jeans. For some reason, I didn't think that would go over so well."

"Like I told you before, it's not a problem."

"Trust me," Jones said, "I'd rather be wearing jeans. I feel like a maître d' in this getup."

She reached out and touched his sleeve. "Well, you look great."

"I know I do, but I feel like I should be describing the soup du jour."

"Anyway," Payne said, trying to get back on task, "if

we decided to help, what would be our cover story? Or should we tell everyone the truth?"

"Well," she said, "I gave that some thought on my drive over here and came up with a good idea. During the school year, I sometimes coordinate my lesson plans with teachers from other subjects. It's called cross-curricular teaching. I figured we could do something like that. Maybe call it an academic experiment, or a cultural riddle. You could say it's designed to promote unity among the people of the world. I'm sure your experts would eat that up."

Payne smiled at the concept. It was a brilliant idea, one they could pull off with very little deception. All they needed to do was make some copies, then they could sit back and relax while some of the best academics in the world went to work. "What do you think, D.J.?"

"What do I think? I'm kind of mad I didn't think of it myself."

"So, you're willing to help?"

"Of course I'm willing to help. However, I'd like to make a small suggestion. I think it would be best if we compartmentalized the data. Instead of passing out the full document, I think we should attack this in much smaller chunks. Maybe break it down, line by line."

"Why's that?" she asked.

"Who knows what the document says? Heck, it might be something confidential, something only you were meant to read. If that's the case, it would be best if we were the only ones who got to see the full message."

Ashley nodded in agreement. "So, what should we do first?"

Payne glanced at his watch. "My event will last another two hours. The first thing we need to do is make some copies. If I remember correctly, we can do that in the Cathedral basement. Let's go down there and figure out how to break up the document."

"Actually," Jones suggested, "why don't Ashley and I take care of that? You should probably go back to your party. I'm sure your guests are missing you by now. The last thing we want is for everyone to leave early."

"Yeah, you're probably right," Payne said as he helped Ashley with her coat. "Is that okay with you?"

"Of course it's okay. I'm just thrilled you're willing to help. It means a lot to me."

The three of them walked toward the rear of the chapel. Jones led the way, followed by Ashley, then Payne. "As soon as we're done," Jones said, "I'll call you and we can meet in the Commons Room. Maybe you can get some students to help."

Payne nodded. "I'm sure they'd be willing."

"Here," Jones said, opening the door for Ashley, "let me get that for you."

"Thank you. In fact, thanks for everything. I appreciate it."

As she stepped into the cold night, rock salt crunched under the heels of her leather boots. She lingered on the stone steps for just a second, slowly tilting her head back to admire the falling snow as it danced in the swirling wind.

It was a simple act, completely innocuous, but one that led to her death.

10

One moment she was standing there, enjoying the winter scenery. An instant later, her head erupted in a burst of pink mist.

The gunman's shot had been perfectly placed, just under her chin at a slight upward angle. The bullet tore through her throat, the roof of her mouth, and finally her brain, before it blew out the top of her skull and embedded itself in the chapel door.

Death was instantaneous and completely unexpected.

Her heart stopped, her knees buckled, and she toppled into Jones, who managed to catch her before she hit the ground. His dress shirt, which had been crisp and white, was now stained with blood and chunks of her hair. Splatter covered his face. Despite his years of experience, a few seconds passed before his shock faded and his adrenaline surged. Once it did, Jones transformed into a MANIAC, ready to hunt down whoever was responsible for her death.

Payne recovered a half second quicker. He grabbed Jones by the back of his collar and yanked him inside as a second shot whizzed by and buried itself in the door. Splinters burst into the cold night as the sound echoed in their ears. While falling backward, Jones instinctively thrust his hands behind him to brace his fall. As he did, he let go of Ashley's lifeless body. She slumped sideways against the door, then toppled forward onto the steps. Within seconds, a puddle of warm blood had oozed from the top of her head.

"Are you hit?" Payne screamed in the interior of the narthex.

Jones shook his head and scrambled to his feet. Just to be sure, he probed his chest and stomach with both of his hands. "I'm fine."

"Are you sure?"

"It's not my blood."

Payne nodded in understanding. Although he had been inside the chapel when the first bullet struck, he had witnessed its impact and the carnage it caused. Unfortunately, that was the only thing he saw. Everything else had been blocked by the door and the people in front of him.

"What did you see?" he demanded.

Jones closed his eyes and replayed the scene in his mind. "Muzzle flash from the lawn, approximately seventy feet ahead. Second shot a little closer. Same line of fire."

"One shooter?"

He paused. "I can't be sure."

"Doesn't matter," Payne said as he slipped his hand

under Jones's jacket and stole his gun. It happened so quickly Jones barely had time to open his eyes before Payne was past him.

"Not cool!" Jones shouted. "Not cool at all!"

Payne ignored him. "Call 911. Make sure they know I'm pursuing the suspect."

"Then what?"

"Go outside and save the janitor."

"I don't even *like* the janitor."

"Save him anyway. He might have seen something."

Jones nodded as he pulled out his phone. "I'll call you with an update."

The main entrance to the chapel consisted of two sets of double doors. A minute earlier, they had used the pair on the right with little success. This time he would try the left. Not only was it corpse-free, but it was slightly closer to a long row of hedges that separated the stone patio outside the chapel and the beginning of the Cathedral lawn. The evergreens were waist-high and draped with a thick blanket of snow. They weren't as safe as a brick wall, but were more than adequate for cover.

After taking a deep breath, Payne burst through the doors and leaped down the steps in one mighty bound. He skidded briefly on the slick concrete but managed to keep his balance as he scurried across the patio and dove behind the bushes. With gun in hand, he scanned the immediate area, searching for threats of any kind. The only person he spotted was the janitor. He was holding his shovel in a death grip, cowering against the side of the chapel.

"Are you okay?" Payne whispered across the courtyard.

"Do I *look* okay? I think I pissed my pants."

"Did you see the shooter?"

The janitor's voice trembled. "Some whitey in a trench coat."

"Young? Old? Short? Tall?"

"I don't know! My eyes ain't great."

"Where was he?"

"Standing in the lawn. That's the only reason I saw him. He was standing out there like a snowman."

"Was he alone?"

"What's with all the fucking questions?"

"Was he alone?" Payne demanded.

"I don't know! I was too busy trying to hide."

"Don't worry. My buddy will be right out. He'll take you to safety."

The janitor mumbled something else, but Payne was no longer listening. His focus had shifted to the man with the gun. Once he found him, everything else would take care of itself.

After flipping onto his stomach, Payne pulled himself underneath the hedge by grabbing one of its lower branches. Pine needles scratched his face as their scent filled his nose, but his sole concern was surveying the lawn from the safest place possible. If he had climbed to his knees and peered over the hedge, he would have been exposed to a head shot, just like Ashley had been. But down below was a different story. Although his sight line was restricted, his exposure was minimal—unless someone crept up behind him. If that happened, he was a dead man.

With his free hand, Payne brushed away some of the

snow that blocked his view. With each additional stroke, his sight line increased until he could see halfway across the lawn. Trees, benches, and lampposts dotted the landscape, but as far as he could see, there were no people.

"Screw it," he mumbled to himself as he scurried backward. He knew if he waited any longer, the shooter was going to get away.

Jumping to his feet, Payne hurdled the hedge and dashed into the lawn. The snow was deep but his traction was good, even better than it had been on the sidewalk. He sprinted forward until he reached the area where Jones had seen the muzzle flash. The snow had been trampled down, as if someone had lingered there for several minutes. Payne dropped to his knees and stared at the surrounding tracks. One set branched to the left; another pointed straight ahead.

The question was, which was more recent?

Payne looked closer, trying to figure out which way the shooter had gone, but the falling snow and the swirling wind hindered his progress. A fine layer of fresh powder had recently coated both sets of tracks. Coupled with a lack of light, Payne couldn't rely on his eyes to pinpoint the escape route. Instead, he used his hand, running his fingertips from one side of the footprint to the other until he made sense of things. Like a blind man reading Braille, Payne located the ridge patterns in the compressed snow and determined which way the heel had been facing.

Just like that, Payne knew in which direction the shooter had fled.

Now his pursuit could begin in earnest.

11

In the summertime, the Cathedral lawn was like a city park, filled with coeds in bikinis and frat boys throwing Frisbees. But on this night it resembled Siberia. The arctic wind was howling, and the snow was drifting high. In some places, it was over two feet deep. But none of that mattered to Payne, who sprinted across the flat terrain with reckless abandon.

With the Cathedral on his left, he followed the shooter's trail for nearly two hundred feet. The entire way he ran parallel to Fifth Avenue, which glowed on his right and provided just enough light to see the footprints. Cars and buses occasionally passed, as did salt trucks and plows. Somewhere in the distance he heard the shrieking of metal as ice was scraped from the asphalt. Other than his breath and his pounding heart, it was the only sound he heard.

Bigelow Boulevard was straight ahead at the bottom

of a small hill. The road ran left to right, just beyond a row of hedges that marked the end of the Cathedral grounds. To slow his forward momentum, Payne went into a controlled slide. He thrust his legs in front of him and slid down the icy embankment, stopping a few feet short of the shrubs. He quickly popped into a crouch and scanned his surroundings, using the bushes for temporary cover.

Payne cursed when he realized the sidewalk and the four-lane road had been recently plowed. From this point forward, he was on his own. No more footprints to follow. Nothing but a vague description of a white man in a trench coat. Even if he spotted a possible suspect, Payne couldn't just shoot him. On a large city campus, there was no telling how many men met that description. That meant Payne would have to approach him and confront him face to face.

Glancing to his left, he saw nothing but parked cars. All of them were covered in a thick blanket of snow, meaning they had been there for a while. With no exhaust fumes in sight, he knew none of the cars was running. On his right, three students were sitting inside a bus shelter, huddling for warmth. They were dressed in jeans and ski jackets, not trench coats.

Across the street was the William Pitt Union. At one time it had been the Schenley Hotel, a glamorous facility that had housed several celebrities over the years—including Theodore Roosevelt, Dwight Eisenhower, and Babe Ruth—but now it served as the student union, one of the major social hubs on the Pitt campus. Despite the blizzard, Payne knew the place would be swarming with students.

If the shooter went in there, things could get ugly.

With no suspect in sight, Payne searched for a gap in the hedges. He found one near the bus shelter and squeezed his way onto the sidewalk. Not wanting to startle the students, he tucked his gun into his pocket and approached the shelter.

"Excuse me," Payne said, "have you seen a guy in a trench coat?"

"Why?" said the smart-ass in the middle. "Are you hoping to get flashed?"

Payne wasn't in the mood for jokes. He took a step closer and stared at the kid, half tempted to pull out his gun in order to stress the urgency of the situation. But the last thing he wanted to do was to threaten them, especially with the news he was about to share.

"Listen very carefully," he said calmly. "There was a shooting near Heinz Chapel. The suspect is wearing a trench coat and he fled this way."

"What?" shrieked the female on the left. The others sat upright.

"Do you have a phone?"

All three nodded their heads.

"Contact the Pitt police and tell them what I said. Have them send a warning message on the campus system. The fewer people outdoors, the better."

Ever since the Virginia Tech shooting in 2007, most American universities had implemented a text-message alert system that could notify students and faculty of impending danger. With the touch of a button, more than thirty thousand phones would receive the warning.

"Do you understand me?"

They nodded their heads in unison.

"Make the call on your way to the Cathedral. Go right now and spread the word."

"Why the Cathedral?" the smart-ass asked.

"Because the shooter just passed the Cathedral and was headed this way. There's no reason for him to backtrack."

"I think I saw him," said the girl on the right.

"Where?" Payne demanded.

"He crossed the street toward the union a few minutes ago."

"Did he go inside?"

She shook her head. "He was heading toward the quad."

"Did you see his face?"

"I only saw his coat. It was long and dark brown."

Payne thanked her, then jogged across the street toward the main entrance of the student union. Three sets of doors sat under a large portico on his left. Just beyond it was a split set of steps that led up to Schenley Quadrangle, a cluster of five residence halls that housed more than a thousand students. On most nights, the quad would be swarming with foot traffic—students heading to class or hanging out with friends—but Payne knew the basketball game on the far side of campus would reduce those numbers, as would the cold temperature.

He darted up the steps, hoping to find an empty quad.

Instead, he found himself in the middle of a war zone.

More than fifty students were in the midst of a massive snowball battle. Everywhere Payne looked, people were running, and throwing, and howling with laughter. Not only in the courtyard between the buildings but also in the windows above. Minutes earlier, a few devious students had dumped buckets of water on the participants down below, and now their room was the main focus of the attack. Snowballs were flying at all angles: up, down, and across the quad. All of it was good, clean fun— students blowing off steam at the end of a semester.

Little did they know, a killer was lurking nearby.

A female student, wearing a knit cap and matching mittens, spotted Payne in his tuxedo. She hustled over to warn him. "If I were you, I'd go another way. It's not safe in here."

Payne smirked at the irony of her statement. "Are you on guard duty?"

She smiled. "Something like that."

"Did you see a guy in a brown trench coat?"

She nodded. "He ignored me and kept on walking."

"How long ago?"

"Thirty seconds. You can catch him if you hurry."

"Which way?" Payne demanded.

She pointed to the right. "Just past Amos Hall, heading toward Fifth."

"Thanks," Payne said as he sprinted across the courtyard. Snowballs whizzed past him like enemy fire, but he wasn't the least bit concerned. His sole focus was catching the man in the trench coat, stopping him before he killed again.

A few seconds later, Payne reached the end of Amos Hall. He skidded to a stop on the slick pavement and pulled out his gun. With his back against the wall, he inched his head around the corner and searched for his target. Unfortunately, the shooter was waiting for him behind a parked car. His muzzle blast sounded like thunder as it echoed off the surrounding buildings. His bullet struck the edge of Amos Hall, less than a foot from Payne's head, producing a tiny wisp of debris. Behind Payne, the collective sound of laughter turned into shrieks of terror as students scattered in all directions, some diving indoors, others running toward the union.

But Payne didn't flinch. He stood perfectly still, gun in hand, waiting to make his move. A moment later he poked his head into the alley a second time, and once again the shooter fired. This time the bullet was even closer, missing Payne's head by less than six inches.

"Shit," Payne mumbled, realizing he was at a tactical disadvantage.

As a right-handed shooter, Payne knew he would have to expose his entire right flank in order to get off a clean shot. And due to his opponent's accuracy, he knew that was a dangerous proposition. With that in mind, he moved his gun into his left hand. Although a kill shot wasn't realistic, he figured he could pump a few rounds into the car that was shielding his target. If his opponent got flustered and ran, Payne could charge forward and take him out.

Payne took a deep breath and inched his gun around the corner. He calmly squeezed the trigger, and the passenger window exploded. Payne made a small adjustment to his aim and fired again. This time the bullet entered the front passenger window and exited the driver's side. Shards of glass rained down on the killer, stinging him like a swarm of angry bees. The man howled in agony as a piece of window pierced the corner of his left eye.

It was the sound Payne had been hoping to hear.

With his shield destroyed and his vision blurred, the assailant ran toward Fifth Avenue, hoping to reach his vehicle on the other side of the street before Payne shot him from behind.

A few seconds later, his escape attempt ended in a puddle of blood.

12

The bus driver had always driven carefully through the Pitt campus. She knew several students had died over the years walking into the bus lane that ran against the flow of traffic on Fifth Avenue. But in this case, her caution didn't matter because the man darted in front of her like a deer on the highway. One second he wasn't visible, the next he was splattered on her windshield.

The noise that the body made was unlike any that Payne had heard before. It was a mixture of a meaty thud and the splash of a spilled drink, all rolled together with the crack of a wishbone. By the time the driver skidded to an icy stop, the surrounding snow looked like salsa.

"Holy shit," Payne muttered as he moved forward to inspect the carnage.

Although he was thrilled that the drama had ended quickly, Payne was smart enough to realize that the man's death had left several questions unanswered. Not only his identity—which would take a while to determine based on his current lack of a face—but also why Ashley had been murdered. Was she the intended target? Or was she simply collateral damage?

During their careers, Payne and Jones had made a long list of enemies. Their time with the MANIACs guaranteed that they would live the rest of their lives looking over their shoulders. Most of their missions had been classified, but rumors about their exploits were well-known in the military community. Sure, some of the stories were untrue—nothing more than lies that had become a part of their legend—but enough facts were sprinkled in to put them in harm's way.

"Oh my God," the driver wailed as she stepped off the bus. She was white and pudgy, the female equivalent of Ralph Kramden from *The Honeymooners*. "I swear I didn't see him!"

Payne walked over to comfort her. "Don't worry, ma'am. It wasn't your fault."

"It doesn't matter," she shrieked. "They're going to fire me for sure! Oh my God, I can't believe I killed a man!"

He put his hand on her shoulder. "I swear, you're *not* going to get fired. In fact, you're liable to get a medal for this."

She looked at him like he was crazy. "What are you talking about?"

"That *monster*," Payne said for effect, "just killed a

woman. And he would've killed several more if it wasn't for you. You, my dear, are a *hero*."

She wiped her nose with the sleeve of her coat. "He killed someone?"

Payne nodded. "In cold blood."

"And I stopped him?"

"With your massive bus."

She glanced at the red pulp that stained the asphalt. "Are you serious?"

"Completely."

She let out a sigh of relief, then broke into a wide smile. "Oh my Lord, thank you, Jesus. I can't believe I'm a hero . . . Do you think I'll be on TV?"

"I'd bet on it."

"Oh my goodness, I gotta call my sister. She's gonna be so jealous."

"Before you do that," Payne suggested, "you better call your supervisor. This lane needs to be shut down for the rest of the night."

"Oh my Lord, I never thought of that."

He pointed toward her bus. "You also need to calm your passengers. Tell them what happened, and tell them they need to stay onboard until the police arrive. The last thing we want is for them to be walking through any evidence."

She nodded in agreement. "What else should I do?"

He gave it some thought. "Tell me, do you wear glasses?"

"Why? Do you think I need 'em? I'm telling you, the guy ran right—"

"No, that's not what I meant. What about sunglasses? Do you have sunglasses?"

"Why? Should I wear them on TV?"

"No, ma'am. I'd simply like to borrow them."

"Why? Are *you* gonna wear them on TV?"

He growled in frustration. "Ma'am, this has *nothing* to do with TV. I need to make sure the guy is dead, and when I do, I don't want any blood to splash into my eyes."

It was a lie, but he didn't have the patience to explain the truth.

She glanced at the body. Chunks of carcass littered the bus lane. "I'm telling you, sweetie, that boy is dead. I caught him flush."

Payne tapped his watch to make his point. "The cops will want a time of death for their report. It can't be *official* if I don't check his pulse." He knew she would believe him. "Of course, if you'd rather do it yourself, go right ahead. I'm not going to stop you."

"No way," she argued, "that's okay. You can have my sunglasses. I'll get 'em right now."

"Thank you, I'd appreciate it."

As she hustled to get them, Payne pulled out his phone and called Jones. He answered on the third ring. "Jon, are you all right? I heard multiple shots."

Payne nodded. "I'm fine. The shooter's dead."

"How?"

"I lured him in front of a bus."

"You *what*?"

"Long story," Payne said dismissively. "The important thing is he's dead."

Jones paused. "Did you recognize him?"

"I'm still working on that. Things are kind of messy here."

"Here, too. The janitor is going ape-shit over the crime scene. I told him he was in charge of cleaning everything up. I even told him to get his shovel."

Payne smirked. Their years of service had darkened their sense of humor. It was a trait they shared with half the military, especially those who saw combat. "Why'd you do that?"

"Why? Because I don't like the guy. He's too lippy."

"Lippy? Look who's talking! Mr. Pot, meet Mr. Kettle."

"Hold up! Is that some kind of a black joke?"

Payne laughed, realizing Jones was teasing. "Have the cops arrived yet?"

"Any moment now. I see their lights on Bellefield."

"Then we better talk quick. What's our story?"

"Our story? I didn't know we needed one."

"Just a second." The bus driver returned with her sunglasses and handed them to Payne. He thanked her, then walked away so she couldn't hear what he was saying. "A mystery woman drives across the state to chat with us and gets her head blown off. I don't know about you, but I'm slightly suspicious."

"Wait. You think this was about *her*, not *us*? I'm not sure about that."

"Me, neither. But until we ID the shooter, what can we say? If he's from our past, we can't tell the cops anything. We'll have to get the Pentagon involved. And if *that* happens, you know damn well our statements will have to be cleared by them."

"And what if he isn't from our past?"

"Then he might've come for the letter. I mean, that's why she was here, right?"

Jones nodded. "By the way, I've got it."

"Good. We'll deal with it later. In the meantime, what should we say?"

"Let's stick to the basics. She showed up at your party and was embarrassed by her clothes. So we went to the chapel to talk. When we came out, she got shot."

"And what were we discussing?"

"You tell me. I came up with everything else."

Payne paused in thought. "Let's keep it simple. She was a schoolteacher interested in Greece, and she asked us about our treasure. Nothing more, nothing less."

"Sounds perfect."

"Anything else to worry about?"

"Just one thing. But it's kind of big."

"What is it?" Payne asked.

"That gun you're holding? I bought it on the street and never registered it because the serial number was filed off."

"What?!" Payne blurted, suddenly panicked. The last thing he needed was to be arrested on a weapons charge.

Jones stayed quiet for several seconds before he cracked up with laughter. "Nah, I'm just messing with you. Serves you right, though. I can't believe you stole my gun. If I'd had a backup piece, I would've shot you in the ass. You sneaky bastard!"

Payne hung up the phone without saying another word, realizing that Jones was fully within his rights to torture him. In fact, he realized he'd probably gotten off easy. Unless, of course, Jones was planning a two-stage attack. A simple joke now, an intricate prank later. It was something he'd be mindful of in the coming days.

In the meantime, he had more important things to worry about.

Like identifying the shooter.

Payne untucked his dress shirt and exposed the bottom of his undershirt. With the soft cloth, he carefully wiped all the smudges off the driver's sunglasses. When he was done, he held them up to a streetlight and inspected the lenses. To his naked eye, they were spotless.

Next, he walked behind the bus and searched for the shooter's torso. The initial impact had killed the man, snapping his spine and ribs like toothpicks. The messy part had come later, when his body got caught on the front axle and had been dragged along the asphalt for half a city block. At some point he had ripped free and was quickly run over by one of the rear wheels, which squirted out his innards like a popped zit. Thankfully, one of the guy's arms was mostly intact, and that was what Payne needed to make his identification.

Grabbing the lifeless hand, Payne made a perfect thumbprint on one of the clean lenses, then repeated the process with the index finger on the other. Afterward, he held the glasses up to the light, just to make sure it worked. Now, no matter what the cops did with the body or how long they took to gather forensic evidence, Payne could run the prints himself.

With any luck, he would know the shooter's background by the end of the night.

13

Jones answered the same questions, over and over, for nearly forty minutes. First it was the campus cops, then the Pittsburgh police came rolling in. One officer after another, each slightly higher up the food chain than the previous one, all of them asking the same things. Not that Jones complained. He had spent too much time in the military to get upset over the chain of command.

The only request that bothered Jones was their final one of the evening. Since he was covered in blood splatter, they asked him to undress inside the chapel and give his tuxedo to a forensics expert for further analysis. Jones wasn't sure why they needed his clothes—the shooter was dead, which meant this case would never go to court—but he complied. He figured, the sooner he got out of the police's spotlight, the better. Because there were things he needed to do.

Illegal things.

Unfortunately, he would be forced to do them in someone else's clothes. The police offered him a paper-thin smock that resembled a hospital gown, but he immediately turned it down. Considering the cold weather and the flock of journalists that had gathered on the lawn, he told the cops he would rather spend the night in his underwear than go outside in a muumuu. After all, he had his reputation to worry about.

With very few options in the lost and found, the police scrambled to find an alternative. The best they could come up with was a khaki jumpsuit a few sizes too small, but all things considered, it was acceptable to Jones. He wondered where they had found it on such short notice until he read the name on the front pocket. The tiny patch read: SAM.

"Thank you, karma," Jones mumbled as he got dressed in the basement.

Upstairs, Sam was waiting for him. He stared at Jones for several seconds, checking him out in his new outfit, then burst into laughter. "Not as gay as your monkey suit."

He took it in stride. "Thanks for the loan."

"Loan, my ass. Report to work at six a.m. sharp. I'll be damned if I'm cleaning up the blood myself. That shit ain't in my job description."

Jones bit his tongue and left before the janitor could tease him further. Outside the chapel, the police were still dealing with the crime scene. The steps and patio had been cordoned off with yellow tape, and the coroner's office was still handling the body. Jones spotted the officer in charge and asked if he could borrow a police jacket for his long walk to his car. A minute later, Jones was handed a navy blue coat. In gold letters on the back, it read: SWAT.

Only a couple letters different from SAM, but way cooler, in his mind.

No way in hell he was giving it back. Not unless they returned his tux.

Ironically, the coat was going to do more than keep Jones warm. It was going to help him break the law, which was why he had asked for it in the first place. If he had been concerned with warmth or style, he would have walked over to the Cathedral and retrieved his overcoat from the coat-check girl. Instead, he wanted to use the SWAT coat to gather intelligence.

During the question-and-answer period, Jones had kept a few tidbits to himself. The first was the existence of the mysterious letter. Since it was in his possession when Ashley was killed, he didn't see the need to tell them about it. And neither did Payne. So Jones stuck with the basic story that they had agreed upon, and he was confident that Payne would do the same.

The second item was a little more dishonest. Not a bold-faced lie, just a simple omission that would slow down the police investigation by an hour or so. It was the time Jones needed to get some information for himself.

Very early on, Jones realized Ashley wasn't carrying any identification. He had figured that out when cop after cop kept asking if he knew her full name. The truth was he didn't. She had introduced herself as Ashley and had never provided a surname during their conversation. If she had, he would have told the police immediately, so they could notify her next of kin.

However, he had failed to mention the location of her car. He knew he should have, since it probably contained her purse, or insurance papers, or something with her name and address, but he decided against it because he wasn't sure what else was out there.

Maybe information about the letter. Or possibly the *actual* letter.

Whatever the case, he wanted to see it first.

WEARING HIS SWAT jacket, Jones ducked under the crime-scene tape and turned left on the Varsity Walk, hoping to figure out why Ashley had been killed. Earlier that evening, he had followed her down the same path and had spotted her from the icy steps. Back then, her movement had stood out on the deserted road. Now S. Bellefield Avenue resembled a carnival midway.

Everywhere Jones looked he saw bright, flashing lights. The entire left-hand lane was filled with police cars and satellite trucks from the evening news. People scurried to and fro, half of them buzzing from adrenaline, the other half from caffeine. Compared with earlier, this seemed like a different place—like Pittsburgh had been magically transformed into Las Vegas.

Only with fewer strippers and a lot more snow.

Glancing across the street, he saw her Ford Taurus. It was parked fifty feet to the right, buried under an inch of fresh powder. To his mind, that was good news, because it would help conceal what he was about to do. He needed to break into her car, right under the cops' noses.

With a smile on his face, Jones walked down the steps like he owned the place. After waving to some detectives, he said hello to a group of paramedics. The entire time Jones acted like he belonged, like he was one of them. And because of that, no one questioned his presence. Although the jacket helped, his attitude sealed the deal. Never nervous or shady, he carried himself with confidence, like a man who was there to do his job.

Reaching into his pocket, Jones pulled out his wallet. Hidden in the crease of the leather was a small set of lock picks that he had carried with him for years. The type that could get him inside a car or building in a matter of seconds. He had learned how to use them in the military and had continued to use them during his career as a private detective—a career that began several years sooner than Jones had ever imagined.

Originally, Jones had planned on staying in the service for another decade or so, but when Grandpa Payne died and left his company to his grandson, everything changed. At the time, Payne wasn't ready to retire, but out of love and respect for the man who had raised him, he left the military and moved back to Pittsburgh to fulfill his familial duties.

To help his adjustment to civilian life, Payne convinced Jones to retire as well. In fact, he bribed him to do it. He gave Jones office space in the Payne Industries complex and loaned him enough start-up capital to open his own business. It had always been Jones's dream to run a detective agency, and Payne had the means to help. So Payne figured, why not?

In Payne's mind, Jones was the only family he had left.

Not surprisingly, the pace of their lives had slowed considerably in recent years. Other than the rare occasions when Payne helped Jones with one of his cases, the only time they got to carry guns and have some fun was when they had their own adventures. The last time had been their trip to Greece. And it had been a life-changer.

Thanks to their historic discovery, Jones suddenly had more money than he could possibly spend in his lifetime. Growing up in a lower-middle-class family, he had lived his life frugally, always saving money for a rainy day. The military had paid for his education at the Air Force Academy and had taken care of his basic living expenses for nearly two decades. This had allowed Jones to build a nice nest egg. Now he had more nest eggs than a chicken farmer.

The first thing he did was pay back all the cash that he had borrowed from Payne. Not only the start-up capital, but also the money that Payne should have been charging for rent, plus interest. Payne had been reluctant to take it—he certainly didn't need the funds—but Jones pestered him so much that Payne eventually agreed.

Unfortunately, there were some drawbacks to their sudden notoriety. For one, crackpots and treasure hunters were constantly approaching them with crazy schemes. And since Jones's clients came from the general public, he had to deal with nut jobs more often than Payne. Sometimes they asked Jones for money, other times they needed his guidance or required a helping hand on some wild adventure, but the sheer number of people that contacted his agency was so large that Jones had to hire extra staff to screen potential clients.

Not that he was complaining.

As someone who loved mysteries, Jones was enjoying his second career. Still, compared to his days with the MANIACs, his current life was painfully boring.

Of course, all of that changed with the shooting at the chapel.

His adrenaline was flowing, and he was craving more.

14

Auto dealerships and law-enforcement personnel call them *tryout keys*—they're universally designed to get inside many makes and models of cars—but on the street, they're called *jigglers*. As the two names suggest, they are grooved pieces of metal that look like keys, but the notches are so worn down that they will fit inside most locks. In order to open a door, the key is jiggled left and right while inching it in and out of the keyhole. With a skilled touch, the grooves will eventually match the mechanism inside, and when that happens, the lock pops open.

During his time with the MANIACs, Jones had broken into more cars than he could possibly remember. Sometimes to acquire an escape vehicle, other times to plant an explosive device. Over the years, those life-or-death experiences had hardened his nerves and steadied his hands, making his current mission seem easy by comparison.

Police across the street? Not a problem.

Even if they started shooting.

To block the cops' view, Jones walked around the front of the car and eyed the passenger-side door. Like most Ford cars, the Taurus required a five-pin jiggler. Jones flipped through his tools as if he was fumbling for his keys and came out with the appropriate one. Handmade in his workshop at home, the jiggler was carved out of stainless steel. He slipped it into the keyhole and wiggled it slightly. Less than ten seconds later, he heard the lock click.

"Not bad," he mumbled as he opened the door and climbed inside.

The interior was cold but not nearly as bad as it had been outdoors. For that, he was thankful. He was also glad he had found a pair of black leather gloves at the chapel. They allowed him to rummage through her car without leaving any prints. Not that it actually mattered. The shooting had taken place across the street, so he doubted that a forensic team would examine the car. But on the off chance they did, he preferred to keep his physical evidence out of the equation.

The first place he searched was the glove compartment. In his experience, that was where most people kept their car registration and insurance card, and all he needed was Ashley's full name and address. With that information, he could go back to his office and run it through every database and search engine imaginable. In a matter of seconds, her entire life would appear on his computer screen, everything from her date of birth to the size of her latest paycheck.

When Jones opened the latch, he expected the storage space to be jammed with personal items—music CDs, cosmetics, a small purse, maybe even some food. Anytime he went on a road trip, he packed peanut-butter crackers or protein bars, so he wouldn't have to stop for snacks. And if Payne, a freak of nature who had to consume more than eight thousand calories a day or he lost weight, was along for the ride, then they brought multiple sandwiches or several containers of beef jerky to keep Payne from getting cranky. Therefore, when Jones looked inside the glove box and it was empty, he was more than surprised. He was borderline stunned.

"What the hell?" he said to himself.

At the very least, Jones had expected to find her paperwork. But nothing? That didn't make any sense. Even the most obsessive people in the world kept *something* in their cars, even if it was just a dust cloth to tidy up. But an empty glove box was suspicious.

Suddenly, all types of paranoid thoughts ran through his mind. Had the assassin gone through the vehicle before the shooting? Worse still, what if the shooter had a partner who had done it? There might be another gunman floating around the Pitt campus, searching for his next target.

It was a concept Jones hadn't considered until that very moment.

For all he knew, a sniper could be eyeing him from a nearby building, patiently waiting for the cops to leave before he pulled the trigger.

Boom! Boom! Boom!

The sound echoed from above like gunshots. With a burst of adrenaline, Jones nearly dove into the backseat until he realized what had made the noise. Someone was on the street outside, pounding on the roof of the car. Jones glanced out the driver's side and saw a muscular man in a tuxedo and black gloves. Only then did his heart rate start to calm.

"Holy hell," he cursed as he leaned over and opened the door. "You almost killed me."

Payne grinned and slipped inside. "Sorry about that. I thought you saw me."

"You know damn well I didn't see you, or you wouldn't have knocked."

Payne shrugged, not willing to confirm or deny anything. "Any luck?"

"With what?"

"Your search."

"Nothing so far. Then again, I just got here."

Payne pointed. "Did you check the glove box?"

"First thing I did. It's empty."

"Any paperwork?"

"Nothing."

"What about food?"

Jones shook his head. "*Nada.*"

"No snacks? Who goes on a road trip without snacks?"

"I was wondering the same thing myself."

"What about a pack of mints?"

"Jon, what is it about *empty* that you can't comprehend?"

"Sorry. It just seems weird, that's all."

As their search continued, they checked the storage compartment under the center armrest and the pockets that were mounted behind the leather seats. But they were empty as well. Next Jones flipped down both sun visors, hoping to find something of value. From the driver's side, a single slip of paper came fluttering out. Payne snatched it in mid-flight and held it up to the window, struggling to read it in the dim light. Slowly, a grimace surfaced on his face.

"Shit," Payne cursed. "This isn't good."

"What is it?"

"A leaflet for Budget Rent A Car."

Jones paused, thinking things through. "Well, that would explain the empty glove box. I guess she rented a car for her road trip. What's the problem?"

"Look at the business address."

Jones opened the glove box and used the interior light to read the details. According to the flyer, the car had been rented from the Pittsburgh airport. "This isn't good."

"I'm pretty sure I just said that."

"I know you did. And I'm agreeing with you."

Payne flipped up both visors and studied the frosty windshield. In the upper-right corner, he noticed a small orange sticker that read: BUDGET. "I wish I had seen that before. It would've changed my entire line of questioning."

"Maybe so, but it was covered with ice and snow. No way it was visible from outside."

"I know that, but I should've—"

Jones interrupted him. "She lied to both of us, and both of us bought it. You weren't the only one who was fooled."

Payne nodded reluctantly. "So, what do we do now?"

"Right now, our only goal is to get as much info about this car as possible before the cops show up. With any luck, Budget will have her name and address on file."

Payne grabbed a pen from his jacket pocket. "I'll start with the registration number."

"And I'll get the license plate."

"While you're back there," Payne said as he hit a button that opened the trunk, "check to see if she had any luggage."

Jones opened his door and walked toward the rear of the car. After brushing away some snow, he wrote the plate number on the back of the Budget leaflet and tucked it into his pocket.

"Find anything?" Payne asked.

"Just getting to that," Jones said as he opened the trunk.

The overhead light popped on, revealing a single carry-on item. Made of black leather, the bag was zipped closed and stuffed full. Instead of wasting valuable time to sort through it there, Jones grabbed the strap and slipped it over his shoulder.

Then, without saying a word, he closed the hatch, and they walked away.

15

François Dubois was obsessed with inside information and had been for most of his life. Like most of his criminal rivals—mafia dons, arms dealers, drug cartels, and so on—Dubois paid top dollar to have well-informed sources at every major law-enforcement agency in the world. He had contacts at the FBI, the CIA, Interpol, MI6, France's Police Nationale, Belgium's Police Fédérale, and in all the other countries where he conducted business. These sources were expensive, but the information he obtained from them was invaluable. Dubois realized that without their warnings he would have been killed or arrested a long time ago.

But Dubois's obsession didn't stop there.

Although he was a highly educated intellectual—the type of man who typically viewed prophets and oracles as scam artists—Dubois fervently believed that some people were blessed with the ability to see the future. This belief stemmed from the fact that he temporarily had the power himself. From the time he was eight until he was nearly eleven, Dubois kept a journal next to his bed, where he recorded his most vivid dreams. On several occasions, those visions came true, right down to the smallest of details.

At first, his ability frightened him. He was afraid something was wrong, that he was some kind of a freak. But his mother, who had been born in Avignon, France, not far from the birthplace of Nostradamus, explained his talent was a gift that many people would love to have. She insisted his knowledge of the future was a powerful tool that he could use to improve his life, and in certain situations, maybe even save it. Then she took him to the library and showed him all the books and articles written about the most famous prophets of all time. Dubois was intrigued by the work of several prophets, but his fascination with Nostradamus bordered on obsession. Partially because he had come from the same region as Dubois's mother, but mainly because of the power that the prophet's name still possessed several centuries after his death.

From that moment on, Dubois was hooked. He read everything he could get his hands on, devouring every last word while trying to determine who had the gift and who was a charlatan. Ironically, his interest in clair-voyance grew even stronger once his own dreams had stopped. No longer able to see the future himself, he realized he was lacking information that other people possessed, so he doubled his efforts to find prophecies that had been verified.

Some of the stories he had read as a teenager were downright spooky.

One of Dubois's favorites involved an American author named Morgan Robertson. Born in Oswego, New York, in 1861, Robertson believed he was possessed by a spirit that helped him write. Before he could produce a single sentence, Robertson had to lie completely still for several minutes in a semiconscious state. Eventually, the entity would dictate stories to him, using vivid images. Then Robertson would translate these visions into words.

Competing with the popular stories of Jules Verne, whose science fiction was filled with an optimistic view of technology and travel, Robertson preferred depressing tales of maritime disasters. This included a novella, published in 1898, titled *The Wreck of the* Titan. As with his other stories, Robertson received the plot from his magical entity, although he told many of his closest friends that this particular vision felt stronger than any other.

In his book, he described a majestic ocean liner steaming across the Atlantic on a foggy night. Robertson wrote of a ship that was twice as long as any ever built, powered by three massive propellers that surpassed the technology of that day. The first line of the story was: "She was the largest craft afloat and the greatest work of man." Over two thousand passengers filled its decks and luxurious cabins on its April voyage from New York to England, a journey that ended in disaster when the *Titan* hit an iceberg just before midnight. A long gash, torn below the waterline, allowed flooding to occur in too many of the compartments for the *Titan* to stay afloat. A short while later, the "unsinkable" ship disappeared into the depths of the cold ocean, and most of its passengers drowned or died of hypothermia.

The story made very few waves in the literary scene until the night of April 14, 1912. While traveling between England and New York on its maiden voyage, the *Titanic*, the largest passenger steamship in the world, hit an iceberg at eleven forty p.m. and sank in the North Atlantic, killing over fifteen hundred passengers. Although a few of the details were different, there were enough similarities between Robertson's story and the actual events of the *Titanic* to capture the world's attention. Within weeks, *The Wreck of the* Titan and some of his other tales were serialized in newspapers across America. It brought him a level of fame he never had a chance to enjoy, because alcoholism and depression ended his life.

Three decades later, another one of his stories proved to be prophetic.

In *Beyond the Spectrum*, a short story he published in 1914, Robertson described a future war between the United States and Japan that resembled the actual events of Pearl Harbor in 1941. Instead of declaring war on its rival, Japan launched a sneak attack on American ships heading to Hawaii. The hero of the story managed to stop the advancing forces by using an ultraviolet searchlight that blinded the Japanese crews. The devastating effects of the searchlight—intense heat, skin blisters, blindness—resembled the injuries caused by the atomic bombs dropped on Japan in 1945, weapons that ultimately ended the war.

Once again, the similarities between fact and fiction weren't perfect, but they were close enough for Dubois to pay attention.

16

The Payne Industries Building sits atop Mount Washington, high above the city of Pittsburgh. According to *USA Today*, it was the second most beautiful place in America, only behind Red Rock Country in Sedona, Arizona. From his office window, Jones could see the Allegheny and Monongahela rivers flowing together to form the Ohio. The confluence of the three rivers defined the Golden Triangle, the name given to the business district, where dozens of skyscrapers glowed in the nighttime sky. More than fifteen bridges, lined with a dazzling assortment of holiday lights, twinkled above the waterways, turning the color of the icy rivers from white to red, then green.

On a clear night, PNC Park and Heinz Field, two of the most scenic ballparks in all of sports, were visible across the rivers on the North Shore. A revitalized section of the city, it featured the Carnegie Science Center, complete with a World War II submarine (USS *Requin*) docked along the water's edge, and the newly opened Rivers Casino. But thanks to the blizzard, Jones struggled to see the city itself, let alone the buildings on the opposite shore.

A beep from his antique desk snapped him out of his daydream.

Dressed in jeans and a sweatshirt, he turned from the window and walked toward his computer. A message on his screen informed him that his search was complete, and no matching entries had been found. Grumbling to himself, Jones sat down in his leather executive chair and clicked his mouse. He had been fishing for clues ever since he had left Ashley's car. Meanwhile, Payne had returned to the Cathedral to apologize to his guests and explain what had happened.

Three hours later, Payne finally made it to Mount Washington.

"Knock, knock," he said as he walked into Jones's office.

Jones barely glanced up from his computer. "It's about time."

Still wearing his tuxedo, Payne collapsed in the chair across from Jones. "Sorry about that. Lots of people to see, lots of asses to kiss."

"How'd it go?"

"Much better than I'd expected. The cops barged in, looking for potential witnesses, and they happened to mention that I chased an armed gunman across campus, potentially saving hundreds of lives. After that, everyone wanted to shake my hand and give me a check."

THE PROPHECY   *101*

"Did you say *hundreds*?"

"Hey, the cops exaggerated, not me."

Jones rolled his eyes. "Let me guess, my name didn't come up once."

"Not true," Payne assured him. "I told everyone you helped."

"Really?"

"Yep! Working as a janitor at Heinz Chapel."

"You're such an asshole."

"By the way, I have a message from Sam. He wanted me to tell you, *six o'clock sharp*. Whatever the hell that means."

Jones growled softly. "I already burned his jumpsuit. I'll send him the ashes tomorrow."

"Speaking of clothes, what'd you find in Ashley's bag?"

Jones pointed to the far side of the room, where the contents were spread out on a glass table. Payne walked over and examined them. Unfortunately, nothing stood out. There was a change of clothes, an overnight kit filled with toiletries, and an unzipped leather portfolio.

"Not much to work with, huh?"

Jones shook his head. "No computer, no wallet, no weapons."

"No wallet? How'd she rent her car?"

"Beats me."

"Any ID?"

"I was working on that when you came in." He grabbed a sealed plastic bag from his desk and dangled it in the air. Inside was a single U.S. passport, already opened to the photo page. "According to this, her full name was Ashley Marie Duvall."

"Ashley was her *real* name?"

"Kind of."

"What does that mean?"

Jones leaned back in his chair. "I ran that name through the State Department computer and got zero hits. It isn't in their database."

"Her passport was fake?"

"Yep, a damn good one. I couldn't spot any flaws."

Payne walked across the room and snatched the bag from Jones's hand. When he did, a fine layer of powder settled on the interior of the plastic. "You dusted for prints?"

"Of course I dusted for prints. I had three hours to kill."

"And?"

"I got two thumbs and several partials. I ran them through IAFIS and got lucky."

IAFIS stood for Integrated Automated Fingerprint Identification System, a national fingerprint and criminal history database maintained by the Federal Bureau of Investigation and intended for law-enforcement agencies, not the private sector. But thanks to his connections at the Pentagon, Jones had full access to the system.

Payne sat down. "How lucky?"

"Very lucky. Our girl had a record."

"For what?"

"She was a lifelong thief." Jones held up a three-page printout, then handed it to Payne. "Her real name was

Ashley Henderson. Born and raised in Camden, New Jersey, she was first arrested at thirteen and was in and out of juvenile homes until eighteen. On the bright side, her last known address *was* in Philadelphia, so she didn't lie about everything."

"See," Payne joked, "there's a little good in all of us."

Glancing at the document, Payne focused on the passport photo on the first page. It was definitely the woman they had met earlier, the victim who had been killed at Heinz Chapel. Ashley the teacher *was* Ashley the criminal. No doubt about it. Of course, some major questions still remained in Payne's mind. Why did she travel across the state to meet with them? What was her motivation? Obviously, she was trying to con them out of something, but what was her endgame? Was she looking for money? Was she looking for a thrill? And why was she gunned down in cold blood on the Pitt campus?

The last question was the one that worried him the most.

"Any thoughts on her murder?" Payne asked.

"Anytime you're dealing with a criminal, there's always a chance she pissed off the wrong person. But considering tonight's circumstances, I'm not sure that was the case."

"What circumstances?"

"Not only was she murdered, it happened three hundred miles from home. That's a long way to give chase if someone had a problem with her in Philly."

"Good point."

"Furthermore, I ran down her travel arrangements.

She flew in this afternoon, under the name Ashley Duvall, and booked a return flight for tomorrow. Her tickets were purchased online within the last twenty-four hours, meaning her killer didn't have much time to set things up. If her trip had been planned weeks in advance, he would've had time to scout things out, but less than a day? That seems unlikely. Especially in this weather. To me, it seems more and more likely that this guy was after us, not her."

"What do we know about him?" Payne wondered.

"I ran his prints, but IAFIS didn't have a match. If he's killed before, he hasn't been caught."

"What about other databases?"

Jones shrugged. "I don't know. I haven't had time to try."

"Wow," Payne teased, "I gave you three hours to wrap everything up, and that's all you got? I thought you were a professional."

"Don't push it, Jon. Or I'll charge you for my time."

"Go ahead and bill me. What do janitors make per hour?"

Jones ignored him. "Anyway, if it's okay with you, I'm gonna call it a night. Let me get some rest, and I'll do more digging in the morning. Maybe something else will turn up."

Unfortunately for them, his words were prophetic.

17

After sleeping in a private suite on the top floor of his office building, Payne stumbled into the spacious kitchen, searching for something to eat. The apartment had been built decades earlier by his grandfather. He used to spend so much time at the office—and had wasted so many hours driving back and forth to his mansion in the northern suburbs—that he finally wised up and converted some office space into his second home.

When Payne took over the business a few years ago, he redecorated the place, eliminating the old décor and adding a touch of luxury. Now, when he or his board of directors needed to impress an out-of-state executive or a foreign client, Payne Industries had the most scenic penthouse in the city at their disposal. And when the suite was empty and Payne didn't feel like driving home, he followed his grandfather's example and spent the night.

With an empty pantry and a growling stomach, Payne put on some jeans, a sweatshirt, and a winter coat. He rode the elevator to the ground floor and exited through the lobby. Just up the street was a local bakery that was known for its fresh bread and pastries. On Sundays, it was always packed with churchgoers, but he knew when services ended and avoided those times.

Strolling up Grandview Avenue, the picturesque road that overlooked the city, he gazed at the river below. The Gateway Clipper steamed across the icy water, shuttling Steelers fans to Heinz Field from the parking lots at Station Square, an old railroad station that had been converted into a bustling entertainment complex. Since it was nearly eleven a.m., tens of thousands of tailgaters had been partying on the North Shore for the better part of three hours. By the time the Steelers kicked off against the Cleveland Browns at one p.m., the local fans would be so rowdy that people could sit on their balconies and, based on the crowd noise alone, tell what was happening at the game over a mile away.

At least that's what Payne had been told by his neighbors. The truth was he wasn't willing to miss a home game to find out. Since Payne Industries had its own luxury box at the stadium, Payne took full advantage. Like many of his peers, he had grown up in the city when the Steelers were the most dominant team in the National Football League, winning four Super Bowls in six years in the 1970s. That had left an indelible mark on his young psyche. Ever since, Payne had bled black-and-gold like everyone else in Steelers Nation, the nickname their fan base had been given by the national media.

Payne bought a box of pastries at the bakery. A couple of fruit Danish would hold him over until he dined on the elaborate spread at the stadium. The doughnuts and croissants would be given to Jones, who was meeting him at noon for the game, and his building's security staff. Unlike most CEOs, Payne identified more with hard-working members of the rank and file than the white-collar types who ran corporate America. His grandfather had been the same way, starting off as a mill worker and slowly building a manufacturing empire. During his life, he had never lost track of his roots, and he made damn sure his grandson didn't, either.

Despite the cold weather, Payne followed his weekend ritual and stopped on one of the half dozen lookouts that jutted out from Grandview Avenue. Held in place by steel girders, the concrete platforms dangled over the steep hillside, giving locals and tourists alike a great place to photograph the scenery below. The view was so spectacular that wedding parties were often seen jostling for position on Saturday afternoons, fighting for the best pictures possible.

With no one around, Payne set his box of pastries on the ground, then fished through his pockets for some change. He found a quarter and slipped it into the coin-operated binoculars that were mounted nearby. As a youngster, he used to come here with his father, who taught him the history of the city by pointing out important landmarks through the viewfinder. The tradition had started a generation earlier when Grandpa Payne had taught Payne's father the exact same lessons. Now, as a way of honoring them both, Payne stopped by and remembered his past.

"Hey," growled a voice from behind. "Show me your hands."

Payne smiled, fully expecting to see one of his friends standing behind him. But when he turned around, all he saw was a silencer pointing at his chest.

"Show me your fucking hands!"

Calmly, Payne raised his gloved hands into the air. As he did, his eyes never left the gunman. He was a middle-aged white male, of average height and build. His slicked-back dark hair and fancy designer suit made him look more like a stockbroker than a criminal. Then again, in today's economy, a lot of stockbrokers *were* criminals.

With his peripheral vision, Payne studied his immediate surroundings. A black Mercedes sedan was running on the nearby street. The windows were tinted, so he couldn't tell if anyone else was inside. Because of the bitter wind, the sidewalk was free of pedestrians. At least for the time being. In approximately ten minutes, the church down the street would be letting out, and when it did, Grandview would be clogged with potential targets.

Then again, ten minutes was an eternity in a holdup.

No way this dragged on that long.

"I've got some cash and a box of pastries. Help yourself to either."

"I don't want your wallet. I want the letter."

Payne took a step back. "What letter?"

"Don't play dumb with me. I know you have it. You got it from the girl."

"What girl?"

"The dead girl."

Payne inched backward until he felt the cold metal railing against the small of his back. Now there was nothing behind him but a great view and a drop of several hundred feet.

"Don't move again!" the man ordered.

"Where can I go?" Payne argued.

The man stepped forward, closing the distance to ten feet. Close enough that he wouldn't miss, but far enough away that Payne couldn't charge him. "Where's the letter?"

"I don't know what you're talking about!"

The man sneered and pulled his trigger. His silencer flashed, and the bullet *pinged* loudly as it struck the railing less than six inches from Payne's waist. It hit so close that he could feel the vibrations in the metal.

"What did you do *that* for?"

He ignored the question. "We already killed the girl. What's one more?"

"Wait a second!" Payne demanded. "Who's *we*?"

The gunman sneered again. "I'll ask you one last time. Where is the letter?"

Payne lowered his hands, grasping the rail behind him. "Honestly," he lied, "I *don't* know what you're talking about!"

"That's a shame, Mr. Payne. Then you must die."

Payne had been around enough soldiers in his lifetime to recognize a killer. Some men had it in their DNA, and others didn't. Sure, most people could be provoked into murder—whether it was the protection of a loved one or self-defense—but it took a special sort of evil to look a defenseless stranger in the eye and savor the opportunity to end his life.

And this gunman had that talent.

With that in mind, Payne did the only rational thing he could think of.

He leaned back and flipped over the railing.

18

The maneuver was so unexpected that the gunman failed to pull the trigger until it was too late. One moment Payne was standing in front of him, the next he was gone.

Stunned by the development, the shooter rushed forward, gun in hand, hoping to see a body splattered on the hillside below. From the edge of the platform to the icy ground was a distance of more than two hundred feet. Several bare trees lined the slope, as did a thick blanket of snow, but neither could save a life from this height. Even a physical specimen like Payne was subject to the laws of gravity. Death would be very likely.

That is, if he had fallen into the valley.

But in reality, that wasn't what happened.

Payne had spent enough time on the concrete platforms to understand how they were built. His grandfather had even taken him underneath one when it was being repaired, so he could teach Payne the basic principles of cantilevers and stress-bearing beams. From the sidewalk, the platforms appeared to be floating on air, hanging over the valley with nothing to support them, but there was actually a network of steel beams underneath each concrete slab. When Payne flipped over the rail, he simply snagged one of the beams on his way down.

Of course, it was more difficult than it sounded.

If not for his leather gloves, he couldn't have pulled off the move without tearing the skin from his hands, but the gloves allowed him to keep hold of the vertical bars in the railing while he slid down the wrong side of the guardrail. Instead of plummeting wildly, his hands never left the metal. At the bottom of the rail, his fingers got pinched in between the support brackets and the concrete, sending a shockwave of pain to his brain, which compelled him to let go. Thankfully, his adrenaline dulled the sensation, and he managed to hold on long enough to survive.

With legs dangling freely, he swung both feet underneath the platform, hoping to make contact with one of the support beams. On his second attempt, his right foot hit steel and he managed to wedge his heel above the lip of the cold metal. Then, before the shooter had a chance to spot him, Payne yanked his left hand free and blindly groped for something to grab. An exposed bolt, jutting six inches from the bottom of the concrete, proved to be ideal.

As Payne ducked his head beneath the platform, the

shooter spotted him from above and fired. The bullet hit the lower corner of the column and sent a small shower of debris toward the trees below. The gunman cursed, realizing that his target was now underneath him, and the only way to get a clean shot was to go after him. It wasn't an appealing proposition.

Wasting no time, Payne shimmied along the steel beam, crawling upside-down toward the anchor point of the concrete. He had learned the technique in the military, using a single cable to cross a ravine or to breach a nearby building. Heels locked above, hips hanging down, then hand over hand until he reached his destination. It took him less than a minute to reach solid ground—a small ledge underneath the platform that had been installed for workers—but when he did, he gasped for breath and considered his predicament.

No weapon. No allies. No help on the way.

And somewhere above was a man with a silencer.

If Payne waited long enough, the church down the street would end its service, and the congregation would pour onto the sidewalk. Although it might give him a chance to slip away, he knew it would endanger a lot of innocent families. In his mind, taking a bullet was bad enough, but watching a kid get killed while he was running for cover was unforgivable.

No way he'd let that happen. Not if he could help it.

Because of his height, Payne was forced to crouch as he moved along the ledge. Slowly, he crept his way toward the right side of the platform, always holding on to the overhead beam to help steady his stride. One misstep on the frozen concrete and he would fall a long way. Not only would death be certain, but cleanup would be a bitch.

At the end of the ledge, he stopped and inched his head away from the platform, leaning back as far as he could to improve his view of above. The shooter must have sensed Payne's presence, because a split second later he was hovering over Payne, ready to pull the trigger.

"Shit!" Payne yelled as he yanked himself underneath the platform. As he did, the bullet whizzed past him, missing his head by inches and slamming into the rocks below.

"Your luck will run out soon," the gunman taunted.

"So will your ammo!" he shouted back.

"I wouldn't count on it."

Payne nodded to himself, realizing the shooter was right. If he had an extra clip or two, he could stand up there half the day, taking shot after shot until he got lucky or a hostage strolled by. Neither scenario appealed to Payne. In the MANIACs, he had been the aggressor, always looking to exploit his enemy, always trying to catch him with his guard down. For him, sitting under a ledge and playing peek-a-boo with a gunman wasn't an option. To survive, he knew he had to spot the guy's weakness and use it against him. But what was it?

After a moment of thought, he figured it out.

"Hey, asshole," Payne shouted. "What's your name? You owe me that much."

"I don't owe you shit!"

"Sure you do," he replied as he listened to the creaking above him. "You snuck up behind me like a bitch. That's a punk move."

The gunman crept to the left side of the platform. "But it worked."

Payne turned his head and shouted to the right. "No, it didn't. I'm still alive."

The killer spun and followed the sound. "You won't be for long."

"Come and get me!"

The gunman paused, then doubled back to his right. Without saying a word, he climbed up on the railing and leaned out as far as possible, hoping he had guessed right.

Ironically, he had, but it proved to be his downfall.

Instead of peeking out from under the platform, Payne leaped out with only one intention: to grab the gunman's tie. He had spotted it earlier when he had narrowly avoided the last shot. It had been hanging there, taunting him, like a leash on a lost dog. Payne knew if he got a hold of it, he would control the gunman. And he would control the situation.

But he didn't expect this.

Stretching as high as he could, Payne snagged the tie with his right hand and gave it a mighty yank. The gunman, who had already been leaning out over the edge, was unable to maintain his balance. Less than a second later, his feet shot skyward, and he flipped over the railing.

In a perfect world, Payne would have held on to the gunman and saved his life, if for no other reason than to question him about his mission. Unfortunately, Payne knew his footing and grip were way too precarious to support any extra weight, so he did the only thing that he could do to survive. Payne let go of the tie and shot his hand toward the railing.

As Payne grabbed the bar, the gunman whizzed past, screaming and flailing the entire way until his life ended with a muffled thud on the icy rocks below.

19

While driving his Cadillac Escalade toward the Payne Industries Building, Jones noticed several police cars parked on the street. Their lights were flashing, and tension seemed high. Two officers stood in the middle of Grandview Avenue, stopping all traffic and checking IDs. A dozen more established a perimeter around one of the scenic lookouts.

Jones rolled down his window. "What happened?"

"Someone fell," said the cop as Jones flashed his license.

"A jumper?"

The cop shook his head. "I wish."

Jones wasn't sure what that meant, but before he could ask, the cop waved him through and approached the vehicle behind him. Jones continued toward his building, unconcerned, until he saw half of Payne's security staff standing on the sidewalk instead of inside the warm lobby. The elderly guard manning the parking garage recognized the black Escalade and opened the gate with a friendly wave. Jones nodded back and parked just inside the mechanical arm.

"Morning, Clyde," he said as he climbed out of his vehicle and slammed the door shut. Jones was dressed for the Steelers game, wearing a black-and-gold Troy Polamalu jersey and a black Pittsburgh ski cap. "What's going on?"

"Don't worry, sir. He's fine. Just fine."

Jones furrowed his brow. "Who's fine?"

The guard stared at him, confused. "You don't know?"

"Know what?"

"Someone tried to kill Mr. Payne."

"What?" Jones asked, incredulous.

The guard nodded. "Pulled a gun on him down the street."

"Where's he now?" Jones asked.

"Inside, I think. Not really sure, though."

"Thanks," Jones said as he hurried to find Payne.

He pushed his way through one of the revolving doors that opened into the atrium. Other than the spectacular view of the city, the building's most prominent feature was the glass-lined lobby. It had been designed by Ieoh Ming Pei, the Chinese-born American architect who had designed the Louvre Pyramid. Normally, Jones took his time as he walked across the marble floor, admiring the way the sunlight danced through the glass ceiling like a prism, but today he had more important things to worry about. Particularly the health of his best friend, whom he spotted across the lobby.

Payne was holding a cardboard box as he talked to two detectives near the security desk. As soon as he noticed Jones, he excused himself and walked over.

"What happened?" Jones demanded.

"It was the strangest thing. I bought a dozen doughnuts and all these cops showed up."

"Come on, man, I'm serious."

"So am I." He opened the box as proof. The only thing left was some powdered sugar on the bottom of the cardboard. "I hope you ate already."

"Jon," he said, annoyed. "What the hell happened?"

"Not here," Payne whispered. "Meet me upstairs."

TEN MINUTES LATER, the two of them had a chance to speak in the privacy of Jones's office—the same place they had discussed Ashley's criminal record the night before. Now they knew something more complicated was going on. Something more dangerous.

Payne filled him in on the basics before Jones peppered him with questions.

"The gunman knew about the letter?"

"Not only did he know about it, that's all he cared about. When I told him I didn't have it, he started shooting."

Jones grimaced. "That doesn't make any sense."

"Sense or no sense, that's what happened."

"Did you recognize him?"

Payne shook his head. "Middle-aged white guy. Slicked-back hair and a fancy suit. He looked European but didn't have an accent."

"Did you get his prints?"

"I tried to as he plummeted past me, but he didn't cooperate."

Jones shrugged. "Shit happens."

Payne reached into his pocket and pulled out a wadded tissue. He carefully unwrapped it, then dumped a shell casing on Jones's desk. "You might get something from this."

"You took this from the crime scene? I'm so proud of you."

"I learned from the best."

"Next time, just let the guy shoot you. It's much easier to ID a bullet."

Payne laughed. "I'll remember that."

Jones used the tip of his pen to pick up the casing. As he studied it under a desk lamp, he asked, "What's our next move?"

"Well, I've been thinking about that, and you're not going to like my answer."

Jones glanced across his desk. "Go on."

"Just to be safe, I think we should skip the Steelers game."

"Come on, Jon! It's not like the guy shot you. I mean, *that* I could understand. But the bastard missed."

"Maybe so, but two shooters in twelve hours makes a guy rethink his priorities. In the grand scheme of things, how important is the game?"

"You're kidding, right? Please tell me you're kidding. Because if you force me to answer that question, you're going to be crushed by my response."

Payne smiled. He knew Jones was teasing. "Normally, I wouldn't skip a game, but let's be honest. We're playing Cleveland. When was the last time we lost to Cleveland at home?"

He shrugged. "Probably before we were born."

"Exactly! So if we have to miss one game, this is definitely the one."

Jones growled softly. "Last night it was Pitt hoops, now it's the Steelers. Next thing you know, you'll be buying tickets to the ballet. I'm warning you, Jon. If that happens, I'll shoot you myself."

"If *that* ever happens, I'll beg you to do it."

Jones nodded. "You can count on me."

"Good," said Payne as he looked to change the subject. "Anyway, as I mentioned earlier, I've been giving this some thought, and I think we have two different issues to worry about."

"The letter and the gunmen."

"Exactly."

"Last night I didn't have a chance to track down the shooter. Let me call the cops and see if they came up with something."

Payne shook his head. "That's one of the things I asked the detectives in the lobby. The shooter is still a John Doe. No ID on him, no prints in the system."

"Which is weird. Most hired guns would have some kind of record."

"Unless . . ."

"Unless what?"

Payne rubbed his chin. "Unless he was a soldier."

"Trust me, I considered that. Unfortunately, my computer doesn't have access to everything. Certain databases are beyond my clearance."

"And . . ."

"And what?"

"And what do we do when something is above our pay grade?"

Jones grinned. "We call Randy."

As a computer researcher at the Pentagon, Randy Raskin was privy to many of the government's top secrets, a mountain of classified data that was just there for the taking if someone knew how to access it. His job was to make sure the latest information got into the right hands at the most appropriate time. Over the years, Payne and Jones had used his services on so many occasions that they had developed a friendship.

"Is it my turn to call or yours?" Payne wondered.

Jones laughed. "It doesn't matter. He'll give us shit no matter what."

Raskin was known to get cranky, especially when they asked him to break the law and track down data they weren't supposed to have. It never stopped him from helping, though. Raskin was a hacker at heart, always looking to circumvent the rules.

"Actually, before we call, there's something else we need to discuss. Something that will take longer than a computer search."

"The letter."

Payne nodded. "Prior to last night's shooting, I was more than willing to ask some Pitt professors for help, but not now. Not if it's going to put them in danger."

Jones agreed. "Do you have someone else in mind?"

"As a matter of fact, I do. Someone far away from here."

"How far?"

Payne leaned back in his chair. "I was thinking Switzerland."

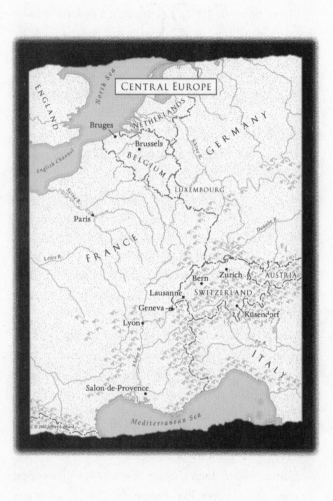

20

Küsendorf, Switzerland
(82 miles southeast of Bern)

P etr Ulster, a round man with a thick brown beard that covered his multiple chins, sat at his kitchen table, scrutinizing the actions of his personal chef. As Ulster nibbled on a hunk of cheese, he heard the private line ringing in his office. With a glass of wine in hand, he lumbered down the long hallway, trying to reach his phone before it stopped ringing. It took most of his energy to get there in time.

"Hello," he blurted, completely out of breath. "This is Petr."

"Hey, Petr, it's Jonathon Payne."

Ulster beamed. Even though he was in his mid-forties, he came across as boy-like, due to the twinkle in his eye and his zest for life. "Jonathon, my boy, it's wonderful to hear your voice."

"Yours, too."

"If I recall," Ulster gasped, still fighting for air, "it's been nearly a month."

Payne grimaced at the wheezing. "Did I catch you at a bad time?"

"No, not at all."

"Are you sure? Because it sounds like you're having a heart attack."

"Sorry," Ulster apologized, "I ran to the phone."

"How far did you run?"

"From the kitchen."

"Wow. No comment."

"I assure you, it's not *me* . . . It's the altitude."

Payne laughed at the explanation, realizing Ulster's shortness of breath was more about the size of his belly than the elevation of Küsendorf, a small village in the southernmost canton of Switzerland. But Payne was willing to cut him some slack. As director of the Ulster Archives, the finest private collection of documents and antiquities in the world, Ulster spent most of his time sitting down, studying important books and relics, not exercising in the Alps.

During the early 1930s, Austrian philanthropist Conrad Ulster, an avid collector of rare artifacts, sensed the political instability in his country and realized there was a good chance that the Nazis would seize his prized library. To protect himself and his collection, he smuggled his possessions across the Swiss border in railcars, using thin layers of coal to conceal them. Though he initially planned to return to Austria after World War II, his new home in Küsendorf eventually became his permanent residence. When he died in 1964, he expressed his thanks to the people of Switzerland by donating his estate to his adopted hometown—provided that they kept his collection intact and accessible to the world's best academic minds.

For the past decade, the Archives had been run by his grandson Petr. He had befriended Payne and Jones a few years ago when they had sought his expertise during one of their missions. Since that time, their friendship had evolved into a mutually beneficial partnership.

After making their startling discovery in Greece, Payne and Jones realized an outside expert should be brought in to catalog the massive treasure, someone they could trust to protect their personal interests. Thanks to his sterling reputation in the academic community, Ulster was approved by the Greek government. He had been handling their affairs ever since.

"Petr," Payne asked, "do you have a moment to talk?"

Ulster took a gulp of wine. "For you, my boy, I have all night."

"If it's okay with you, I'd like to put you on speaker-phone with D.J."

"Yes, of course, put him on."

Payne handed the phone to Jones, who pressed the appropriate button on the unit. As he did, Jones asked, "Can you hear me, Petr?"

"Hello, David, what a pleasant surprise! It's been far too long."

"I couldn't agree more. How were things in Greece?"

"Wonderful, just wonderful! I will be sending you

another check in January. I know how you Americans are. Always deferring your money until next tax year. Isn't that correct?"

"You got that right," Jones said.

"One of these days," Ulster suggested, "perhaps you'll wise up and allow me to deposit your funds directly into a Swiss bank account. It can be our little secret."

Payne smiled. "Millions of dollars is *never* a little secret. Especially on something this visible. If we don't do everything by the book, Uncle Sam is gonna get pissed."

Ulster chuckled. "Perhaps you're right. However, if you change your mind, I have several connections in the banking world. Rest assured, my friends are known for their discretion."

"Great. We'll keep that in mind."

"Speaking of discretion," Jones said, "there's something that Jon and I would like to discuss with you, but only if you're willing to keep it confidential."

"Color me intrigued," Ulster whispered as he closed his office door. "What have you fellows stumbled onto now?"

Payne spoke next. "Just so you know, there have been two attempts on our lives during the last twenty-four hours. If you don't want to be a part of this, we'll completely understand."

Ulster trembled slightly. "Now you've done it, I've got goose bumps!"

"We're serious, Petr."

"I am, too. You guys are so much fun!"

Payne grinned. He knew Ulster would react this way. "Consider yourself warned."

"Yes, yes, I've been warned. Now tell Uncle Petr all about it."

Jones glanced at his computer screen and clicked the send button on his e-mail program. He had been so confident that Ulster would be interested in the project he had already scanned in the document and typed his message. "I'm e-mailing you a one-page letter that we were given yesterday. The woman who gave it to us was shot and killed a short time later."

"How unfortunate! Did you get the bugger who did it?"

"Kind of," Payne admitted. "He was hit by a bus while I was in pursuit."

"Did you say, *bus*? That must have been messy."

"You have no idea."

Ulster took another gulp of wine. "And attempt number two?"

"It happened this morning. A gunman approached me from behind and asked for the letter. When I declined, he opened fire."

"Did a bus get him as well?"

"No bus. Just me."

Ulster cackled with delight. "You are such a brute. I love it!"

"What's the status of the e-mail?" Jones asked.

"It's coming through now." Ulster stared at his screen as his computer downloaded the file. "While I'm waiting, please provide me with pertinent information."

Jones answered. "It is written in a mixture of languages that I can't translate. According to the woman, one of the languages was Middle French."

"If I may inquire, how old is this letter?"

"No idea. Unfortunately, that's part of the problem. The woman who gave it to us was less than reliable. She used a fake name and made up several details about her life."

"Yet you believe this document—whatever it is—is important?"

Payne nodded. "The gunmen who attacked us seemed to think so."

Ulster clicked on the e-mail and smiled at the image that filled his computer screen. "Interesting, very interesting. I see Latin, and Greek, and Middle French, too. Not to mention a few other dialects that are no longer spoken."

"Then you can help us?" Jones wondered.

"Of course I can help you. I love academic puzzles, and this one is a doozy. May I call you later with my results?"

"Later is fine."

"Wonderful!" Ulster said as he glanced at his watch. It was a few minutes past six p.m. in Switzerland. "I'll tackle it before dinner, then get back in touch."

21

Randy Raskin sat in his basement office, surrounded by next-generation computers and paper-thin digital screens that would be the envy of every hacker in the world. Unfortunately, due to his classified position at the Pentagon, he wasn't allowed to mention anything about his work or his equipment to his friends. As far as they knew, he was nothing more than a low-level programmer, working a dead-end job in the world's largest office building, because that's what he was required to tell them. But in reality, he was a high-tech maestro, able to track down just about anything in the world of cyberspace.

"Research," he said as he answered his phone.

"Is this Raskin?" the voice growled on the other end of the line.

"Yes, sir."

"Where the hell is my data?"

Raskin leaned forward in his chair. "What data, sir?"

"Don't mess with me, son! Not today!"

"I'm sorry, sir," Raskin stuttered, as he frantically glanced through the files on his desk. "I don't recognize your voice, sir. Who am I speaking with?"

"Sandecker!" the voice barked. "Admiral James Sandecker!"

Raskin gulped. He was familiar with the name but couldn't quite place it. And in a building like the Pentagon—where admirals and generals wielded all the power—that was dangerous. He knew if he pissed off the wrong officer, his life would become a living hell. Frantically, he typed Sandecker's name into one of his military search engines but came up empty.

"Sir," he apologized, "I'm having trouble finding your files. If you tell me who called in your request, I can check his name as well."

"Gunn. Rudi Gunn. My second in command at NUMA."

"Rudi Gunn," Raskin repeated. That name sounded familiar, too, but once again, he got zero hits in his network search. Obviously, there was something wrong with his system. "Sir, what type of research am I looking for? Perhaps I can—"

"What type of research?" the admiral barked incredulously. "You better find my data *now*, before it's too late. Dirk Pitt is in serious trouble!"

"Dirk Pitt?" he mumbled into the phone. Suddenly, Raskin realized why all those names sounded familiar. They were fictional characters in the novels of Clive

Cussler. "You asshole! Don't *ever* do that to me again! I thought the entire Atlantic fleet was waiting on me."

"Asshole? Who are you calling an asshole?"

"Both of you," Raskin blurted. Very few people had his direct line, and the only guys he knew who had the guts to mess with him were Payne and Jones. "Seriously, you idiots should hear my heartbeat right now. It sounds like a machine gun."

Jones laughed, finally willing to speak in his normal voice. "How would you know what a machine gun sounds like? You never leave your desk."

"Dude, video games are *very* realistic nowadays. Especially on this setup. It's practically the same thing as being a MANIAC. Except, you know, the whole asshole thing."

"Come on," Payne said into the speakerphone, "you have to admit it was funny. Besides, considering all the pranks you've pulled on us, you got off rather easy."

Raskin broke into a wide grin, remembering everything he had done to Payne and Jones in the last year. His all-time favorite was creating a fake personal ad for Jones, which he simultaneously posted on over five hundred dating sites around the world—including one that specialized in Eastern European transsexuals. To this day, Jones was still getting messages from preoperative men named "Olga" and "Svetlana."

"So," Raskin said, "was there a reason you called, or can I hang up on you now?"

Jones answered. "No, there's an actual reason. Someone tried to kill us last night."

Raskin scoffed at the news. "Someone tries to kill you every week."

"Good point, but they tried again this morning."

"Fine." Raskin yawned. "What do you need me to do?"

"A couple of things," Payne said. "I got some prints from last night's shooter, but IAFIS came up empty. We were hoping you could check some of your military databases."

"You think he was a soldier?"

"Maybe."

"One of ours?"

Payne shrugged. "I don't know. I didn't talk to the guy. He was too busy shooting at me."

"What's your point? When I'm shooting at a guy, I talk smack all the time."

"Yeah, but you're doing it online. That's slightly different."

"Not really," Raskin said as he opened the necessary program on his system. "Our games are pretty damn intense. The loser has to pay for beer."

"Oh," Jones mocked, "that sounds just like Iraq."

Raskin grinned, glad he was getting under their skin. It was the least he could do after the whole Sandecker episode. "Are you sending me the prints or what?"

"I already did. Check your e-mail."

Raskin clicked on the message, then went to work. Within a few seconds, he had opened up the digital scans of the prints and started running them through multiple databases, spread across several of his computer screens.

Faces and fingerprints flashed all around him, yet his eyes stayed glued to the monitor in front of him. "This might take a while. What else did you need?"

"Can you access data on active criminal cases?" Payne wondered.

"Of course I can."

"What about a homicide that happened this morning?"

"God," Raskin groaned, "who did you kill now?"

"Actually, that's what I want to find out."

"Please tell me it wasn't another hooker."

"Hey," Jones joked, "the first two had it coming."

"Time-out," Payne said, putting a stop to the humor. "We're trying to ID this morning's shooter, and I was unable to get his prints before the cops showed up."

"How long ago was that?"

"Less than two hours."

Raskin gave it some thought. "Where did this happen?"

"In Pittsburgh, near my office."

"Then the answer is *maybe*."

"Maybe?"

Raskin nodded. "CSI units in most major cities have handheld scanners that can take fingerprints at the crime scene. With a touch of a button, they can upload the data to their station, where an officer can run the prints. No ink, no smudges, no waiting."

"So," Jones said, "if the Pittsburgh police have uploaded the data—"

"Then I can pluck it off their system. If not, we'll have to wait."

"Can you check—"

"Already on it," Raskin said as the clicking of his keys filled the room. He remained quiet for a few seconds as he circumvented multiple firewalls and searched for back doors that would give him access to the files that he required. Eventually, he found what he was searching for.

"Gotcha, you little bastard!" Raskin taunted.

"Got what?" Payne wondered.

"Right now," Raskin answered, "I'm e-mailing you a digital copy of the victim's fingerprints for your personal scrapbook. I know how you serial killers love your precious mementos." He chuckled as he continued working. "In addition, I'm piggybacking my original search, which will allow me to look for both of your shooters at the exact same time. Kind of a buy-none-get-two-free sale, Randy Raskin style."

Jones glanced at Payne. "Did he just say *Randy Raskin style*?"

"I think he did."

"Does he know he said it aloud?"

"I think he does."

"Should we get him some help?"

"I think we should."

Raskin ignored them and kept on typing. "God, I'm good."

"Randy," Jones asked, concerned, "when was the last time you left the office?"

"I don't know. What month is this?"

Payne laughed and shook his head. "Hey, Randy, we

have some leads we need to pursue on our end. Can you give us a call if you find something?"

"Will do, Admiral. Call you later."

"Thanks, man. We appreciate it."

Randy continued typing long after they hung up the phone.

22

The Ulster Archives was nestled against a sturdy outcropping of rock, one that shielded the wooden fortress from the Alpine winds that roared through the region during winter. Nut-brown timber made up the bulk of the chalet's framework and blended perfectly with the broad gables and deep over-hangs of the roof. Square windows were cut into the front façade at regular intervals and were complemented by a triangular pane that had been carved under the structure's crown. A large picture window ran vertically through the middle of the chalet, giving people on the main staircase a spectacular view of the Alps.

But Petr Ulster ignored the view as he trudged up the steps toward the document vaults on the upper floors. It was a journey he made several times a day, moving from room to room, helping researchers from around the world with their pursuit of historical data. Although he didn't consider himself an expert in any particular field, Ulster had a working knowledge of every significant historical subject from A to Z.

It was a skill set that served him well as curator of the facility.

The main goal of the Ulster Archives—unlike that of most libraries—wasn't to provide books to the general public. It was to bridge the ever-growing schism that existed between scholars and connoisseurs. Typical big-city museums displayed fifteen percent of their accumulated artifacts, meaning eighty-five percent of the world's finest relics were currently off-limits to the public. That number climbed even higher, closer to ninety percent, when personal collections were factored in.

Thankfully, the Ulster Foundation was doing something about it. Since the Archives had opened in the mid-1960s, they had promoted the radical concept of sharing. In order to gain admittance to the facility, a visitor had to bring something of value—whether it was an ancient ornament or unpublished research that might be useful to others. Whatever it was, it had to be approved in advance by the Archives' staff. If, for some reason, they deemed the item unworthy, then admission to the facility was denied until a suitable replacement could be found.

Breathing heavily, Ulster paused on the second-floor landing. He fumbled through his pockets for his ID badge, then swiped it across the electronic sensor that was mounted on the nearby wall. Once he had typed in his pass code, he stepped forward for an optical scan. A moment later, the unit beeped, a light turned green, and the electronic lock buzzed open. Without delay, Ulster hustled inside and pulled the door shut. If it had stayed open too long, a team of armed guards would have been notified of a possible breach. In a building that housed some of the most valuable artifacts in the world, there was no such thing as too much security.

Especially after the events of three years ago.

A violent squad of religious zealots had tried to burn the Archives to the ground. Their goal had been to destroy a series of ancient relics that threatened the foundation of the Catholic Church, including evidence about the True Cross. Thankfully, the attack had been thwarted by Payne and Jones, who had been at the Archives conducting research of their own. Without the duo's heroism, Ulster and his staff would have been slaughtered, and everything at the Archives would have been lost forever.

Though they expected nothing in return for their bravery, Ulster would feel indebted to them for the rest of his life. Because of this, Ulster always gave them the highest priority, dropping whatever he was working on if they needed his services. Tonight, that meant postponing dinner while he worked on the academic riddle they had sent to him. Despite his growling stomach, snacking wasn't an option on the upper floors, due to the no-drinking/no-eating/no-smoking policy in all the document vaults. Even for Ulster.

The books and artifacts were far too valuable to put in harm's way.

With another swipe of his ID card, Ulster entered the

Renaissance Collection room. Similar to the other document vaults at the Archives, the floors were made out of fireproof wood—boards that had been coated with an aqueous-based resin—while the white walls and ceilings had been treated with a fire-retardant spray. The texts themselves were kept in massive fireproof safes that were protected behind bulletproof security doors.

Beeps filled the air as Ulster entered his ten-digit security code on the digital keypad. The sound was soon replaced by the low rumble of the partitions as they inched across the floor in their motorized tracks. Once the glass had disappeared into the walls, the dials on the individual vaults—which were thick storage drawers that had been embedded deep into the walls—started to spin in unison until all of the locks popped open, one after another, in perfect synchronization. Now he had access to any file that he required, without having to constantly unlock drawers.

From the supply cabinet in the corner, Ulster grabbed a notebook and a box of colored pens and placed them on the wooden table that sat in the middle of the room. If he had been handling an ancient manuscript, he would have lined the table with a plastic laminate that was similar in texture and strength to Formica. But since he would be using modern textbooks to translate the riddle, a sterile liner wasn't necessary.

Ulster had printed the letter in the center of a crisp sheet of paper. It consisted of four lines of text, written in fancy calligraphy, composed in a multitude of ancient dialects that had been scrambled together in one message. On the top page of the notebook, Ulster made a list of words that he recognized. He made a second column for the modern translation of the terms, followed by a third column where he identified the language. Older forms of French, Latin, Greek, and Italian were obvious, because he had worked extensively with them over the years. Hebrew was slightly more difficult, due to his lack of practice and expertise, but he stumbled his way through it with the help of a translation guide.

The final language, Provençal—which was a dialect spoken in southern France—took the longest to classify because of its similarities to other Occitan dialects. But once he had identified it through trial and error, Ulster called his elderly assistant, Hans, who brought him a language primer from Ulster's personal library in his residential suite.

After that, it was just a matter of time before he deciphered the cryptic text.

Ulster knew every language utilized a unique word structure that determined where different parts of speech (adjectives, pronouns, etc.) should fall in a sentence. He also realized that a sentence's meaning often hinged on two parts of speech in particular: nouns (people, places, and things) and verbs (actions). Because of this, he temporarily ignored all the minor words like articles and prepositions and focused on the words that he considered important.

Slowly but surely, the hidden message came into view.

23

Payne and Jones were good at many things, but waiting wasn't one of them. So instead of sitting around all day, doing nothing while their friends did all the heavy lifting, they decided to reexamine the situation, starting at the very beginning.

"Let's talk about Ashley," Payne suggested. "I tossed and turned all night long, trying to answer one question about her, but I kept coming up empty."

"What's the question?" Jones wondered.

"What was her endgame? Something motivated her to buy a plane ticket and fly across the state to meet us, and I'm wondering what that was. If she was trying to con us out of money, why did she have a return ticket for today? That's a very narrow window to pull off a con."

"Actually, I thought about that, too, and I have a theory I'd like to run by you. Don't hold me to this, though. It's just a guess."

"Go on."

"What if she wasn't there to meet us?"

"Why do you think that?"

"I'm not saying I believe it. I'm just saying it's a possibility."

Payne leaned back in his chair. "Explain."

"First of all, she snuck into the Cathedral and hid during your speech. If she had wanted to speak to us, why didn't she just pull us into a room for a quick chat?"

"According to her, she was embarrassed by her clothes."

"Yeah, well, she also said she was a schoolteacher. So I wouldn't put too much credence into anything she claimed."

"Good point."

"Secondly, do you know where she was when I called you?"

"I have no idea. I wasn't with you at the time."

"She was standing in the English Room, right beside the door to the French Room."

"What's your point?"

"Maybe she was going there to get the Middle French translated. But before she had a chance, she noticed me and I spooked her."

Payne grinned. "You've been known to spook women."

Jones ignored the insult. "Anyway, my point is this: Maybe she wasn't there for us. Maybe she was there for a French professor or some other expert, but we intervened before she had a chance to talk with them. I mean, she flew in before the event and was scheduled to fly out today. That makes me believe she came here for the event, not to spend quality time with us."

"I don't know. That sure is a lot of maybes, especially when you consider how many colleges there are in Philadelphia. Why fly all the way to Pittsburgh when she could have gone to an Ivy League school like Penn and gotten help there?"

Jones shrugged. "Like I said, it was just a theory."

"Trust me, I'm not dismissing it. For all we know, she *might* have been there to meet someone else. Maybe even one of my guests. At this point, it's too early to rule anything out. Especially since we don't know much about the man who killed her. Once we get his identity, I'm sure things will make a lot more sense."

"I hope so. Because right now we're just grasping at straws."

RASKIN CALLED with the shooter's identity less than an hour later, but it wasn't the smoking gun they were looking for. In fact, it confused them even more.

"You were right," Raskin said through the speakerphone. "Last night's shooter *was* a soldier. But you'll never guess where he was from."

"France," Jones blurted.

"Sparta," Payne joked.

Raskin smiled at the reference. "Nope. The guy was Belgian."

Jones furrowed his brow. "Belgian? Like the waffles?"

"Exactly like the waffles. And nearly as flat, if these crime-scene pictures are accurate. Why didn't you tell me he got hit by a bus?"

"Because you never asked."

"Come on, dude. That's not the type of question that comes up—"

Payne cut them off. "Was he still on active duty?"

Raskin stared at his computer screen. "No, he was discharged from the Composante Terre three years ago."

"The what?"

"The Composante Terre. That's the Land Component of the Belgian armed forces."

Payne nodded in understanding. "In other words, their army."

"Exactly."

"What was his specialty?"

"He was a sniper with their Special Forces Group in Flawinne."

Payne glanced at Jones. "A sniper? Why in the hell was a sniper on the Pitt campus?"

Jones shrugged. "Campaigning for a Belgian Nationality Room?"

"Well, I'm not going to vote for him."

"Neither is Ashley."

"I've got a better question for you," Raskin said over the phone.

"What is it?" Payne wondered.

"If this guy was a sniper, why are you guys still alive?"

"Two reasons that I can think of," Jones surmised. "Number one was last night's weather. Visibility was next to nil. No way he could have picked us off from a distance, not with the wind, snow, and darkness working against him. On a sunny day, he could've planted himself across the street and taken us out. Last night, he had to get up close and personal."

"Makes sense to me," Raskin admitted. "What's number two?"

"Simple. He wasn't gunning for us. He was gunning for the girl."

Payne nodded in agreement, realizing a trained sniper would have waited for all of his targets to exit Heinz Chapel before he started shooting. "Randy, do me a favor and e-mail his file to us. I want to look over his record, just to be sure I'm not missing something. Who knows? He was Belgian Special Forces. Maybe our paths crossed on the battlefield somewhere."

"I'm sending it right now."

"By the way, what was his name?"

"Jean-Pierre Allard."

Jones grinned. "I just thought of reason number three. No way a guy named Jean-Pierre kills either one of us. I'd be fine with an assassin named the Butcher. But Jean-Pierre? That would be embarrassing."

Payne agreed. "You got that right."

"Speaking of names," Jones said to Raskin, "any word on this morning's shooter?"

"Not yet, but my search engines are still chugging along. As soon as something turns up, I'll be sure to give you a call."

"Great. We'll be here all day."

"Really?" Raskin looked at the clock on his computer screen. "Shouldn't you be knee-deep in beer and chicken wings by now?"

"Don't get me started," Jones whined. "Last night Jon made me skip Pitt hoops for his charity event. Today it's the Steelers. If he asks me to bail on a playoff game, I'll be in the market for a new best friend."

"If that happens, give me a call. I'd be more than willing to go to a game."

"Hold up! They let you leave your desk?"

Raskin sighed. "I don't know. I've never tried to leave."

24

To better explain his translation of the letter, Ulster took his materials into the teaching studio, located in the basement of the Archives, and set up a secure video conference with Payne and Jones. An antique desk and leather chair sat in the middle of the soundproof room. On the wall behind Ulster was a dry erase board and a silver tray filled with a rainbow of markers. In front of him was a video camera mounted on top of a large monitor. It allowed the trio to have a confidential conversation, protected by the latest firewalls and encryption programs.

Meanwhile, Payne and Jones sat next to each other in the main conference room at the Payne Industries Building. The chestnut-lined chamber was equipped with the newest audiovisual gadgetry—computers, plasma screens, and fiber-optic connections. On the lacquered table, they had set up a camera and monitor that worked the same way as Ulster's. Thanks to their screen, they could see him and speak to him as if he were sitting across from them.

Ulster stared at Payne and Jones via his monitor. "First of all, please allow me to apologize for the lengthy delay. Your riddle was a stubborn beast, one that took me a while to slay."

Jones smiled at the colorful metaphor. Only a few hours had passed since their initial conversation. "To be honest, we're surprised you finished the translation so quickly. I wasn't expecting to hear from you until late tonight or tomorrow."

Ulster waved his hand dismissively. "Tomorrow? I should think not! How could I have slept knowing armed men are running around your city, gunning for your blood?"

"The same way I slept on the battlefield. Left eye closed, right eye closed, good night."

Payne pointed his thumb at Jones. "He's not exaggerating. I've seen this guy sleep through a mortar attack. Enemy shells dropping from the sky like rain, and he's curled up in a trench, snoozing away. Must've been dreaming, too, because he had a big-ass grin on his face."

Jones shrugged. "What can I say? I love naps."

Ulster chuckled at the image, amazed that they could stay so cool under pressure.

"Anyway," Payne said, "we appreciate you getting back to us so quickly. We can't wait to hear about the letter."

Ulster held up his copy. "As you know, the original

message was a mixture of several ancient languages, none of which seemed more important than another. Therefore, I'll list them in alphabetical order: French, Hebrew, Italian, Latin, and Provençal."

"What is Provençal?" Payne asked.

"Provençal is a dialect named after the Provence region in southern France. Today it is spoken by fewer than a half million people, mostly in France, Spain, Italy, and Monaco. Strangely, it is also used by a few wine communities in and around Napa, California."

Jones grunted with surprise. "Really? I'll have to remember that."

"Centuries ago, Provençal served an important role in French culture, for it was the language used by troubadours in medieval literature."

"Is Provençal different than Middle French?" Payne wondered.

"Linguistically speaking, they are both Gallo-Romance languages that were shaped in France, but there are some major differences between the two. Let's start with a timeline."

Without warning, Ulster swiveled in his chair. One moment he was staring at the camera, the next he was facing the board behind him. After selecting a black marker from the tray, he drew a horizontal line across the center of the white surface, then divided the line with three vertical slashes, approximately two feet apart. From left to right, he labeled the slashes A.D. 1000, A.D. 1500, and A.D. 2000. Next he grabbed a red marker and drew a horizontal bar that ran parallel to the timeline for its entire length. Drawn two feet above the timeline, the red bar started just before A.D. 1000 and extended slightly past A.D. 2000. He labeled it PROVENÇAL.

"Can you read my writing?" Ulster asked.

Payne stared at the screen. "Yes."

"Good," Ulster replied as he grabbed a green marker. "Then I shall continue."

A foot below the red bar and a foot above the timeline, Ulster drew a green bar. It started eight inches to the left of A.D. 1500 and stopped four inches past it. He labeled the bar MIDDLE FRENCH. When he was done, the long red bar was on top, the short green bar was in the middle, and the black timeline was on the bottom.

Turning his head toward the camera, Ulster said, "The red bar represents Provençal. The green bar is Middle French. Jonathon, what can you tell me about them?"

Payne suddenly felt like he was back in grammar school, getting picked on by his teachers because he was the biggest student in his class. "Provençal has been around much longer."

Ulster nodded. "Records show that it has been spoken for more than a thousand years. Furthermore, as I mentioned earlier, it is still spoken today in some parts of the world."

"I'm guessing that isn't the case with Middle French."

Ulster pointed at the green bar. "Middle French evolved from *langue d'oïl*, also known as Old French, somewhere in the middle of the fourteenth century. Many grammatical changes occurred at that time—technical things that I won't bore you with. However, it is important to understand that these changes can be traced to this particular era. In fact, it is crucial."

Jones grimaced. "I don't get it. Why is that crucial?"

Ulster smiled into the camera. "Because it gives us a starting point."

"A starting point?"

"Tell me, David, what do you know about the letter's origin?"

He shrugged. "Not a whole lot."

"Do you have the original in your possession?"

"No, just a photocopy."

"What about the name of the author?"

"Nope."

"How about the date it was written?"

"No idea."

Ulster smiled wider. "Are you sure about that?"

Jones furrowed his brow and studied his copy of the letter, carefully searching for a date. Meanwhile, Payne sat next to him, doing the same thing.

"Gentlemen," Ulster said, "the answer *isn't* in your hands. It's on the board behind me."

The duo glanced at each other, confused, then focused on the monitor, each of them trying to figure out the answer before the other. Several seconds passed before one of them caught on.

Jones asked, "You're not talking about a specific date, are you?"

"No, not a specific date. More like a window of time."

"Then I got it. Middle French started in A.D. 1350, give or take an inch. The person who composed this letter used words from Middle French. Therefore, we know that this letter was written *after* A.D. 1350."

Ulster clapped his hands toward the camera. "Bravo, David! Bravo! Thanks to the inclusion of Middle French, we have our starting point. We know, without question, that this letter was composed sometime between the mid-fourteenth century and yesterday."

Payne nodded in understanding, not the least bit surprised that Ulster had taken so long to make such a minor point. He had been around Ulster long enough to realize that his rambling was actually a part of his teaching process. Instead of giving a two-minute briefing where he summarized the key facts, he preferred to work in layers, slowly providing background information until an academic foundation had been established. Once he was confident that everyone had working knowledge of a topic, he would discuss the major points.

But in a situation like this, where time was critical, Payne knew he would have to stay on top of things or Ulster's digressions would go on all day.

"Don't get me wrong," Payne said, "I'm thrilled that you narrowed things down, but six hundred and fifty years is a large chunk of time. Did you learn anything else from the letter?"

Ulster grinned in triumph. "Fear not, my boy. I'm just getting started."

25

While standing with his back to the camera, Ulster grabbed a blue marker from the tray and wrote two words at the top of the board, a few feet above his timeline. To emphasize his frustration, he added three large question marks, then returned to his seat with a sigh.

Finally, Payne and Jones could see what had been written.

WORD ORDER???

"Gentlemen," Ulster explained, "I was able to translate the individual words in your letter in a short period of time. Unfortunately, I struggled tremendously with the word order."

"Why is that?" Jones asked.

"As you're probably aware, every language has grammatical tendencies that define its basic sentence structure. In English, nouns usually fall before verbs, adjectives typically fall before nouns, and so on. For example, *the red ball bounces*. Obviously, there are many exceptions to these rules, but over time most people recognize the quirks of their chosen language and follow the established patterns."

Payne nodded. "We're with you so far."

"Occasionally, these patterns are distorted by topography and distance. In America, for instance, people who live in the north talk differently than people from the south."

"You mean accents?"

"Although accents are quite noticeable, they are merely tonal. I was actually referring to regional dialects. Simply put, the location of your home influences the words that you use and the way that you structure sentences."

Jones smiled. "Down south, they say *y'all*. In Pittsburgh, they say *yinz*."

"*Yinz*," Ulster repeated. "I've never heard such a word. How bizarre!"

"For the record," Payne said defensively, "I grew up here, but I don't say *yinz*."

"And since you are highly educated," Ulster explained, "I wouldn't expect you to. Typically, the more education a person receives, the less likely they are to use regional dialects. Unless, of course, a colloquial term has been absorbed by all levels of society."

"Can you give me an example?" Jones asked.

Ulster nodded. "Of course I can. In fact, I'll give you a test that is favored by linguists around the world. If you were to order a carbonated beverage, what would you call it?"

"In Pittsburgh, we'd call it *pop*."

"In other parts of America, it would be called *cola*, a *soft drink*, or simply *Coke*. Now tell me, if you heard any of those being ordered, would you look down upon the person?"

Jones shook his head no.

"That's because those terms have been accepted by all levels of society. On the other hand, if someone ordered *soda water* or *soda pop*, what would you think?"

"I'd think they grew up on a farm. Or live in the 1950s."

"That's because *those* expressions have been phased out of high society."

"Very interesting," Jones said. "I never thought of that."

Payne cleared his throat in frustration. He knew if he didn't interrupt them soon, they would talk about regional dialects all day. And, considering the recent shootings, he realized they didn't have time to waste. "Sorry to cut in, Petr, but what's your point?"

Ulster smiled sheepishly. "Ah, yes, my point. When I translated your letter, I didn't detect any words that I would consider slang or colloquialisms. This leads me to believe that the author was well educated. And the more educated a person is, the more likely he is to follow proper grammar in all means of communication—whether that be speech or word puzzles."

"Go on," Payne urged, trying to stop Ulster's rambling.

"As I mentioned earlier, all languages have a wide variety of nuances that make them unique. And because of this, I ran into all sorts of problems with your letter."

"Such as?"

"First of all, Greek uses one alphabet, Hebrew uses another, and so on. Second, Hebrew is written right to left, not left to right, which hindered my initial efforts until I got comfortable with the flow. Third, a few of these languages have conflicting sentence structures. Some of them require their articles and prepositions to be placed *here*, and others require them to be placed *there*. Not to mention adjectives and verb tenses, which were particularly troublesome."

Payne grimaced, suddenly understanding the challenges that Ulster had faced. He knew the letter had been written in six languages, but he never factored in the grammatical issues. "So, what did you do next?"

"The first thing I did was toss away the minor words in the letter. Since I didn't know where to place them, I pushed them aside and concentrated on the major words."

"By major words, do you mean nouns and verbs?" Jones asked.

"Precisely!"

With a burst of excitement, Ulster grabbed the black marker from the tray and made a simple chart—two columns with eleven rows—on the board behind him. Then he picked up an orange marker and started filling in the left column with the English translation of all the major words. After that, he used a purple marker to identify the original language that the author had used in the letter. Amazingly, Ulster did the entire chart from memory, never turning around or glancing at his notes. When he was done, he exhaled loudly and collapsed into his chair, as if every ounce of energy had drained from his body.

WORDS	LANGUAGE
city	French
brother	Greek
lover	Italian
lost	Hebrew
line	Latin
mare	Provençal
mother	French
choice	Hebrew
place	Provençal
time	Italian

Both Payne and Jones wrote the chart underneath their copies of the letter while Ulster caught his breath. Thirty seconds passed before he spoke again.

"As you can see," Ulster said, "the author varied his language throughout the message, never using the same language consecutively. Obviously, this added to the complexity of the letter because his grammar rules were constantly changing."

"Did you learn anything by his choice of language?" Jones wondered.

"Hypothetically, yes. Conclusively, no."

"Theories are fine, Petr. This isn't a court of law."

Ulster smiled. "In that case, I would surmise that the author was a French Jew."

"Really?" Jones said, surprised by the precision. "Why do you think that?"

"Simple math, my boy. Simple math." Ulster remained seated as he pointed at his chart. "Please focus on the right-hand column. Forty percent of his major words were either Middle French or Provençal, both of which were spoken in France. In addition, Latin and Greek provided the backbone of a classical education during medieval times, so if the author was educated, and I suspect that he was, then those languages would have been a part of his training."

"And the Jewish part?"

"Since the advent of Middle French in A.D. 1350, the major religion in France has always been Christianity, so much so that Jews would have been persecuted for their beliefs. Therefore, if the author studied Hebrew, he was probably a Jew."

Payne nodded. It made sense to him. "What about a location? Are there any Jewish settlements inside of France?"

"None that I can recall, but I shall certainly check."

"What about places outside of France?"

Ulster rubbed his chin in thought. "Well, French is an official language in Switzerland and Luxembourg. It is also spoken in Malta, Monaco, and Québec. Then there are a hundred million people spread across Africa who speak the language in one form or another—"

"And Belgium," Jones said, interrupting him.

"That is correct. Forty percent of Belgians speak French."

Payne leaned forward in his chair. "Last night's shooter was Belgian."

"Is that so? I don't know why, but I've never thought of Belgians as dangerous." Ulster patted his large stomach and grinned. "For some reason, I think of waffles."

"Us, too," Jones admitted. "With fruit and powdered sugar."

"Anyway," Payne said, trying to move things along, "the Belgium connection might be a coincidence, but we'll keep it in mind as we move forward."

"Don't worry, Jonathon. I'm nearly done. And the best part is yet to come."

26

Ulster grabbed the black marker from the tray and stood near the left side of the board. For the next step, he wanted to make sure that Payne and Jones could see everything he did.

"Based on the assumption that the author was from France, I translated every word in the letter into Middle French. Unfortunately, the words were still jumbled and made little sense. I had the same issue when I used Old and Modern French. Next I tried Provençal, but the results were similar—nothing but chaos. I also tried Latin, Greek, Italian, and finally Hebrew. But guess what? None of the languages seemed to fit. If I pushed and pulled and finagled a bit, I was able to see some semblance of structure, but I doubt this is what the author had intended."

Jones agreed. "You're probably right. Most codes are pretty straightforward. If you know the cipher, then the rest is easy."

"Thankfully," Ulster said, as he tapped on the board with his marker, "I was preparing this chart for you. Otherwise, I might not have seen it."

"Seen what?" Jones asked.

"The rhythm."

Payne furrowed his brow. "The rhythm?"

With his marker, Ulster drew an asterisk next to four words: *brother, line, mother,* and *time.* "Take a look at your copy of the letter. How many lines are there?"

"Four," Payne replied.

"That is correct. Four lines. The words I have identified are the final words of those four lines. Now tell me, what do these words have in common?"

Payne knew it wasn't their language, because all of them were different. According to the chart, *brother* was Greek, *mother* was French, *line* was Latin, and *time* was Italian. Other than that, he wasn't quite sure what to look for. "I have no idea."

"Of course not," Jones teased. "In the future, never ask a white guy about rhythm. If you have a choice, turn to a brother for help."

Payne rolled his eyes. "Okay, Brother Jones, what's the answer?"

"The words rhyme. *Brother* and *mother* definitely rhyme. And *line* and *time* mostly rhyme. At least they would in a rap song."

"You are correct, David. The vowel sounds in those words *do* rhyme. But strangely, they do not rhyme in French. Or Latin. Or any of the other languages. They only rhyme in English."

"No shit?"

"No, I'm quite serious. Your letter is a simple quatrain with alternate rhyming verses."

"Are we talking Middle English like *The Canterbury Tales*, or Early Modern like *Macbeth*?"

Ulster grinned. "I'm talking this decade, like Harry Potter or *The Lost Throne*."

"This message is current?"

"Very current. And once that had been determined, everything else fell into place. I suddenly realized that some of the words that appeared to be nouns—for instance, *choice*—were meant to be verbs. In this case, *chosen*. Once that was resolved, the message became quite clear to me."

"Wait," Payne ordered, slightly annoyed by the turn of events. "Let me see if I got this straight. We just spent fifteen minutes discussing regional dialects and the sentence structure of Provençal, but you're telling us the message was meant to be deciphered in English."

Ulster nodded. "It appears that way, yes."

"Then why didn't you tell us that to begin with?"

"Why? I'll tell you why. Because someone tried to kill you for this letter!" Ulster's voice had an edge to it that hadn't been there before. "And I'm quite confident, once I read the translation, that you'll focus solely on the message and nothing else. However, in my professional opinion, I think that would be a grave error. I believe this letter was created by a brilliant man, a craftsman with a gift for puzzles. And unless I'm terribly mistaken, everything I have told you about this letter will eventually be important to your search—wherever that may lead."

"Oh," Payne said, trying to ease the tension, "in that case, thanks."

Ulster took a deep breath, then cracked a smile. "Sorry, Jonathon, I shouldn't have raised my voice like that. I'm simply hungry, and tired, and craving waffles."

Payne shook his head. "Actually, Petr, I'm the one who should apologize to you. You're doing us a favor here. Without your knowledge, we would've been screwed."

Ulster waved his hand dismissively. "Well, the good news is that we're nearly done. At this point I feel I have adequately prepared you for my translation."

"Are you positive? Because I'll gladly wait some more if you want to discuss dangling participles in Ancient Rome."

Ulster smiled wider. "No, I'm quite sure. Let me write it above my chart."

With a purple marker, he carefully printed the quatrain in English on the top of his dry erase board. Four lines. Two couplets. Twenty-one words in total. Composed in six ancient languages but translated into a sixth language. When he was done, Ulster sat down and admired his handiwork, making sure that he had made no errors. It read:

> *From the city of brothers,*
> *A lover from the lost line.*
> *A mare with no mother,*
> *Chosen for her place in time.*

Payne and Jones copied the translation, word for word, then took a moment to examine it. When they were done, they shifted their focus back to Ulster.

Jones asked, "Any thoughts on what it means?"

"Sadly, English literature is not my forte and never will be. Therefore, if you are looking for deep artistic meaning, I'm afraid you are asking the wrong man. However, if you are searching for a literal translation of these words, I'd be happy to chime in."

Jones nodded. "I'm with you, Petr. My brain was built for facts and numbers, not artistic interpretation. I can read a poem and tell you if I like it, but I can't dissect one to save my life."

Payne cleared his throat. "There's no need. I'll save your life. Like always."

"Will you now? And how are you going to do that?"

"I know what the message means."

"You solved it, just like that?" Jones snapped his fingers for effect.

Payne smiled confidently. "Plus, I think Petr made a mistake in his translation."

Jones laughed. "Oh, man, this is gonna be good! Please enlighten us, *Brother* Payne."

"Yes, Jonathon, I must admit I'm rather intrigued by your insinuation. Please continue."

Payne pointed at the screen. "This poem is about someone in Philadelphia."

Jones rolled his eyes. "Philadelphia? How do you figure?"

Payne stared at Jones. "What's Philadelphia's nickname?"

"The City of Brotherly Love."

"Exactly. Just like the first line. *From the city of brothers.*"

Jones argued, "Wait, where's the love? It doesn't say anything about love!"

"Look at the next line, D.J. You'll find your love there."

"Oh," Jones grunted.

Payne turned his attention to the screen. "Petr, in the third line, are you certain about the word *mare*?"

Ulster looked at the board and nodded. "Fairly certain, why?"

"By *mare*, did you mean a female horse?"

"Yes."

"An adult female or a baby female?"

Ulster shrugged. "Just a female. An age was not specified."

"In that case, may I suggest a substitution?"

"You may."

"How about *filly* instead?"

Ulster considered the word. "Yes, *filly* would fit. *A filly with no mother.*"

Payne smirked at Jones. "Hey, D.J., what's the abbreviated name for Philadelphia?"

Jones stopped smiling. "Philly."

"And the name of their professional baseball team?"

"The Phillies."

"How about that? A *Philly* with no mother. That's two references to the city. I have a strange feeling that isn't a coincidence."

Ulster stood and changed the word in his translation. "So do I."

"While we're at it," Payne said to Jones, "why don't you tell Petr about the woman who gave us the letter? Where was she from?"

"Philly," Jones mumbled, unhappy with his friend's success.

Payne grinned, glad he could finally contribute something to the conversation instead of listening to Ulster and Jones going on and on about historical events.

"Last, but not least," he exclaimed. "When we're done talking to Petr about the letter, where do you think we're going next?"

Jones swore under his breath, refusing to answer the question.

27

Throughout history, many people have exploited the work of Nostradamus for personal gain. Perhaps the most notorious was Joseph Goebbels, the Reich minister of propaganda in Nazi Germany from 1933 to 1945. He was one of Adolf Hitler's closest associates and a master of psychological warfare. One of his most effective tools during World War II was the use of *black propaganda*—fake documents that were designed to destroy the morale of the enemy.

Because of Nostradamus's popularity in Europe, Goebbels hired Karl Ernst Krafft, a prominent Swiss astrologer and an enthusiastic Nazi supporter, to interpret Nostradamus's prophecies in such a way as to cast a positive light on the Third Reich. Their goal was to create the illusion that Nostradamus had predicted a German victory, which would make their opponents believe they were fighting an unwinnable war. Goebbels published the Nazi prophecies on leaflets, and then dropped them out of airplanes over France in advance of the German army. Many French soldiers and civilians became so demoralized they willingly surrendered to invading troops.

As soon as the British learned of the Nazi tactics, they quickly produced their own set of fifty false Nostradamus prophecies, which foretold of Allied victories. These verses were printed and dispersed throughout Nazi-occupied territories, in the hopes of counteracting Goebbels's efforts.

Not to be outdone, the American government commissioned MGM Studios to produce a series of short films to be shown before movies. The counterpropaganda films—which had titles such as *Nostradamus Says So*, *More About Nostradamus*, and *Further Prophecies of Nostradamus*—were narrated by acclaimed screenwriter Carey Wilson and included prophecies that could be connected to World War II. Some of the quatrains were presented in their original state, and others were edited to seem as though Nostradamus had predicted an Allied victory. The films were so successful that *More About Nostradamus* was nominated for an Academy Award in the Best Short Subject category in 1941.

A few years later, *Nostradamus IV* was released in the United States. The short film began with the headline "Mussolini Kicked Out," and it stressed that this prediction by Nostradamus had already been presented earlier in the series. The film then examined the prophecies that supposedly foresaw the rise and fall of Hitler. To emphasize the important part (i.e., the eventual death of Hitler), the movie poster featured a Hitler look-alike getting his throat cut from behind.

Needless to say, the poster and the film were very popular in America.

BACK WHEN François Dubois was still trying to come to grips with his visions of the future, he asked his mother why she viewed his dreams as a gift. Her explanation was a simple one. She said: "Knowing the future is a tool you can use to conquer your environment. The more you know, the better off you'll be—especially if you possess information that no one else has."

From that moment on, he became fixated on the concept.

As a teenager, whenever he was interested in a female, he would study her for weeks in advance, long before he even talked to her. Later, when he planned his first heist, he bribed city officials for blueprints, paid security guards for patrol routes, and conducted surveillance on his own friends to make sure that none of them had been compromised. Eventually, when he set up his first arms deal, he gathered enough blackmail material on the other party involved—including a series of compromising photos—to guarantee a smooth transaction.

The more he knew, the better off he would be.

That was one of the reasons he had established a network of spies in universities around the globe. Dubois realized how much information was available on college campuses, particularly schools with strict academic standards, such as Oxford, Princeton, and Yale. Places where the best and the brightest would matriculate. He also knew how broke some graduate students were and how desperate they were for money.

For a man like Dubois, it was a match made in heaven.

Over the years, he had learned about corporate mergers long before they were announced, which allowed him to invest wisely and make millions. He had been warned of impending military actions, which enabled him to protect his assets in several foreign countries. And he had compiled dirty laundry on enough politicians and royal families to ensure political favors whenever he needed them. However, of all the tips he had ever received, the one that had excited him the most had come less than a week ago.

Martin Müller was a doctoral student in finance at the Faculté des Hautes Études Commerciales. Often referred to as HEC Lausanne, it was the highly respected business school at the University of Lausanne in Switzerland. Having attended the university as an undergrad and a graduate student, Müller had developed personal relationships with most of the faculty and was often asked to help exchange students get acclimated to the campus. A few months earlier, a student from France had told him about François Dubois and the type of information he was looking for. Müller had laughed it off, realizing he wasn't the type of person who consorted with criminals, but he wrote down Dubois's hotline number, just in case.

On the night of December 9, Müller was glad that he did.

One of Dubois's associates answered the phone, but as soon as Müller explained why he was calling, he was immediately patched through to Dubois.

"I understand you have some information for me," Dubois said in English.

"Yes, sir."

"And it has to do with Nostradamus?"

"Yes, sir."

"Well, what is it?"

Müller paused, nervous. "Sir, I have to admit I've never done this before. Shouldn't we talk about money first?"

Normally, Dubois wouldn't have the patience to explain his setup, but due to the urgency of the subject matter and the fact that Müller had been screened in advance, the last thing he wanted to do was spook the caller. "Before we can settle on a price, I need to know what type of information you offer. Therefore, I need for you to provide the basics. Afterward, if I feel it is worthy of my attention, my associate will make financial arrangements."

"Okay. That sounds fair."

"Now please, if you don't mind, tell me what you've learned."

"Earlier tonight, I was studying on campus, and I overheard two of my professors talking about an ancient document they were hoping to sell. I don't know all of the specifics, but I know it's really old and it's connected to Nostradamus."

"Connected in what way?"

Müller shrugged. "I'm afraid I don't know. I couldn't hear everything."

"But you're certain they mentioned Nostradamus?"

"I'm *positive*. As soon as I heard the name, I immediately thought of you."

Dubois wasn't the least bit surprised. His contacts made sure everyone knew Dubois was a collector who was willing to pay top dollar for documents pertaining to Nostradamus.

"Do you know the names of these professors?"

Müller nodded. "Yes, sir."

"What about their phone numbers?"

"Yes, sir. And their addresses, too."

Dubois smiled. It was information he would gladly pay for.

28

NASJRB Willow Grove

Horsham, Pennsylvania

(12 miles north of Philadelphia)

Naval Air Station Joint Reserve Base Willow Grove is a military airfield near Philadelphia that has undergone many transitions over the past century. In 1926, it was nothing more than a grass airstrip and a single hangar in a small rural township. But all that changed during World War II. Shortly after the Japanese attack on Pearl Harbor, the United States bought the grounds and launched a classified antisubmarine program at the base, which stayed active until the late 1940s. Since that time, it has served as a training and operational base for several reserve units.

On this night, though, it had a much different purpose.

It allowed Payne and Jones to fly secretly across Pennsylvania.

In order to keep their names off passenger logs and to let them carry weapons, Randy Raskin had found them two seats on a Naval Reserve jet out of Pittsburgh and had arranged ground transportation—a custom-armored Chevrolet Suburban, normally used by politicians and visiting dignitaries—for their time in Philadelphia. The flight took over an hour but would have been quicker if not for the lingering snowstorms. By the time they had left the base and driven into the city, it was nearly eight p.m., and they were starving.

Back when they were in the military and constantly traveling, Payne and Jones had a long-standing tradition. If their mission allowed it, their first meal in a new city would feature local cuisine—whether that was fish tacos in San Diego, paella in Spain, or Cuban sandwiches in Ybor City. Over the years, they had spent a lot of time passing through Philadelphia, and every time they did, they ordered the same thing: Philly cheesesteaks.

Although it was one of the greasiest, least nutritious meals on the planet, cheesesteaks were also one of the tastiest. Thinly sliced rib-eye steak was placed on a lightly oiled griddle, where the meat was browned and chopped into smaller chunks with an iron spatula. Then, depending on the establishment, slices of provolone or white American cheese were melted over the steak. Once everything was hot and bubbly, the molten mass of meat and cheese was scooped into a small loaf of Italian bread, known in Philly as a hoagie roll. It was then garnished with grilled onions and peppers, lettuce and tomato, or even mayonnaise. In certain locations, a ladle of Cheez Whiz replaced "normal" cheese, but neither Payne nor

Jones was a fan of its viscous texture and mysterious chemical ingredients.

The two most famous eateries in Philadelphia were Pat's Steaks (credited with creating the cheesesteak) and Geno's Steaks, a rival located directly across the street. Both joints were open twenty-four hours a day, seven days a week, and served thousands of hoagies per day. Since Payne and Jones were hoping to maintain a low profile, they skipped both places and drove to the University of Pennsylvania (Penn) campus, where they ordered their food from one of the vendor trucks that catered to hungry college students. Jones ordered a traditional cheesesteak with provolone, onions, and peppers, but Payne opted for a pizza steak—crumbled mozzarella and pizza sauce were added to the grilled meat and roll before it was toasted in a broiler.

To avoid some calories (and to save their arteries), they split an order of French fries and bought two bottles of water instead of soft drinks. Just to be safe, both of them swallowed an antacid tablet before they consumed their feast inside the heated SUV.

"Holy hell, this is friggin' good!" Cheese and grease dribbled down Jones's chin, scalding the top layer of his skin, but he couldn't have cared less. "This is how I want to die."

Sitting in the passenger seat, Payne admired the bulletproof glass. "From the look of this armor plating, that sandwich is the only way you *can* die in here."

"Well, if I start choking, please don't save me. I swear

to God, Jon, I'm gonna walk through the Pearly Gates, carrying my cheesesteak with me."

"If that happens, *don't* take the fries. Remember, we're splitting the order."

Jones wiped his chin. "No promises."

AFTER THEY finished their meals, their focus shifted to the mission at hand. According to the criminal database, Ashley had lived in an apartment near Spruce Street, fairly close to the Penn campus. Because of her proximity to the school, Payne and Jones wondered why she had flown to Pittsburgh to visit the Cathedral of Learning. Perhaps it had been to maintain her anonymity, or to meet someone at the charity event, or to talk to them, as she had claimed. Whatever the reason, they realized the best way to find the answers they were looking for was to visit her place. At night. Without a key. Or permission.

Simply put, they were going to break in.

Dressed in dark sweaters and jeans, they drove around the block a few times, memorizing the exits, looking for guards and security cameras. Doing most of the things they used to do when they had planned an urban assault. Because that was what this situation required. Although it had started off as a simple conversation with a mysterious woman, it had evolved into something complicated and violent. Belgian snipers blowing off heads, trained assassins searching for a letter, and a coded message pointing back to the city where the woman had lived.

None of it made any sense to them. Or Ulster. Or Raskin. None of them understood what was going on, why Ashley had been targeted, or what to make of the puzzling poem.

However, all of them agreed on two things.

The best way to solve the mystery was to charge forward.

And, if the situation called for it, shoot with prejudice.

THE APARTMENT building was nineteen stories high with a tan brick exterior. Overall it was a nice complex, but not *too* nice, meaning they wouldn't have to worry about a pompous doorman or an overzealous security staff. The surrounding streets and sidewalks were fairly busy for a Sunday night, filled with students and nonstudents alike. Snowflakes danced through the air, yet there was little accumulation on the concrete walkway that led up to a maroon awning.

Payne and Jones wore ball caps and gloves—partly because of the cold, but mostly to protect their identities as they sneaked inside Ashley's apartment. If the Pittsburgh police hadn't contacted the local authorities about her homicide already, they would in the near future. And once that happened, the Philadelphia cops would swing by, looking for clues of any kind.

The last thing the duo wanted was to be linked to the scene and her apartment.

That was the type of coincidence that would be tough to explain.

As they walked toward the front door, Jones reached into his back pocket for his lock picks. Payne shook his head, though, and pointed to the intercom off to the side. Jones nodded and smiled. This would be easier than they had thought. Both of them had been in enough high-rise buildings to understand how easy it was to get past this type of security system. Simply press the ringer on a few random apartments, and some sucker was always willing to buzz the electronic lock open without asking questions.

In this case, it took less than thirty seconds for them to get inside.

The lobby was warm and well lit. No security cameras in sight. Several rows of locked mailboxes filled the left-hand wall. Beyond it was a long corridor that led to a workout center, laundry facilities, and a private parking lot. On their right, a fire door opened into an emergency stairwell. Just past it was a bank of three elevators and a small sitting area, filled with a couch and two chairs. A bulletin board, covered with flyers and a local bus map, hung on the back wall.

Jones pressed the elevator button, and the middle doors sprang open without delay. He walked inside first, followed by Payne, who pressed floor number six.

The doors slammed shut, and the next phase of their journey began.

29

When the elevator opened on the sixth floor, Payne stepped out cautiously while Jones stayed behind, holding the door open. Ashley's apartment number was 615, which was approximately halfway down the hall on the right. Payne crept toward it while clutching his gun inside his coat pocket. Jean-Pierre Allard, the Belgian sniper, had tracked her down in Pittsburgh, so it stood to reason that he knew all about her apartment in Philadelphia. Obviously, Jean-Pierre was no longer a threat, but who knew if he had partners?

For that reason, they proceeded with caution.

As Payne walked toward the door, he studied it out of the corner of his eye. The lock and door frame appeared intact, and no police tape was visible. As far as he could tell, the apartment was undisturbed. Without advanced recon, there was no way of knowing if Ashley had a roommate or a deadbeat boyfriend who stayed over all the time. Just to be safe, Payne knocked on the door and slowly walked past. If someone answered, he would apologize over his shoulder and keep on moving until he reached the stairs at the far end of the building. He figured, no sense turning around and showing his face to a potential witness. On the other hand, if no one answered, they would move on to part two of their plan.

A minute later, after no response, Payne was confident the apartment was empty. Of course, they wouldn't know for sure until they got inside.

With a quick whistle, he signaled to Jones, who left the elevator and strolled casually down the hall. Inside his coat pockets, he held a gun in his right hand and his lock picks in his left. No matter which hand was needed, Jones would be prepared. Outside her door, he put his ear against the surface and listened. No sound at all. The door was cold and hollow. Made from some type of galvanized steel that had been painted the same shade of tan as the building's exterior. The knob was outfitted with a simple cylindrical lock. Nothing too fancy. A click here and a twist there, and Jones popped it open. Less than fifteen seconds from start to finish.

From their military training, they realized the next step was the most dangerous. Although they had downloaded the floor plan from the building's website and knew the basic layout of the apartment, they still didn't know who or what would be waiting for them. A dog seemed unlikely, since there had been no barking when Payne knocked on the door. But a dog would be better than a gunman, who would be on full alert because of the knocking.

Ultimately, it was a risk they had been willing to take.

The odds of a roommate were higher than the odds of an intruder.

As an added precaution, Jones would fling the door open while taking cover in the hallway, just in case a shooter was lying in wait. Sometimes an inexperienced adversary would fire at the first sign of movement instead of the first sight of prey. And this tactic was a way to avoid those bullets. After a brief pause, Payne and Jones would then breach the room in tandem, carefully scouring the apartment for trouble before they searched for evidence.

With their weapons drawn, Payne stood to the left of the door while Jones stood on the right. From this point on, Payne would be in charge—as he was in the MANIACs.

"Ready?" he whispered.

Jones put his left hand on the knob and nodded.

Payne counted softly. "Three . . . two . . . one . . . go."

With a quick push, the door swung open and bumped against a coat rack with a muffled thud. Light from the hallway spilled into the dark apartment, revealing a carpeted floor and little else. While keeping their backs against the hallway wall, they struggled to detect movement of any kind, but neither man heard a thing. The apartment was completely silent.

If someone was inside, he was a professional.

But not as deadly as Payne and Jones.

Communicating through hand signals, Payne explained what Jones needed to do. No words were necessary. Years of experience and hundreds of missions had prepared them for this moment. Jones simply nodded, letting Payne know he was ready to breach the room.

Payne moved first, dashing through the door and to his right. A moment later, Jones cut behind him and headed left into the darkness. Both men stayed low and under control, their eyes sweeping for targets and their guns at the ready. Without flashlights or night vision, Payne flicked a switch on the far wall and scanned his surroundings, searching for immediate threats. Much to his surprise, the apartment looked like a tornado had swept through it. Everywhere he looked, furniture was overturned and debris was scattered.

"What the hell?" Jones whispered from across the room.

Payne signaled for Jones to shut up and cover him while Payne checked the back rooms. Jones nodded and moved into position. With his gun leading the way, Payne eased down the hall and glanced into the bathroom on the left. It had been wrecked as well. The shower curtain had been ripped down and the cabinets had been emptied, but it was devoid of threats. Next, Payne entered the bedroom on the other side of the hall and checked the closet and under the bed, looking for targets. The room was secure but completely in tatters.

"We're clear," Payne said as he glanced back. "Go get the door."

Jones hustled to the other side of the room and closed the door so curious neighbors couldn't see inside. Then, just to be safe, he locked it and used the security chain, too.

"What the hell happened here?" Jones asked.

Payne shrugged as he stared at the wreckage in the front room. Everything had been pulled off the shelves, and a knife had been taken to all of the furniture cushions. A thin layer of stuffing that looked like snow covered the carpet in front of the TV. Actually, where the TV *used* to be—because it had been overturned and torn apart as well.

"You know," Jones said, "I've only seen this once before."

"What type of case?"

"It wasn't a case. It was on a cartoon. The Tasmanian Devil ripped shit up!"

Payne smiled at the image. "Somehow I doubt Taz was here."

"Yeah, you're probably right. It's too friggin' cold for a marsupial."

Both of them laughed at the absurdity of his statement as they waded through the debris, looking for anything that would explain what had happened there, or why.

Jones asked, "What do you think they were searching for? The letter?"

"That depends."

"On what?"

"When this happened."

Jones kicked aside a broken lamp. "What do you mean?"

"If this happened yesterday, they might have been looking for Ashley's travel plans so they could track her down. If this happened today, they were probably looking for the letter."

"Who are *they*, by the way?"

Payne shrugged. "Who knows? Maybe the Belgian Gun Club."

"The notorious BGC. Kinda sounds like a rap group."

"Hopefully, we'll find something that points us in the right direction."

"Such as?"

"What's with all the questions? Aren't *you* supposed to be the detective?"

Jones stopped searching. "Are you paying me for my time?"

"No."

"Then I'm *not* a detective. I'm merely your lieutenant."

"In that case, go get a broom and clean this mess up."

"I will, right after you kiss my ass."

The two of them searched the apartment for over ten minutes, not finding anything of value until Jones wandered into the kitchen. He had gone in there for some water—the salt from the fries had made him thirsty—but found something better.

"Hey, Jon," he called, "you need to see this."

Payne left the bedroom and walked down the hall toward the cluttered kitchen. Strangely, he found Jones just standing there, completely silent, pointing at the refrigerator. Payne shifted his gaze toward its door and saw a single item hanging there, held in place with tiny magnets. Taking a step forward, he leaned in for a closer look and was stunned by what he saw.

It was a photograph of him and Jones.

30

Payne pulled the article from the refrigerator door. In his hands he held a newspaper clipping from the *Philadelphia Inquirer*. It described his upcoming charity event at the Cathedral of Learning and provided a brief synopsis of their adventures in Greece, complete with a photograph from some random press conference. He and Jones had done so many during the past year they all ran together in his mind.

"That really pisses me off," Jones growled.

"What does?"

"That they used *that* picture for the story. It makes my ass look fat."

Payne shook his head. He was amazed that Jones was a year older than he was and not twenty years younger—because Jones sure acted like a teenager at times. "Are you finished?"

"With what?"

"Being an idiot."

Jones nodded. "I guess you want to talk about the article, huh?"

"That would be nice."

"Not much to discuss as far as I'm concerned. It simply means that Ashley wasn't lying about everything she told us at Heinz Chapel. Remember, she mentioned the article there."

"True," Payne said, "but in my opinion, it means more than that."

"Such as?"

"Because of this, I think the odds are pretty good she came to Pittsburgh to meet with us, not someone else. It also might explain why a second gunman showed up today."

"How so?"

Payne explained his theory. "Let's assume both gunmen are on the same side of things. The first one went to Pitt to eliminate Ashley. He did his job with a shot to the head, then fled the scene. Unfortunately for him, a bus killed him before he could retrieve the letter. Meanwhile, a second team comes here, trying to find it. From the looks of this place, they didn't find much. So what do they do next? They go to plan B."

Jones nodded in understanding. "They noticed our names in the article and realized she had flown to Pittsburgh to meet us. They can't ask Jean-Pierre for help because he's dead, so they send gunman number two. He finds you and asks for the letter, which you deny having. After that, he has no use for you, so—"

"He tries to take me out."

Jones paused in thought. "So, what's their next move?"

"If I was them and wanted the letter, I would send more troops to Pittsburgh to chat with you and me. No doubt about it."

"Well, that settles it."

"Settles what?"

"I'm *never* going back to Pittsburgh."

Payne grinned at the comment. "Not even for the playoffs?"

"Shit! I forgot about the playoffs!"

"How could you forget about the playoffs?"

Jones shrugged. Unable to think of a clever retort, he did the next best thing. He changed the subject. "Let me ask you a question. Where did Ashley get the letter?"

"Where do thieves usually get things?"

"They steal them."

"That would be my guess."

Jones nodded. "You think she stole it from the Belgians?"

Payne shook his head. "First of all, we've only identi-fied *one* Belgian, not two. We have no idea if the second gunman was a Belgian, an American, or something else, so don't get sloppy and automatically assume we're going after Belgians. Second, my guess is she didn't take it from them. My guess is that she took it from someone before they could steal it."

"Why do you say that?"

"Mostly just a gut feeling. There's something about

their desperation that leads me to believe they don't know what it says. I'm guessing they never had it in the first place."

"If that's the case, whom did she take it from? You saw her rap sheet. She stole all the time, but nothing too big. Mostly shoplifting and petty thefts, not museum heists. If this letter is important enough to kill for, someone must have reported it missing."

"You're probably right."

Payne gave it some thought as he walked out of the kitchen and headed for the bedroom. Other than Petr Ulster, he didn't know anyone associated with historical artifacts who could provide them with rumors about items for sale on the black market. At least no one he would trust with their lives. Randy Raskin was already searching for the identity of the second shooter. If he discovered a name, he would look at the gunman's known associates and try to figure out if he was tied to Jean-Pierre. But Raskin's reach only extended as far as his computer's. He could pluck data out of cyberspace but he couldn't track down gossip about ancient relics or the names of people who sought them.

Even though they'd tattered the furniture in the other room, the intruders hadn't used a knife on her mattress. They had leaned it against the wall to look under it, but they hadn't slashed it open. For that, Payne was grateful. It allowed him to examine all the books and papers on the floor without having to brush away a thin layer of stuffing.

Payne spent the next five minutes searching through

her belongings and found two items that interested him. The first was a recent photograph of Ashley. It had been taken at the top of the "Rocky Steps" in front of the Philadelphia Museum of Art, the location that Sylvester Stallone, aka Rocky Balboa, had made famous in his *Rocky* movie series. Ashley was just standing there, smiling—not raising her arms in triumph as hundreds of tourists do every day. But for Payne's purposes, it was perfect. He needed a photo he could casually show around to people, and her driver's license photo and mug shots were a little dated.

The second item was even more helpful to Payne, because it explained why Ashley had been in such a rush to get back to Philadelphia and why she had used a fake name to book her flight.

He spotted it hanging in the corner, right above a card table she had used as her desk. Thumbtacked to the wall, the calendar had been printed on a bright yellow sheet of paper. A black star filled the tiny box for Monday, December 14, which was the following day. Next to it, she had written *8:00 a.m.* in red ink and circled it more than once.

This was an appointment she couldn't afford to miss.

Nothing else had been written in the box, so Payne didn't know why it was so important until he noticed *PBPP* at the top of the paper. It was a set of initials that he was familiar with.

Suddenly, several aspects of Ashley's cover story started to make sense.

31

ayne rushed into the other room to share his discovery with Jones. Coincidentally, Jones had found something of his own that he wanted to share with Payne.

"Look at this," Jones said as he flipped through a stack of mail he had assembled on the kitchen counter. He handed an envelope to Payne. "Check out the name."

The letter was addressed to Megan Moore in Apartment 617, not Ashley Henderson in Apartment 615.

Payne shrugged. "What's the big deal? The mailman screwed up."

"If that's the case, he's retarded, because all of these belong next door."

"All of them?"

Jones nodded. "It looks like a few days' worth, maybe more."

"Ashley was stealing her mail?"

"Not exactly a shock, considering her track record."

"I guess not."

"When we came through the lobby, did you notice the setup? All the mailboxes had simple key locks. A good thief could've picked one of those in two seconds flat."

Payne furrowed his brow. "Kind of ballsy to steal from your neighbor, isn't it? Why not steal from someone you'll never see in the hallway?"

"Who knows? Maybe Megan played her music too loud, and this was Ashley's way of getting revenge. Or maybe it was just a matter of convenience. If Megan's mailbox was right next to Ashley's, she could empty both without looking suspicious."

"Speaking of stealing," Payne said, "I think I know why Ashley booked a return flight for today. She had a meeting tomorrow morning that she couldn't miss."

"Oh, yeah? With who?"

"Do the initials PBPP ring a bell?"

Jones shook his head. "Should they?"

"I figured a detective like yourself would know that type of thing."

"Apparently not. What do they stand for?"

"Pennsylvania Board of Probation and Parole."

Jones smiled in understanding. "No wonder she had to get back today. She had a meeting with her parole officer. If she missed that, they would've sent her back to prison."

"It also explains why she booked her flight under an alias. Many parolees have to stay within their county. If her name turned up on a passenger log, she would've been busted."

"Slowly but surely we're getting a better understanding of Ashley's background."

"Maybe so, but nothing about the letter. I was hoping we'd find something here. I'm guessing someone beat us to it."

Jones glanced at the debris. "Either that, or she was the worst housekeeper *ever*."

A loud knock on the door ended their conversation. Immediately, the duo shut up and scrambled into position. Payne hustled behind the door and readied his weapon while Jones did the same thing behind the counter. If the apartment had been a few floors lower or there had been a fire escape, Payne and Jones would have gone out the back window to avoid a possible confrontation with the police. But from this height, their best option was to stay put.

"Open up," said a female voice in the hallway. "I know you're home. I heard you in there."

Payne raised his gun in front of him, prepared to use it, if necessary.

"Come on, Ashley," the woman whined. "Open the door!"

He stayed perfectly still, controlling his breathing as he had been taught in the military. Not only to stay quiet, but also to manage the adrenaline that was surging through him.

"I hope you're decent," the woman said as she put a key in the lock. "Because I'm coming in."

Payne cursed under his breath as he watched the doorknob turn. Obviously, it was someone—maybe a relative or a friend—who knew Ashley well enough to have her key. Whoever it was, he would have to deal with her quickly, quietly, and without violence.

"Ready or not," she called out, "here I come!"

The door cracked open a few inches before the security chain snagged against its fastener. The door stopped abruptly, and the female slammed into it.

"Son of a bitch!" she mumbled in the hallway. "I can't believe I did that."

Payne cracked a smile, realizing he wasn't dealing with the most graceful person in the world. And definitely not an assassin.

"Come on, Ashley! The chain's on the door, so I know you're home. If you're busy, that's fine. I just came for my mail."

Payne glanced back at Jones, who was standing in the kitchen, unsure of what to do. It was pretty obvious to both of them that this female wasn't leaving anytime soon, and the longer she stood in the hall making a commotion, the worse it would be for them. Still, they couldn't let her in, because if she saw the wrecked apartment, she would freak out.

With that in mind, Payne decided to get creative. He quickly took off his shirt, shoes, gloves, and socks and put them in the corner. Then he placed his gun underneath the pile and messed up his hair—as if he'd been having sex in the bedroom. To look convincing, he slapped his face a few times to put some added color in his cheeks, then crept toward the kitchen.

"What the hell are you doing?" Jones whispered.

"Shut up, and stay hidden."

"Screw that. I want to see this shit."

Payne signaled for him to duck behind the counter. Once he had complied, Payne was ready to start his charade. "Hold your horses," he grumbled. "I'm coming!"

From a distance, he could see the woman trying to peek through the crack in the door, but the angle didn't give her a clean view of the apartment. If it did, his ruse wouldn't have worked.

"Can I help you?" he said as he put his face near the door.

A gorgeous brunette was standing in the middle of the hallway. From her body language, he could tell that she had been caught off guard by the unexpected presence of a stranger.

"Is, um, Ashley home?" she asked.

"Of course she's home. She's in the shower. Who are you?"

"I'm her neighbor, Megan."

"Hey, Megan. We're kind of busy right now. Can you come back later?"

She took a step closer. "And you are?"

"A friend."

"Yeah, I kind of gathered that. I meant your name."

"Jon."

"Nice to meet you, Jon." With a grin on her face, she reached her fingers through the crack and tried to shake his hand. He willingly obliged, just to speed things up. "So, have you known Ashley long?"

Payne cleared his throat. "Not to be rude or anything,

but I'm half dressed here and kind of embarrassed. Can I have Ashley call you later?"

Megan leaned in closer and whispered, "From what I can see, you have *nothing* to be embarrassed about."

Payne laughed. "Okay, now I'm *really* embarrassed. Time for me to go."

"Wait," she said, giggling. "Don't close the door. I was just teasing."

"Don't worry, I wasn't offended. I just need to get back to Ashley."

"Before you go, can you *please* do me a favor? Can you get my mail for me?"

"Your mail?"

Megan nodded. "I've been out of town, and Ashley's been picking up my mail. Can you grab it for me? My name is Megan Moore."

"Hold on. Let me see if I can find it."

"Look on her table. It should be there in a neat little pile."

Payne turned around and mumbled, "There's nothing neat in here."

"What was that?"

He called over his shoulder. "Something smells sweet in here."

"That's probably my new scent. Do you like it?"

"It's wonderful," Payne said as he walked toward the kitchen, where Jones was grinning and shaking his head. "What?"

Jones whispered, "The goal is to get rid of her, not pick her up."

"I know that, but she won't leave."

"Is she hot?"

"Excuse me?"

Jones noticed Payne blush ever so slightly. "Oh my God, she *is* hot. Does she have a friend?"

"Yeah, her name was Ashley, and she was shot in Pittsburgh."

"I meant *another* friend. I don't like dead chicks. Does that make me a racist?"

Payne growled softly. "Just give me her mail."

Jones handed him the stack, loving every minute of Payne's embarrassment. "If the topic comes up, ask her about a threesome. Maybe we can do some ebony-and-ivory shit."

Trying to control his emotions, Payne took a deep breath, then turned back toward the door. Once he got rid of the neighbor, he was going to take care of Jones. One way or another, he would make him pay.

"Who were you talking to?" Megan wondered. "Was that Ashley?"

"Nope," he said, handing her mail through the crack. "Just talking to myself."

"Really? Do you know who else does that?"

"No, who?"

"Serial killers."

Payne grinned. "Then I guess I better stop. I don't want to tip off my victims."

She returned his smile. "Nice talking to you, Jon."

"You, too, Megan."

"And thanks for my mail."

"You're welcome."

She started to walk away, then stopped. "Wait! I think you're forgetting something."

"I completely disagree. A good-night kiss would be inappropriate."

She laughed. "You know, you're pretty funny—for a serial killer."

"I hear that all the time. So, what did I forget?"

"There should be a package of some kind."

"A package?"

She nodded. "I was expecting a package."

"Sorry, I didn't see any package. I'll let Ashley know you're looking for it, and she can drop it off later. Okay?"

"Are you sure?"

"Megan, I swear, there is nothing on the table. Absolutely nothing."

"Okay, I can take a hint. I'm leaving now. But please let Ashley know I stopped by."

Payne nodded, then closed and locked the door.

32

While Payne got dressed in the front corner of the room, Jones stayed silent in the kitchen. He stood still, biting his tongue, patiently waiting for the appropriate time to make a joke. But because of their mission, he refused to do it if it would distract Payne. There would be plenty of time to tease him outside, once they were far away from Ashley's apartment.

Payne walked toward his friend, bracing for the onslaught that would eventually come. "Go on. Get it out of your system."

Jones started to laugh. "Man, I've seen a lot of crazy things during our time together, but the whole I-just-got-done-banging-your-neighbor tactic has got to be the craziest. Did you learn that shit at the Academy or during SEALs training?"

Payne shrugged off the comment. "It worked, didn't it? That's all that matters."

"I guess *worked* depends on your distorted definition."

"What do you mean by that?"

"Did it buy us some time? Yes. But now we have another issue to deal with."

"Which is?"

"Miss Moore saw you and talked to you. Who do you think she's going to blame for wrecking this place? I'll give you a hint. He just finished boning a dead chick."

Payne disagreed. "She saw three inches of me through the crack in the door. No way she can ID me from that."

"Dude, I've seen you in the shower. Three inches is all you got."

Payne ignored the insult, trying to decide if he had anything to worry about. Ideally, he would have preferred not to talk to anyone who could place him inside the apartment, but considering the unique situation he had been facing, he utilized an unconventional tactic to do what he had to do—he kept Megan away from the apartment without harming her.

"Listen," Payne declared, "it's my ass on the line, not yours. So tease me all you want; I really don't care. I made a gutsy, spur-of-the-moment decision that proved to be successful. And if I had a chance to do it over, I would do the same damn thing."

"Are you sure? Because next time I'd suggest the full Monty. If you show 'em the package, they won't look at your face as much."

Payne shook his head. "I swear to God, I need to get a new best friend."

"If you don't mind, can you order one later? For the time being, it's probably best if we get out of here as soon as possible. Megan might come back for a second viewing."

PAYNE WIPED down the door, making sure all of his prints had been removed, before he peeked into the hallway. He glanced left and right and saw nobody out there. Jones stood behind him, waiting to exit the apartment, but he wouldn't leave until Payne was holding the elevator at the far end of the hall. In their minds, it was the best way to minimize their exposure time.

Moving quietly, Payne slipped out of the apartment and turned left. He clutched his gun inside his coat pocket, ready to fire at all times. The odds were against the intruders returning—they had already trashed Ashley's apartment—but he was prepared, just in case.

He pushed the down button and watched the numbers move above the three elevators, trying to time things perfectly. The one on the right had been in the lobby but was now climbing toward the sixth floor. It would be there any second. He glanced behind him, looking for interlopers, but saw no one in the corridor. With a quick whistle, he let Jones know that everything was clear.

Jones heard the signal and opened the door softly. Wasting no time, he slipped into the hallway and closed the door. Unfortunately, his timing couldn't have been worse. A split second after the lock clicked shut, Megan stepped out of her apartment, carrying a large bag of recyclables. Years of training had taught Jones to trust his senses, so he immediately pivoted toward the noise behind him and raised his gun in a shooting stance, fully expecting to see an armed gunman. Instead, he saw a gorgeous brunette wearing a silk robe and bunny slippers.

Their eyes locked for a full three seconds before all hell broke loose.

Stunned by the development, Megan dropped her bag and unleashed a scream that caused dogs to bark a block away. Realizing his mistake, Jones tucked the gun into his pocket as quickly as he could and immediately started to apologize, but Megan was too frazzled to comprehend what he was saying.

"Take the bag," she screamed. "You can have it! It's just garbage!"

"I'm sorry! I don't want the bag!"

"Then what do you want?"

"Jon!" he yelled, realizing he needed backup. "Come here!"

One by one, doors started to open throughout the sixth floor as nosy neighbors stuck their heads into the hallway like prairie dogs looking for predators. Completely exposed, Jones was tempted to run, but realized that would result in twenty people dialing 911 before he even reached the lobby. So he followed Payne's lead from before and decided to improvise, even if it meant exposing himself to several potential witnesses.

Of course, his exposure would involve less nudity than Payne's.

Jones whipped out his credentials, issued by the Pennsylvania Association of Licensed Investigators, and held it above his head. "Relax, everybody, I'm a detective. The woman startled me, and I overreacted. It's completely my fault."

Despite his apologies, Megan backed away from Jones, not willing to trust the man who had just pulled a gun on her. She stared at him the entire time, reluctant to shift her gaze from him until her neighbor across the hall opened his door. Brad was a scrawny man with a large Adam's apple that bulged from his neck like a massive ravioli, but at least he was a friendly face to Megan. She rushed to his side even though he couldn't have protected her from a gust of wind, let alone an ex-MANIAC like Jones.

Meanwhile, Payne hustled down the center of the hallway, trying to calm everyone else on the floor. As he did, he held his wallet in the air—even though he didn't have a badge of any kind. He did it all for show. "Don't worry, people, everything is fine. We didn't mean to disturb your evening. Please go back inside, and we'll get things settled."

"I'm sorry," Jones said. "I didn't know it was you."

She slid behind Brad, who didn't seem pleased by the development. "Who did you think it was?"

Jones shrugged, not sure how to answer. "I heard a noise behind me and my instincts took over. I'm sorry if I scared you. I really am."

"Who let you in?" she demanded.

"Excuse me?"

"This is a *secured* building," she explained. "Who let you in the building?"

"Yeah," Brad said, puffing out his chest. "Who let you in?"

Jones stammered. "I, um, don't—"

"I did," Payne said as he stepped in front of Jones.

"And who the hell are you?" Megan demanded.

Payne pointed to Ashley's apartment. "I'm Jon. We talked earlier."

She blinked a few times, trying to absorb the information. "Ashley's friend?"

"Yes, Ashley's friend."

She stared at Payne, sizing him up. "And you know this guy?"

Payne nodded. "Yes, he's a friend of mine. He came to give me a ride."

"A *ride*? Why does he have a gun?"

"Like he said, he's a professional detective." Payne grabbed Jones's ID and showed it to Megan and Brad, who was now standing behind her as if he were the one who needed protection. "He's fully licensed and has a permit for the weapon. I assure you, he's not a threat."

"I'll be the judge of that," she said tersely. "He pulled his gun on me in my hallway."

"I know he did, and he's obviously sorry about it. Just look at him. He looks like a puppy dog that peed on the carpet."

She stared at Jones, who appeared mortified by everything that was going on. "He does look kind of pathetic."

Payne nodded. "Completely pathetic."

"And you're willing to vouch for him?"

"I've known him half my life. I promise, he's not dangerous."

"Yeah, well, he seemed pretty dangerous with that gun in his hand."

"I bet he did, but I swear to you he's *not* a threat. In fact, if you want, we can take him into the alley and kick the shit out of him together. Will that make you feel better?"

She smiled. "No, that isn't necessary. But thank you for asking."

Payne took a step closer and lowered his voice. "Megan, if it's all right with you, please do me a favor and tell everyone you're okay. The sooner that happens, the sooner everyone will leave the hallway, and we can get out of your life for good."

She glanced at her neighbor. "What do you think, Brad?"

Payne glared at him. "Yeah, Brad, what do you think?"

Brad gulped and nodded.

"Fine! I'll forgive him. But keep him away from me. I don't trust the guy."

Payne quickly agreed. "No problem at all. D.J., go wait by the elevator."

Jones scurried away as quickly as he could.

As he did, Megan cleared her throat and stepped into the middle of the hallway so everyone could see her. "Excuse me, everybody! Thank you for coming to my rescue, but I swear I'm okay. It was just a false alarm. Feel free to go back to your TVs. Everything is fine."

She looked at Payne for his approval. "How was that?"

He glanced down the hall and watched her neighbors retreat, one by one. "That was perfect."

"Well, I aim to please."

Payne flashed a smile. "That's good to know."

"So," she said as she blushed slightly, "the show's finally over. I guess you and your driver can leave now."

"I guess so. Thanks for being so understanding. You, too, Brad."

Brad gulped again, then slipped into his apartment without saying a word.

Megan smiled at Brad's skittish behavior. "So, where's Ashley? Is she inside?"

Payne nodded, not sure how to respond. He had lied to Megan enough already, and the more he did, the guiltier he felt about it—especially since her friend was dead and he was keeping that from her. Not only that, but if the intruders returned, Megan could be in harm's way.

She took a step toward Ashley's door. "Good. That means I can *finally* get my package."

"Actually," Payne said as he touched her arm, "that's not a good idea."

"Why not? Did you wear her out?"

Payne shook his head, realizing he owed her the truth. No matter how painful it was.

33

Megan was the type of woman who attracted attention without even trying. A natural beauty, who dressed conservatively and wore little makeup yet always stood out in a crowd. Dark brown hair, light blue eyes, and a slender frame with the perfect amount of curves. When she entered a room, all heads turned toward her, as if she were royalty.

Not surprisingly, most men were intimidated by her presence. They ogled her from afar, practically drooling, but when given the chance, they lacked the self-confidence to approach. Even when she smiled at them or met their gaze, they tended to freeze, or stutter, or look away.

Like boys with a schoolyard crush.

But Jonathon Payne was different. She sensed that from the moment she had met him. As did nearly every person he had ever encountered. In the entertainment field, it was called the "it" factor—an innate quality that couldn't be taught or learned but ultimately determined who became a star. Either you had "it," or you didn't. And Payne definitely did. Which was one of the reasons he had been handpicked by the Pentagon to run the MANIACs. His mixture of looks, intelligence, size, and charisma made him a natural-born leader.

Not to mention a hit with the ladies.

When Payne turned on the charm, he could sell steak to a vegetarian. Or, in this case, convince Megan to have a chat with him a few minutes after Jones had pulled a gun on her.

Of course, she wasn't stupid about it. She didn't invite Payne inside her apartment. Instead, she suggested a recreational lounge on the second floor. It had a pool table and video games and, most important, several neighbors who could protect her better than Brad.

Payne went downstairs first and grabbed a booth while Megan changed into jeans and a sweater. To help keep her calm, Jones stayed on the far side of the lounge, where he kept his eye on the door. By the end of her chat with Payne, Jones knew she would understand why he had pulled a gun on her, but until then, he was willing to give her the space she needed to stay comfortable.

Ten minutes later, Payne spotted Megan in the doorway. Before she entered, she glanced around the lounge, making sure there were plenty of witnesses. Three college-age guys played pool while their girlfriends sat to the side, gabbing about holiday shopping. Four senior citizens played poker for pennies at a card table in the corner. A few other people were scattered around the room, reading the Sunday paper and surfing the Internet.

Taking a deep breath, she walked across the room toward Payne's booth, holding items in both hands.

He stood as she approached. "Thank you for coming, Megan."

"Just so you know," she warned, "I've got my pepper spray in one hand and my cell phone in the other. One false move, and I'll use both."

Payne pretended to shield his eyes. "If I get a vote, start with the phone."

She smiled and took a seat. "So, what's this all about?"

Payne was surprised the chatty girl from before was now all business. But considering the events of upstairs, he could understand why. "How well do you know Ashley?"

"Why is that important?"

"Why? Because it will help me decide the tone of this conversation."

She stared at him. "I'm not liking this already."

"I need to know if you were like sisters or just neighbors."

"The second, I guess. Ashley moved next door about six months ago. We're roughly the same age and have some common interests, so we're friendly. We don't hang out all the time or anything like that, but we keep an eye on each other's apartment when one of us goes out of town. You know, getting mail, watering plants, and so on."

"But you had her key."

She nodded. "Her spare key—just in case she gets locked out. Our building manager is never around, so we exchanged keys for an emergency. She has mine as well."

Payne listened to her explanation, trying to gauge how he should break the news about her neighbor's death. Normally, he'd come right out and say it, but in this situation, he wanted to learn as much information about Ashley as possible, since there was always a chance Megan would clam up when she learned about her neighbor. "And did she—"

"Wait," Megan said, interrupting him. "Did you call me down here to find out dirt about Ashley? Because if you did, that's *really* sleazy."

"No, Megan, that's not why I wanted to talk to you."

"And if you're about to ask for my number, that would be even sleazier. I mean, you were just with her upstairs."

"Actually, no, I wasn't."

She looked at him, confused. "What are you talking about? I walked in on you."

He shook his head. "On me. Not us."

Instinctively, she clenched her pepper spray. "You better start explaining, or I'm leaving."

Payne nodded, then filled her in on everything that had happened, starting with her neighbor's trip to Pittsburgh and ending with the incident in the hallway upstairs. About the only thing he didn't mention was the translation of the letter. That information was too important to share with someone he had just met.

ONCE PAYNE HAD FINISHED, Megan sat quietly in the booth, considering everything she had been told. Normally, she was the skeptical type, requiring all kinds of evidence before she was willing to accept anything, but because of the level of detail in Payne's story, she believed his account of things—at least for the time being.

"I don't know how to feel about this," she admitted. "I should be distraught over her death, but at the same time, I just found out that she's been conning me for the last sixth months. I knew nothing about her background, or prison, or anything. Everything she told me was a lie."

Payne nodded in empathy. "I doubt this will make you feel any better, but I'm a pretty good judge of character. Normally I can spot a liar or a phony a mile away. Yet for some reason, I believed everything she told me. And so did my partner. The woman was *very* convincing."

"Speaking of convincing, how do I know you're not lying to me as well?"

He shrugged. "I guess you don't. But if you want, feel free to check up on me right now. It wouldn't bother me at all. Tell me, does your phone have an Internet browser?"

"Yes, why?"

He pulled out his wallet and showed her his driver's license. "Google my name, Jonathon Payne, and see what pops up. Same thing with David Jones, the idiot who tried to shoot you. You'll get all the proof you're looking for."

"Are you serious?"

"Completely serious. The sooner you trust me, the better—and the sooner D.J. can join us." Payne paused for a moment and grinned. "Actually, I take that back. I kind of like him sitting in the corner. He deserves a time-out after pulling a gun on you."

She smiled. "He deserves more than that. I should have kicked him in the nuts."

Payne laughed. "Wow, I have to admit you're handling this a lot better than I thought you would. When I saw your bunny slippers and heard your scream, I pegged you for a crier. A loud, theatrical, over-the-top crier."

She shook her head. "I cried myself out at an early age."

"Let me guess. Guy trouble?"

"No," she said quietly, "family trouble. I lost my parents when I was young."

His face flushed. "Me, too. Eighth grade."

"At the same time?"

He nodded. "Drunk driver. How about yours?"

"My dad died when I was two. I can't even remember him . . ."

"And your mom?"

"A mugger shot her when I was ten. They never caught the guy."

He nodded in understanding. "I guess that explains it."

She looked at him, confused. "Explains what?"

"The volume of your scream. You saw the gun and had a flashback to your mom's death. The more emotion involved, the louder the scream."

"Are you psychoanalyzing me?"

He held his thumb and forefinger an inch apart. "A little bit."

"Well, Jonathon, I'll have you know my scream had *nothing* to do with my mom's death. I'm simply a loud screamer. I always have been."

He grinned. "Good to know."

"Stop flirting with me."

He scrunched his face. "Come on! Why would I flirt with you?"

"Why? Because I'm awesome."

"Who said I even like awesome?"

She sneered at him. "*Everyone* likes awesome."

"Good," he said as he stood up, "then you'll love me."

34

Megan used her touch-screen phone to get background information on Payne and Jones—everything from a *New York Times* article about their discovery in Greece to their biographies on Wikipedia. By the time she was done, she felt comfortable with both of them, despite the fact that Jones had pulled a gun on her less than an hour before.

While she investigated them, they returned the favor in the back corner of the room. They figured, her neighbor had already burned them; they weren't about to let it happen again. Jones called one of the detectives at his agency and asked him to do a quick background report on Megan Moore. Using her name and current address, he was able to track down everything from her personal information (single, never married, no family) to her credit score (excellent).

Once she was satisfied with her digging, she signaled

for them to join her. Payne led the way, followed by Jones, who raised his hands as he approached the booth.

"I come in peace," he assured her.

"Relax, I'm no longer mad at you. And considering the circumstances, I can understand why you were a little bit jumpy."

"Still," he said as he pulled up a chair, "I'm sorry if I scared you."

"Speaking of scared, do I scare you?"

"What do you mean?"

She smiled. "I mean, there's plenty of space next to me in the booth, yet you choose to pull up a chair. Or is that your way of telling me that I need a mint?"

Jones laughed. "No, nothing like that. I promise."

"What is it then?"

"Safety," he said.

"Oh, so you *are* scared of me!"

He shook his head and pointed. "Actually, I'm afraid of what might come through that door. If I sit next to you, a pillar obstructs my view. From here, I can see the room."

She glanced at Payne, who was sitting across from her. "Is he serious?"

Payne nodded. "We're always serious about safety. Especially in a place like this."

She looked around the room. It was well lit and filled with several neighbors, none of whom appeared threatening. "Am I missing something? I feel perfectly safe in here."

"Good," Payne said, "then we're doing our job."

"You're doing your *job*? What do you mean by that?"

"I mean, we're soldiers. When we enter a room, we automatically look for ways to minimize threats. It's part of our training."

"You minimize threats? What does that mean?"

Jones glanced at Payne, requesting permission to speak. He gave him a simple nod, and Jones launched into a monologue. As he did, he never took his eyes off Megan, letting her know that he knew everything going on around him without even looking.

"First of all," he told her, "turn around. There's a fire door behind you that leads to an emergency staircase. From Jon's seat, he can't see it clearly because of the pillar over your left shoulder, and if I had joined you on your side of the booth, the door would've been at my back. Right away, we're in a position of weakness."

She took a quick peek at the door, then refocused on Jones.

"Second, check out the windows behind me. We're on the second floor of a building, which is a floor below my comfort zone. Pull a truck under the window, stand on its roof, and you have a clean shot in here. Thankfully, the windows are coated with a protective film, used to keep the sun out during the summer and the heat inside during the winter. Because of that, it would be tough for a gunman to see more than shadows inside the room, which is one of the reasons that Jon chose this booth. Away from the windows, away from the exits, yet partially shielded by the pillars to the front and back."

She looked at Payne, who nodded in agreement.

Jones continued. "Obviously, the biggest threat is the door behind Jon. It leads to the elevators and the main hallway, which means it gets the most traffic. At first, I questioned Jon's choice of seats. I would've selected the seat you're in, allowing me to keep an eye on the door. Then it dawned on me, when he originally sat down, he knew I would be positioned in the corner, keeping an eye on all traffic in the hallway. In addition, I could see clear of the pillars that would've obstructed his view from the bench. Therefore, he chose the seat that offered *you* the best protection from the main door. The two pillars would act as shields."

She stared at Jones, amazed. "How long did it take you to figure that out?"

He shrugged. "About a second. Any longer and we were at risk."

"Are you serious?"

Payne answered for him. "Like I said earlier, we're always serious about safety."

Megan considered his statement. "Then what happened to Ashley?"

Jones leaned back in his chair, frustrated by the question. "For the record, she flat-out lied to us about everything—her name, her background, her motivation, everything! That put us at a serious disadvantage. We thought she was a schoolteacher with a word puzzle, not a career thief with a stolen artifact. If we had known differently, we would've been better prepared."

She nodded in understanding. "In other words, tell you the truth at all times."

"Yes. That's *exactly* what I mean. Always tell us the truth. *Always*."

"That's a two-way street, you know."

Payne studied her. "Meaning?"

"You didn't invite me down here to break the news about my neighbor. You could've done that upstairs in the hallway. You brought me down here for another reason— one that involves *my* welfare. Otherwise, you wouldn't be so paranoid about safety, and you certainly wouldn't have positioned me in the safest seat in the room. There has to be a reason for that."

Payne shrugged. "Maybe we're just chivalrous."

"Or maybe you're full of shit."

"Damn," Jones said, "I like this gal. She's smart *and* sassy. I'm glad I didn't shoot her."

"Me, too," Payne joked. "Shootings are always messy. And there's so much paperwork."

Megan stared at him, unwilling to look away until she had conveyed how truly serious she was. She knew something dangerous was going on and wasn't about to back down until they told her everything. "I'm waiting."

"For what?"

"The reason you think I'm in danger."

"You're pretty persistent, you know that?"

"You have *no* idea."

He paused for a moment, weighing the pros and cons of telling her. Eventually, he decided she was right. Trust was a two-way street. "Fine! In the spirit of honesty and full disclosure, I'll tell you what has us worried. I hope you can handle it, because you aren't going to like it."

"Don't worry, I can handle it."

Payne nodded. "The odds are pretty good the shoot-ings in Pittsburgh were done by the same people who broke into your neighbor's apartment. They must've seen our article plastered on her refrigerator and figured out she had come to talk to us."

"And?"

"And guess what else was in her apartment? A stack of mail belonging to you. How long do you think it will be before they pay you a visit? In fact, I'm kind of surprised they didn't tear up your place when they were done with hers. That's what most people would've done."

Some of the color drained from her face, but other than that, she took the news in stride. "If you had to guess, why didn't they?"

"Honestly, they probably didn't want to spook you."

"They didn't want to spook me? Why in the world would they care about that?"

"Why? Because if they'd trashed your apartment, there's a decent chance you would've stayed somewhere else for a while. Or invited someone over to protect you. Or purchased a gun for safety. By doing nothing, they lulled you into a false sense of security, which will ulti-mately make it easier to get to you."

Fear flashed in her eyes. "To get to *me*? Why do they want *me*?"

"Simple. By getting to you, they improve their odds of finding the letter."

Megan shook her head in denial. "That makes no sense

at all! I don't know anything about a stupid letter. Or anything about Ashley! At least nothing that was true."

Jones chimed in. "But they don't know that. They'll assume you two were tight."

"Great! This is just great! Gunmen are after me for information that I don't have. I'm sure they'll really believe that, if they find me."

Payne studied her, looking for signs of shock or panic. Surprisingly, she was holding up pretty well. "Megan, let me ask you something. Where were you for the past few days?"

"I was in New Orleans."

"On vacation?"

"Not really."

"What does that mean?"

She explained. "Every year during the holidays, I take a week off to do charity work. I don't have any family to visit at Christmas, so I spend my vacation helping others. This year it was Habitat for Humanity, rebuilding homes that were lost in Hurricane Katrina."

Payne smiled at her compassion. He had spent a lot of time in New Orleans, before and after the hurricane, and realized how much damage had been done. The city's continuing struggle had convinced him to spearhead a campaign that encouraged manufacturing companies, like his own, to donate equipment and building supplies to help with the reconstruction process. In fact, Megan had probably used materials that Payne had provided to Habitat for Humanity.

Not that he would ever tell her. Bragging wasn't his style.

"So," Jones said, "you don't have any family. What about friends?"

"Of course I have friends, but I'm not going to stay with any of them, if that's what you're hinting at. Why would I want to put them in harm's way?"

"That's okay," Payne said. "You can stay with us."

She shook her head. "No way! I don't even know you guys."

Payne signaled for her to calm down. "Don't worry, Megan. I didn't mean in the same room as us. I just meant in the same hotel. It's been a long day, and it's probably not a good idea for you to sleep upstairs."

"Yeah," she admitted, "you're probably right."

"Therefore, if you're willing to put up with us for a little while longer, D.J. would like to get you a room for the night."

"Excuse me?" Jones blurted. "Why me?"

"Why? Because you almost shot her. It's the least you can do."

Jones growled softly. "Fine! I'll pay for one night, but no room service or movies."

Megan shook her head. "One movie, and I can order dessert."

"Deal!" he blurted. "But no porn. That shit is expensive."

35

Jones drove the Chevy Suburban into the heart of the city, where the three of them checked into the Westin Philadelphia, a luxury hotel within walking distance of some of the most famous historical landmarks in America. Normally, Jones would have taken the long way around, driving past Independence Hall, the Betsy Ross House, and the Liberty Bell, but none of them was interested in sightseeing with armed gunmen possibly lurking around every corner.

To conceal their whereabouts, Payne used a fake ID and cash to rent two connecting rooms on one of the upper floors. Megan wasn't comfortable sleeping with her connecting door open—she had known Payne and Jones less than two hours, and one of them had pulled a gun on her—so they reached a compromise. The guys' door would stay open all night, always giving her a secondary exit, if she needed it. They doubted it would come to that, though. They had been on high alert during their drive to the hotel and were confident they hadn't been followed.

By the time they finally got into their rooms, it was nearly eleven p.m.

Payne unzipped his overnight kit. "I've been thinking about the letter, trying to figure out where Ashley got it from."

Jones put on a T-shirt. "What'd you come up with?"

"Nothing yet, but I know somebody who can help. What time is it in France?"

He glanced at his watch. "Almost five a.m. Why?"

"Never mind. It's too late to call him now."

"Call who?"

"Nick."

Jones smiled at the mere mention of the name. He was the perfect guy to give them information about their mission, plus they could trust him with their lives. "Come on! This is Nick we're talking about. The chances are pretty damn good he isn't even in France. Every one of his cases takes him somewhere new. Besides, we saved the guy's life and made him a millionaire to boot. I assure you, he won't be pissed if we call."

NICK DIAL rolled over in his bed in Lyon, France, and stared at the clock on his dresser. He was a very unhappy man. Not only was it the middle of the night, but he had an important meeting scheduled for the morning.

Groaning loudly, he snatched his cell phone from his nightstand and answered it. "Who the hell is this, and what the fuck do you want?"

Payne's eyes widened at the unexpected use of profanity. He moved the phone from his lips and whispered to Jones, "Oh, shit. He's pissed."

"Hang up!" Jones urged.

"I'm not gonna hang up. I'm not in middle school."

Dial shouted into his phone. "Who the hell is this?"

Payne took a deep breath and answered. "Hey, Nick, it's Jonathon Payne. Sorry to call you so late, but something important came up."

There were very few people in the world Dial truly respected, but Payne and Jones were at the top of the list. The trio had met several years ago at Stars & Stripes, a pub in London that catered to Americans who worked overseas. Payne and Jones were in the MANIACs at the time, and Dial was rising through the ranks at Interpol. The three of them hit it off, and they had kept in touch ever since—occasionally bumping into each other in the strangest places. Once, at an airport in Italy. Another time, in the mountains of Greece.

After years of fieldwork, solving some of Interpol's most important cases, Dial had been selected to run the newly formed Homicide Division at Interpol. Since it was the largest international crime-fighting organization in the world, he dealt with death all over the globe. His job was to coordinate the flow of information between police departments any time a murder investigation crossed national borders. All told, he was in charge of a hundred and eighty-six member countries, filled with billions of people and hundreds of languages.

Dial sat up in his bed, groggy. "How important are we talking?"

"Pretty important, Nick. Someone tried to kill us."

"Give me five minutes, and I'll call you back on a secure line."

ONE OF the biggest misconceptions about Interpol was their role in stopping crime. They seldom sent agents to investigate a case. Instead, they used local offices called National Central Bureaus in the member countries. The NCBs monitored their territory and reported pertinent information to Interpol's headquarters in Lyon, France. From there, facts were entered into a central database that could be accessed via Interpol's computer network.

Unfortunately, that wasn't always enough. Sometimes the head of a division (Drugs, Counterfeiting, Terrorism, etc.) was forced to take control of a case. Possibly to cut through red tape. Or handle a border dispute. Or deal with the international media. All the things that Dial hated to do. In his line of work, the only thing that mattered to him was *justice*. Correcting a wrong in the fairest way possible. That was the creed he had lived by when he was an investigator, and it had continued in his new position. If he focused on justice, he figured all the other bullshit would take care of itself.

Still waking up, Dial stumbled into his kitchen and

returned Payne's call, using a landline that was routinely checked for listening devices. "Who'd you piss off now?"

Payne laughed at his directness. "You mean, besides you?"

"Sorry about that. As you know, I'm not a morning person."

"Which is why I called you now. It's not even morning yet."

Dial shook his head as he turned on his coffeemaker. "With that kind of logic, no wonder someone wants you dead."

Payne shrugged. "It's happened before; it'll happen again."

"So, how can I help?"

"Let's start with the people I've killed."

Dial rubbed his eyes. "Before you say another word, let me remind you what I do for a living. I arrest guys who kill people. Are you sure you want to tell me this?"

"Don't worry, I won't be charged. One shooter fell off a cliff, the other got hit by a bus."

"Were you driving the bus?"

Payne laughed, then explained the incident on the Pitt campus, the mysterious letter, and everything that had happened on Mount Washington. He also mentioned the nationality of the first shooter.

"The guy was Belgian?" Dial said as he sat down at his kitchen table. "We rarely run across killers from Belgium. Crime-wise, Brussels is on par with most European capital cities of the same size. There is some violence there, but most of their crimes center on the tourist trade—

pickpockets, purse snatching, street drugs. Not hit men and homicides."

"What about Antwerp or Ghent?"

"As the cities get smaller, so do the crime rates. Rural areas are virtually crime-free."

"We're still waiting for an ID on the second shooter. Once we get that, we might have a clearer picture of what we're up against."

"Until then, what would you like me to do?"

"Do you have any trustworthy contacts in the world of antiquities?"

"I have several," Dial said. "Over here, art forgery is a billion-dollar business. We have an entire floor at headquarters devoted to nothing else."

"If you have the time, I'd appreciate it if you could poke around a little bit—maybe see if anyone is familiar with the type of letter that I described."

"Not a problem. I know who I'm going to call already. Of course, I'll wait until the guy is actually awake before I bug him."

"Sorry about that. I wasn't sure what time zone you'd be in."

"Relax. I'm just busting your balls. Do me a favor, though. Try to stay out of trouble."

"I'll try," Payne said. "Two shootouts in one weekend are more than enough for me. I'm supposed to be retired."

"Yet you still manage to kill more bad guys than any cop I know."

Payne shrugged. "What can I say? Old habits are hard to break."

36

When it came to sleep, Payne and Jones were polar opposites. Payne had always been a troubled sleeper. Even as a child, he had struggled to turn off his brain at night, constantly thinking about all the things he had accomplished during the day and all the stuff he had to do tomorrow. Jones, on the other hand, could flip an internal switch that allowed him to power down like the Terminator. In fact, the MANIACs always teased Jones about it, claiming he would be the best prisoner of war ever, because he could sleep through all the torture.

Therefore, it was no surprise that Payne was still awake at 2:13 a.m. when he heard a soft tapping on the connecting door from Megan's room. There was no urgency to the sound, so Payne didn't leap out of bed with his gun drawn. And Jones didn't flinch, either—although one of his eyes popped open, just to make sure everything was all right. Payne told him to go back to sleep, and just like that, Jones closed his eye and slipped back into robot mode.

Wearing lounge pants and a long-sleeved T-shirt, Payne crept across the dark room and put his ear to the door. "Are you okay?" he whispered.

"I'm fine," Megan said. "Are you decent?"

"I think so. And you?"

Instead of replying, Megan opened her door, revealing the soft glow of a lamp on her bedside table. She was dressed in silk pajamas and a hotel robe, her hair pulled back with a white scrunchie. "Do you have a minute to talk?"

"Of course," Payne said, looming in the doorway like a palace guard. At six foot four and two hundred forty pounds, he was a foot taller than she was and more than double her weight. "Do I need to wake my chaperone, or will you behave?"

"I will, if you will."

"No promises," he teased.

She moved aside and smiled. "Keep in mind, I still have pepper spray."

He stepped into her room. "Duly noted."

Her queen-size bed was a tangle of blankets and sheets, as if she had been tossing and turning nonstop since she had said good-night over three hours earlier. Her TV was on with its volume down low, barely audible above the rumble of the heater. In the right corner of the room, there was a leather chair with its back against the drawn curtains. Payne pointed to it, and she nodded, giving him permission to sit down. As he did, she plopped on the soft mattress, tucking her bare feet underneath her for warmth.

"Did I wake you?" she asked, concerned.

"Not at all. I'm something of a night owl. Have been my whole life."

"Me, too," she admitted. "But even if I wasn't, I would be tonight."

He smiled. "To be honest, I would've been shocked if you had fallen right to sleep. Guns and virgins rarely mix."

"Did you say *virgins*?"

"Sorry. It's a military term for new soldiers in the field. Rookies, virgins, newbies, fresh meat—they all mean the same thing. Whatever you call them, they rarely sleep well."

She shook her head. "I can't even imagine how scared I'd be."

He shrugged, not sure how to explain it to someone who had never served in the armed forces. "If you're interested, I have some heavy-duty sleeping pills in the other room. Take one of those, and you'll be out until Tuesday."

"Wow," Megan joked, "we just met, and you're already trying to corrupt me. First it was guns, now it's drugs. What's next? Are we going to rob a bank together?"

"That depends on you, *Bonnie*. Can you handle a get-away car?"

"Not a problem, *Clyde*—as long as it's an automatic. I'm a little rusty with a stick."

"A beautiful woman like you? I find that hard to believe."

She blushed at the innuendo, her blue eyes shining in the dimly lit room. "There you go again. Always flirting."

He raised his hands defensively. "Sorry about that. From here on in, I swear I'll be on my best behavior."

She giggled at his claim. "Don't become a Boy Scout just for me. Your best behavior is probably too boring for my taste. I'd settle for pretty good behavior with an extra side of compliments. I mean, a woman always likes to hear she's beautiful."

"Strangely, D.J. said the same thing about himself. He's such a pampered little princess."

She laughed at the comment. "I wish I had a best friend like that."

"Actually, he's more than a friend. He's family. The only family I've got."

She nodded, envious. "Like I said, I *wish* I had a friend like that."

The two of them talked for another ten minutes, learning about each other's backgrounds—including Megan's job as a hostess at one of the nicer restaurants in Philadelphia. Eventually, Payne changed the topic of the conversation, focusing on something that had been bothering him.

"When you knocked on my door," he said, "I had the feeling that you wanted to talk about something in particular. Was I imagining that?"

"Not at all. I actually remembered something that

might be important, and I wanted to tell you guys before I forgot."

"Go on."

Megan crossed her legs in front of her, resting her elbows on her knees. "The people who searched Ashley's apartment were looking for your letter, right?"

Payne shrugged. "We think so, but we don't know for sure."

"Well, if she was hiding it, I think I know where it might be."

He leaned forward in his chair. "Where?"

"In the basement."

"What basement?"

"The one in my apartment building. For a hundred bucks a month, you can rent a storage closet. They aren't very big, but they're perfect for storing boxes and junk. They're pretty safe, too. All of them come with a lock."

"And Ashley rented one?"

Megan nodded. "I helped her carry a table down there once. Her space was jammed with all kinds of stuff. At least it was a few months ago."

Payne considered the information. "You know, the odds are pretty good the intruders wouldn't have known about it. Obviously, that doesn't mean she hid the letter there—for all we know she might have a safe-deposit box somewhere in the city—but if she wanted round-the-clock access to it, that would be a lot safer than under her bed."

"That's what I was thinking, too."

He smiled. "I'm glad you thought of it. We can check it out first thing in the morning."

"And then what?"

"Well, I guess that depends on what we find."

"Actually, I was hoping for more of a long-term prognosis."

"Oh, you meant when can you safely go back to your life?"

She nodded. "Something like that."

Payne shrugged. "To be honest, I'm not really sure what to tell you. Right now I have some contacts researching the gunmen who attacked us in Pittsburgh. If we catch a break or two, we might be able to wrap things up in a couple of days."

"And if we don't?"

He grinned. "There's a decent chance we'll be spending Christmas together."

37

After eating breakfast in Payne and Jones's room, the three of them checked out of the hotel and drove back to Megan's apartment building. Thanks to the tinted windows on the Suburban, they felt safe as they circled the block twice, searching for any signs of an ambush. Confident that the area was clean, they parked the SUV across the street and planned their next move.

Ideally, Jones would have entered the basement alone while Payne and Megan stayed hidden in the vehicle. With his lock-picking skills, Jones figured he could break into the storage closet and search it in less than five minutes. Unfortunately, that plan wasn't feasible because Megan didn't know the unit number. She was pretty sure she could identify it by sight—Megan had been there only once, a few months back—but she wouldn't know until she looked for herself.

Following much discussion, the trio split in two. Jones and Megan entered the complex together, and Payne kept watch from the driver's seat of the Suburban. He held his gun in one hand and his cell phone in the other, ready to signal a warning or answer a distress call at a moment's notice. For him, it was a position he wasn't used to. Normally, Payne would have been on the front line, taking the biggest risk, while the rest of his squad watched his back. But on this mission, it made a lot more sense for Jones to go inside. Not only was he better with locks, but he also knew a lot more about historical artifacts than Payne—a skill that might come in handy if Ashley's storage unit was filled with more relics than the mysterious letter.

Not that they were expecting a roomful of treasures.

The truth was, they didn't know what to expect from a career thief like Ashley. The unit might be filled with a shipment of stolen goods, or it might be emptier than Al Capone's vault.

Whatever the case, they wanted to get in and out as quickly as possible.

AS JONES led the way into the lobby, he held his gun inside his coat, ready to fire at the first sign of trouble. Megan walked closely behind him, suspiciously eyeing everyone around them as the two of them opened the door to the stairs. Jones paused and searched for signs of an ambush before he stepped inside. Wasting no time, they hurried down one flight and entered the basement through a thick fire door. Fluorescent bulbs hummed overhead, lighting the concrete corridor.

"Which way?" Jones whispered.

"Up ahead on the left."

Jones nodded, then hustled forward, trying to minimize the time they spent in a hallway that had no exits or places to take cover for nearly twenty feet. At the end of the stretch, Jones poked his head into the storage area and saw nothing that worried him. Locked doors, approximately twenty in all, lined both sides of the hallway that ran directly into a cinderblock wall. As far as Jones could tell, extra security measures had not been installed, meaning he didn't have to worry about cameras or alarms. All things considered, he couldn't have been happier.

"You're clear," he said to Megan. "Which one is hers?"

"Let me check," she said as she walked forward.

Megan knew it was roughly two-thirds of the way back on the right. Ashley had needed her help carrying a breakfast table that was more cumbersome than it was heavy. She remembered the two of them had struggled to get it through the closet door. Eventually, they had been forced to turn the table on its side and angle it in. As they did, they had laughed hysterically at their clumsiness, which made their task even more challenging.

The memory brought a bittersweet smile to Megan's face. A few days ago, she had considered Ashley a friend. Now she didn't know what to think. Obviously, Ashley was not the person she had claimed to be. That much was certain. Ashley's background was bogus, and she had kept her criminal record from Megan. Still, despite all the lies, the Ashley she knew simply didn't match the person Payne and Jones had described. And because of that, Megan didn't know how to feel about her neighbor.

Should she grieve her death, or be thankful Ashley was out of her life for good?

"Any luck?" Jones asked from the doorway.

Megan blinked a few times, then nodded. "It's this one here. I helped make all these scuff marks on the door frame."

"Trade places with me," he said as he moved forward. "If you see or hear *anyone*, let me know right away."

"No problem."

Brushing past Megan, Jones pulled out his lock picks and eyed the closet. It was protected by a simple keyed knob, one that took him little time to defeat. With a quiet click, he opened the door a few inches and eyed the interior for booby traps. Thieves were typically a paranoid lot, mostly because they knew how easy it was to steal things, but also because they were concerned about the police finding their goods. The last thing Jones wanted was to swing the door open and have his face blown off by a homemade explosive.

He knew the odds of that happening were pretty slim. But Ashley had fooled him in Pittsburgh, and it had nearly cost him his life. He wasn't about to let that happen again.

"What are you waiting for?" Megan asked.

"Patience," he said to her. "Never rush into the unknown."

A few seconds later, he was confident the door was clear.

PAYNE EYED the traffic as it flowed in both directions past the apartment complex. Even though the snow had stopped falling and the temperatures had climbed above freezing, the gray skies remained. People streamed past on the slush-filled sidewalk, trekking through puddles that had been layers of ice the night before. Most walkers shivered as they moved, their faces red and chapped from the bitter winds. Instinctively, Payne turned up the heat in the Suburban.

In Pennsylvania, it was a miserable time of year.

Up the street, a group of six huddled together for warmth inside a bus shelter, waiting for a SEPTA bus to pick them up and whisk them to another part of the city. Payne stared at them, thinking back to the tragic events of Saturday night. If not for the bus accident on the Pitt campus, he could have questioned the shooter, all but eliminating his need to be in Philadelphia.

Not that Philly had been all bad. Without this trip, he never would have met Megan, the first woman to pique his interest in a very long time. Due to his wealth and celebrity status, he rarely met anyone in his hometown who wasn't familiar with his life story—at least the details that weren't classified. Because of that, he found it difficult to meet people who wanted to get to know him instead of people who knew about him. In his world, gold diggers and smooth talkers were around every corner, always trying to get a piece of him. For that reason and a few others, he spent most of his time walled off from the rest of the world.

Out of the corner of his eye, Payne noticed a vehicle turning into the circular driveway in front of the complex. He blinked once, then shifted his gaze to his left.

"Shit," he mumbled. "This can't be good."

AS JONES peered into the storage closet, his cell phone started to vibrate. He quickly fished it out and glanced at the screen. The call was from Payne.

Jones answered. "What's wrong?"

"A squad car just pulled up to the building."

Jones cursed under his breath. "How many cops?"

"Two. Right now they're sitting in the car."

"Let's hope they stay put for a while."

"What's your status?" Payne asked.

"I just picked the lock. I still have to search."

"How long do you need?"

"At least ten minutes. Ashley was a damn pack rat. This place is full of boxes."

Payne nodded. He was familiar with the type. His grandfather had been the same way. "Work as quickly as you can. I'll keep you posted on their movement."

"If they're here because of Ashley, they'll probably go

to her apartment to look for clues. That should give me all the time I need."

Payne agreed with his assessment. "Wipe your prints before you leave."

"No worries," Jones said as he adjusted his gloves. "Already done."

38

Jones stared at the crowded space and wondered where to begin. The room was eight feet wide, nine feet high, and ten feet deep. A wide variety of boxes were stacked from the cement floor to the unfinished ceiling. A single bulb, affixed above the door and controlled by a switch on the wall, filled the front half of the room with light. Everything in the back was either masked by shadows or too far out of reach to worry about. In the limited time he had, Jones would focus his search on the boxes near the door. In his mind, those were the only ones that Ashley could have accessed on a moment's notice, so the odds were pretty good the letter would be hidden there.

That is, if the letter was down there at all.

Wearing leather gloves, Jones opened the first box and looked inside. It was filled with T-shirts, shorts, and an assortment of summer clothes. Apparently, she had been forced to make room for her winter wardrobe in her closet upstairs. The second box was crammed with much of the same. The only difference was a layer of sandals underneath her skirts and blouses.

To give himself a little extra room to maneuver, Jones hauled both boxes outside the door as Megan watched from the hallway. "Any trouble?" he asked.

She shook her head. "Need a hand?"

"Nope."

She smiled. "Nice talking to you."

"Yep," Jones said with a grin.

The third box was half the size of the first two. It was made out of thick cardboard and had been placed on top of some larger boxes along the right-hand wall. With a black marker, Ashley had written STUFF on the side of the box. It wasn't the most descriptive noun in the world, but unlike the first two boxes, at least she had taken the time to mark it.

THE PASSENGER door swung open on the squad car, and a brawny officer climbed out. Dressed in dark blue pants, a turtleneck sweater, and a long patrol jacket, he adjusted his hat and holster, then slammed the door shut. A few seconds later, he was walking toward the lobby like a sheriff from the Wild West.

Although Payne couldn't see his face from across the street, he assumed the cop was in his twenties, based on his muscular torso and his cocky stride. During his time in the military, Payne had learned to recognize this particular model of meathead. Even now, he did everything in his power to avoid them. Their tempers ran hot, their brains were rarely used, and their experience was far too limited to understand the world around them. Most of the time, they relied on their bulging biceps to get them out of trouble. Ironically, it was that line of thinking that usually caused their problems to begin with.

For the time being, Payne wasn't concerned with the young cop's presence. As long as his partner stayed in the car, he wasn't going to venture deep into the building. Especially if they had come here for a murder investigation.

Flying solo was simply too risky when a homicide was involved.

JONES OPENED the box and smiled at what he saw. Sitting on top of several photo albums was a manila envelope with a strange-looking postmark. He couldn't tell where it had originated—the stamps were exotic, the postmark had been smudged, and there was no return address—but the name of the recipient was visible. As expected, it hadn't been sent to Ashley.

Still wearing gloves, he turned the envelope around and was surprised to see the flap completely intact. Whoever had opened it—probably Ashley—had done so carefully, possibly steaming it open to prevent any damage. If so, did she know what it contained before she had taken it? Or had she been planning to return the envelope before anyone knew it was missing?

They were all good questions, but Jones knew he didn't have time to answer them now. Instead, he focused on the task at hand. He needed to make sure that the letter was inside.

With a delicate touch, he tapped on the bottom of the envelope and emptied its contents on top of a nearby box that he had brushed clean. Two pieces of cardboard, attached with clear tape that had been broken on one side, formed a protective shield around a single sheet of parchment that had yellowed with age. Although Jones was no expert, the letter appeared to be quite old. At least a century, probably more.

Next, his eyes drifted to the body of the letter. A grin quickly surfaced on his face. He was confident that he was staring at the original. The handwriting was distinct, and the shift in ancient languages was unique.

PAYNE KNEW there was trouble as soon as the meat-head cop waved his partner inside. A minute later, they were greeted by an elderly man who had a gigantic set of keys dangling from his hip. The cops handed him a sheet of paper, which he studied intently before he started fiddling with his key ring. Whether he was a janitor or the building's superintendent, it was pretty obvious that he had been summoned to give the police access to some part of the complex.

The only question was, would they be going up or down?

Just to be safe, Payne called Jones before the officers had revealed their decision, hoping to give him as much notice as possible. He answered on the second ring.

"I found the letter," Jones announced.

"I'm glad, because the cops just produced a warrant."

"That's not good. Which way are they heading?"

"I don't know yet. They're standing in the lobby with someone who looks like the Keymaster."

Jones smiled at the *Ghostbusters* reference. "We have nothing to worry about until the Gatekeeper shows up. After that, all bets are off."

"Actually," Payne said as he watched them from afar, "you need to worry now. They're heading toward the stairs, not the elevator."

"Shit!"

Both men realized the police wouldn't trudge up six flights of stairs to Ashley's apartment, but they might walk down one flight to her storage unit in the basement.

"What's wrong?" Megan asked from the hallway.

Jones hung up the phone. "The cops just showed up. We have to clear out."

The color drained from her face. "What can I do?"

"Tuck this under your shirt," he said as he handed her the envelope. "I've gotta move these boxes."

It didn't take him long to carry the two boxes inside. He realized their placement wasn't important, so he tossed them against the others without rhyme or reason. The only thing that mattered was turning off the light and closing the door before he was spotted in the closet. The moment the lock clicked shut, Jones figured they were in the clear.

At least he thought they were—until he met the meathead.

39

The meathead's name was Vinnie Agostino. He was a local boy, who grew up in South Philadelphia, a section of the city that was rooted in Italian-American culture. Like many people from his part of town, he was fiercely proud of his heritage. Vinnie and his cousins worshipped Rocky Balboa, the Italian Stallion. Ironically, his first job was stocking produce at the Italian Market, a place made famous by the *Rocky* films.

In recent years, a population shift had occurred in South Philly, one that has been the source of racial tension among some of the locals. A few of the smaller sections—most notably Grays Ferry, Point Breeze, and the areas closest to Center City—were no longer "white" neighborhoods. For most people, racial diversity wasn't a problem, but it didn't sit well with Vinnie and his racist friends. Ultimately, that was one of the main reasons that Vinnie had become a cop after a two-year stint in the Marines. In his mind, it was an opportunity to "clean up" the city he loved.

Vinnie's partner was Italian as well, but Paul Giada was nothing like the meathead he had been stuck with for the past three months. Paul was a book-smart, divorced father of two, who mostly kept to himself while Vinnie shot off his mouth and acted tough. Paul was unremarkable in many ways—medium build, average looks, and a bland personality—but he was a good cop with a good heart. Unfortunately, he was something of a pushover, especially when it came to Vinnie, who was the alpha dog in their partnership.

Wherever Vinnie went, Paul followed—whether he liked it or not.

BECAUSE OF Payne's warning, Jones knew the cops were taking the stairs to the basement. Grabbing Megan's arm, he hustled her to the opposite end of the hallway, hoping the elevator would arrive before the cops did. But it wasn't to be. Vinnie threw the door open with a bang and marched down the corridor like he owned the building. The Keymaster, the elderly complex manager, was directly behind him, trying to keep pace, and farther back was Paul.

"Stay calm," Jones whispered as he studied the trio out of the corner of his eye. "We're not doing anything wrong. We're just waiting for the elevator."

"Don't worry," she assured him. "I'm fine."

Vinnie saw the two of them whispering in the distance and was sickened by the sight. A gorgeous woman like *her* had no business being with a guy like *him*. In Vinnie's mind, it went against the laws of nature. In his old neighborhood, their coupling would have resulted in a brutal beat-down that would have left blood on the street—something he and his friends had done many times before. It was their way of keeping the *mulignan*s off of their turf.

"Where's the closet?" Vinnie demanded.

The Keymaster pointed ahead. "Up there, on the left."

"Open the door. I'll be there in a minute. I need to check on somethin'."

"Where are you going?" Paul wondered.

"Don't worry 'bout it," Vinnie growled. "Go with him."

Paul nodded and followed the Keymaster toward the storage unit. Meanwhile, Vinnie marched toward the elevators where Jones and Megan were waiting.

"Hey," Vinnie called from a distance, "what are you *ladies* doin' down here?"

"Stay calm," Jones warned her. "Let me handle this."

"Okay," she whispered.

The closer Vinnie got, the more he looked like a bull. He was six feet tall and made of thick muscles. Like many ex-Marines, he wore his hair shaved tight on the sides, and his gaze was piercing. "Hey! I asked you a fuckin' question. Do you ladies belong down here?"

Jones responded, "Megan lives here. She was giving me the tour."

"Of the basement? Why show *him* the basement?"

"I've got a lot of stuff. I need somewhere to put it."

Vinnie stared at Jones. "Was I talkin' to *you*? No, I was talkin' to *her*."

"Sorry," Jones apologized, hoping the elevator would hurry.

"So?" Vinnie growled as he focused on Megan. "Why are you down here?"

"I'm just giving him the tour. He might move here."

"Great, that's all we need. Let me see your ID."

"Why?" she squeaked. "We haven't done anything wrong."

"That's for *me* to decide. Let me see your ID." He glared at Jones. "Yours, too."

Both of them fished their IDs out of their pockets and handed them to the cop. He barely glanced at Megan's— he simply made sure she lived in the building, as Jones had claimed—before he returned it. Jones, however, was not nearly as fortunate. The only identification he had was his investigator's license, which he kept in a small leather case next to his permit to carry a concealed fire-arm in Pennsylvania. As soon as Vinnie spotted that, he knew he had the right to check Jones for weapons.

"Against the wall and spread 'em," he told Jones. Then he looked at Megan and said, "Stand over there, Jungle Fever, and don't move."

Jones rolled his eyes and turned away from the eleva-tor as its doors opened with a clang. Unfortunately, cops had pestered him a few times over the years, so he was familiar with the procedure. Hands on the wall, legs wide apart, no backtalk of any kind. If he played by the rules and stayed cool, the meathead would probably let him go. If Jones fought back or did anything stupid, the cop would have him in cuffs before the elevator doors closed.

Jones was bound and determined not to let that happen.

"Where's your gun?" Vinnie demanded.

"Right coat pocket," Jones answered calmly.

Vinnie reached in and grabbed it. He took a moment to inspect the Sig Sauer P228 before he tucked it into his belt. "Any other weapons?"

"No, sir."

"We'll see about that."

Vinnie started his search high, patting down Jones's shoulders and sleeves before he moved to the rest of his jacket. First he reached into Jones's right pocket, making sure it was completely empty, then he did the same thing on the left. A moment after his hand went in, a huge smile surfaced on Vinnie's face. "My, oh my. What do we have here?"

Jones closed his eyes and cursed under his breath.

The cop had found the lock picks he had used to break into the storage closet. In the state of Pennsylvania, the only citizens legally allowed to carry picks were certified locksmiths, which Jones was not. Therefore, the meathead could charge him with possession of an instrument of crime, a first-degree misdemeanor.

Grinning widely, Vinnie snatched the handcuffs from his service belt and pulled Jones's right arm behind his back. "For a licensed detective, you sure are stupid." He leaned closer and whispered into Jones's ear, "Then again, you are a fuckin' *mooley*, so what'd I expect?"

Jones sneered but remained silent. This wasn't the time to lose his cool.

"What are you doing?" Megan screeched, stunned this was happening.

Vinnie yanked Jones's left arm back and slapped on the cuffs. "What's it look like I'm doin'? I'm arrestin' your boyfriend."

"But he didn't do anything!"

"Hey, Paulie," Vinnie shouted as he finished searching Jones.

A few seconds later, his partner ducked his head around the corner. "Yeah?"

"Get your ass over here. This eggplant was carryin'."

"Drugs?" Paul asked as he hustled forward.

"Nah, he had a Sig and a set of picks."

"I'm licensed for the gun," Jones clarified. He wanted to make sure the other cop was aware, just in case his permit vanished before he was booked. "You saw my license. It's valid."

Vinnie laughed. "It won't be for long, asshole. Not after I file my report."

Paul stopped next to Megan. "What about the closet?"

"Fuck the closet," Vinnie said as he pushed Jones toward the elevator. "I'm takin' this monkey to the zoo."

40

ayne started getting nervous when Jones and Megan didn't appear in the lobby shortly after the cops had entered the front stairwell. He knew if everything had gone smoothly, the two events should have occurred nearly in unison. Through his years of experience, he realized unforeseen variables often popped up during a mission, but they weren't always disastrous. So Payne wasn't about to overreact and charge forward with his guns blazing.

Perhaps Megan knew the Keymaster, and the two of them stopped to chat in the hallway. Or maybe the cops didn't even go into the basement, which would give Jones more time to continue his search.

Whatever the case, Payne wasn't truly worried about things until the elevator doors popped open and his best friend emerged in handcuffs.

Vinnie the meathead appeared next, followed by his

partner, and then Megan. Thankfully, her hands were free, which meant she wasn't under arrest and would be able to explain everything that had transpired. For the life of him, Payne couldn't imagine what had happened, because he knew Jones wasn't the type to lose his cool under pressure. Were there security cameras that they didn't know about? Or did Megan panic and do something stupid? If that were the case, she would have been the one in cuffs, not Jones, unless he had tried to intervene.

Payne leaned forward in the Suburban, trying to get a better view of Jones as he was pushed out the main entrance toward the police car. For an instant, the two friends made eye contact from fifty feet away. Jones simply shook his head in frustration, as if to say he had done nothing wrong. Like he was sorry for letting Payne down.

Ironically, Payne felt even worse than Jones. The guilt he felt for sitting on his ass and watching his friend get hauled off to jail was overwhelming. But what choice did he have? If he had been permitted, Payne would have willingly traded places with Jones, just to spare his friend the humiliation of being taken into custody. But that wasn't the way the system worked. And he knew if he rushed forward and told the cops that he was friends with Jones, there was always a chance Payne would be arrested, too—which would do neither of them any good.

No, Payne knew the best thing for him to do was to pick up Megan and follow Jones to the police station, where Payne could use every connection he had to get Jones released.

With any luck, they'd be back on the street in less than an hour.

Of course, that plan became moot when the first shot was fired.

One moment, Vinnie was shoving Jones into the back of the squad car, the next his meat head was splattered all over the door and window. The kill shot was so unexpected it took Payne a moment to process what had actually happened. By the time he did, bullet number two was airborne and headed his way. A split second later, he heard a loud crack and flinched as the front windshield of the Suburban absorbed the impact of the round. Thankfully, the bulletproof glass held firm, saving Payne from near-certain death.

It also helped him figure out where the gunman was positioned.

Using simple geometry, Payne knew the shooter had to be somewhere near the street; otherwise, he couldn't have hit the cop and the Suburban in rapid succession. Leaning to his right, Payne tried to see around the web-like fracture in the glass, hoping to spot the gunman. But before he got a clean view of the road, another shot hit the windshield, pushing the glass to its breaking point. There was a loud *thwack* followed by a soft crinkling that reminded Payne of ice cracking on a frozen pond. One more shot, and he knew the window might collapse.

Wasting no time, Payne shifted the SUV into drive and punched the gas. The Chevy shot forward and clipped the bumper of the BMW sedan that was parked in front of it, knocking it into oncoming traffic. Tires screeched loudly as Payne turned the wheel hard to the left and rocketed across the road to a chorus of blaring horns. Yet none of that mattered to Payne. His only concern was surviving long enough to rescue Jones and Megan.

BUT JONES didn't need rescuing. He was quite capable of saving himself.

Covered in blood splatter in the back of the police car, Jones pulled his knees toward his chest and slid his wrists beyond his feet. A moment later, his cuffed hands were in front of him, giving him the freedom to run or fight.

Jones opted to run now, fight later.

The racist cop had fallen facedown on the sidewalk, his body twisted against the side of the car. Blood and brains coated the door, telling Jones everything he needed to know about the guy's condition. The bastard couldn't be saved. The meathead was dead.

A black polymer handle dangled from the back of the cop's belt. Jones recognized it at once. It was his Sig Sauer P228. With a smile on his face, he stretched forward and grabbed his gun.

Suddenly the playing field was a lot more even.

A shot rang out from the nearby street, followed by the crack of glass. Jones turned and glanced at the road but couldn't see the gunman. He was definitely back there, but where? Realizing he was in a position of weakness—pinned down in the back of a squad car, unable to reach the ignition because of an iron partition between the seats—Jones knew he had to move before the shooter came any closer.

The front entrance to the building was roughly twenty feet away. A long distance to run with bound hands. He stared through the blood-streaked window, trying to gauge how long it would take to cover the ground and where he should go once he got inside. In his opinion, the entire lobby was a tactical nightmare. Furniture was sparse. Counters and barriers were nonexistent. And the front of the building was lined with windows. If not for the back hallway and the shielded space near the mail-room, it wouldn't be worth the exposure time. But he knew if he remained stationary in the car, he would be a sitting duck.

"Screw it," he mumbled as he got ready to run.

Taking a deep breath, Jones burst from the car like a sprinter from his starting block. A gunshot echoed behind him, followed by the screeching of tires and the honking of horns, but his sole concern was getting indoors as quickly as possible.

To hasten his entrance, Jones raised his gun and fired two shots at the front window of the building. The glass shattered on impact, sending tiny shards crashing to the lobby floor. They tinkled and clanked in a melodic song, one he didn't notice as he leaped through the empty window frame and scrambled for cover.

Originally, he had planned on running left and hun-kering down by the mailroom, using its angled wall for protection. But out of the corner of his eye, he noticed the middle elevator had just arrived and its doors were sliding open. Taking that as an omen, he cut sharply to his right and dove inside the car before the gunman could clip him from behind.

Unfortunately for Jones, the elevator wasn't empty.

PAUL WAS ten feet behind his partner when Vinnie's head erupted like a pink volcano.

The shot had come from their left, somewhere near the busy road, not from the suspect they had in hand-cuffs, although there was a chance he had an accomplice who had pulled the trigger. With that in mind, Paul did what he had been trained to do—he grabbed the near-est civilian and dragged her to safety in the opposite direction. And Megan was thankful he did; otherwise, she would have remained standing in the middle of the sidewalk, too stunned by the graphic nature of the kill shot to react rationally.

She had never seen someone murdered before. It took a moment for her to recover.

When she finally snapped out of her haze, she was already halfway across the lobby, running toward the sitting area beyond the bank of elevators. Paul pulled her arm and yanked her behind a faux-leather couch that would temporarily shield them from the gunman outside.

"Stay down," he warned as he pulled his Glock 21,

a .45-caliber semiautomatic handgun, from his holster. "I'm calling for backup."

Megan said nothing as she cowered next to him on the floor.

With his free hand, Paul clicked the button on his transmitter and called in a *ten double zero*, police code for *officer down, all patrols respond*. A few seconds later, Jones fired two shots at the window and sprinted across the lobby.

Suddenly, Paul had more important things to worry about than backup.

He had an armed suspect to take out.

41

Ann and Mary Choban were senior citizens. They lived with their sister Sally in a small apartment on the tenth floor. Despite their advancing age, they roamed the city every day, riding public transportation and searching for bargains. Today they were headed to Taco Bell, followed by a trip to a local casino where they would play the cheapest slots available.

At least that had been the plan until Jones dove into their elevator.

The two seniors shrieked with surprise and moved to the far corner of the car, where they huddled against the wall. Jones spotted them while still on his back and assured them they were safe, despite the fact that he was pointing a loaded gun toward the lobby.

"Don't worry, I'm a cop," he lied.

Mary stared at him, confused. "No, you're not. You *can't* be a cop."

Jones glanced up at her. "What's *that* supposed to mean? I'm *black* so I can't be a cop?"

Ann stammered. "No, but . . ."

"Hold up!" he said, annoyed. "This is *supposed* to be the City of Brotherly Love. Well, I'm a brother, so show me some love. I can't believe how racist everyone is!"

"But . . ."

"But *what*? Spit it out, Grandma."

Ann finished her thought. "But you're wearing handcuffs."

"Oh," he mumbled, suddenly realizing how he appeared to them. The meathead cop had pissed off Jones so much he was actively searching for racism, even in places it wasn't present. "Ladies, the lobby isn't safe right now. You should go upstairs for a while."

Mary grumbled, "But we're going to lunch."

"To get tacos," Ann added.

"Not today," Jones said as he sprang to his feet. "What floor?"

Both women sighed and answered in unison: "Ten."

Jones pushed the appropriate button. "Don't come back until dinner."

THINKING THINGS THROUGH, Paul realized there was a decent chance that Jones had an accomplice who had killed Vinnie. It would certainly explain why Jones was now armed and running free. Furthermore, it probably meant the woman he had dragged behind the couch was actually the enemy. After all, she had been with Jones at the time of his arrest.

"What's your name?" Paul demanded.

"Megan Moore," she said, curled up on the floor.

"Are they coming for you?"

"Who?"

He pointed his gun at her. "Your friends."

"My friends?" she shrieked, confused by the turn of events.

"The ones who killed my partner."

She backed away from him. "We didn't kill your partner. They tried to kill us!"

"Bullshit!"

"I swear to God, someone is trying to kill us. They already killed my neighbor."

The comment made him pause. "Who's your neighbor?"

"Ashley Henderson. She lived in 615."

That was the same woman Paul and Vinnie had been sent to investigate. The one who had been killed on the Pitt campus for no apparent reason. "Who are your friends?"

"Jonathon Payne and David Jones. They're investigators from Pittsburgh."

Paul peeked over the couch, looking for trouble. "Why are they here?"

"They're here to protect me."

"Did you hire them?" he demanded.

"No, I didn't hire them."

"Then that *doesn't* make sense. They must be here for some other reason."

"I'm telling you, they're here to protect me!"

A moment later, Paul found out that was true.

AS HE SLAMMED on the SUV's brakes outside the lobby, Payne thought about his best course of action. Jones and Megan had dashed inside the building, which was temporarily the safest place for them. Unless, of course, there were more gunmen approaching from the rear. If that was the case, then everyone inside was going to get caught in the crossfire.

Not a pleasant thought.

Thinking quickly, Payne tapped on the driver's side window, trying to figure out what kind of material had been used in its design. From his time in the military, he realized that high-profile vehicles in war zones were now being fitted with one-way bullet-resistant glass because it allowed security details to fight back without leaving their vehicles.

He had never used it during combat, but he had tested it during drills.

The glass was made of dual layers, a brittle layer on the exterior and a flexible one on the interior. When a bullet was fired from the outside, it hit the brittle layer first, shattering a section of it. This absorbed some of the bullet's energy and spread it over a large area. When the slowed bullet hit the flexible layer, it stopped. However, when a bullet was fired from the inside, it hit the flexible layer first, easily penetrating it because the bullet's energy was focused on a smaller area. The brittle layer then shattered outward due to the flexing of the inner layer and did not hinder the bullet's progress.

Based on what he knew about the Suburban and all the high-ranking officials who had used it before him, Payne decided the vehicle would be equipped with all the latest features.

Only one way to find out, he thought.

Payne twisted in the driver's seat and stared out the back of the SUV. He put his finger in one ear while pressing his shoulder against the other to protect his ears from the sound of a gun firing in an enclosed space. Thirty seconds passed before the gunman inched around the corner. He swept his gun from side to side, searching for possible targets on the street and near the building. Due to the tint in the SUV's windows, the gunman had no idea Payne was still inside the vehicle, staring at him over the tip of his handgun, patiently waiting to strike.

Second after second ticked by as the gunman crept forward. Finally, when he was no more than five feet from the Suburban, Payne calmly pulled his trigger.

The shot ripped through the rear window as though it were passing through paper. It struck the gunman just below his left ear and rattled around the interior of his skull before it settled in his temporal lobe. The bastard didn't feel a thing. He was dead before he hit the sidewalk.

FROM HIS position near the elevator, Jones saw a gun pointing at Megan, who was cowering away from the weapon. Considering everything that had transpired during the past couple of minutes, Jones wasted no time before he sprang into action. Sprinting across the lobby, he dove headfirst over the couch and tackled the man who was threatening her.

No warnings. No threats. Just a forearm and his opponent's head.

One moment Paul was questioning Megan, the next he was on the floor with a set of handcuffs wrapped around his neck like a hangman's noose. Kneeling on the cop's back, Jones applied constant pressure, slowly but surely choking the life out of Paul.

"Drop the gun or die!" Jones hissed.

Paul did as he was told, and it clanked to the floor.

"Don't kill him," Megan said as she scrambled forward. "He saved my life."

"That doesn't give him the right to take it."

She touched Jones's shoulder. "Ease up. Please, ease up."

Begrudgingly, Jones let him breathe. "Why'd you pull a gun on her?"

"Someone killed Vinnie," Paul gasped, fighting for air.

"What's your point? We didn't do it. You were with us the whole time."

"I thought you might have a partner."

Jones considered the cop's answer. It was a valid point. If their roles had been reversed, he would have assumed the same thing. "We're the good guys. We don't kill cops."

Megan nodded. "That's what I was telling him before you kicked his ass."

"Come here," Jones said to her. "Get his keys and unlock my cuffs. Once my hands are free, I'll let him go. I've got no beef with him."

"Left hip," Paul mumbled as he tasted the floor.

Megan grabbed the keys from his belt and undid the lock. Still not in a trusting mood, Jones picked up the cop's gun and handed it to Megan, who stared at it with a mixture of fear and confusion. "What do I do with this?"

"Point it away from us," Jones said as he climbed off the cop and turned him over. Ironically, Paul had the same look in his eye as Megan. "Listen to me. I am a licensed investigator from Pittsburgh. I did not kill your partner. My partner did not kill your partner. In fact, none of us killed your partner. Do you understand?"

Paul nodded his head, still catching his breath.

"Whoever killed your partner wants us dead. They already killed her neighbor, and they've been gunning for us all weekend. Do you believe me?"

Paul nodded again.

"Good," Jones said as he snatched the gun from Megan and handed it to Paul, "because we need all the firepower we can get. My partner's name is Jon, and he's a big white dude."

The color returned to Paul's face once his Glock was back in his hand. "I called for backup. They should be here soon—"

Just then they heard a loud rumble, followed by a deafening crash as the back end of the Chevy Suburban fishtailed through the lobby entrance and shattered the remaining windows. As the vehicle skidded to a stop, the SUV's trunk slowly rose open.

Payne stared at them from the driver's seat. "Need a lift?"

Jones grinned at the stunned cop. "Feel free to stick around, but my backup just arrived."

42

For Nick Dial, it had been a day from hell. Starting with the early morning wake-up call from Payne and continuing with a breakfast meeting that lasted until mid-afternoon, Dial was not in the mood to be messed with. Unfortunately for Henri Toulon, he did not realize that when he broke into his boss's office and used his couch for an afternoon nap.

Toulon, the assistant director of the Homicide Division, was a wine-loving Frenchman who practically lived at headquarters yet spent half of his time avoiding the tasks of the day. In some ways, he was a great employee, able to speak at length on every subject under the sun—whether it was history, sports, politics, or pop culture. But sometimes he got lost in his own thoughts, and when that happened, he could usually be found outside the building, smoking a cigarette and preaching to his coworkers about some random topic. Back in school, he had been the student everyone loved to hate. He never studied, rarely showed up for class, but always had the best grades.

Dial unlocked his office door, looking forward to a few minutes of peace and quiet before he responded to a handful of messages. Unfortunately, he was greeted by the sound of snoring.

"You've got to be shitting me," he mumbled to himself.

Wasting no time, Dial walked across the room and tipped the couch forward, dumping the unsuspecting Frenchman onto the floor. Toulon awoke on impact and then launched into a string of profanities that Dial couldn't understand. Eventually, Toulon shifted to English.

"Why did you do that? I have done nothing wrong."

"Say that again."

"I have done nothing—"

"Stop!" Dial growled, cutting him off. "That's the problem right there. I've been busting my ass all day, and you have done *nothing!*"

Toulon ran his fingers over his gray hair, which was pulled back in his trademark ponytail. He certainly didn't look the part of an Interpol officer, but his brilliance usually made up for his attitude and attire. "I am detecting tension in your voice. Perhaps *you* need a siesta?"

"Henri, I'm telling you right now: Do not mess with me."

Toulon ignored the warning. "Why are you so cranky? Are you mad you are not French? I know if I was an American, I would be tempted to slit my wrists."

Dial stared at him, fuming.

"*Excusez-moi*," Toulon apologized. "I did not know you were serious."

"Do I sound like I'm joking around?"

He shook his head. "On reflection, you do not."

"And do you know why I'm so pissed?"

"Several jokes come to mind, but I shall keep them to myself."

"I'm pissed because I gave you an important task this morning, and as far as I can tell, you haven't taken care of it."

Toulon fiddled with his ponytail. "And what task is that?"

"You were supposed to identify the second gunman who tried to kill Jonathon Payne in Pittsburgh, and then talk to our contacts in antiquities about that mysterious letter."

"Have you no faith in me? I completed those tasks long ago."

"Really? Because you were *supposed* to send the information to my cell phone, so I could forward it to my friend."

Toulon groaned. "That I did not do. But two out of three is pretty good, no?"

"Not good enough."

"If you'd like, I can send it to your phone right now."

Dial growled. "How does that make any sense at all? You're standing in front of me. Just tell me what you learned, and I'll call Jon myself."

"In my defense, it makes perfect sense, because I do

not remember all of the details. If you give me a moment, I can run to my desk and get my notebook."

Dial waved him off. "Go!"

Toulon nodded and walked away. He returned a few minutes later and sat in one of the chairs across from Dial, who was using the phone on his desk. Normally, Toulon would have cleared his throat and pointed to his watch, just to piss off his boss, but he realized if he did either, there was a decent chance that Dial would shoot him.

"So," Dial said as he hung up, "what did you learn?"

"The Pittsburgh police have identified the second shooter. He is an American named Chad Wilkinson. His criminal record is quite long, but not very distinguished. On the surface, there does not appear to be a connection with the sniper from Belgium."

"What about *below* the surface?"

Toulon scrunched his face. "What do you mean?"

"Your notebook says there isn't a connection, but sometimes detective work isn't about paperwork. Sometimes it's about hunches and gut feelings."

"Do you know where the term *gut feeling* originated? Soothsayers from ancient civilizations, particularly those near the Mediterranean Sea, used to read animal entrails in order to prophesize the future. They literally used to *feel* an animal's *guts* in order to work their magic."

Dial rolled his eyes. He didn't give a damn about the term's origins, but he knew if he had interrupted Toulon, it would have wasted more time than the explanation itself. "Are you done?"

"*Oui*, I am done. I kept my story short because you are angry."

"I'll be a lot happier if you answer my original question."

"Your original question? Ah, yes, you wanted to know if I had a theory."

"Well? Do you?"

Toulon smiled. "What if shooter number two was a last-second substitute?"

"How so?"

"The first shooter was from Belgium, but he was killed before the job was done. Whoever hired him refused to wait for a replacement to be flown in from Europe, possibly afraid that the letter might be taken out of the city. So he hired a substitute, someone who lived near Pittsburgh. According to our files, the American was from a small town in Pennsylvania. Obviously, he would be more familiar with the region, and he would not have to worry about smuggling a weapon aboard a flight."

Dial nodded. "Makes sense to me. Wilkinson was a pinch hitter. Of course, that leads me to the next question. Who hired him?"

Toulon shrugged. "This, I do not know."

"What about the letter? What did our contacts in antiquities say?"

"They said nothing. The letter you described is one they are not familiar with. But they will ask around. If they learn anything, they will let me know."

"If that happens," Dial stressed, "call me immediately. No more of this forgetting-to-tell-me bullshit. Understand?"

"*Oui*, I understand."

"And no more naps in my office. If I can't sleep here, neither can you."

PAYNE'S PHONE rang several times before going to voice mail. Normally, Dial would have been reluctant to leave confidential information in a message, but considering the urgency of the situation, he explained everything he had learned and apologized for the delay.

"If you have any questions, give me a call back."

Dial smiled and added, "Preferably at a decent hour."

43

Once they were a few blocks from the apartment complex, Payne called Randy Raskin at the Pentagon and briefed him on their situation. "I've got some good news and some bad news."

Raskin leaned back in his chair. "What's the good news?"

"Whoever bulletproofed the Suburban did a wonderful job."

Raskin rubbed his eyes, trying to massage away the migraine that was starting to form. "Please tell me you're joking. A senator reserved that vehicle for tomorrow!"

"No problem. He can pick it up at a parking garage near the Penn campus."

"And what's the bad news?"

"He can pick up the rest of it along a half-mile stretch of Spruce Street."

Raskin growled softly. "I can't believe you guys. Every time I help out, I always end up paying for it."

"Gosh, I hope not, because the repair bill is gonna be ridiculous."

He growled louder. "What happened this time?"

Payne told him the basics about the shootout, including the murdered cop. The death of an officer always struck an emotional chord with Raskin. Over the years, he had met a lot of people who later died fighting for their country or had lost someone who had. Somehow it helped Raskin keep things in perspective. Even though he worked grueling hours in the Pentagon basement, he never faced the threats that field operatives did on a daily basis. And because of that, he was more than willing to help Payne and Jones whenever he could—even if it meant risking his job by circumventing rules and regulations on occasion.

"How can I help?" Raskin asked.

Payne explained. "There was a cop at the scene named Paul Giada. As a favor to us, he let us leave before the cavalry arrived. In return, I promised him that someone from the Pentagon would explain who we were and the mission we were on. Obviously, there isn't an *actual* mission, but if you could make it sound good, it will keep our names out of the newspapers."

"Consider it done."

"We also need a lift back to Willow Grove, preferably an armed escort. There are some things we need to sort out, and I'd feel a lot safer if we were at a military airfield."

"I hope you realize it's not a secure facility."

Payne nodded. "Secure or not, it has to be safer than the closest Starbucks."

"Definitely. Four bucks for a cup of coffee is highway robbery."

TWO HOURS LATER, Payne was shown a cramped back office at NASJRB Willow Grove. It was a windowless room lined with cinderblocks that had been painted white ten years earlier. A musty scent filled the air. Inside was a cheap desk, three chairs, a phone, and a dry erase board—all the things Payne had requested. He thanked the guardsman and asked him to retrieve Jones and Megan, who were finishing their lunches in the small cafeteria down the hall. Years in the field had taught Payne and Jones one of the key rules to surviving a mission: Eat whenever you had a chance, because your next meal might be days away.

Payne took his spot behind the desk and waited for the others to arrive. The last forty-eight hours had included three attempts on his life by three different gunmen. The first one had been a Belgian soldier. According to Nick Dial, the second one was an American. Unfortunately, because of Payne's hasty retreat from the apartment complex, he didn't have time to get prints from the most recent shooter. Not that he actually needed to. Since an officer had been killed, he realized that the Philadelphia police would make the case a top priority.

And the moment they discovered the gunman's identity, Raskin would get him the information.

Jones walked into the office, carrying the envelope he had taken from Ashley's storage locker. Megan had stored it under her shirt right before the cops had arrested Jones, but he took it back from her as soon as they were inside the Suburban. Not only for the letter's protection, but because he didn't want Megan to see what he had discovered.

It was something he wanted to spring on her when the time was right.

And that time was now.

Megan sat across the desk from Payne, and Jones sat on her right.

"How are you holding up?" Payne asked.

"I'm okay," she said. "I've got a horrible headache, but other than that I'm fine."

Payne nodded knowingly. "Probably from the excess adrenaline. It's tough to get used to. Thankfully, the food you ate should help. So would a shot of bourbon."

She grimaced. "The only thing bourbon would help is the odds of me puking."

Jones scrunched his face. "Now that's a pretty image."

She shrugged. "Sorry, I'm just being honest."

Payne smiled at the segue. "Speaking of honesty, we were hoping you could explain something for us."

"I'll certainly try."

"When we first arrived at the airfield, D.J. pulled me aside and showed me something that confused the heck out of me. Ever since then, I've been trying to come up with a rational explanation for it, but I've been unsuccessful. In fact, both of us have failed."

She arched her eyebrow. "What are you talking about?"

Jones replied, "When I was in the storage unit, I found the mysterious letter that compelled Ashley to track us down in Pittsburgh."

"I know. You gave it to me when the police arrived."

"Did you look at it?"

She shook her head. "There wasn't time. I stuffed it in my shirt like you told me to, and I gave it back to you once we'd left the building. Why? Did I damage it? If I did, I'm sorry. I kind of forgot about it while I was running—"

Payne interrupted her, "Megan, relax. You didn't damage the letter. Then again, even if you had destroyed it, we wouldn't have the right to complain."

She looked confused. "Why not?"

Jones handed the envelope to her. "Because it was addressed to you."

Megan blinked a few times, then focused on the center of the manila envelope. Shocked, she saw her name and mailing address, penned in fancy calligraphy. "Is this a joke?"

Payne stared at her from across the desk. "Do we look like we're joking?"

"No, but . . ."

"But what?" Jones demanded. "Isn't that the envelope I gave you?"

"I think so, but I can't explain this."

Jones grunted. "That's too bad because we can't explain it, either."

A few days earlier, Payne would have considered himself a great judge of character, but after the whole ordeal with Ashley, he was slightly less confident in his ability to detect a con artist. However, based on the bewilderment on Megan's face, he was pretty damn certain she was being honest with them. She had no idea why the letter had been sent to her.

"Let me ask you something else," Payne said. "When you first knocked on Ashley's door, you said you were expecting some kind of package. What were you expecting?"

"I wasn't expecting anything."

Payne leaned back in his chair, annoyed. "See, I find that hard to believe. You asked me about the package several times. It had to be important to you."

She shook her head. "I asked because I was curious. Not because it was important."

"What's *that* supposed to mean?"

Megan pulled out her cell phone. "May I show you something?"

Payne and Jones nodded their heads.

She touched a button and started scrolling through her messages. "When I was in New Orleans, I worked from sunup to sundown, so my phone was never with me. But on one of the nights—Wednesday, I think—I got a strange text message. Here, take a look at this."

She handed the phone to Jones, who studied the

screen, trying to make sense of the cryptic message. Unlike the mysterious letter, the entire text had been written in English.

> *Your fortune waits for you.*
> *Protect it with your life.*
> *Death shall visit those untrue.*
> *Blood of his first wife.*

44

Jones slid Megan's phone across the desk to Payne, who read the text without comment. Although he wrote the cryptic quatrain in his tablet, his main concern was finding the phone number of the sender and the time it had arrived. While Payne searched for that information on the phone, Jones took over the questioning.

"I consider myself an educated man," he said to Megan, "so when I read poetry I tend to ask myself certain things. For instance, what was the central theme of the piece? Why did the writer choose this particular rhyming scheme? Occasionally, I even like to speculate on which schools of thought influenced the poet's word choice."

Payne glanced at Jones, trying to figure out where he was going with his line of questioning. He knew damn well that Jones didn't read poetry—apart from the lyrics of his favorite rap songs.

"That being said," Jones continued, "do you know what question popped into my mind while I read your text message?"

She shook her head. "No, what?"

Jones leaned closer. "Why the fuck didn't you show us this last night?"

"Pardon me," she blurted.

Payne cleared his throat. "Language."

Jones raised his hands defensively. "Sorry for being so crass, but vulgarity isn't nearly as offensive as gunfire. I mean, curse words sting and all, but bullets freakin' kill!"

Payne cleared his throat even louder.

"What?" Jones snapped. "I said *freakin'*, not *fuckin'*."

"I know you did, but calm down."

"Calm down? Why should I calm down? Personally I think *you* should be more upset!"

"And what good would that do?"

"What good?" Jones asked incredulously. "Maybe it would help her understand that she shouldn't keep intel from us. That keeping us in the dark is a good way to get us killed."

Megan had heard enough. She wasn't the type of person who was going to let two people argue about her while she was in the room—especially since she didn't feel she had done anything wrong. "Wait a second! Do you mean like not telling *me* about the translation of the letter? I'm not stupid, you know. I heard you guys whispering about some Petr guy translating it for you.

Why should I tell *you* everything if you're not going to tell *me* everything?"

Jones glared at her for a few uncomfortable seconds. As much as he hated to admit it, she had a valid point. They had been keeping things from her. Important things. Of course, that was the way it had been for them during their military careers. Information was compartmentalized. Everything was on a need-to-know basis. And since Payne and Jones were at the top of the MANIAC pyramid, they got to pick and choose when intelligence was passed to their men. Unfortunately, now that they were in the real world, they occasionally struggled with the concept of give-and-take. Sometimes information had to be shared for trust to be earned.

"Listen," Jones said, suddenly not as loud or angry as a moment before, "I can understand your point of view, but you have to understand mine. When it comes to safety, there are no secrets. If you get a text message or a phone call that mentions death or threatens anyone in any way, you tell us ASAP. In return, we'll do our best to keep everyone safe."

Megan nodded in agreement. That sounded like a fair deal to her. "In hindsight, you're right. I should have shared the message with you sooner. However, in my defense, I received this message way before anyone tried to kill me. I honestly thought it was some kind of a prank. It never dawned on me that it was actually important until earlier today."

"Well, now you know."

She nodded and stuck out her hand toward Jones. "Still friends?"

He smiled and gave her a fist bump. "Still friends."

For Payne, it was a major struggle not to tease Jones. He had never seen one of his rants cut so short. Normally, Jones spouted on and on until he eventually ran out of steam, but Megan had managed to disarm him with a well-timed rebuttal and a few kind words. To Payne, it was like watching a woman use the Jedi mind trick. Only better. Because this wasn't fiction.

"Hey, D.J.," Payne said, "do you feel like working your magic?"

"With what?"

Payne handed Megan's phone to Jones. "The message was sent to her on Wednesday night from a restricted number. Can you access her account and find out who sent it?"

"I can, but I'll have to do it in the other room. It's the only place I can hook up my laptop to a high-speed connection."

Payne nodded. "That's fine. I think I can handle things from here."

"Scream if you need me," Jones said as he walked through the door.

Megan glanced over her shoulder to make sure he couldn't hear what she was about to say. "Well, that was interesting."

Payne leaned back in his chair, impressed. "I have to admit, you showed a lot of moxie. Not only did you stand up to him, but you managed to calm him down."

She smiled slyly. "What can I say? I have a gift."

"What gift is that?"

"The ability to soothe the savage beast."

"Well, I—"

She cut him off. "Choose your next words wisely. If you say *anything* about a beast in your pants that needs soothing, I'm leaving and never coming back."

Payne laughed. "Although I'm flattered that you're thinking about my pants, I was actually going to say your gift probably comes in handy at work."

As hostess of one of the fanciest restaurants in Philadelphia, Megan was often forced to deal with angry clientele—everyone from the snobby rich to the obnoxious drunk. "As a matter of fact, I have handled some of the most delicate reservation snafus in the history of this fine city. Perhaps you've heard of the Fagan Fiasco of 2006? Or the Hennessy Debate of 2008?"

He shook his head. "Actually, I haven't."

She playfully slammed her fist on the desk. "That's because I handled them."

Payne grinned at her playfulness, trying to remember the last time he had felt so comfortable around a woman in such a short amount of time. "As much as I'd like to hear all the details, let's focus on the text message for a moment."

She nodded. "Whatever you need, just ask."

"Out of curiosity, what did you do when you received the message?"

"I did what most people would do: I tried to figure out who sent it. Unfortunately, as you know, it came from a restricted number. And when I replied to it, my text got bounced back."

"Then what?" Payne asked.

"I tried to make sense of the riddle."

Payne, who had written the poem on a tablet, read it aloud. "*Your fortune waits for you. Protect it with your life. Death shall visit those untrue. Blood of his first wife.*"

"Strange, huh?"

"More than strange. It was prophetic."

"In what way? Please tell me there's a big check in that envelope."

"Actually," Payne explained, "I was talking about Ashley. She came to Pittsburgh, claiming the letter had been sent to her, and she was killed because of her deceit."

Megan opened her mouth to argue how preposterous that was, then realized Payne was right: Death had visited Ashley for that very reason. Suddenly, a chill went down her spine. "Jon, that is *so* creepy. Look at my arms. They're covered in goose bumps."

"If you think that's creepy, hand me your envelope. Since it was addressed to you, I think it's time I told you what the letter said."

Standing from his chair, Payne carefully removed the mysterious letter and laid it on the desk. As he did, she walked around to his side and stared at the ancient languages, trying to understand why it had been sent to her.

"Is this my fortune?" she asked.

Payne shook his head. "If the letter is as old as we

think it is, it's probably valuable, but I doubt it's worth a fortune."

"Oh well, it's probably for the best. Most rich people are assholes."

"Hey," he argued.

She patted him on the back. "Relax, big guy. I said *most.*"

"Anyway," he said as he flipped his tablet to the notes he had taken during Petr Ulster's lecture, "the main reason we came to Philly to investigate Ashley's death was because of the cryptic message of the poem. She didn't know it, but it talks about Philadelphia."

He set the tablet on the desk and allowed Megan to read the modern translation.

> *From the city of brothers,*
> *A lover from the lost line.*
> *A filly with no mother,*
> *Chosen for her place in time.*

Payne focused on Megan's face as she read the poem, hoping to see how she reacted to the letter that had been intended for her. Would she be surprised? Or confused? Or maybe some other emotion that would allow him to learn more about her?

He watched her lips as they moved silently, slowly sounding out the words as she tried to decipher their meaning. In the middle of the message, she paused, as if she'd noticed something that no one else had and needed to read it again and again to make sure that she wasn't imagining things. Finally, after several seconds of bewilderment, she grabbed Payne's arm.

"Who wrote this?" she demanded, her voice filled with concern.

"Why? What's wrong?"

"Who wrote the letter, Jon?"

Payne shrugged. "We don't know who wrote it. Why? What's bothering you?"

"The letter," she said as she sank into Payne's chair. "I know who it's describing."

He stared at her and noticed the blood had drained from her pale face. "Who?"

Megan glanced up at him. "The letter is about *me*."

45

From the look in Megan's eyes, Payne knew she was serious. She truly believed the letter had been written about her. Unfortunately, he wasn't as certain.

"Not to doubt you," he said, "but what makes you so sure?"

She didn't speak. She simply pointed to the third line, tapping it repeatedly.

Payne put his hand on her shoulder. He could feel the tension building in her neck and back. "A filly with no mother? That's what has you so shaken?"

He thought back to their late-night conversation at the hotel. They had talked about losing their parents at such an early age and how tough it had been on them. If he remembered correctly, a mugger had killed her mom when Megan was only ten.

"Trust me when I tell you this," he said, "I know exactly what you're going through. I truly do. Not a single day has passed since the death of my parents that I haven't thought of them. And sometimes the emotions catch me completely off guard. I can't tell you how many times I've been watching a movie or a TV show and started getting misty because one of the characters lost a parent. For some reason, my childhood memories just overwhelm me. And this is coming from a guy who has spilled a lot of blood over the years. I'm telling you, nothing in my life has affected me like my parents' deaths. Not war. Not 9/11. *Nothing*."

Megan grabbed his hand and squeezed. Somehow she felt better knowing he cared enough about her to open up even though they had just met. For an ex-soldier like Payne—someone who had been taught to bury his emotions in order to survive—she knew that was probably a difficult thing to do.

"Come here," she said as she tugged on his arm and urged him to sit down on the corner of the desk. She wanted to look him in the face while she spoke to him. "I appreciate you telling me that. That had to be tough for you."

Payne said nothing. He simply focused on her eyes, which were moist with tears.

"Last night," Megan said, "when we talked about our parents, I didn't tell you everything about my family history. We had just met and all, and there's only so much that you want to share with a stranger. Actually, I haven't shared this with anybody in a very long time. Not my friends, my coworkers, or my neighbors. But as D.J.

pointed out, I shouldn't keep secrets from you guys, not if I expect you to help me through this."

"What is it?" he asked gently.

"The parents I told you about were my *adoptive* parents. They took me in when I was just a newborn, so they were the only ones I ever knew. But they weren't my biological parents."

Payne studied her face, trying to figure out why this detail seemed so important to her—why it had knocked her off her feet and shaken her so deeply. But before he had a chance to ask, she wiped her eyes and continued her explanation.

"When I was still a little girl, my mom decided it was time to tell me that I had been adopted. I'm not quite sure why she chose that particular moment—maybe she was afraid that I was going to find out from someone else, and she wanted to make sure that didn't happen. Whatever the reason, she came into my bedroom, sat down on my pink bed, and told me that I was her precious little gift from heaven. Keep in mind I was only eight at the time, so I didn't know much about adoption or childbirth, but she took her time and explained that sometimes parents were unable to take care of their children, and whenever that happened, someone else was given that gift. By the end of the conversation, I felt like the luckiest kid in the world for having such a loving mom."

Payne smiled warmly, appreciative that she had shared such a wonderful memory with him. Yet in the back of his mind, he couldn't help but wonder what her story had to do with the letter. Why had the line *a filly with no mother* affected her so deeply? Obviously, there were thousands of adopted women from Philadelphia, and many of them had lost their adoptive parents over the years—just like Megan had—so why was she so confident the message was about her?

Couldn't it have been about any of them?

Unless, Payne reasoned, he had been focusing on the wrong aspect of the story. Maybe her emotional connection with the third line of the poem had nothing to do with her adoptive mother. Maybe it had something to do with her biological parents.

"I don't mean to pry," Payne said, "but what do you know about your birth mother?"

Megan blinked a few times, and when she did, tears ran down her cheeks. Slightly embarrassed, she brushed them away with the sleeve of her sweater. "Sorry about that. I swear I'm normally not a blubbering mess. I promise I'm not."

"That's quite all right. Take your time. I'm not going anywhere."

She managed a slight smile. "Ironically, I never even knew my birth mother, yet she's the reason I'm crying. She's the reason I'm so certain the poem is about me."

"Go on."

"You've heard of mothers dying during childbirth? Well, my birth mother has that beat. She actually died six hours and seventeen minutes before I was even born."

Payne furrowed his brow. "Excuse me?"

"Yeah," she said, sniffling, "I thought that would get your attention."

"Wait. How did, um, I mean—"

Megan explained. "According to medical records, my birth mother was eight and a half months pregnant with me when she had a severe brain aneurysm. They rushed her to the hospital and tried to save her life, but she passed away in the emergency room. For the next six hours or so, machines kept her heart beating while they pumped her full of drugs that would help me survive a cesarean section. Whatever they did must have worked because I came out healthy."

Payne shook his head in disbelief. "Every once in a while, you hear about stuff like that on the news, but you never expect to meet the person who has lived through it."

"There aren't a lot of us, that's for sure. That's why I got so emotional when I saw the third line of the poem. *A filly with no mother*—that has to be about me, right?"

Payne stood from the corner of the desk and walked around the room, trying to figure out some other explanation for the quatrain. Yet the more he thought about it, the more he became convinced it was referring to Megan. It simply had to be. But why would someone take the time to write a poem in a series of ancient languages and send it to a total stranger?

Furthermore, why were people willing to kill for it?

None of it made any sense.

46

François Dubois had enough money to live anywhere in the world, but he chose the city of Bruges because of its Old World charm. In the summertime, he often took long strolls along the scenic canals and watched the boats as they glided past stone buildings and ducked under ancient bridges. During the golden age of Bruges, the rivers and canals were constantly dredged, allowing trader ships to carry their goods into the heart of the city, where they could be unloaded in large water halls or sold in the market. Centuries later, the covered halls no longer exist, but the marketplace continues to thrive—although its purpose has changed over the years.

Once the commercial hub of the city, the Grote Markt is now a traffic-free square, surrounded by picturesque buildings and small cafés with matching green awnings. Whenever the weather cooperated, Dubois would sit outside for hours at a time, conducting business by phone while his bodyguards looked for potential trouble. The crowds here seldom provided any sense of a threat. Understandably, most tourists would be focused on the twelfth-century belfry, which towered over the market like a medieval guard. Made of tan brick and stone, it stood over two hundred and seventy feet high and housed a series of bells that had a distinct sound and function. Some indicated the time, but others had been used to warn the citizens of Bruges of impending danger. Of course, that was long ago, back when the belfry served as a watchtower. Otherwise, the warning bell would ring every time Dubois entered the marketplace.

Recently, tourism in the city had increased significantly, thanks to the award-winning movie *In Bruges*, which starred Colin Farrell and Ralph Fiennes. Much of the movie had been filmed in the Old City and Grote Markt, including a climactic scene at the top of the belfry. Dubois had never seen the film and never would—he preferred operas and symphonies to the silver screen—yet several filmgoers had told him the movie had presented the city in a favorable light. To Dubois, that was a blessing and a curse. He was delighted the rest of the world could see the beauty that he got to see every day, but he loathed the sudden influx of tourists.

In his line of work, the appearance of strangers was rarely a good thing.

Because of the falling temperatures and the chance of flurries, Dubois bundled himself in a tailored coat and made his way to the marketplace for an early dinner.

His driver stopped the car as close to the café as possible, and Dubois waited for one of his bodyguards to open his door. A few minutes later, Dubois was sitting in a window seat, staring at the neo-Gothic Provincial Court on the northern side of the plaza. The building had been built on the site of the old water halls and was reconstructed in 1878 after a fire destroyed most of the complex. Critics argued that the neo-Gothic style conflicted with the medieval architecture found in the rest of the city. Ironically, that was the reason Dubois found comfort in the building. In many ways, it reminded him of the cathedrals back in Paris, a city he loved deeply but rarely got to visit.

"Good evening, Mr. Dubois," the waitress said in Dutch.

He nodded but refused to address the help. It was beneath him.

She unfolded his cloth napkin and carefully placed it on his lap. Then she handed him a leather-bound menu. "Would you like to hear our specials?"

Dubois shook his head and waved her aside, letting her know that he would summon her *if* and *when* he needed assistance. Until then, he didn't want to be disturbed. Glancing at his Vacheron Constantin watch, he realized it was time to make his call. First, he would handle his business in America, and then he would order dinner and a nice bottle of wine.

Dubois dialed the number from memory and waited for his intermediary to pick up. This was standard procedure for Dubois, who preferred for his subordinates to get their hands dirty anytime they were operating outside the letter of the law.

The phone rang three times before Haney answered.

"Hello," he said in English. Haney wasn't his real name, but it was the one they used when they were talking on the phone—even though their phones were encrypted.

"Where do things stand?" Dubois asked.

"I'm afraid we've had some trouble."

"What kind of trouble?"

"We've had some . . . interference."

"Please explain."

This was a moment that Haney had been dreading. Up until now, he had let his boss believe that everything was under control in Pennsylvania. He knew how Dubois could get whenever he was upset, and Haney didn't want to be the one to feel his wrath. He figured if he kept the bad news to himself until the situation was handled, then he could give Dubois nothing but good news. Unfortunately, things didn't work out the way he had hoped.

"The girl from Philadelphia passed the document to two outsiders before we got to her. Since that time, we have been unable to retrieve it."

Dubois's nostrils flared with anger. "Why not?"

"Unforeseen circumstances."

"Meaning?"

"The outsiders have a special set of skills that we weren't anticipating."

"What type of *skills*?"

"Special Forces, sir."

Dubois snatched the napkin from his lap and flung it against the window. His bodyguards, who were positioned a few tables over, scanned the room for an impending threat, but they quickly realized Dubois's outburst was related to his conversation.

"When did this happen?" he demanded.

"Saturday night."

"You've known about this for two days, yet you're telling me now?"

"No, sir. This information has recently come to light, after two failed attempts."

"Define *failed*."

Haney cleared his throat. "My associate silenced the girl, but died in a traffic accident shortly thereafter. I sent a replacement to retrieve the document, but he failed as well."

"Another *accident*?" Dubois said sarcastically.

"Actually, sir, it was. He fell off a cliff."

Dubois shook his head, the anger building inside him. "Two associates in two days, yet not an utterance from you. May I ask why?"

"I, um," Haney stuttered. "I'm sorry, sir. I should've called earlier."

"You're *sorry*? Well then, I guess all is forgiven. Haney is *sorry*, so everything is okay!" Dubois took a deep breath, trying to control his temper. "Don't tell me you're sorry. Tell me what you're going to do to fix this! Where are these men now?"

"In Philadelphia."

"And *what* are they doing there?"

"They're protecting the girl."

Dubois furrowed his brow. As he did, his eyes looked like slits. "What girl?"

"We're still figuring that out, sir. We think maybe the document belongs to her."

"Who is this *we* you keep referring to?"

"Me, sir. I think maybe the first girl—the one who tried to get the letter translated at Penn—wasn't the actual owner. I think maybe she was working on behalf of this new girl."

Dubois smirked. "An intermediary who ended up *dead*. It's funny how that happens on occasion."

Haney gulped at the implied threat. "I sent an associate to investigate her, but her guardians intervened. They killed him in broad daylight. A cop also got killed in the crossfire."

Dubois stood abruptly and walked toward the door. He flung it open with a violent push. "The news keeps getting better and better! I ask you to retrieve a single document, and you turn it into World War III. How many people have died so far? Five, maybe more? Do we even know the names of these interlopers?"

"Yes, sir, we do."

"And?"

"And we'll find them soon. I promise."

47

Jones walked into the tiny room, shaking his head. "Bad news on the phone."

Payne looked at him. "How bad?"

"The mystery text came from a prepaid cell phone. It was purchased last week at Charles de Gaulle Airport. The buyer, who obviously paid in cash, could have been arriving in Paris or flying to just about anywhere in the world when he bought it. Also, according to computer records, only one text was sent from the phone—the message that was sent to Megan."

"How about phone calls?"

"Nope. Not a single call to anyone."

Megan frowned. "In other words, someone bought the phone to text me."

Jones nodded. "It sure seems that way."

"Why not call from a pay phone? Or send me an

e-mail from a public terminal? Buying a cell phone seems pretty extreme."

Jones smirked. "If you think *that's* extreme, what do you consider armed gunmen?"

She conceded his point. "You're right. I guess I need to lower my standards."

Jones glanced at Payne. "Hey, Jon, it's your lucky day. If she *lowers* her standards, you might have a chance with her."

She snickered at the comment, which brought an immediate reaction from Payne. "Please don't encourage him. If you laugh at his wisecracks, he simply won't stop."

She smiled. "You have to admit, it was kind of funny."

"No," Payne said, "I'll admit nothing. One time back in the mid-nineties he said something mildly amusing, and I barely cracked a smile. The guy hasn't shut up since."

Jones stroked his chin, as if deep in thought. "You know what? I remember that day. That was during my Eddie Murphy phase. First I made you laugh, then I picked up a transvestite prostitute in West Hollywood." He paused for effect. "No, wait, that was Eddie who did that, *not* me. Come to think of it, that was actually the day my Eddie Murphy phase ended."

Payne shook his head as he looked at Megan. "See what you did? You got him started. Now I have to listen to him for *another* decade."

She covered her smile with her hand, not willing to say anything else.

"Anyway," Payne said, trying to change the subject, "it's pretty apparent that someone is going to great lengths to send you a coded message. If not for the violence, my advice would be to ignore them until someone picked up the phone and called you like a normal person. However, since people keep trying to kill us, I think it's probably best to play his little game and figure out the meaning of the letter."

Megan frowned. "I thought we already did that. The poem is about me."

Payne shook his head. "Actually, we figured out *half* of the poem. You're from the city of brothers, and you're a filly with no mother. But what about the other two lines? What do they mean?"

She asked, "What were the lines again?"

Jones walked behind the desk and wrote the poem in black in the center of the dry erase board, so they could examine it as a group.

Payne immediately grabbed a red marker from the tray and wrote asterisks on both sides of lines one and three. He did it to signify they had already figured them out. "If we're correct, these two lines are about you. Now all we have to do is decipher the other pair."

> * From the city of brothers, *
> A lover from the lost line.
> * A filly with no mother, *
> Chosen for her place in time.

Megan nodded in understanding. "I'm pretty good

with word games and puzzles. If you ever feel like losing, challenge me to Boggle or Scrabble."

Jones looked at her. "Decipher now, talk smack later."

She gave him a mock salute then focused on the words. "How confident are you with the translation? Do you trust the person who did it for you?"

Payne answered, "Do we trust him? Definitely. He's a good friend of ours. Are we confident in his ability? I'd say ninety percent sure. In his original translation, he had the word *mare* instead of *filly*. Not a grievous mistake, but a mistake nonetheless."

"In Petr's defense," Jones added, "we asked him to do a word-for-word translation of the message. We didn't know it was a word puzzle where we were supposed to look for puns and other sorts of twists."

Megan scrunched her face. "What pun are you talking about?"

Payne tapped on the word *filly*. "An abbreviation for Philadelphia."

"Philly! I get it. Very clever. And you think there might be more puns?"

Payne shrugged. "At this point we don't know. Could be anything."

"Well," she said, "at first glance I don't think lines two and four go together."

"Why? Because they don't rhyme perfectly?"

Megan shook her head. "Actually, that doesn't bother me. If you want to get hypercritical, lines one and three aren't perfect, either. *Brothers* is plural, and *mother* is singular."

"True," Payne admitted. "Then what troubles you?"

"The verb."

"What verb?" Jones asked.

"What do you mean?" Megan grabbed a green marker and underlined *chosen*. "It's the only verb in the whole poem. Don't they teach grammar at the service academies?"

Jones reread the quatrain. "You're right. One verb. But why does that bother you?"

She made a giant circle around lines one, two, and three. "I'm pretty sure the first three lines are supposed to be describing me. I'm from the city of brothers, and I'm a filly with no mother. And just because of the context of the poem, I think they're saying that I'm a lover from the lost line—although I don't know what that means."

"And the fourth line?"

Megan answered, "It's *not* talking about me. It's telling us *why* I was selected. It's actually giving us an explanation."

Payne nodded in agreement. "I think you're right. The first three lines go together."

"If that's the case," Jones concluded, "then there's a good chance we're missing something in the second line."

"Like a meaning?"

"Well, yeah," Jones admitted as he removed the cap from his black marker. "A meaning would be nice, but I think the reason we don't understand the line is because we're missing a word trick. Remember what Petr told us? He felt the author of this piece was a brilliant puzzle maker, so it stands to reason the three lines that go together would utilize similar tactics."

"Oh," Payne said, "I see what you're saying. Lines one and three used word tricks, so line two probably does as well."

Jones nodded. "Let's hope so, because I have no idea what it's talking about."

To help them focus, Payne erased the other three lines, leaving line two by itself.

A lover from the lost line.

Megan scrunched her face as she focused on the words.

"What's wrong?" Payne wondered.

"Two things off the top of my head. I realize old guys like you haven't been in school this millennium, but are you familiar with alliteration?"

"Ouch! Why so mean?" Jones demanded.

Payne ignored her jab. "Alliteration is the repetition of a sound at the beginning of a word. In this case, *lover*, *lost*, and *line*. What's your point?"

She answered. "For some reason, alliteration is used in this line but none of the others. That seems fishy to me."

"Bad fishy or good fishy?"

"What's the difference?"

"Wow," Payne said sarcastically, "I was beginning to think you knew everything. D.J., please tell her the difference."

"With pleasure," he said. "Bad fishy is when you get a girl naked and—"

Payne interrupted him. "On second thought, I'll explain it myself. Bad fishy means we did something wrong. In other words, our translation is off. Good fishy means the author used alliteration on purpose in order to attract our attention to this line."

She nodded in understanding. "In that case, I'm going to go with bad fishy."

"Why's that?"

"Because there's something about the word *lover* that just seems off to me."

"Off in what way?" Payne asked.

"I don't know. It's just a gut feeling. I get those sometimes, and I'm normally right."

Payne smiled at her comment. "Trust me, I know the feeling. No pun intended."

Jones sighed. "Awwww, isn't that sweet? You're both psychic. In that case, why don't you put your freak brains together and figure out how Petr screwed up his translation? Meanwhile, I'll focus on the end of the verse. I think I might know what *the lost line* means."

48

ayne pointed to the two chairs on the other side of the desk. Megan walked over first and sat in the far seat. He gave her his tablet as he joined her. "Take a look at my notes. On the left are the words in English. On the right are their original languages."

WORDS	LANGUAGE
city	French
brother	Greek
lover	Italian
lost	Hebrew
line	Latin
filly	Provençal
mother	French
choice	Hebrew
place	Provençal
time	Italian

Megan glanced at the two columns, amazed by the effort that everyone had put into this project. Since she was unfamiliar with Provençal, Payne explained it was a dialect still spoken in parts of France. Jones could have told her a lot more about the foundation of the language, but he was busy solving the second half of line number two.

"Where should we start?" she asked.

"Let's start with your gut feeling. You said something feels off about the word *lover*, so let's begin there."

"Great. So how do we do that?"

He shrugged. "Actually, I have no idea."

She laughed at his honesty. "A guy who isn't afraid to admit how clueless he is. That's a very attractive quality in a man."

"Really? Then you'll *love* me. I don't know squat about anything."

"Keep in mind, I didn't say stupidity was attractive. I simply said that . . ."

Payne stared at her, waiting for her to finish her thought, but she didn't seem to notice. Instead, her gaze had shifted to the notebook she held in her hands. "What is it?"

"What?" she asked, not looking up at him.

"What's wrong?"

"Nothing's wrong. It was just something you said."

A quizzical expression filled his face. "What did I say?"

She ran her finger down the left column. "You mentioned the word *love*."

"And?"

Megan glanced at him. "The list is wrong."

Payne inched his chair closer. "How so?"

"On your chart, you have the word *choice*. But in the poem, you use the word *chosen*."

Payne nodded, then explained that Ulster was forced to change the form of certain words for the poem to make sense. This was necessary because some of the languages had conflicting rules when it came to grammar. For example, where an adjective needed to be placed in order to modify the appropriate word in a sentence. "Does that make sense?"

"Perfect sense. It also explains what's wrong with the second line."

Payne put two and two together. "Does this have to do with *love*?"

She flashed him a smile. "Everything has to do with love."

"Wow, my flirting must have been contagious."

"Tell me," she said, "how much Italian do you guys know?"

Payne shrugged. "A few words, here and there. Mostly related to food."

Jones said, "I know a lot more than Jon, but I'm not exactly fluent."

"Trust me," she said, "you don't have to be fluent to know this. When you mentioned *love*, it got me thinking about the second verse. What if the word *lover* was the wrong form of the word? What if it was supposed to be *love* instead?"

With his finger, Jones erased the *r* from the board. Now it read:

A love from the lost line.

Payne studied the subtle change, but the solution still didn't click in his head. "I don't get it. How does that help us?"

"And," she added, "what if the word was never meant to be translated? What if it was meant to be read in its original *Italiano*?"

Jones wasn't an expert, but like many people he knew the Italian word for *love*. He erased the English version and wrote it in its original language.

Amore from the lost line.

"I'll be damned," Payne said from his chair. "That's really clever."

"What's clever?" Jones demanded, still not connecting the dots. He took a few steps away, hoping the big picture would come into focus. "What's clever?"

"Certainly not you," Payne teased, "or else you'd see it."

"See what?" Jones snapped.

Payne smiled at Megan and encouraged her to speak. "Go on. Tell him why you're so confident this line is about you."

"I don't care *who* tells me," Jones growled. "Just give me the damn answer!"

Smiling from ear to ear, Megan stood up and walked

to the board. She grabbed a red marker and made a slash through the middle of the Italian word. Now it read:

A/more from the lost line.

"Do me a favor," she said to Jones. "Read this phonetically."

He did as he was told. "A more from the lost line."

A few seconds passed before Jones understood the pun. "Holy shit! They used your name in the verse. A *Moore* from the lost line. I have to admit, that's pretty cool."

Megan bowed theatrically. "Thank you very much."

"It's cool," Jones admitted, "but is it good news?"

"What do you mean?"

Jones smiled. "Now that we know the poem is about you, there's no getting rid of us. You're gonna be stuck with us until the bitter end."

49

lthough Payne and Megan's work on the first half of the verse was impressive, Jones wasn't going to let them steal all the glory—especially since Payne had figured out "Philly" the day before. If Jones didn't start pulling his weight soon, he knew he'd never hear the end of it.

"So," Payne taunted as he took a seat next to Megan, "I vaguely remember you saying something about understanding the significance of *the lost line*. Or was that just bullshit?"

Jones smirked, enjoying the added pressure. Over the years he had developed a friendly rivalry with Payne in just about everything they did, whether it was golf, bowling, or guessing the names of total strangers. Neither man liked to lose, which was one of the reasons they had worked so well together in the MANIACs. Their drive to be the best made everyone better. "No, I'm pretty sure I know what it means. In fact, your discovery actually strengthened my case."

"Glad we could help. Now quit stalling."

Jones grabbed a tissue from the desk and erased everything on the board. Once it was clean, he wrote the second line in black marker and underlined the last three words.

A Moore from the lost line.

Jones asked, "What's the first thing that comes to mind when you read this line?"

Payne shrugged. "Something to do with Megan's ancestry."

"That was my first guess, too. *Line* stands for *lineage*. Pretty simple, right?"

"Right," Megan agreed.

Jones continued. "Furthermore, if you think about the final word in lines one and three—*brothers* and *mother*—they have to do with family as well. Which fits in nicely with the theory that the first three lines *are* connected. Remember, none of them have verbs."

Payne nodded. "We're all in agreement. Those lines are talking about Megan."

Jones smiled cryptically. "And yet we're still missing a key piece of information. How does Megan's lineage fit into all of this? What has actually been *lost*?"

"I'm guessing you have a theory."

"Of course I have a theory." Jones grabbed the black marker and wrote the four lines of the text message on the board. "I think the information we're searching for is in the second poem."

> *Your fortune waits for you.*
> *Protect it with your life.*
> *Death shall visit those untrue,*
> *Blood of his first wife.*

Payne skimmed the quatrain. "Care to narrow it down for us?"

"I could," Jones said, "but I think it's pretty obvious. Only one line talks about family."

Megan pointed at the board. "The fourth one. It mentions someone's wife."

"Not only that," Jones said as he underlined three words: *waits*, *protect*, and *shall*. "It's the only line in this poem that doesn't have a verb." He paused for a moment, then glanced at Megan. "How about that? I guess they *do* teach grammar at the service academies."

She smiled, remembering her earlier wisecrack. "Touché."

"Okay," Payne admitted, "you make a pretty strong case. The fourth line seems to connect with the first three lines from the other poem. But unless I'm mistaken, you still haven't solved the mystery of what's been *lost*."

"Don't worry. I was just getting to that."

Jones used the same tissue as before and erased the first three lines of the poem. When he was done, only two lines remained on the board:

A Moore from the lost line.
Blood of his first wife.

Wasting no time, Jones explained how they were connected. "As soon as I saw the word *line*, my mind jumped to *bloodline*. I mean, when you're discussing someone's lineage, that's what you're actually referring to: their bloodline. Then it dawned on me that *line* ended one verse and *blood* began another. That led me to believe that the two statements could be combined. All you have to do is tweak the word order a tad, and you get the following . . ."

A Moore from the lost bloodline of his first wife.

Jones grinned in triumph. "Not too shabby, huh?"

Payne nodded. "Not bad at all."

Jones turned his attention to Megan. "Of course, now the ball is back in your court. We know nothing about your family tree, so whose first wife are they talking about?"

Megan shrugged as she read the line. "I have absolutely no idea. My adoptive parents were high school sweethearts, so they weren't married beforehand. And as far as I know, neither were my biological parents. Then again, I never met either of them. My mom died in childbirth, and my father split right after conception. At least, that's what I was told."

"Although you never met them, do you remember their names?"

She nodded, as if the memory was a painful one.

"Then I can probably help. Let's go into the other room and run some data searches on my laptop. I've tracked down several deadbeat dads over the years. If we're lucky, we'll find something useful."

She stood from her chair. "Sounds good to me."

Jones walked toward the door. "Please tell me their names weren't Jesus and Mary Magdalene. Because if this is some kind of *Da Vinci Code* bullshit, you're on your own."

She laughed at the suggestion. "I drink water. I don't walk on it."

He shrugged. "That's too bad. I'd pay big bucks to see that trick."

PAYNE REALIZED Jones and Megan didn't need his help, so he sat behind the desk and used his encrypted cell phone to contact the Ulster Archives. Even though it was nighttime in Küsendorf, Petr Ulster answered the call in his private office.

"I'm so glad you called," Ulster said. "I was beginning to worry about your safety."

"Don't worry. We're fine."

"No more run-ins with gunmen?"

"Only one, so it's been an easy day."

Ulster laughed at the comment. "Oh, Jonathon, you slay me!"

"Ironically, that's what he was trying to do to us. I'm

not quite sure where they're coming from, but they're persistent."

"So," Ulster said, "were you simply checking in, or did you need further help?"

"Believe it or not, I was calling to give you an update. We put our heads together and figured out these poems. As you suggested, the author was pretty clever."

"Did you say *poems*, as in plural?"

Payne rubbed his eyes. "That's right. I haven't told you about the text message. Sorry about that. My days are starting to run together."

He took a few minutes to explain everything to Ulster, starting with Megan's text and ending with the solutions to the puzzles. During the explanation, Ulster said very little, but he wrote all the deciphered codes in a notebook so he could reexamine them later.

"What about the letter? Did you find the original letter?"

Payne nodded. "Sorry, I should have mentioned that, too. I'm looking at it right now."

"Tell me about it," Ulster said excitedly. "What type of paper?"

"I don't know. I'm not an expert. Some kind of parchment, I guess."

"Does it look old?"

"Yep. Pretty fancy, too. It's held up well over the years."

"Tell me, do you have a black light on your person?"

"Excuse me?"

"It's a device for seeing bloodstains and such."

Payne laughed. "I know what is it, Petr. Why in the world would I have a black light on me? I *make* bloodstains. I don't examine them."

"Yes, of course, how silly of me. In that case, are you near a police station? Or maybe a discothèque?"

"A discothèque? No, Petr, we're at an airbase, not Studio 54. Why?"

"An airbase might work! Do they have warplanes? Perhaps something from the forties?"

Payne furrowed his brow at the line of questioning. "Police stations? Discothèques? Warplanes? What in the heck are you rambling about?"

"Your letter," Ulster explained. "I have a theory about its author, but I need a black light to prove my hypothesis."

"Tell me what you have in mind, and I'll see what I can do."

Ulster leaned back in his office chair. "Since 1282, papermakers have been using watermarks to identify their products. The first technique was called the Dandy Roll Process, a pressure roller developed in Bologna, Italy. In time, governments started protecting their products as well, using special paper for stamps and currency in order to discourage counterfeiting."

"And what does that have to do with the letter?"

"Eventually, the art world followed suit. Painters protected their works by using special types of canvas, marked in ways only they knew about. And writers often used their own personal stock, a way to guarantee the authenticity of a piece."

Payne grabbed the corner of the letter and held it up to the light, searching for a watermark of any kind. "Sorry, Petr, this letter is watermark-free."

"Wonderful! Just wonderful!"

"Are you being sarcastic?"

"No, Jonathon, not at all. In fact, I'm thrilled with the news. As I mentioned, I have a theory about the puzzle maker. If the author is who I think he is, the only way we can be sure is with a black light."

"Wait. Who do you think it is?" Payne wondered.

Ulster shook his head. "For the time being, I'd rather not say. But if my hypothesis is correct, I can understand why people are willing to kill for that letter."

50

While Ulster waited on his cell phone, Payne used the office telephone to call the base commander. The gray-haired supervisor answered on the second ring. After a moment of small talk, Payne got right to the point.

"Let me apologize in advance, but I need to ask you a strange question."

The commander smiled. "You mean stranger than being smuggled into Willow Grove and setting up shop in a back office?"

Payne laughed. "Well, when you put it like that . . ."

"What can I do for you, son?"

"I was wondering if you had a black light anywhere on the base."

"As a matter of fact, we do. Handheld and battery-powered."

"Seriously? Why in the world do you have one?"

The commander explained. "Every year we have one of the biggest air shows in the country. Sometimes we get in old bombers from World War II. The type we built for night flights. Whenever we do, we break out the black light to show off the panels. The kids love it."

"Sir, I'm confused. What type of panels are you talking about?"

The commander grunted. "How disappointing! I figured an Academy man like you would know this stuff. You soldiers nowadays need to learn your history."

"You're right, sir. If you have a moment, please fill me in."

The commander smiled, happy to impart his knowledge to a younger generation. "Back in the old days, the bright glow of our instrument panels used to give away the position of our planes during night raids. During the war, we experimented with UV-fluorescent dials and black lights. We even printed charts in UV-fluorescent inks and designed special UV-visible pencils and slide rules for the navigators."

Suddenly, Ulster's comment about warplanes made sense to Payne. "That's pretty fancy gear for the forties. Was it effective?"

The commander laughed. "Not really. That's probably why you never heard of it. The damn power-inverters kept blinking out on takeoffs. And no power meant no instruments."

"Ouch! Flying blind is a bitch—especially during combat."

"A series of crashes forced us and the Brits to abandon

the program back in 1945. Surprisingly, some of the old birds are still functional. Not the inverters, though. That's why we have to break out the wand. To light those panels up."

"If it's all right with you, could I borrow the wand for an hour or two?"

"Not a problem, son. Someone will bring it to you in a few."

"Thank you, sir, I appreciate it. And, sir? Thanks for the history lesson."

AS PROMISED, the UV wand was delivered less than five minutes later. It was nearly a foot long, and the casing was made of black plastic. There was a thumb switch near the handle, which turned on the UV lamp—a single UV bulb that shined light over a limited space.

Jones saw the device being delivered and was immediately intrigued. As soon as the airman left, Jones and Megan hustled into the office.

"Close the door," Payne whispered as he covered the mouthpiece on his cell phone. Jones did as he was told, then took a seat next to Megan. "I'm on the phone with Petr. He wants us to run a test on the letter."

"What kind of test?" Jones asked.

Payne signaled for Jones to hold on for a moment. "Petr, the wand just got here. If it's okay with you, I'm going to put you on speakerphone. I'm here with D.J. and Megan."

"Hello, everybody," Ulster said through the speaker. "This is *so* exciting!"

"What's exciting? What are we checking?" Jones wondered.

"I have a theory on the identity of your mysterious writer. If I'm correct, your letter will have a special UV watermark in the parchment."

Jones scoffed at the notion. "Petr, none of us are experts in the field, but this letter looks several centuries old. I doubt UV technology was available when it was written."

"Technology, no. Ink, yes."

"I don't understand."

"Believe it or not, phosphorescent ink is older than modern man. Several forms of it can be found throughout nature. For instance, there are many species of fish that glow under UV lighting. Insects, too. Have you ever seen a scorpion under a black light? Very creepy!"

"Maybe so, but—"

Ulster finished his thought: "But without the technology to read it, why use the ink?"

Jones smiled. "Exactly."

"Because that's what forward thinking is all about. Some of the greatest minds of all time designed contraptions long before we had the technology to build them."

"In other words, you're telling us that ancient writers used UV watermarks to verify their work for future generations?"

Ulster clarified his point. "No, I never said *writers*. Just *one* in particular."

"And why would he do that?"

"Because his most important work focused on the future."

"The future, huh? Care to give us a name?"

"In a moment," Ulster promised, "but first, you need to do something for me."

"What's that?" Payne asked.

"Turn off the lights, turn on the wand, and tell me what you see."

Despite being highly skeptical, Jones walked toward the door and put his hand on the light switch. Megan slid around the desk next to Payne, who anxiously held the wand over the letter.

"Ready?" Jones asked.

Payne nodded and turned on the wand. The device emitted a faint purple light, but it wasn't very visible until Jones flipped the switch on the wall. Suddenly, darkness filled the room, and the letter on the desk started to glow like a prop from a science fiction movie.

"Holy shit!" Jones blurted as he rushed over to read it.

Payne echoed his sentiment, "Holy shit indeed."

"What do you see?" Ulster demanded.

Jones answered, "It's glowing. The damn thing is glowing!"

"But what do you see? Words? Shapes? Numbers?"

"All of the above."

"The shape! Tell me about the shape."

Payne moved the lamp closer and did his best to

describe it. "The object is in the center of the page. It's roughly two inches in diameter and looks like a crescent moon on its back."

Jones growled in the dark. As he did, his teeth glowed. "Please tell me it's not Islamic. The Saudis are still pissed about what we did in Mecca."

"No, it's not Islamic," Ulster assured them. "In fact, it's not even a moon."

"What is it, then?"

"It's a bowl."

"A bowl? Like for Frosted Flakes?"

Ulster ignored the question. He'd explain everything soon enough. "Tell me, Jonathon, is the bowl being cradled?"

"Yes," Payne said. "It's being held in the air by some kind of support."

A loud belly laugh filled the line. "Brilliant! Bloody brilliant! I simply knew it!"

Payne smiled at Ulster's excitement. "Knew what, Petr?"

"The tripod. It *had* to be the bowl and tripod! What else could it be? A long time ago, I had read that—"

"Petr!" Payne said forcefully.

"Jonathon?"

"We're here in the dark. *Literally* in the dark. Please tell us about the bowl and tripod."

Ulster took a deep breath, trying to calm himself. "Yes, of course. Sorry for my babbling. I won't let it happen again. Are you familiar with the concept of scrying?"

"Scrying? Nope, never heard of it."

"Scrying is a technique used by soothsayers to predict the future. It involves seeing things psychically in a reflective or translucent medium, such as a crystal ball or a mirror. The watermark you described is an illustration of a popular method. A brass tripod supports a bowl of water above the ground or table. A single flame is placed nearby, and the seer interprets the images that appear in the rippling surface of the water. This technique was used by many famous psychics, including the Oracle of Delphi."

"If scrying is so common, how do you know who wrote our letter?"

"How? Because of the watermark! Only one man in history used UV ink in that manner and had the talent to pull off such an elaborate puzzle for a future audience. Obviously, we won't know for sure until I test the parchment and sample the handwriting, but as far as I'm concerned, I've seen enough to hazard a guess. In fact, it's more than a guess. I'm ninety-nine percent sure I know who wrote that letter."

"Give me a name," Payne demanded.

Ulster grinned. "Your pen pal from the past is none other than Michel de Nostredame. Of course, you probably know him by the Latinized version of his name: Nostradamus."

51

Everyone's eyes widened in the dark. For the next few seconds, no one made a sound as they pondered the significance of Ulster's claim.

Finally, Payne ended the silence. "Did you say *Nostradamus*?"

Ulster's laugh filled the room. "Yes, Jonathon, I did."

"You mean the prophet from the Middle Ages?"

"The one and only."

"Nostradamus wrote *this* letter?"

Ulster laughed some more. "Yes, I'm fairly certain he did."

Jones jumped in. "Did he send the text, too? Because *that* would be some freaky shit."

"No," Ulster clarified, "I think he had some help on that one. I would imagine whoever mailed the letter to Megan also sent the text."

Hearing her name, she entered the conversation.

"Why would someone do that? Why would someone send me a letter written by Nostradamus?"

"That, my dear, I do not know. Nor do I understand why he referenced you in his poem. But perhaps the answer is within our grasp. Now that we've verified the watermark, let's examine the rest of the document for clues . . . Jonathon, are you still there?"

Payne smiled at the question. Where else would he be? "Yes, Petr, I'm still here."

"Wonderful! Perhaps you would be kind enough to describe everything that is glowing. I believe David mentioned there was a series of letters and numerals."

Payne repositioned the UV wand above the letter and leaned in for a closer look. "Up near the top, he wrote some initials and some numbers: *C.S. 1566.*"

Ulster jotted it down. "Interesting. Very interesting. What else?"

"His watermark is in the center of the page."

"Yes, yes, I knew that already."

"Toward the bottom of the letter, he wrote something in French: *Quai du Mont-Blanc.*"

Ulster repeated it back to him, making sure his notes were accurate. "Any numbers?"

"Nope. No numbers."

"Strange. Very strange. What else do you see?"

"Underneath that, there's a single word. I think it's a name. Genève."

"Genève?" Ulster blurted. "You're sure of this?"

Payne nodded in the dark. "Positive."

Ulster sought a second opinion. "David, do you concur with Jonathon?"

Jones, who knew basic French, read the entire document aloud. "C.S. 1566. Quai du Mont-Blanc. Genève."

"Wonderful! Just wonderful! This is exceptional news!"

"How so?" Payne wondered.

"First, before I answer your query, is anything else glowing?"

"No, Petr, that's everything."

"In that case, you should turn off the wand now. The sooner, the better."

"Why?" Payne asked as Jones walked across the room and turned on the overhead lights. "Will it damage the letter?"

"No," Ulster explained, "the parchment is quite durable. However, without proper eyewear, long-term exposure to UV light can cause blindness in humans."

"Excuse me?" Payne snapped.

"Relax, Jonathon, relax. A few minutes are fine. Twenty minutes, not so much."

Payne rubbed his eyes as he readjusted to the brightness in the room. "Next time, warn us in advance. I could've used the wand alone while they waited outside."

"And robbed your friends of this memory? I should think not. Do you know how many people in the world worship Nostradamus? Millions upon millions read his prophecies like scripture. To some, he is the Muhammad of the Middle Ages—not quite a god, yet more than a man. Someday the three of you will look upon this moment as one of the highlights of your lives."

Although Payne doubted it, he didn't want to debate Ulster's statement or the importance of eyesight. There would be plenty of time for that later. For now, he wanted to know about the document. Specifically, what Nostradamus had written.

"Petr, tell us about the message. I get the feeling you understood it."

"The second half, yes. The beginning, no."

"Then let's work backward. Tell us about the ending."

"As you surmised, Genève is a name. Not the name of a person, but a city. Genève is the French spelling of Geneva, Switzerland."

"I'll be damned. How close is that to the Archives?"

Ulster smiled. "It's only a few hours away. Which is why I am familiar with Quai du Mont-Blanc. It is one of my favorite roads in all of Switzerland. It is short, but very scenic. It runs along Lake Geneva, overlooking the marinas and the Jet d'Eau. That's the tallest fountain in the world. Have you seen photos of it? Water is shot over five hundred feet into the air. It is quite spectacular."

"How old is the road?"

Ulster paused in thought. "Honestly, I can't recall, but the city itself is quite old. At one time it was part of the Roman Empire. In fact, the man who named it Genua was Julius Caesar."

"In other words, the city is much older than Nostradamus."

"Good heavens, yes! Nostradamus lived in the mid-sixteenth century, during the time that John Calvin first arrived in Geneva to preach his faith. If my memory is correct, it seems to me that Nostradamus died in 1565 or 15—" Ulster stopped in mid-sentence, suddenly aware of the number's significance. "The number at the top of the page. I'm fairly certain that Nostradamus died in 1566. Somehow I doubt that's a coincidence."

"Probably not."

Jones was excited by the revelation. "What about C.S.? Any theories on C.S.?"

"Sorry, David, none at the moment. Perhaps something will spring to mind as I browse through my library. I have several wonderful books about his life and prophecies. Once we're done conversing, I'll see what I can find."

"Petr," Megan said meekly, "may I ask you a question?"

"Of course, my dear."

"Would your books include information about his personal life?"

"They certainly would."

"In that case, will you do me a favor? While you're searching for C.S., can you keep an eye out for my surname? Maybe Moore is a part of his family tree."

Ulster smiled at her request. In truth, he was surprised she had taken so long to ask. "It would be an honor, my dear. And if I find anything, you shall be the first to know."

PAYNE HUNG UP the phone and looked across the desk at Jones and Megan. For the past few hours, they had been reasonably safe at the airbase, yet he realized as soon as they left Willow Grove, they would be back in the line of fire with huge bull's-eyes on their backs. Unfortunately, it was a condition that wouldn't change until they found the "fortune" that had been mentioned in the text message or they figured out who else was gunning for it. Or preferably both.

He had broached the idea of stashing Megan in a safe house for her protection, but she objected fiercely. There was no way in hell she was going to let them risk their lives for her while she rested comfortably. She was a fighter and had been as long as she could remember. In her mind, it was pointless to stop now—even if the violence escalated.

In Payne's opinion, the best way to accomplish their goal was to become aggressive. No more detective work behind the scenes. No more treading lightly. He and Jones were two of the best-trained soldiers in the world, but over the past forty-eight hours they hadn't been playing to their strengths. Instead of searching for targets, they had become them. Instead of firing first, they had been fired at. If that trend continued for much longer, it was just a matter of time before someone got lucky and picked them off. That was the law of averages.

No, if Payne was going to die, it wasn't going to be solving puzzles in Pennsylvania. It would be overseas— with Jones by his side and blood on their hands.

52

The private jet was chartered by Petr Ulster, who paid for it with funds from one of his confidential Swiss bank accounts. The name of a fictitious company had been used during the transaction, and a fake flight plan to Paris had been filed, thereby minimizing the possibility of detection. As long as the workers at NASJRB Willow Grove kept quiet, no one would know Payne, Jones, and Megan had boarded the transatlantic flight to Geneva without the proper paperwork.

Once they landed in Switzerland, things would get a bit more complicated. Due to its proximity to the French border, the Geneva International Airport was divided into two sections. The majority of the facility was in Switzerland—where Ulster had plenty of clout—but a small part was known as the "French sector." This area allowed passengers on certain flights to enter or leave France without a Swiss visa. Normally, this wouldn't be a problem, because Ulster's jet was supposed to land in Switzerland, where he had several connections who could help sneak them into the country. Unfortunately, bad weather sometimes forced private planes to land on auxiliary runways monitored by French personnel, officers who weren't influenced by Ulster. In that scenario, there was little he could do for them. They would be stuck in diplomatic limbo until the U.S. embassy intervened.

Of course, Payne and Jones weren't the least bit concerned. Sneaking across borders was a way of life for them. And because of their confidence, Megan was able to relax and focus on more important things—like her connection to Nostradamus.

"I still don't understand how he could've written a poem about *me*. He lived in the sixteenth century. That's before Philadelphia was even a city!"

Reclining in a plush leather seat, Jones glanced up from a book about the French prophet that he had been reading. It was one of several that an airman had bought for them at a bookstore near Willow Grove. The titles ranged from the academic (*Nostradamus and His Prophecies*) to the simplistic (*Nostradamus for Dummies*). They figured the more they knew about Michel de Nostredame, the better.

"Honestly," Jones admitted, "I've been a casual fan of Nostradamus ever since I saw a movie about him back in the mid-eighties. It was called *The Man Who Saw Tomorrow* and was hosted by a fat Orson Welles, who smoked a cigar through half of his narration."

Payne, who was sitting next to Megan, laughed at the

memory. "I remember that film. The first time I saw it I was just a kid. When they started talking about our impending war with the third Antichrist, I pulled the blanket over my head. It scared the crap out of me."

Megan giggled at the image. She found it hard to believe that anything scared him, even as a child. "I've never seen the movie. Was it any good?"

"Way back then, I thought it was awesome. Unfortunately, I saw it again a few years ago and couldn't believe how cheesy it was. Everything was so over the top. Then again, that's Nostradamus in a nutshell. Some of his prophecies were accurate; others were way off base."

"Or maybe they haven't happened yet," Jones joked.

Megan pondered Payne's comment. "I have to admit I don't know much about him. Obviously, I'm familiar with his name—I think everyone is—but I'm clueless about his predictions. For instance, you just mentioned the third Antichrist. Who were one and two?"

Jones answered, "The first was Napoleon. The second was Hitler."

"He predicted *them*?"

"Kind of," Payne admitted.

"What does that mean?"

"It means his prophecies weren't written in straight-forward language that could be easily read. Like your letter, his quatrains were coded and ambiguous."

"Why do fortune-tellers always do that? If they *really* know what's about to happen, why don't they come right out and say it?"

Jones smiled at the question. "Why? Because most

fortune-tellers are charlatans. They speak in generalities to preserve their ruse for as long as possible."

"Is that what Nostradamus did?"

"Maybe, maybe not. He wasn't reading tea leaves at the local carnival, trying to string along some sucker for an extra buck. Nostradamus was writing verses for the masses. By doing so, he opened himself up to a world of trouble. In fact, that's the main reason he wrote in riddles. He did it to save his life."

"What do you mean?" she asked.

"Nostradamus wrote his prophecies in the sixteenth century, during the same time as the Roman Inquisition. Tribunals, established by the Vatican, prosecuted people throughout Europe who were accused of sorcery, witchcraft, and other offenses. If he had written his thoughts in simple French, he would have been burned at the stake. Instead, he coded his messages, sprinkling in Greek, Latin, and other languages, in order to protect himself. That way he could claim they were puzzles or poetry, not prophecies."

"Okay," she said, "I guess I can understand that. But if his writing is so vague, why is he famous?"

"Because there's a beauty in his ambiguity. Take Hitler, for example. In the passages that describe the second Antichrist, Nostradamus claimed that the evil one would come *from the Rhine and Hister*. Well, guess what? The Rhine River runs through Germany, and the Hister is the Latin name for the Danube. Later, he mentions Hister again in connection with armies and fighting. Most people go nuts over that one."

Megan scrunched her face. "What's your point?"

"When Adolf was a young boy, he played along the shores of the Lower Danube in Austria. Furthermore, *Hister* is only one letter different than *Hitler*. If Nostradamus had written the river's name in French, Italian, or a dozen other languages, the two names wouldn't have been similar. But for some reason, he chose the Latin name of the waterway. Some view this as coincidence. Others see it as prophetic."

"And what do *you* think?"

Jones pointed to himself. "Me? I think most of his verses have been pushed and pulled and contorted so much that his believers could make his words fit any historical event. I also think his critics have plenty of ammunition to poke holes in every quatrain he's ever written."

Payne smirked. "That wasn't an answer."

Jones laughed. "I know it wasn't. But like Nostradamus, I'd like to remain mysterious."

Megan glanced at Payne. "And what about you?"

He shrugged. "Like D.J., I think some of his verses have been distorted to fit certain world events. That being said, I've heard enough stories about him to think maybe he had a gift that can't be explained in simple scientific terms."

"Such as?"

"Did you hear the one about Nostradamus and the pope?"

"Is this a joke?" she asked.

Payne shook his head. "No, it's *not* a joke—although my setup made it seem that way. This is a story I've read many times over the years. Obviously, I don't know if it's true or not, but if it is, you'll have to admit it's pretty freaky."

She smiled. "Cool. I love freaky stories."

"While traveling through Europe, he came across a group of lowly Franciscan monks in Italy. Despite his advancing years, Nostradamus immediately threw himself on his knees and kissed the feet of one of the monks, a man named Felice Peretti. When asked why he was doing this, Nostradamus said one must kneel before His Holiness, the pope. Peretti, who was much younger than the prophet, was deeply embarrassed by this and helped the old man to his feet. Amazingly, more than thirty years later, Peretti was named Pope Sixtus the Fifth."

"Are you serious?" she shrieked.

Payne shrugged. "Like I said, I don't know if it's true or not, but I've heard it many times over the years. From many different sources."

"I've heard it, too," Jones admitted. "But that story pales in comparison to the one about his burial. If you want freaky, that shit is *freaky*!"

"Wait! Is this the one about the French soldiers?"

Jones started laughing. "Yeah! Ain't that some crazy shit?"

"I forgot about that one! You're right. That blows the pope out of the water!"

"Tell me," Megan said excitedly.

Jones launched into his story. "When Nostradamus died in 1566, he was buried in a cemetery near his hometown. Back then, he was fairly well-known, but not the celebrity he is today—mostly because the bulk of his prophecies were just starting to come true. Anyway, somehow a rumor got started that said anyone who drank from Nostradamus's skull would be able to see the future, but would die shortly thereafter."

She grimaced. "They had to drink from his skull?"

He nodded. "More than two hundred years later, during the French Revolution, three drunk soldiers stumbled upon the grave of Nostradamus. Wanting to know how the revolution would turn out, they decided to dig up his body to see if the stories were true. Under the cover of darkness, they grabbed some shovels, and they started digging. Several minutes later, they finally got down to the wooden coffin and pried that sucker open. Once they did, guess what they saw?"

"What?" she demanded.

"Hanging around the skeleton's neck was a simple sign that said *May 1791*—the exact month and year of their excavation."

"No way! Are you serious?"

"I'm serious, but I'm not done. Obviously, this sign freaked them out, but they'd been drinking so much they decided this was actually a good omen. They figured Nostradamus was expecting them, so the rumors must've been true. With a simple drink, they'd be able to see the future. Anyway, the bravest of the bunch stepped forward and poured a bottle of wine into the prophet's skull. Getting swept up in the moment, he mumbled a drunken toast in the dead man's honor then took a big gulp from the hollowed-out head. Just then a bright light flashed in the distance! His friends assumed it was the spirit of the prophet returning from the great beyond, but it *wasn't* Nostradamus. Instead, it was rifle fire from a nearby skirmish. Unfortunately, one of the stray bullets sailed through the night and pierced the drunken soldier right between the eyes. The poor sucker dropped dead on the spot before he had a chance to reveal the future."

"Come on! The guy died?"

Jones shrugged. "According to legend, the guy actually fell into the grave. Of course, that's the beauty with most stories about Nostradamus. Who knows what to believe?"

"I don't know," she said, "that one seems pretty far-fetched."

Payne smiled. "Actually, I think it's a lot easier to accept than Nostradamus writing a poem about you, but what the hell do I know? I'm not a historian. Or French."

She laughed. "To tell you the truth, I'm still doubting that one myself. I guess we'll know a lot more once Petr tests the ink and parchment."

Payne nodded. "Tests like that would normally bore the hell out of me, but in this case, I can't wait to hear the results. Personally, my gut's undecided, but not my heart."

"Meaning?"

"I think it would be pretty cool to know what's going to happen in the future. Especially if we're given a chance to change it."

"You think we can change the future?" she asked.

Payne shrugged. "Who knows for sure? But let's be

honest, that's one of those philosophical debates that is bound to rage on for centuries. However, some of the greatest thinkers of our time believe that we control our own destiny. Not God. Not the stars. And certainly not Nostradamus. It's our decisions—and nothing else—that influences our lives and future. I'm normally not the kind of guy to quote literature, but Shakespeare wrote something that's always stuck with me. He said, *men are masters of their fate*. That's something I truly believe."

53

TUESDAY, DECEMBER 15

Geneva, Switzerland

Payne, Jones, and Megan had departed Pennsylvania on Monday evening and arrived in Geneva on Tuesday morning. Although the temperature was below freezing and flurries fluttered through the sky, the plane was able to land on a Swiss runway far from the French sector. One of Ulster's associates met them as they hustled across the tarmac and led them into a nearby hangar, where a silver Mercedes SUV and a black Mercedes sedan were waiting for them.

The sight confused Payne. "Why two vehicles?"

The associate, whom he had met several times, explained: "One is for your time in Geneva. The other will deliver the document to Küsendorf, where testing will be done."

Payne pointed at his choice. "If it's okay with you, we'll take the SUV."

The associate nodded. "Petr assumed as much. That is why he is waiting inside."

Jones overheard the comment. "Petr's *here*? He didn't tell us he was coming."

"I believe he wanted it to be a surprise."

"Great! I haven't seen him in a while."

Jones hustled over to the late-model SUV, admiring its heavily tinted side windows. Peeking through the windshield, he saw Ulster sound asleep in the front passenger seat. A drop of drool oozed from the corner of his mouth. Jones grinned at the sight and decided to play a trick on his friend. He put his face next to the windshield, then rapped loudly on the glass, hoping to scare him. The loud noise spooked Ulster, who tried to leap from his seat but was restrained by his seat belt. His arms flailed wildly and spittle flew in all directions like a broken sprinkler. Due to Ulster's girth, the entire SUV shook as though a small tremor had just hit Switzerland.

Payne noticed the movement as he approached. "What the hell was that?"

"It wasn't me," Jones claimed as he slowly backed away.

"For some reason, I don't believe you."

Jones picked up his bag. "You can drive. I'll sit in back where it's safe."

Ulster opened his door a few seconds later. He was unsure of what had happened, but knew it wasn't important. All that mattered was his friends had arrived safely. "Jonathon! It's so good to see you." He rushed forward and gave Payne a bear hug. "How are you, my friend?"

"I'm great, Petr. How about yourself?"

"Wonderful. Just wonderful!"

Jones walked over timidly. "Hey, Petr. Good to see you."

"David! I just had a dream about you."

"Really?"

Ulster paused and pointed. "Strangely, you were wearing those same clothes."

Jones hoped his host wouldn't put things together. "All this talk about Nostradamus, and now you're seeing the future. How crazy is that?"

Ulster laughed. "Yes, that must be it!"

"So," Jones said, trying to change the subject, "why are you here?"

"Why? Because this is my home. Wherever you go in Switzerland, I go."

Payne put his hand on Ulster's shoulder. "I appreciate the offer, but I'm afraid we have to refuse. People have been hunting us since Saturday, and I get the feeling they're not going to stop anytime soon. I'd never forgive myself if you got hurt in the crossfire."

"And *I'd* never forgive myself if you got hurt in my homeland."

"But Petr—"

Ulster cut him off. "Jonathon, this *isn't* open to debate. I know the streets of Geneva like my own backyard, and I have trustworthy friends who can help us throughout the city. Furthermore, I can speak and read all of the languages that Nostradamus used, plus my knowledge of the prophet is greater than all of yours combined. Pardon me for saying so, but you'd be foolish to turn down my expertise."

Jones glanced at Payne. "He's got a point."

"But—"

Ulster cut him off again. "And take a look at this." He trudged toward the back of the SUV and opened its hatch. Inside the trunk, there was a wide assortment of guns and ammunition. All of the weapons looked brand-new. "I come bearing gifts."

Jones rushed over and eyed the merchandise. "Merry fuckin' Christmas."

Ulster laughed. "I took your advice after the last attack on the Archives. Now we have a modern armory at our disposal."

Jones grabbed a Benelli semiautomatic twelve-gauge shotgun. "Much better than those war relics we used a few years ago. With this thing, Santa and his reindeer wouldn't stand a chance."

Payne took a few seconds and considered their options. Although he didn't like the thought of Megan and Ulster in the fray, he realized neither of them would be deadweight. Megan had been invited by name and might be the key to whatever they were searching for, and Ulster was one of the few people in the world who could interpret all the clues along the way.

"Fine," he said reluctantly, "you can tag along. But in the field, I'm in charge. If I say something, you do it. No questions, no quarrels, no hesitation."

Ulster nodded and grinned.

"One more thing, and this *isn't* negotiable. Both of you need to wear bulletproof vests."

Ulster grinned even wider as he pulled up his sweater. Hidden underneath was the largest Kevlar vest that Payne had ever seen. Custom-built to protect Ulster's massive stomach and flabby chest, it had been decorated with red and blue paisley. "I'm ready to rock and roll!"

Jones grimaced at the sight. "And I'm ready to throw up."

THE AIRPORT was located northwest of Geneva, a short drive to Quai du Mont-Blanc, the road whose name was inscribed on the Nostradamus document. Jones drove the SUV while Payne rode shotgun. In this case, it wasn't just a nickname. He actually had the Benelli in his lap as he surveyed the surrounding terrain. While navigating from the backseat, Ulster described all the research he had done during the night, which explained why he had been napping at the airport.

"As soon as I got off the phone with you, I hustled to the Renaissance Room at the Archives and located a copy of *Les Prophéties* in its original French and all the materials I had on Nostradamus. That included some handwritten correspondence to his son. Although nothing will be conclusive until your document is tested at the Archives, I can assure you the handwriting is a perfect match. If your letter wasn't written by Nostradamus, it was done by a master forger."

Sitting next to Ulster in the backseat, Megan shook her head in disbelief. "You mentioned he had a son. Did you find any connections to my family?"

Ulster patted her on the leg. "If I had, my dear, I would have called."

"So where does that leave us?" Payne wondered.

"Actually, it leaves us in a very good place."

"How do you figure?"

Ulster explained. "Although I found nothing definitive about Megan's family, I uncovered a few tidbits about his family that might come in handy. First of all, his son's name was César. According to some accounts, he was named after Nostradamus's mentor, a man named César Scalinger, who was a famous philosopher and botanist."

"Why is that important?" Jones asked in his rearview mirror.

"Because his initials were C.S., just like the initials on your document."

Payne tried to make sense of it. "So the letters might stand for César Scalinger, and the number is the year that Nostradamus died. Any thoughts on what that might mean?"

Jones guessed. "Maybe there's a statue or a plaque on Quai du Mont-Blanc honoring them?"

"I don't think there is," Ulster said, "but we can certainly look. As I mentioned yesterday, it's a very short road. We can cover it on foot in less than an hour."

"Anything else?" Payne asked.

Ulster nodded. "The last line of Megan's text message mentioned *the blood of his first wife*, so I tried to find all the information I could about this woman. During my search, I found something rather surprising. No one knows the woman's name. At least not with any certainty. A few sources claim it was a woman named Henriette d'Encausse, but most sources say that it is incorrect and her actual name has been lost over time."

Megan looked puzzled. "How is that possible? Nostradamus was famous."

"Remember, my dear, this was his first wife. At the time they were married, Nostradamus was a physician, not a celebrated prophet. According to my research, they married for love, not convenience, and the couple had two children whose names are not known."

"What happened to them?" she demanded, hoping one of them had carried on the bloodline of his first wife.

"Sadly, there was an outbreak of Black Death in France, and Nostradamus was called away from their home in Agen to help heal the afflicted. While he was off helping others, his entire family caught the plague and died before he returned. Obviously, this devastated him on a personal level, but it also ruined his professional reputation. Nobody wanted to be treated by a healer who let his own family die from the plague."

"You're right," Jones said. "That wouldn't look good on a business card."

Ulster continued. "Because of this stain on his résumé, he left Agen and roamed throughout France and Italy for the next six years, helping the sick and grieving his loss. For him, it was a deep period of reflection and personal growth that altered his life forever."

"In what way?" Payne asked.

"No one knows when and no one knows why, but at some point during his travels, Nostradamus found his gift for prophecy."

54

Ulster wasn't exaggerating about the short length of Quai du Mont-Blanc. It ran for two thousand feet along the northwest shore of Lake Geneva. Sandwiched between Rue du Mont-Blanc to the south and Quai Wilson to the north, Quai du Mont-Blanc was a picturesque road filled with banks, monuments, and luxury hotels. It offered a distant view of Mont Blanc, Europe's highest mountain, which towered above the Alps on the French-Italian border.

After parking on the quay near the Genève-Pâquis ferry terminal, the foursome climbed out of the SUV and felt the cold sting of the Geneva winter. All of them were bundled up in warm clothes and Kevlar vests, but they were no match for the frigid wind that whipped across the water.

"From now on," Jones mumbled to Payne, "we only take missions near the beach."

Payne turned up his collar and nodded. When he was younger, he used to love downhill skiing and snowmobiling at the great resorts near Pittsburgh—Seven Springs, Hidden Valley, Snowshoe, etc. But the more he aged, the more his body ached in the cold weather. Years of sports injuries, martial arts, and bullet holes had slowly taken their toll. Now when he visited a ski lodge, he spent half the time on the slopes and the other half in the hot tubs.

As they walked along the water, Ulster pointed toward the eastern shore, which was less than a half mile away. "The Jet d'Eau fountain is over there. During the warm season, it shoots water five hundred feet into the air."

"I find that hard to believe," Jones said.

Ulster stopped. "I'm serious, David. It shoots the water very high."

"No, I meant the part about a warm season. Right now I'm freezing my ass off."

Ulster laughed and started walking again. As he did, Megan moseyed up to Jones and locked her arm in his. "You know, for an ex-soldier, you're kind of wimpy."

He shrugged. "Maybe so, but at least I'm not a . . . um . . . Ah, fuck it! It's too cold to be funny."

"That's fine," she teased. "No need to talk. Just shut up and look pretty."

Jones grinned and leaned closer. "Same to you."

STARTING NEAR the Pont du Mont Blanc, the scenic bridge that crosses the Rhône where it flows from Lake Geneva, they explored the north bank of the city. During the first block, most of the buildings looked remarkably similar. Made of stone and painted neutral colors such as beige and white, they housed storefronts on the ground floor and living quarters above. Most of the residences had porches with iron railings that offered great views of the scenery below, but due to the cold weather, the balconies were empty except for a thin layer of snow.

Cars whizzed by as they walked past several Swiss banks and businesses on the busy street. A few blocks later, they came across the Beau-Rivage, the only privately owned hotel in Geneva and one of the most famous hotels in all of Europe. It was so luxurious it served as the headquarters for Sotheby's, the most prestigious auction house in Europe. Even from the sidewalk, the hotel overflowed with extravagance.

"Have you heard of the Beau-Rivage?" Ulster wondered.

Jones answered, "I've been to the Beau Rivage Casino in Biloxi, Mississippi, but I'm going to guess it's not affiliated."

Ulster smirked. "I truly doubt it. This is the finest hotel in all of Geneva."

"Does it have slot machines in the lobby?"

"Certainly not."

"Then it can't beat the one in Biloxi."

Payne, who considered himself a hotel aficionado, was quite familiar with the Beau-Rivage, a lavish five-star hotel. If not for the task at hand, he would have strolled through the marbled atrium and the Sarah Bernhardt Salon, soaking in the history and enjoying the decadence. Despite his personal wealth, he rarely bought expensive toys like gold watches or fancy yachts, but whenever Payne was traveling abroad, he always stayed in the grandest of hotels. It was one of the few luxuries he truly enjoyed. "Have you ever eaten at the Chef's Table?"

Ulster's eyes widened with surprise. "You know of the Chef's Table?"

"Who doesn't?" Payne joked.

Megan raised her hand. "I don't. What's the Chef's Table?"

"The Beau-Rivage has a special table inside the kitchen of Le Chat Botté, its famous restaurant. Those who dine within have their meal specially created for them by its world-class chef. All done tableside."

Ulster gushed, "Not only does he prepare the meal for you, but he describes every ingredient, explains his advanced culinary techniques, and allows you to sample dishes along the way."

Payne smiled. "I guess that means you *have* eaten at the Chef's Table."

"Indeed I have. Many times. It's a magical feast for all your senses!"

Jones cleared his throat. "If you guys are done salivating, can we get back to our mission? I mean, what's this world coming to when *I'm* the guy trying to keep us focused?"

Payne rolled his eyes. "You're just cranky because you're cold."

"I'm fucking freezing, but that's beside the point."

"Fine. What's your point?"

Jones explained, "While you guys are bragging about eating in the kitchen—something black people have been *forced* to do for centuries—I'm over here solving mysteries."

"And what mystery is that?"

"I just figured out what C.S. stands for. And it's *not* his mentor, César Scalinger."

Payne furrowed his brow. "What is it then?"

Jones motioned toward a building up the street. "I think it's a bank."

"A bank?"

Jones nodded. "Ever heard of Credit Suisse?"

Ulster answered for Payne. "Heard of it? I have several accounts there. In my country, there are two major banks that handle more than half of all Swiss deposits. Union Bank of Switzerland is number one. Credit Suisse is number two."

"Have you been inside this branch?" Payne asked.

"Many times. It is where I do my banking when I'm in Geneva." Ulster paused for a moment. "I'm sorry I did not think of it sooner. I was focused on landmarks, not businesses."

"Don't worry about it," Payne said. "We still don't know if D.J.'s right. It might simply be a coincidence."

"Maybe so," Jones admitted. "But the text message said something about her *fortune*. It seems to me that a bank would be a perfect place to stash it."

"If that's the case, what does 1566 stand for?" Megan wondered.

"Don't ask me. I've done my heavy lifting for the day. What do you guys think?"

Ulster shrugged. "It can't be an account number. It's way too short. Besides, unless Megan's name is on the account, she wouldn't be able to access the funds."

Payne considered other possibilities. "Was Nostradamus a wealthy man?"

Ulster shook his head. "He was an apothecary and an author, not a duke or a king."

"In other words, he wasn't rich."

"Comfortable, but not rich."

"If that's the case, what's his fortune?" Payne asked. "It can't be cash or jewels. It has to be something else."

"Like what?" Megan wondered.

"I don't know. Maybe something he cherished. Something priceless."

Ulster gasped softly. "His journal."

"What journal?" Payne asked.

Paranoid, Ulster glanced in both directions. "During the past few days, I've come across several rumors about a secret journal that Nostradamus might have been keeping. Although he never admitted to its existence, it was widely believed that he wrote all of his prophecies in a single notebook and stored it somewhere safe. Since it was never intended for publication, all of his visions were written in simple, straightforward language. No puzzles, or codes, or verses of any kind. Nothing but his most vivid predictions, all compiled in one journal."

Payne frowned. "What happened to it?"

Ulster shrugged. "No one knows for sure, because it's

never been found. Some scholars have speculated that Nostradamus destroyed it on his deathbed, afraid that his immediate family might be charged with heresy if the Inquisition ever discovered it. Others believe that Nostradamus died before he had a chance to retrieve it from wherever it was hidden."

"And what do you think?"

Ulster smiled. "If the man could see the future—and that's still a very big *if*—then he didn't die without a plan. If Nostradamus was a prophet, I'm sure he realized that future generations would cherish his work, not condemn him for it."

Payne continued the thought. "If that's the case, then he definitely figured out a way to get his journal into the hands of someone he was connected to. Perhaps a distant relative."

Megan gasped in understanding. "Someone like me."

55

The four of them strolled past Credit Suisse, giving Payne and Jones an opportunity to inspect the exterior of the nineteenth-century building. Made of tan stone, the bank was four stories tall and equipped with modern security. Cameras had been mounted above the main entrance, which gave guards a panoramic view of Quai du Mont-Blanc and the waterfront. Unlike most of the taller buildings on the street that housed several businesses and residences, the bank was a stand-alone structure, designed to be impregnable.

"What do you think?" Payne whispered.

Jones answered, "I think any facility with that type of camera on the outside is going to have even better technology on the inside. Maybe even facial-recognition software."

"In other words, we can't go inside without risking detection."

"Not only that, but my lock-picking skills would be useless. I'm sure their safe-deposit vaults are equipped with digital-scan security. Probably not retinal scans, but something more complex than fingerprints."

"Yes," Ulster said, "the security at Credit Suisse is top-notch. Although I don't have a box in this branch, I've seen customers entering that section of the bank. First they enter a password into a computer system, then their entire hand is scanned. Fingertips, palm, everything. After that, they go downstairs where the vaults are. Who knows what kind of system they have down there? They might even take DNA samples."

Jones smiled. "Somehow I doubt that, but you'd know better than I. You're the one who has been bragging about the Swiss banking system for as long as we've known you."

Ulster patted him on the back. "I brag because I care. I want my friends to have the best."

"Speaking of friends," Payne said, "do you have any buddies who work at this branch? Maybe someone in management who can provide us with some inside information."

"What type of information?"

"For instance, does this bank have a safe-deposit box with the number 1566? And if so, what's the name and address of the person who rents it?"

Ulster chuckled. "You're joking, right? Swiss bankers pride themselves on one thing above all others, and that's their ability to keep a secret."

Jones leaned in and whispered, "Ironically, Jon and I

pride ourselves on making people talk. If push comes to shove, whose side do you think will win? The bankers or us?"

Payne forced a laugh to defuse the tension. "He's kidding! Just kidding! No one's going to make anyone talk. Tell him you're kidding, D.J."

"Sorry, Petr. I'm cold, and I'm cranky. I promise, no torture today."

"And what about tomorrow?"

Jones shrugged, unwilling to commit. "Depends on the weather."

Slightly concerned, Ulster glanced at Payne. "Is he joking?"

Payne put his arm around Ulster's shoulders and led him away from the others. "Petr, you need to keep something in mind. We're not here because of Nostradamus. We're here because people are trying to kill us. For the time being, we're off the grid, but our status can change at any moment. The last time we were spotted, a cop was killed in Philadelphia, and we were lucky to get away. Next time, we might not be as fortunate."

Slowly but surely, Ulster nodded his head in understanding. Despite the guns and the Kevlar vests, he had been viewing their excursion as a historical field trip, not the life-or-death struggle that it actually was. To him, it was an adventure. To them, it was the best way to stay alive.

"What do you need me to do?" he asked.

Payne answered, "If you have a friend, call him. If you have a connection, use it. I don't care what rules they have to break, but I need all the info you can get on box 1566."

Ulster looked him in the eye. "Give me one hour, and I will get your information."

WHILE ULSTER did some digging inside the bank, Payne, Jones, and Megan killed time at the Hotel Beau-Rivage, where they ordered hot beverages and freshly baked pastries inside the L'Atrium Bar. Located next to the five-floor atrium, the bar continued the same theme with its chandeliers, mirrors, candelabras, and sculptures. High stools filled with guests lined the long marble bar, but the trio preferred a more private setting, comman-deering the plush loveseat and upholstered armchairs near the roaring fireplace.

Halfway through a mug of authentic Swiss hot chocolate—made by melting pieces of chocolate bars in hot milk—Jones was back to his old self. As soon as the chill had left his body, his irritability faded away. "I'm telling you, this is the best hot chocolate *ever*. There's no way in hell that blond chick on the Swiss Miss box is actually from Switzerland. Because compared to this stuff, her cocoa tastes like shit."

Payne smiled. "Next time I see her, I'll be sure to mention it."

"Please don't piss her off. For some reason, I still want to bang that chick. I think it's her cartoon braids."

Megan laughed at the absurdity of the comment. "Welcome back, David."

"Welcome back?" he said, confused. "Oh, you mean my crankiness? Sorry about that. In case you haven't figured it out, I'm not a fan of the cold."

"Don't worry, I figured it out. Helen Keller could have figured it out."

Payne nodded in agreement. "D.J.'s the best soldier I've ever met from forty degrees to one hundred forty. Never bitched. Never moaned. Never needed sunscreen or extra fluids. The guy was like a black Terminator. But thirty-nine and below? He was a pouty little princess. Thankfully, during Hell Week—the roughest part of Special Forces training—the temperature never dipped below forty or he would have washed out for sure. Ain't that right, buttercup?"

Jones smirked. "No comment."

"Nowadays, he'd be screwed. All candidates are forced to live in the mountains of Kodiak, Alaska, in near-arctic conditions to prove their worth. They're tossed from tiny boats into the coastal waters and have to swim to shore. Over the next three weeks, they climb cliffs, traverse gorges, rappel down mountains, and sleep in the snow. All in hopes of preparing them for extreme conditions like Afghanistan."

Jones sipped his hot chocolate and sighed. "I don't know about *screwed*, but I'd be pretty damn cranky. If I had to guess, I'd say the odds are fifty-fifty that they'd feed me to a bear, just to shut me up."

Megan was about to question him further when Ulster entered the room. His cheeks were flushed, and he was out of breath.

Payne stood, concerned. "What are you doing here? You were supposed to call, so I could meet you at the bank."

Grinning, Ulster collapsed into an armchair. "No need, my boy. I have great news, so I hurried straight here."

Payne growled softly as anger filled his eyes. "Everyone stay put. You got me? *Everyone*."

A few seconds later, he hustled out of the bar and into the atrium.

Confused, Ulster and Megan looked to Jones for answers.

"Did I do something wrong?" Ulster whispered.

Jones nodded as he eyed the room. "You were supposed to call us from the bank. That was the plan. You deviated from the plan."

"I know, but it was only a block. I might be plump, but I can walk that far by myself."

"Maybe so, but how do you know you weren't followed?"

Ulster's eyes widened. "Followed? Who would follow me?"

"The same people trying to kill us," Jones explained. "If they know about the letter, there's a possibility they know about Geneva, too."

"Yeah, but—"

Before Ulster could utter another word, Payne hustled back into the bar. The look on his face and the gun in his hand told them everything they needed to know.

They had company.

56

Urban warfare is particularly tricky, especially in a delicate environment like a five-star hotel. Before the first trigger is pulled, the combatants have to decide whether their impending battle is more important than the collateral damage that is bound to occur. Not only to the artwork and the architecture, but to all the people who might get caught in the crossfire.

Ideally, Payne would have preferred a gunfight in the mountains or a desolate stretch of desert where he could utilize his training and minimize civilian casualties. However, when the enemy initiates a fight, a soldier has no choice in the matter. The field of battle has already been determined. All that is left is to make the best of a bad situation.

"How many?" Jones demanded as he pulled his gun from his belt.

Payne answered. "Four out front. Maybe more in the back. Didn't have time to check."

"How do you want to play it?"

Payne yanked Ulster from his chair and grabbed Megan's arm. "I'll stow these two while you secure the atrium. This is gonna get messy."

Jones said nothing as he hustled out of the room.

Meanwhile, the people at the bar realized that something bad was about to happen. Payne sensed their anxiety and did his best to quell the panic. "You, behind the counter."

The bartender froze. "Me?"

"Call the cops and tell them armed gunmen are about to storm the hotel."

"What?"

"I'm a U.S. soldier on vacation. My partner and I will stop the gunmen, but we need reinforcements. Got it?"

The bartender nodded and picked up the phone.

"White guy, green sweater," Payne said as he tugged on his own clothes. "My partner's a black guy in a beige coat. Tell them not to shoot us."

The bartender nodded again. "White in green . . . black in beige . . . got it!"

"What do we do?" said a middle-aged woman on a nearby stool.

"Get behind the bar." Payne quickly scanned the room, calculating how much space the remaining customers would occupy. "All of you! Get behind the bar and keep your heads down!"

"What about us?" Megan asked.

Payne ignored her and focused on Ulster. "Where is Sotheby's located?"

"What?" Ulster asked, confused.

"The auction house! Where are their offices in this hotel?"

Ulster pointed toward the Sotheby's headquarters on the other side of the building, where some of the most spectacular auctions in Europe had been held. Over the past few decades, they had sold the celebrated jewels of the Duchess of Windsor, the Princely Collection of Thurn und Taxis of Germany, and a pear-shaped diamond weighing more than a hundred carats. In addition, they also auctioned art masterpieces and a variety of precious collectibles.

Payne asked, "Do they have a walk-in vault where they store their treasures?"

Ulster nodded, too panicked to speak.

"Listen to me," Payne growled as he grabbed him. "You got us into this mess, now you gotta get us out."

Ulster blinked a few times. "How?"

"I can't fight the bad guys if I'm worried about you and Megan, so you need to take her to Sotheby's. Tell them what's happening and tell them the safest place for everyone is inside the vault. You got me? Get inside the vault and don't come out until I come and get you."

Megan overheard the instructions. "But what if—"

Payne cut her off. "No ifs! You got me? There are no ifs when I'm involved! I will come to the vault and get you. That's a promise."

JONES WARNED everyone in the lobby of what was headed their way and then dashed up the nearest staircase. He exited on the third floor and positioned himself in the back right corner of the five-story atrium, lying on the carpet near a marble banister. From there, he had a bird's-eye view of everyone who entered the plush atrium. Grand columns supported the surrounding walkways. Marble busts and tiny figurines filled the alcoves. A circular fountain, lined with Christmas flowers, sat in the middle of the tiled floor. Like the calm before the storm, the soft trickling of water would soon be replaced with the echoing blasts of gunfire.

Three days earlier, Jones would have displayed tactical restraint, refusing to fire until he had been fired upon. However, he had learned a lot about his enemy in the past seventy-two hours. They were cold-blooded and deadly. Whenever they had a chance to shoot, they took it—whether their target was a defenseless woman like Ashley or a preoccupied police officer. They had established the rules of the game, and Jones was willing to play.

Two men with buzz cuts crept across the deserted vestibule. Both carried F2000 assault rifles, manufactured by Fabrique Nationale of Belgium. The weapon has a unique ejection system, where spent casings are ejected in the front through a tube running alongside the barrel. Gas-operated, the F2000 is capable of firing eight hundred and fifty rounds per minute. In the right hands, it is the type of weapon that could bring down a herd of elephants.

As soon as Jones saw it, he knew he wanted one for himself.

Armed with nothing but a Sig Sauer handgun—their larger weapons were locked in the SUV—Jones waited until both thugs were within range. They split up as they inched around the circular fountain, but as soon as they reunited, Jones fired his weapon with two quick bursts. The first bullet penetrated the gunman's throat, severing his carotid artery and nicking his spinal cord. He staggered back from the bullet's impact, and when he did, the lip of the fountain tripped him up. A moment later, he was falling backward into the water, which quickly turned a shade of red from the geyser in his neck.

The other gunman was far more fortunate, because the second bullet didn't kill him. Instead it merely struck him in the right cheekbone with so much force that it snapped his optic nerve, blinding his right eye. In a wave of agony, he pulled the trigger of his F2000, sending a random burst of rounds from his barrel. Marble and tile exploded in its wake as tiny wisps of debris filled the air. But the blitzkrieg ended a few seconds later with a third bullet from Jones.

And this time, his shot was lethal.

PAYNE WAS positioned near the entrance to the L'Atrium Bar, waiting for Jones to eliminate the first wave of intruders. As soon as the second corpse hit the floor, Payne peeked around the column and tried to spot the next batch of gunmen. As far as he could tell, no one was coming.

"Hold your fire!" he yelled to Jones.

Tentatively, he moved deeper into the atrium, trying to get a better view of the surrounding corridors that spread throughout the hotel like a tangle of veins. The building itself occupied half a city block, and neither of them was familiar with its layout. During the next few minutes, the enemy could come from any direction, and if they did, they would have to be ready.

"Am I clear?" he shouted.

Jones scanned the terrain and saw nothing. "Clear!"

"Coming out!" Payne hustled across the lobby floor and ripped the F2000 from the dead man's hands. He quickly searched the guy's pockets and grabbed two thirty-round magazines. Suddenly, he felt a whole lot better about their predicament. "Incoming!"

Jones stood from his perch, and Payne tossed him their bounty. The magazines went first, one after the other, and then Payne sent the rifle skyward. It weighed roughly ten pounds, so it took some effort to throw it to the third-floor balcony. Jones snagged it cleanly and quickly scrambled toward the left corner of the atrium, where he repositioned himself along the floor, just in case some unseen spotter had locked onto his previous location.

While Jones scrambled into position, Payne dropped to the floor behind the fountain, hoping to buy a few seconds of cover. He was highly exposed in the center of the atrium, but he knew what was at stake. If he got his hands on the other F2000, they could do some serious damage.

"Come on," he mumbled to himself. "Hurry."

"Clear!" Jones yelled as soon as he was settled.

Without delay, Payne leaped into the bloody water and fished out the rifle and as much ammo as he could find. While Jones covered him from above, he stuffed the thirty-round magazines into his cargo pants, then climbed out of the fountain, dripping wet. He quickly scanned the ground floor, searching for shooters that Jones might not be able to see. As he did, he heard a door open near the front of the hotel, followed by an army's worth of footsteps.

"Shit," he cursed under his breath.

Whoever was out there was coming en masse.

57

Payne had less than a second to decide his next move before he was spotted. If he sprinted across the lobby and sought cover behind the front desk, he would risk being detected and possibly shot from behind. His Kevlar vest might protect his torso—although that was questionable, with their advanced weaponry—but his head and legs would be fully exposed during his flight. Worse still, he would be pinned behind a counter with a limited view of the room and no exits. On the other hand, if he stayed in the atrium, he would be exposed from all angles (including above), yet he would have a full three-hundred-and-sixty-degree field of fire. Plus his partner could cover him at all times, something he found very comforting.

In his mind, it was an easy decision. He opted to stay and fight.

Without delay, Payne dove into the bloody water and

pulled the corpse on top of him. The carved stone fountain was nine feet in diameter with a water depth of two
feet. The curved lip of the pool extended a foot above
the waterline, giving Payne three feet of protection on
all sides. In addition, a stone column jutted out of the
center of the fountain. Water bubbled out of the top tier,
slowly trickling over the edge of the bowl and into the
pool below. If not for his current predicament, Payne
might have found the sound calming.

The enemy poured into the hotel in groups of two and
three. All of them white, all dressed in black. Ten soldiers in total, armed with an array of weapons manufactured by Fabrique Nationale of Belgium. A few handled
tactical shotguns, but most carried pistols. Strategically
speaking, it made a lot of sense. Too much firepower in
an enclosed space was a dangerous combination. Send
in the big guns first to clear the path, and then send
in the precise weaponry to clean up the survivors. Of
course, their plan would have been a lot more successful
if their opponents hadn't taken the F2000s before they
had done any damage.

JONES TWISTED the fire selector on his new rifle to
the letter *A*, which stood for *fully automatic fire*. As he
did, he realized that his weapon had been outfitted with
a lightweight underslung grenade launcher. Normally, it
was the type of modification he would have spotted right
away, but the F2000 was a unique weapon, one he had
never handled in the field. At first glance, it looked more

like a prop from *Star Wars* than an actual assault rifle, yet he quickly figured out its technology.

The launcher was a single-shot pump-action weapon, capable of firing a standard low-velocity 40×46mm grenade. When loaded with a HELLHOUND—a round from the High Order Unbelievably Nasty Destructive series by Martin Electronics—the launcher could stop a moving truck from a hundred yards away. Indoors it was even nastier. Loaded with more shrapnel and explosives than standard ordnance, the HELLHOUND had a ten-meter kill radius.

Grinning like a butcher's dog, Jones eased the barrel of the F2000 between the slats of the balcony and aimed at the soldiers as they stormed through the main entrance of the hotel. Quickly, he glanced into the atrium. Payne was still in the water, where he was shielded by the fountain and the first casualty. In a matter of seconds, Jones knew there would be several more.

ALTHOUGH PAYNE'S rifle wasn't equipped with a grenade launcher, he had spotted the modification on the weapon he had tossed to Jones. And being familiar with his friend's taste in tactics, Payne knew it was only a matter of time before he used it.

Hotel architecture be damned.

An ominous *pop* from above announced the impending firestorm. Taking no chances, Payne took a deep breath and slipped completely underwater, realizing how lethal a HELLHOUND could be. A half second later,

the wrath of Lucifer erupted in the lobby of the Beau-
Rivage. There was a burst of light followed by a wall of
thunder that surged across the tiled floor and up through
the atrium like a geyser. Water rippled all around him
from the impact, and shrapnel soared overhead, cutting
through the advancing horde like a firing squad.

One moment they were charging forward, looking for
potential victims. The next they were sprawled on the
floor in various states of disrepair. Some were missing
limbs; others were missing faces. More than half were
missing a pulse.

The four who survived scrambled for cover. One dove
behind some overturned furniture. Another staggered to
his feet and hid behind a marble pillar in the left corner.
The third one crawled toward his pistol, which had been
knocked free by the blast. Jones spotted him from above
and quickly pulled his trigger. The rapid *thwap-thwap-
thwap* of automatic fire echoed throughout the hotel.
The bullets shredded the lobby floor, one after another,
until the strafing eventually tore through the soldier's
gut and chest, ripping him open like a hungry wolf.

The last soldier made the mistake of seeking cover
next to the fountain. He was so focused on Jones that he
neglected to see Payne easing his head out of the bloody
water. From a crouch position, the soldier fired a few
shots at the third-floor balcony. Although they missed
their mark, they were close enough to Jones that he temporarily stopped shooting. Gaining confidence, the soldier took a step forward to improve his angle, and when
he did, Payne pulled his trigger.

From close range, automatic fire wasn't necessary; in fact, it would have been a waste of ammo. A single round fired from an assault rifle was more than capable of killing a man, especially if it caught him under the chin. And thanks to Payne's accuracy, he hit his target with precision, blowing his brains through the top of his skull.

One of the other two survivors—the soldier who had hustled behind the pillar—saw Payne in the water and tried to clip him from the side. He pulled his trigger twice in rapid succession. The first bullet struck the lip of the fountain, sending a chunk of stone toward Payne's face. The fragment, which was small but sharp, nicked his cheek. Within seconds, a thin rivulet of blood was streaming down his face and trickling into the water. The second shot sailed wide, ripping through an upholstered chair before it embedded itself in the far wall.

Ignoring the sting, Payne turned toward the line of fire and spotted the gunman by the column. Both men pulled their triggers at the exact same time, but there was a major difference in the outcome. A single bullet left the barrel of the soldier's pistol while multiple rounds left Payne's F2000. A moment later, the soldier was dropping to the floor in tatters, his body mangled by multiple hits, and Payne was thanking the Belgians for making such a quality rifle and for being such poor shots.

The remaining soldier, who was cowering behind an overturned table, tossed his pistol forward and raised his hands above his head. "Don't shoot!" he begged with a faint accent.

Jones readjusted his aim, waiting for the guy to do something stupid. "Jon?"

Payne stayed in the fountain, not saying anything until he scanned the room for more hostiles. Once he was confident everyone else was dead, he answered. "Coming out!"

With his rifle pointing forward, Payne stepped out of the fountain and hustled across the lobby. Bodies and debris littered the floor. After kicking the pistol away, he dragged the lone survivor to the middle of the atrium, where Jones could keep an eye on him.

Payne growled, "If you move, you die. Understand?"

The guy nodded, then sprawled on his stomach in a submissive position.

"Is anyone else coming?" Payne demanded.

"No! I'm all that's left!"

"If you're lying to me, I swear I'm gonna—"

"I'm not lying!" the survivor screamed. "He only sent us! I swear to God he only sent us!"

Payne dropped to one knee and put the rifle in the man's face. "Who the fuck is *he*?"

The man gulped, trying to decide whom he feared more: his boss or Payne.

And Payne sensed the hesitation. "Righty or lefty?"

"What?" the man asked, confused.

Payne got closer. "Are you a righty or a lefty?"

"Why?"

"Because I'm a nice guy."

"I don't understand!" the man whimpered.

Payne took a deep breath, annoyed. "I'm about to

shoot off one of your fucking hands, and I'm willing to start with the hand you use less. So, which is it? Righty or lefty? Or do you want me to take a guess?"

"François!" the guy shouted. "François Dubois! He lives in Bruges!"

Payne smirked. The ruse worked every time. "What was your mission?"

"To kill you and your friends."

"What else?" Payne demanded.

"Nothing! That's all we were supposed to do!"

"What about the letter?"

"What letter? I don't know anything about a letter!"

Payne stared at him. He seemed to be telling the truth. "Your *only* goal was to kill us?"

"I don't know what you did, but François wants you dead!"

58

Jones remained on his perch until he heard the squawking of police sirens in front of the Beau-Rivage. Only then was he willing to stand and survey the scene. The front half of the lobby had been heavily damaged by the HELLHOUND. Not quite obliterated—because it was still structurally sound—but several levels beyond scarred. It would take more than a paint crew to whip it back into shape. The same thing with the atrium. Everywhere he looked, Jones saw blood and bodies, not to mention dozens of bullet holes and a few stray limbs.

Simply put, the housekeepers were going to be pissed.

"Hey, Jon," Jones called from above. "I don't want to pay for this shit. Let's blame the grenade on them."

Payne nodded and looked down at their prisoner. "You got that, Lefty?"

"It was François!" he shouted. "François did it!"

"That's the spirit. Keep saying that, and we'll get along fine."

After warning Payne, Jones leaned over the railing and tossed his F2000 into the fountain. It hit the water with a loud splash. "Let the cops find it there."

"Speaking of cops," Payne said, "we should have Nick back our story. Can I borrow your phone? Mine's kind of wet."

Jones shook his head as the Geneva police stormed through the front entrance. "*I'll* call Dial. You handle the cops. For some reason, they always blame the black guy."

Payne laughed. "In this case, they'd be right!"

JONES DUCKED into the stairwell and hustled up to the fifth floor. He figured the higher he was in the hotel, the more time he'd have to make his call before the cops found him.

Sitting in his office at Interpol, Dial answered on the third ring. He was pleasantly surprised to hear Jones's voice. "It's about time you guys called me at a decent hour. Did you finally figure out the time difference?"

"Nope. We're actually in Geneva."

"Switzerland? I thought you were in Philly."

"We were, until someone tried to kill us. So we snuck over here."

"Define *snuck*."

Jones smiled. "I'd rather not."

Dial sighed. "Fine. Then why are you calling?"

"Why? Because they just attacked us again. And this time, we hit back."

"How hard?"

Jones did the math in his head. "Eleven dead, one captured."

"You killed *eleven*? Any civilians?"

"None that I know of. But I haven't checked the wreckage yet."

"Wreckage? What wreckage?"

Jones didn't want to lie to Dial about the grenade, so he skirted the question. "Let's just say the Beau-Rivage is no longer a five-star hotel."

Dial took a deep breath and tried to remain calm. But it was tough since he knew he was about to be pulled into this mess. He just wasn't sure how. "What do you want?"

"Surprisingly, not much. Maybe a few kind words to the Swiss police, if they don't believe our story. Other than that, I think Petr Ulster will be the only character witness we need. He's considered royalty in these parts."

"Petr was there? Is he all right?"

Jones feigned anger. "I can't believe you! I spent the last minute telling you about a major firefight with eleven casualties, yet you never asked if Jon and I were okay. But as soon as I mentioned Petr, you got all weepy and concerned. What's up with that?"

"Fine. Are you guys all right?"

"Actually, Jon got a small cut on his cheek. It might require a bandage. Oh, and his phone got soaked. It might not make it."

Dial smiled. "And Petr?"

"I think he's fine. I'm not sure, though. Jon got pissed and locked him in a safe."

"Did you say *safe*?"

Jones grunted. "Damn, I hope there's air in that thing. If not, we might need—"

"D.J.," Dial said, cutting him off. "Why are you calling?"

"Why? Because we got the name of the asshole who keeps trying to kill us."

Dial picked up a pen. "Great! Who is it?"

"Some dude in Bruges named François Dubois."

"You're shitting me!"

Jones noticed his excitement. "I take it you know the guy."

Dial nodded. "Know him? We've been after him for years. Murder, weapons, drugs, you name it. Don't let his fancy French name fool you. That guy is bad news. His nickname on the street is Frankie Death."

"Really? Then I guess Christmas just came early. Come to Geneva, talk to the injured guy who fingered him, then pick up Frankie Death. In return, we expect something nice. How about a Swedish hooker?"

"Hold on," Dial said as he closed his office door. He didn't want anyone in his office to hear what he was about to say. "You *don't* want me to do that."

Jones smiled. "Relax, I was kidding about the hooker. I can get my own hooker."

"Knock it off! I'm not talking about a hooker. I'm talking about Dubois. Trust me, you *don't* want me to arrest him. That's the wrong move."

"How so?"

Dial explained. "Do you know how he got the name Frankie Death? Every time he was arrested—and it happened a lot when he was younger—everyone involved with the case ended up dead. I'm talking witnesses, cops, their families, *everyone*. He even took out a few reporters who had covered his story. After a while, people stopped messing with him."

Jones shook his head in disgust. "I can't believe what I'm hearing. You're scared of the guy. Too scared to arrest his ass."

Dial was offended by the insinuation. "Fuck that, and fuck you! You should know me better than that. I'm not scared of the prick! I'd fucking arrest Hitler if the bastard was still alive!"

"Then what are you saying?"

Dial lowered his voice. "Do I have to spell it out for you?"

"I guess so, because I don't know what the hell you're talking about."

Dial growled in frustration, not wanting to say anything illegal. "Arresting him won't save your ass. In fact, it'll do the opposite. If you think he's coming after you now, you just wait. He'll put a bounty on your head that's so large, every thug in Europe will fly to Pittsburgh to take you out. And if you're not there when they arrive, they'll burn down your building for bonus points before they slaughter everyone you know. And I mean *everyone*. Frankie Death even kills pets."

Jones grunted in understanding.

Once they were done in Switzerland, they'd be forced to visit Bruges.

PAYNE TALKED to the first officers on the scene. He explained who he was and whom he was with. As soon as he mentioned Petr Ulster, the Swiss police treated Payne like he was one of their own. In Switzerland, few surnames were held in higher esteem than Ulster's. Over the years, his family had donated millions of dollars to local charities, and the incredible work they did at the Archives was a source of national pride—even to those who knew nothing about history.

"Where is Monsieur Ulster?" asked the ranking officer.

"I secured him in the vault at Sotheby's."

"Good thinking," the officer said as he grabbed Payne's arm and pulled him toward the section of the hotel where the vault was located. "He is a treasure to my country."

A few minutes later, the door to the massive vault swung open, and several people came streaming out. One of the first was Megan, who ran over to Payne and gave him a big hug.

"Are you okay?" she demanded. "We heard the explosion and assumed the worst."

"We're fine. Both of us are fine."

"No, you're not," she said as she pulled out a tissue from her pocket. Then, ever so carefully, she dabbed the cut on his cheek. "What happened here?"

He shrugged, not really sure. "Bullet, shrapnel, who knows? It doesn't hurt."

She lowered her voice. "Then why are you sweating like a pig?"

He laughed. "It's not sweat. It's water. I was forced to take a dip." He was about to explain what happened when he saw Ulster out of the corner of his eye. For some reason, he was standing off to the side with a remorseful look on his face. "Petr, are you all right?"

Ulster trudged forward like a schoolboy heading to the principal's office. "Jonathon, I am so sorry for disobeying your instructions. If you had been hurt or killed, I don't know what—"

"Petr, relax. I'm fine, and I'm no longer mad at you. In fact, your mistake turned out to be a blessing. We got the name of the guy who's been coming after us."

"That's wonderful," Ulster said, breathing a sigh of relief. Then, as if he was afraid the whole room was filled with spies, he crept closer to Payne and Megan. "Guess what?"

Payne studied the cryptic look on his face. "What?"

Ulster leaned in and whispered. "You aren't the only one who got a name. Credit Suisse was very cooperative."

59

It took a few hours to work through the political mess at the Beau-Rivage. Payne and Jones had entered Switzerland illegally and had just gunned down eleven people, but they had saved many more with their heroism—including Petr Ulster, a personal friend of Geneva's mayor.

A phone call from Nick Dial helped strengthen their case. He explained that Payne and Jones had been attacked in Pittsburgh and Philadelphia, and the only reason they had entered Switzerland unofficially was to figure out who was trying to kill them. He assured the police that Payne and Jones had worked closely with his office in the past, and Interpol would soon be involved in the investigation due to the international nature of the shootings. In addition, he told the Geneva police they should announce the death of twelve criminals, not eleven, in order to protect a valuable informant in a very important case.

Once the duo was finally allowed to leave the scene, Jones hustled across Quai du Mont-Blanc and retrieved their SUV near the waterfront. Somehow they had been spotted in Geneva, so they would take extra precautions until they were safely away from the city. Jones pulled onto the sidewalk next to Rue du Fossé Vert, a tiny road behind the hotel, and scanned the nearby buildings before he signaled for his friends to come out a back exit. The three of them climbed into the vehicle and quickly closed their doors.

Over the next forty minutes, Jones used every driving tactic he could think of to ensure they weren't being followed. He crossed several lanes of traffic to exit the highway at the last possible second. He ran red lights and made illegal U-turns. He even drove down a one-way street in the wrong direction. The entire time Payne focused on their surroundings, memorizing cars and faces, even searching the skies for aerial pursuit. At one point, they pulled into a parking garage, where they searched the SUV for listening devices and tracking beacons.

In the end, they were confident they were clean.

"ACCORDING TO Credit Suisse," Ulster explained, "box number 1566 was closed on December first by a man named Louis Keller. That was the main reason they were willing to give me his personal information. He is no longer one of their customers."

Jones read between the lines. "What was the *other* reason they helped?"

Ulster grinned. "I threatened to pull my family fortune from their bank."

"Well played!" Megan said, laughing.

"What do we know about Keller?" Payne wondered.

"He is fifty-two, never married, and lives in Lausanne. It is a French-speaking city on the shores of Lake Geneva, roughly thirty miles to the northeast."

Jones frowned. "I've heard of Lausanne, but I'm not sure why. Does it have anything to do with Nostradamus?"

"Not that I'm aware of," Ulster admitted. "Lausanne is in the Swiss wine region. We refer to it as *capitale olympique,* because the International Olympic Committee is located there."

"That's why I've heard of it. Every time an Olympic athlete gets busted or a new host city gets announced, the IOC issues a statement from Lausanne."

Payne barely heard Jones's comment, because he was focused on something far more important. "How far did you say it was from Geneva?"

Ulster answered, "Thirty, maybe forty miles. Thankfully, we can take the A1 motorway all the way there. It's part of the Swiss autobahn."

"How big is Lausanne? A hundred thousand people?"

"Larger than that. I'd say, closer to three. Why do you ask?"

Payne ignored the question. "In other words, it has dozens of banks."

Jones glanced at him. "What are you getting at?"

"Why would a man from Lausanne have a safe-deposit box in Geneva?"

"He wouldn't," Jones joked. "That's why he closed it on the first."

"I'm serious." Payne turned in his seat and spoke to Ulster. "When you were at Credit Suisse, did you read Keller's file? Or did they just write down his contact info?"

"Neither. They pulled up his account and printed everything on the screen."

"Can I see it?"

"Of course you can. But it won't do you much good."

"Why not?"

Ulster unfolded the paper and showed it to him. "It's written in French."

"In that case, do me a favor. We know he closed the safe-deposit box on December first. Try to find out when he opened it."

Ulster glanced at the document, looking for the requested information. As soon as he spotted the answer toward the bottom of the sheet, his eyes widened. "I can't believe I missed this."

"Missed what?"

"I was so excited about getting his name and address I didn't even bother to read the paper they gave me."

"Missed what?" Payne repeated.

Ulster looked at him. "Louis Keller *didn't* rent the box. A man named Maurice Keller did."

"Maurice Keller? Is it a relative of his?" Megan asked.

"I would bet on it, but . . ." Ulster hesitated, trying to figure out the significance of what he had discovered. "But a relative who Louis had never met."

Confusion filled Payne's face. "They never met? Why do you say that?"

Ulster tapped on the paper for emphasis. "Because Maurice Keller rented the box on December first—exactly one century before Louis closed it."

Megan gasped. "Are you serious?"

"One hundred years to the day," Ulster said. "But that's not all. According to this, the annual fee for the box was paid by some kind of trust fund. I'm not sure who set it up, but it appears the bill has been handled in this manner since the very beginning."

Payne was quite familiar with family trusts, since one had been established in his name—although he didn't know anything about it until after his parents had died. A week after their funeral, his grandfather sat him down and explained the basics to Payne so he wouldn't be worried about his future. He was told his inheritance was being held for him at a major bank until he was old enough to handle "the financial responsibility."

In order to encourage his growth as a person, his parents had placed several incentive clauses in the document. They included high school and college graduation, mandatory charity work, and a number of other things Payne would have done anyway. Surprisingly, he never rebelled or complained about his obligations. Deep down inside, he knew his parents had been looking out for his long-term interests. They tried to do everything they could to ensure he didn't turn into one of those trust-fund celebrities who were always getting drunk or arrested. To proud people like his parents, that would have been a fate worse than death.

Eventually, Payne and his grandfather even joked about the clauses.

They called it *parenting from beyond the grave.*

"Hey, Petr," Payne said, "does that document say anything else about the trust fund? Who started it? How much it was worth? Anything like that?"

Ulster shook his head. "I'm afraid not. Why do you ask?"

"I was wondering if the trust fund might be the fortune that was mentioned in the text message. I figure if Nostradamus is behind all of this, there's always a chance that his life savings have multiplied over the years. After four centuries of prophetic investments, there could be a lot of money socked away."

Ulster shrugged. "We'll find out soon enough. We'll be in Lausanne shortly."

60

L ouis Keller lived in a nice chalet near the University of Lausanne, where he had taught business and economics for the past decade. With its steeply sloped roof and its overhanging eaves, his timber house looked like many others in the quiet neighborhood. Of course, looks could be deceiving, which was why Payne and Jones studied the nearby streets before they were willing to park their SUV near Keller's home.

Snowflakes filled the air as the four of them walked up the stone steps of his front porch. Payne led the way, followed by Megan, Ulster, and Jones, who lingered several strides behind with a pistol in his hand. Payne was armed as well, but he kept his weapon concealed as he approached the house. Since they still weren't sure how Keller fit into all of this, the last thing Payne wanted to do was spook the guy and have him clam up before they got the answers they were looking for. That is, if Keller even had any answers.

A half second before Payne could knock on the door, he heard the lock being opened from the inside and the security chain being jostled. Unsure of who it was, Payne raised his closed fist in the air, the military signal to halt. Everyone behind him stopped, as if a cold wind had blown in from the nearby mountains and turned them into ice. For the next few seconds, the tension continued to build until the door finally swung open.

A middle-aged man wearing a sweater vest, slacks, and slippers stood in the doorway. He neither smiled nor frowned, his face a blank mask, his eyes devoid of emotion. He stared at the foursome in front of him, not the least bit surprised they were there. Strangely, his gaze sought them out, one after another, as if he were trying to match their faces to the names he had known for years. A moment later, his comment seemed to confirm that.

"I was told you were coming," Keller said in English.

"By whom?" Payne wondered.

"Nostradamus."

With that, Keller turned around and walked back inside his house, leaving his door open so they could enter. Confused by the remark, Payne glanced over his shoulder and shrugged, not completely sure what they should do. Surprisingly, Megan was the first one to react. She had come too far and had too many questions to wait any longer. Without asking for permission, she wiped her feet on the mat and walked inside, where she spotted Keller standing in front of a roaring fire. He signaled for her to sit on the couch, and then waited for the others to follow.

One by one, they entered the house without saying a word. Payne roamed around the ground floor of the chalet, searching for anything that troubled him, but his gut told him they weren't in danger. In fact, for the first time in the past several days, he felt as though their path were free of obstacles. As though their quest had finally come to an end. As though they were meant to be there.

In an unpredictable world, it was a feeling Payne wasn't used to.

Keller waited for Payne to join his friends before he spoke again. When he did, there were no introductions or small talk. Keller launched into an explanation, starting with some background information about himself.

"I am not a whimsical man," Keller informed them. "I don't like literature, I don't watch movies, and I never play games. For as long as I can remember, I have loved the structure of numbers. To me, they are the only constant in my life, the one thing I can depend on. Numbers never lie. They are always black and white, never gray, and somehow I find comfort in that."

Keller walked across the room and sat in a worn leather chair that looked older than he was. Brushing the gray hair away from his eyes, he took a deep breath and blew it out slowly, as if he could finally relax now that his guests knew he wasn't fanciful or the least bit crazy. Seemingly, that was important to him. He needed everyone to know he was a rational man with rational thoughts, not some random loon who searched for Bigfoot in his spare time.

"Thirty-two years ago, my father drove me to Geneva under false pretenses. He told me we were going to the city to celebrate my twentieth birthday. Instead, he took me to the bank and added my name to his safe-deposit box. At least I thought it was his box. Later in the day, he told me that wasn't the case. It was our family box and would be until December of this year."

He glanced around the room, making eye contact with everyone.

"On our drive home, my father explained that one of our forefathers, a man named Maurice Keller, had been given a sealed wooden box for safekeeping. As long as he protected it and never opened it, he would be compensated for his time and effort. Furthermore, he was told the same arrangement would hold true for future generations of Kellers. If we followed a simple set of instructions, we would be paid an annual stipend to offset any inconvenience that we incurred."

Keller stood again and began to pace about the room. "At first, I was annoyed by it all. My father had the only key, and he told me he would keep it until it was supposed to be mine. I had no idea what he meant by that and even resented him for it. Why did he waste half of my birthday to drag me to some bank in Geneva? None of it made any sense. I just thought it was a stupid game, a silly bonding moment between father and son."

He paused for an instant, gathering his thoughts.

"A few months later, when I was off at school, my father passed away from pancreatic cancer." His voice cracked slightly when he said it. "I never even knew he was sick."

Nothing was said for the next minute or two. No one knew what to say, including Keller, who walked back across the hardwood floor and collapsed onto his chair. After that, the only sound in the room was the soft crackling of the fire.

Eventually, it was Megan who got things started again.

"What happened then?" she asked.

"Then I waited," Keller said bitterly. "For thirty-two years, I waited. And do you know why I waited? Because that's what I was told to do. My father didn't even have the decency to tell me he was dying, but he made damn sure he wrote a letter explaining what was expected of me. He left me a key and a letter, yet he never even said good-bye. How pathetic is that? Do you know how many times I wanted to destroy that box just to spite him? If it had been kept in Lausanne instead of Geneva, I probably would have done it. I would have gone to the bank in a fit of anger and smashed it with a hammer."

He shook his head in frustration. "In the end, I always talked myself out of it because of the money. The yearly stipend, it always came in handy during the holidays."

Payne had several questions about the trust fund. How much was Keller paid? Who handled the payments? How did the keepers of the fund know he had followed their instructions? But in the end, he realized there were more important issues to focus on, starting with the obvious.

"Out of curiosity, what happened on December first?"

Keller smiled at the question. Relief filled his face. He was thrilled to be done talking about his father and eager to discuss the contents of the mysterious box.

61

K eller sat forward in his chair. As he did, everyone leaned closer. They realized he was about to share a secret that had been guarded for more than four hundred years, a secret penned by Nostradamus himself. None of them wanted to miss a word.

"I was the first customer in the bank that day," Keller explained. "I couldn't sleep the night before, so I drove to Geneva quite early and sat in my car until Credit Suisse opened. Frankly, I've been anxious for several months now—but not for the reasons you might expect. I felt very little excitement about the contents of the box. How could it possibly live up to three decades of expectations? In truth, I simply wanted it out of my life. However, I was afraid I was going to open it and there would be a letter telling me to pass its contents on to my children. Obviously, that would have been a major problem since I don't have any."

Keller smirked at his own comment.

"Despite my need for closure, I didn't feel comfortable opening it in a viewing room at the bank. I figured my family had protected the box for a hundred years. The least I could do was wait another hour and open it in the safety of my own home."

"You opened it here?" Ulster asked.

Keller nodded. "Two weeks ago today."

"Do you still have it? I would love to see it."

"In a moment," Keller assured them, "but not until I've fulfilled my obligation. Not until I tell you everything you're supposed to be told."

Megan stared at him. "Why us?"

"Because you were the ones who showed up," he answered cryptically. "The four of you were chosen for a reason beyond my understanding, by a man who died long ago. I am not a prophet, nor a medium of any kind. I am simply a proxy. I've been given a job, which I intend to do to the best of my ability. But after today, I will be done with this nonsense forever."

For some reason, Payne winced when he heard the word *chosen*. Somehow it made him feel like a pawn in a game he didn't want to play. Thinking back, he realized the word had also been used in the letter to Megan. According to the translation, she had been *chosen for her place in time*—whatever that meant. Now Keller was using it to describe them. If the foursome had been picked, Payne wondered why, and by whom. Could it actually have been Nostradamus? Or was there something else going on that was beyond his current understanding?

Keller continued his story from where he had left off. "As soon as I returned home, I took a few minutes to examine the box. Even though it had been in my possession for years, I'd never taken the time to study it. I know that probably sounds strange, but I figured the more I knew about the box, the more fixated I would become. And I didn't want to be tempted to open it. Hell, I didn't even want to think about it."

His voice faded slightly. The last few years had been difficult for Keller. In some ways he had felt like an addict, always battling a demon he couldn't kill. He could only push it away. No matter where he went or what he did, temptation was always lurking.

"At first I thought I would have to pry the lid open, but then I noticed the corners of the box. Three numbers had been carved into each. One on the top, and one on each side. That's when I realized the corners were tiny pyramids that could be turned like knobs. Over the years the wood must have warped slightly, which made the knobs seem like solid corners, but once I figured out what they were, I applied enough pressure and spun them like dials on a lock."

"What are the numbers?" Ulster demanded.

"Somehow I knew I would be asked." Keller reached into his vest pocket and pulled out a list that he handed to Ulster. It contained four sets of three numbers. Each number had been placed in a column that had been labeled by the corner's location on the box.

Front Left	Front Right	Back Left	Back Right
03	01	15	09
07	02	19	66
12	25	20	82

Ulster studied the chart as Megan and Jones looked on. Meanwhile, Payne remained focused on his surroundings. Although he felt safe, it didn't mean they were. Every once in a while during their visit, he would stand from his chair and walk over to the window, where he scanned the street and the nearby terrain. Eventually, he decided to remain standing near the front door. Close enough to listen to Keller, but in a much stronger tactical position.

"Did you figure out the combination?" Megan asked.

A smile surfaced on Keller's face. "As I mentioned earlier, numbers are a passion of mine. I have always loved the power that they possess. They are often overlooked, yet they bring structure to a world filled with chaos. I find beauty in that." He pointed at the list. "After I created that chart, it didn't take long for certain numbers to stand out. Four in particular."

"Which four?"

"Twelve, one, twenty, and nine."

The foursome pondered the numbers, trying to understand their significance. Eventually it was Ulster who expressed his confusion. "What do they represent?"

Keller smiled even wider, temporarily forgetting all the anguish the box had brought him over the years.

After all this time, he was proud his expertise was being put to good use. "They represent the date that I was supposed to open the box."

"The date?" Ulster said, glancing back at the list.

Keller explained his discovery. "Each of the knobs has a meaning. One knob represents the month. One represents the day. One represents the year's prefix. The other represents the suffix."

Megan was confused by the terminology. "What do you mean by prefix and suffix?"

"Fifteen represents the fifteen hundreds. Nineteen represents the nineteen hundreds."

"I get it," she said. "And twenty represents *this* century."

Keller nodded. "As soon as I determined their meaning, I twisted the dials until the numbers on the top of the box read twelve, one, twenty, and nine. Those numbers represented December first of this year—the date I was supposed to open the box."

"Why did he use the American date format instead of the European?" Jones asked.

Keller shrugged. "Perhaps because you were involved."

"Perhaps," Jones said. "What happened next?"

"I immediately heard a click on the inside, and the lid popped free."

Ulster grinned. "A puzzle box! How marvelous!"

Megan furrowed her brow. "What's a puzzle box?"

"They are wonderful contraptions that can only be opened through a precise series of movements and manipulations," Ulster explained. "Sometimes the codes are rather simple, and other times they are unbelievably complex. I have seen some from Japan, known as *himitsu-bako*, that require more than two hundred movements to unlock the interior. Occasionally, it's not even movement that is required. Some puzzle boxes require pressure on certain parts of the wood to activate other mechanisms on the inside. Thankfully, by comparison, it seems like we have gotten off rather easy. Then again, I can't remember any puzzle boxes being built as early as the sixteenth century. Perhaps this box is the first of its kind."

"Do you think it's my treasure?" she asked, and then instantly regretted it. Keller had spent most of his life protecting the box, only to give it to her. She imagined it would upset him to hear it might be worth a fortune.

Ulster shrugged. "That depends on the contents of the box. What did you find inside?"

Keller answered, "I found a letter written by Nostradamus."

"Oh," Megan said in understanding, "the letter you sent to me."

Keller grimaced as confusion filled his face. He had no idea what she was talking about. "To *you*? I didn't send anything to you."

"What do you mean?" she demanded.

"The letter I found was written to *me*."

62

Surprised by the comment, Payne stared at Keller from across the room. The bewilderment in his eyes told Payne everything he needed to know. The guy was telling the truth.

"What about the text message?" Payne demanded.

Keller's gaze shifted to Payne, who was standing near the door. "What text message? What are you people talking about?"

Payne moved closer. "You didn't send her a letter or a text message?"

"I didn't send *anything* to *anyone*! How could I? I don't even know your names!"

Jones straightened in his seat. "And we're going to keep it that way."

Keller stood from his chair. "That's fine with me. In fact, I'd prefer it. Now that I've completed my task I want to wash my hands of this nonsense and get on with my life. For the first time in thirty-two years, I can finally move on."

"Wait!" Megan blurted. "How can you be *done*? You haven't told us anything yet! What are we supposed to do now?"

Noticing the emotion in her voice, Keller felt pangs of empathy. He was familiar with the confusion and the hopelessness she was displaying. He had suffered through the same maladies over the years. "I'm sorry, but I don't know what to tell you. The instructions from Nostradamus were short but explicit. The letter said four strangers would show up at my door, precisely two weeks after I opened the box. It asked me to describe the events of December first, starting with my vault at the bank, and then I should explain how the puzzle box worked. After that, I was to give you the box and bid you adieu."

"Nothing else?" Jones asked.

"Actually, there was one more thing, but it doesn't pertain to you. I was told to sell the letter for a tidy profit. The money would be my reward for faithful service."

"Have you done that already?" Ulster asked, hoping to see the letter.

Keller shook his head. "Not yet. But I gave it to a friend of mine at the university. He is currently getting it appraised. Once we have confirmed its worth, I will hold an auction at Sotheby's."

Jones laughed at the coincidence. "You *might* want to rethink your plan. I heard Sotheby's was a wreck."

"Really? I've heard nothing but good things."

"Trust me on this one. The hotel needs some major work."

"Anyway," Payne said, trying to cut things short, "just give us the box, and we'll leave you alone. We've got a flight to London later tonight, so we need to get going."

"Just give me a moment," Keller said, hustling toward his steps. "I hid the box upstairs."

Megan waited until he was gone before she spoke. "We're going to London?"

Payne shook his head and whispered, "Nah, I'm just throwing him off the scent in case someone comes looking for us. Better safe than sorry."

"Then what are we going to do?"

He shrugged. "I don't know. We'll figure it out on the road."

ZÜRICH, THE LARGEST CITY in Switzerland, was less than a three-hour drive from Lausanne and had everything that Payne and Jones were looking for: a major airport, dozens of hotels, and a diverse populace to hide in. Ulster recommended the Baur au Lac Hotel, located in its own scenic park on the shore of Lake Zürich. Not only was it near the Paradeplatz, the city's bustling financial district, but it was adjacent to the Bahnhofstrasse, one of the most expensive shopping districts in the world. The exclusivity of the area guaranteed around-the-clock security and special attention from the city's police force, which made it safer for them.

Using a false identification and cash, Payne booked

the River Suite at the hotel. With a living room, kitchen, and multiple bathrooms, it allowed the foursome to spend the night together comfortably. While Ulster ordered room service for the group, Payne hopped in the shower, desperate to wash off the bloody water that had dried on him in Geneva. Afterward, he felt like a new man. Wide awake and ready to plot their next step.

Wearing a plush hotel robe and shorts, he strolled into the living room, where Jones, Megan, and Ulster had gathered around a mahogany coffee table. Sitting in its center was the puzzle box. Measuring just under a foot in height, width, and depth, the exquisitely carved box had been crafted out of light-brown linden wood. Its lid, decorated with astrological patterns that helped to conceal the corner knobs, was currently locked in place.

"Did you open it yet?" Payne wondered.

Megan shook her head. "We were just about to."

"You didn't have to wait for me."

"Don't worry, we didn't," Jones said. "Keller stored this thing in so much bubble wrap it took us an hour to break through. In addition, a certain historian who shall remain nameless refused to use a blade of any kind for fear of damaging the box."

Ulster defended his caution. "If this artifact was actually built by Nostradamus, I can't begin to fathom how valuable it might be. In the world of antiquities, there are very few names that create a bigger buzz than his. It seems everyone wants a glimpse of the future."

Payne plopped down in a nearby chair. Now that he

was clean, his stomach was growling for attention. "Do you think the box is Megan's fortune?"

"Possibly," Ulster said, "especially when you consider how long it's been hidden. According to Louis Keller, his family had this box in their possession for a hundred years. That leaves more than three hundred years unaccounted for. How many people guarded the box before them? And how many people were asked to contact Megan?"

Payne had broached the topic during the drive to Zürich, but the group hadn't reached a consensus of any kind. "At least one, maybe more."

Jones counted them off. "The text message was sent from a French cell phone, so that's one. The letter was mailed from Asia, so that's two—unless the same person did both."

"Or," Payne suggested, "the letter could have bounced from country to country beforehand, offering layers of insulation along the way. If that's the case, there's no way of knowing who leaked word of Megan's letter to François."

"Guys," she said anxiously, "I appreciate everything you've done for me, but if it's okay with you, can we play with the box now? I want to see how this thing works."

Payne laughed. "It's your box. Play away."

"But gently!" Ulster urged. "We don't want to break it."

Megan smiled and slid the box toward her on the coffee table. As she did, her heart rate quickened. She still didn't understand how she fit into everything, but she realized she was part of something special. Even if their search had ended in Lausanne, she still had been given a puzzle box that might be worth a small fortune, certainly more than a hostess from South Philly could make in a lifetime. "I'm nervous," she admitted.

Ulster patted her knee. "Don't be, my dear. I'm sure the box will hold up fine. I truly doubt Nostradamus would have left it to you if he foresaw you breaking it."

"You know, that's a very good point."

She took a deep breath and then turned the knobs to twelve, one, twenty, and nine. When the final knob clicked into place, the lid popped open, as Keller had described. The sides of the box housed a complicated series of pins and latches that held the ten-inch square in place. With the latches released, the inner lid simply popped up from the center of the box top. Pushing the lid flush against the surface and turning any of the knobs to an incorrect number would once again seal the device. Viewed from the side, the box appeared solid. Viewed from the top, the intricately carved designs concealed the seam between the lid and the outer edge.

Megan pulled the lid off and handed it to Ulster for safekeeping.

"Thank you," he said as he examined the underbelly of the lid. Unlike its outer surface, it had no carvings or patterns of any kind. It was unadorned linden wood with four slots for the latches. Unimpressed, he quickly put it aside and focused his attention on the box.

Much to everyone's disappointment, the interior of the box was just as plain. It consisted of a small storage compartment that was cramped because of the locking mechanism in the box's walls. The space was large enough to hold a few trinkets—or, in Keller's case, a folded letter—but it certainly couldn't hold anything larger than a Rubik's Cube.

Jones peeked inside. He was less than impressed. "Wow, nice box. I hope you kept the receipt. Maybe you can return it for something useful, like, a box filled with . . . *stuff.*"

Payne rolled his eyes. "On that note, I think all of us should take a break. It's been a very long day, and we have a lot to figure out—including our next move. Once we get some food and rest, I'm sure the big picture will make a lot more sense."

63

A few hours later, after dining on a gourmet meal in their suite, Ulster and Jones had fallen asleep in opposite corners of the room while Payne and Megan stayed awake, talking on the couch. Their conversation had covered a wide range of topics but had slowly shifted back to the events of that day, particularly the time they had spent in Lausanne.

Megan said, "The thing I don't fully understand is Keller's role in this."

Payne shrugged, still not sure about several things. "The guy was good with numbers. I guess he was picked to figure out the combination, so he could show us how the puzzle box worked."

She shook her head. "That's not the part that bothers me. I want to know why Nostradamus asked him to do everything else. Remember what Keller said? Nostradamus was explicit in his instructions. Before giving us the box, Keller was supposed to tell us about his bank vault and explain what he did on December first. Why was that stuff important?"

"You know what? That's a good point. I think I over-looked the first part of Keller's instructions because I was focused on the box and getting us to safety. But now that you mention it, there has to be a reason he explained everything to us."

Megan leaned forward and touched the puzzle box. "If I had to guess, it has something to do with this. I'm not sure what, but *something*."

Payne rubbed his eyes in thought, trying to remember everything Keller had told them. Replaying the conversation in his mind, he focused on a fact that Ulster had brought up while describing the history of puzzle boxes. Some of them were so complex they required over two hundred moves to open. He even mentioned they had gotten off easy, opening the box in only four. "What are your thoughts on Keller?"

"In what sense?"

"How he acted today. His overall state of mind."

"I don't know. He seemed kind of burdened, like all of this was weighing him down. He definitely has some father issues. That much is certain."

"Did his mood change during the course of our conversation?"

She nodded. "He was *much* happier at the end. He couldn't wait to give us the box and get us the heck out of there."

"Yeah, I noticed that, too."

She glanced at Payne. "What are you thinking?"

"Don't worry about it. It might be nothing."

"Jon," she said sharply, "what are you *thinking*?"

He smiled at her. There was something about her feistiness that he really liked. "In my opinion, there are three likely scenarios in play. We just need to figure out which one makes the most sense."

"Okay. What's the first one?"

"Keller did everything he was supposed to do, and the box is actually your treasure."

"I guess that's possible. What's number two?"

"Keller couldn't wait to get the box out of his life, so he stopped studying the numbers after he figured out the first combination. Remember what Petr said? Some puzzle boxes utilize hundreds of moves. What if there's more than meets the eye to this contraption? What if there are several hidden compartments?"

She pondered his comment. "Maybe that's why Nostradamus asked Keller to tell us everything he did, so we could figure out what still needs to be done with the box."

Payne smiled. "Or something like that."

"Wait, what does *that* mean?"

"Call me cynical, but I'm still not sold on the whole Nostradamus thing. And I probably won't be until Petr verifies the age of your letter and the origins of the box. Actually, I take that back. Even then, I'll still have my doubts about Nostradamus."

She laughed. "O ye of little faith. I can't believe you're doubting my grandfather!"

"Your grandfather? I think you better take a closer look at your family tree. You missed a few dozen generations."

"Maybe so, but you have to admit this stuff is pretty mysterious."

"Mysterious, yes. But that doesn't mean it's factual. We're still a long way from factual."

"Anyway," she said, not wanting to argue about it, "what's scenario number three? Or have you forgotten it already?"

He shook his head. "Nope, I haven't forgotten. In fact, of the three choices, this is the one that worries me the most."

"It worries you? What is it?"

"What if Keller conned us?"

"In what way?"

Payne explained. "What if he figured out multiple combinations and unlocked parts of the box we haven't seen yet? Who knows what he might have found? It would certainly explain why his mood brightened at the end of our visit. He wasn't thrilled the box was out of his life; he was thrilled that *we* were out of his life."

"But he willingly gave us the box."

"True, but it's a small price to pay if he removed the description of the actual treasure and its location. Remember, the best con jobs are the ones where the victim doesn't even know he's been conned. What if he sacrificed the box to remove us from the equation?"

"Why would he do that?"

"Simple. Now he has all the time in the world to go after the treasure himself."

LOUIS KELLER never even heard them coming. One moment he was sleeping peacefully in his bedroom, the next his hands and feet were being tied to his bed frame. He tried to scream, but their gag prevented it. He tried to see, but their flashlight blinded him.

He was completely at their mercy.

A few minutes earlier, he had been dreaming about the profits he would make from the sale of the items. He felt the money was rightfully his—no matter what the letter had claimed. Fuck his father, and fuck Nostradamus. They had put him through hell over the past thirty-two years. In his mind, the cash was compensation for all the suffering he had endured.

Then again, suffering was a matter of perception. For all he knew, the next few minutes might be far worse than the last three decades combined.

The mere thought of it made him wet his bed.

Although he couldn't see them, Keller knew they were hovering nearby. There were at least two of them, maybe more. They moved around the room with unbelievable agility. Like ghosts. Keller closed his eyes, trying to block the potential horrors out of his mind, but that didn't last for long. One of them tapped Keller on the bridge of his nose with the flashlight. Not hard enough to hurt him, but hard enough to get his attention.

"Listen to me," a deep voice growled. "I'm about to remove your gag. If you scream, you'll regret it. Understand?"

Keller nodded enthusiastically. As soon as the gag had been removed, he sucked in a gulp of air, praying it wasn't the last breath he would ever take.

"What do you want from me?" he said meekly.

"The truth. As long as you tell us the truth, you will *not* be hurt."

"Anything! I'll tell you anything! Just don't hurt me!"

"Where's the box?" the voice growled.

"I gave it away! I gave the box away!"

"To *who*?"

"I don't know their names, but there were four of them! Three men and a woman. I swear, I don't know their names! They showed up this afternoon!"

"Describe them."

"Two Americans. One was big, and one was black."

"And the other man?"

"He was fat."

"And the woman?"

"She was young. And thin. She had brown hair."

"Where are they now?" the voice demanded.

Keller paused, trying to remember. "London! They were flying to London!"

"And they have the box?"

"Yes! I gave them the box."

"Shit!" he cursed. "What about the other items? Did you give them *everything*?"

"No! I still have them!"

"Where are they?" the voice growled.

"Behind you! In a plastic case on the shelf!"

"Check it out." Footsteps moved across the room in the darkness. Suddenly, a second flashlight was turned on. The beam bounced from shelf to shelf in the interior of the closet until it settled on the top shelf. A moment later, the light clicked off. "Well?"

"Got it," the second intruder replied. "One item."

"I told you," Keller blurted. "See, I was telling you the truth!"

"Keep it up, and you'll be fine," the voice whispered.

"I will! I promise! Ask me anything!"

"Does the box have multiple combinations?"

"Yes! It has two!"

"What are they?"

"They're dates! One is December first. The other is the day he died!"

"The day *who* died?"

"Nostradamus!"

The voice paused. "Where are the other items?"

"There were only two! And you have one!"

"What's the other item?"

"A letter of instructions! It was written to me!"

"Where is it?"

"A friend has it at work. I'm supposed to pick it up before my flight!"

"Your flight? Are you meeting the Americans?"

"No! I told you, I don't know them!"

"Then *where* are you taking it?" the voice snarled.

"I'm taking it to Bruges!"

"What's in Bruges?"

"A buyer! I found a buyer in Bruges! He's a Nostradamus freak! Totally obsessed!"

"What's his name?"

"François! His name is François!"

"What's his last name?"

"I don't know!" Keller whimpered. "I swear I don't know."

"Bullshit! How can you meet him if you don't know his name?"

"He sent me a phone! He said he'd call with directions once I landed!"

"Where is it?"

"Behind you on the shelf!"

"Take a look," the voice ordered.

Five seconds later, his partner responded, "Got it."

"See!" Keller said. "I'm not lying. I swear I'm not."

"What time are you expected?"

"Seven. He'll call tonight at seven."

"He'd better. If he doesn't, we'll come back and finish the job."

"He'll call! He'll definitely call! He wants the item badly!"

The voice paused. "What aren't you telling us?"

"What?" Keller asked, confused.

"You're hiding something from us. What is it?"

Keller shook his head furiously. "Nothing! I swear on my life!"

"That's exactly what you're doing!"

Keller's eyes widened. "I swear, there's nothing else. You know everything!"

"If you're lying, you'll see us again real soon. Do you understand?"

Keller nodded, terrified of that possibility.

"Time to go," his partner whispered. "The camera's in place."

"Good," the voice said. "Cut him free so we can leave."

"Camera?" Keller asked. "What camera?"

The voice explained the device as his partner worked on Keller's hands. "We've placed a wireless camera in your room. It is very small but very powerful. It works in darkness and in light. Our associate will be monitoring the feed from nearby. Until midnight tonight, you are to remain in this room at all times. If you leave, he will visit you. If you call or signal for help, he will visit you. If you do anything to piss him off, he will visit you. And trust me, that is something you do not want. We are gentle compared to him. Do you understand?"

"I understand, but . . ."

"But *what?*" the voice growled.

"What if I have to use the bathroom?"

"You already pissed the bed. One more time won't hurt it."

PAYNE AND JONES CREPT through the woods near Keller's house. They had managed to get him to talk without roughing him up or threatening specific acts of violence. They might have insinuated it, but the threats had not been defined. They threatened "to return" or "pay him a visit," instead of saying they were going to kill him. Early on, they even promised he *wouldn't* be hurt if he told the truth, yet they never said they would hurt him if he had lied.

It was a fine line, but they did their best not to cross it.

In reality, even if they had roughed him up a little bit, it would have been understandable. Criminals were trying to kill them, and Keller had stolen an item from them that might help solve their problems. Of course, they wouldn't fully understand the item's significance until they reached the SUV, which had been parked a quarter mile away. Megan and Ulster were patiently waiting for them, not really sure what Payne and Jones had planned for Keller, although they had been promised he wouldn't be harmed. A promise the duo had kept.

As they slipped through the night, Payne cleared his throat. Disguising his voice for so long had made it sore. "Do you think he believed the stuff about the camera?"

Jones laughed. "Definitely! I bet he's shitting his bed right now. I'll be shocked if he calls the cops or tries to warn anyone. You bought us all the time we need."

"Did you like my questions about the Americans?"

"Those were sweet! There's no way he'll ever suspect it was us."

64

As the sun climbed above the Alps in the eastern sky, Payne and Jones decided a quick trip to Geneva made a lot more sense than a long drive to Zürich. Not only were they familiar with the airport, but Ulster had multiple connections at the facility, which would come in handy. With a few phone calls, they were given access to the same hangar as the day before. He also arranged a mid-morning charter flight to Ostend-Bruges International Airport.

One of the security guards at the hangar unlocked a small office. It resembled the one Payne and Jones had used at NASJRB Willow Grove. It was a windowless room with cinderblock walls that hadn't been painted in years. As far as they were concerned, it was perfect, because it gave them a chance to examine their recent acquisition in private.

To protect the document, Ulster waited to unveil it

in a semicontrolled environment instead of a moving
SUV. He was worried the cold air coupled with the warm
heater might create enough condensation to damage the
parchment. Ideally, he had hoped to examine it at one of
his document vaults at the Archives, but he realized they
didn't have that kind of time. Payne and Jones wanted to
know what it said before they left for Belgium.

Keller had stored the document in a plastic case that
was roughly the same size as a laptop computer. The case
had been sealed in several layers of bubble wrap, similar
to how Keller had wrapped the puzzle box. Thankfully,
this time Ulster was willing to open it with a knife, since
the parchment was safely ensconced in hard plastic. Once
he had sliced through the wrapping, he placed the case
on the desk and opened it like a book.

A single sheet of parchment had been sealed inside a
clear plastic sleeve. Although it was designed to hold an
oversize photograph, it was large enough to house the
document.

"What's it say?" Megan asked as she peeked over
Ulster's shoulder.

From his seat at the desk, he glanced back at her.
"Patience, my dear. Give me a chance to read it first."

She blushed slightly. "Sorry."

Payne and Jones smiled from the other side of the
desk. They, too, were anxious to hear the translation,
but they knew she had a lot more to gain than they
did. Whatever people had been killed for—whether it
was the puzzle box, the new document, or some yet-to-

be-discovered fortune—probably belonged to Megan. And since the initial letter had already mentioned her by name, there was no telling what this one might say. Maybe it even revealed her future.

"Good news," Ulster said as he scanned the four lines of text. They had been written in ink in the center of the page. "This quatrain is Middle French, not a series of ancient languages. Give me a moment or two, and I should be able to translate it."

"Is it the same handwriting as before?" Jones asked.

"To the naked eye, it appears so. Of course, we won't know for sure until I take it back to the Archives and put it through its paces. But give me a moment, and I shall know more."

While they waited for the translation, Megan played with the puzzle box, testing the combination Keller had revealed to Payne and Jones. She entered 7, 2, 15, 66— the date of Nostradamus's death—and a secret panel opened inside the center compartment.

"Pretty cool," Payne admitted.

Megan smiled. "It would have been even cooler if the parchment was still inside, but I guess I shouldn't complain. Thanks to you guys, we have it in our possession."

"Speaking of the parchment, how's it coming?" Jones asked.

Ulster didn't even hear the question. He was too focused on the document itself. Every once in a while he grunted with surprise, but at no point during the process did he actually say a word. After that, neither did anyone else. The last thing they wanted to do was ruin his concentration.

Nearly five minutes passed before he translated the final word.

"Goodness," Ulster muttered as he read the translation to himself.

"What is it?" Megan demanded. She moved around the front of the desk so she could stand next to Payne. "Does it mention me?"

Ulster nodded, still not ready to speak.

She grabbed Payne's arm. "Oh, God. Is it bad?"

"Honestly, I'm not certain . . . But it *is* surprising."

Payne stared at him, trying to figure out why someone who rarely shut up was suddenly at a loss for words. Whatever it was, it had to be monumental. "What's surprising?"

"The quatrain," he stammered. "Megan's not the only one mentioned."

The comment intrigued Payne. "What do you mean? Who else is mentioned?"

Ulster looked him in the eye. "You."

Payne blinked a few times. "Excuse me?"

"You *and* David. Both of you are mentioned."

"It mentions our names?"

"No, but I'm fairly sure he's describing you."

"Read it," Jones ordered, suddenly excited.

Payne nodded in agreement. "Read it."

Ulster glanced at the paper and read it aloud. Although the quatrain had been written in Middle French, the English translation followed the same rhyming scheme as Megan's letter:

The fortune belongs to my heir,
Who will be chased 'til out of breath.
Hidden in ink inside his lair,
Where black and white shall conquer Death.

As soon as Ulster was done, he handed the paper to Payne so he could examine the translation in closer detail. Megan and Jones leaned in next to him and read it at the same time.

Several seconds later, Jones made the first comment. "Now *that* is some freaky shit. I'm talking Merlin the Magician, Wicked Witch of the West kind of—"

"Enough," Payne said, cutting him off. "We get your point."

"Good! Because that shit is freaky."

Megan smiled at Payne. "You have to admit, this verse is rather specific. You guys *are* black and white, and you're flying to Bruges to find Frankie Death."

"And apparently we're going to kill the bastard," Jones added.

"Sure," Payne said, "that's *one* interpretation. But there's another."

Jones snatched the paper from Payne's grasp. "If we're going to die, I *don't* want to know. I want it to be a secret. Like a gift from Santa."

"Actually," Payne said, "the other interpretation has nothing to do with us. It has to do with a book."

Ulster stared at him. "A book?"

Payne grabbed the paper and handed it back to Ulster. "Read line three."

He did as he was told. "*Hidden in ink inside his lair.*"

"Didn't you tell us that Nostradamus might have been working on a book of prophecies before he died? Some kind of journal?"

Ulster nodded. "I read several rumors about it. Nothing certain, but a lot of speculation."

"And if he wrote it in ink, wouldn't it be in *black and white*?"

"I guess it would, but—"

Payne continued, "And if someone finds it and reads his words after all this time, wouldn't his journal be beating death? After all, Nostradamus has been dead for several centuries."

Ulster groaned. "I suppose so, yes."

"What about the first two lines? Are they about me?" Megan wondered.

Payne shrugged. "Maybe. Of course, we still don't have any proof that you're related to Nostradamus. Despite the letter you received, we don't have any verification that he's actually talking about you. Maybe he is, maybe he isn't. But as I've said all along, that's the beauty of Nostradamus. *Everything* is ambiguous."

"I have to admit, I'm kind of relieved. When I read that *out of breath* part, I thought it meant I was going to die."

Jones grinned. "I thought you were a goner for sure."

Payne shook his head. "Even if she *is* the heir, it simply might mean that people will always be chasing her, trying to get an interview or trying to borrow money."

"Which brings us to the fortune," Jones said.

"What about it?"

"It's been mentioned more than once."

"True," Payne said, "but something dawned on me while I was reading this poem. What if the fortune *isn't* monetary? After all, Petr told us that Nostradamus wasn't a wealthy man. So maybe he's not talking about money. Maybe he's talking about the type of fortune that he was known for. Maybe he's leaving his heir information about the future."

"Oh," Megan muttered, disappointed. "Maybe he's right."

"Or maybe I'm wrong," Payne admitted. "For all I know, Nostradamus might have been talking about a giant treasure in your future, and he might have been talking about D.J. and me killing Frankie Death. Or maybe we're just seeing things in his words that aren't really there. The truth is we don't know what's going to happen—who's going to live and who's going to die. For that reason alone, I need to approach this thing like any other mission."

"Meaning?"

He stared at Megan. "I'm sending you and Petr to the Archives."

"The hell you are!" she argued.

"I don't care what you say or how loud you scream," he said in a calm tone. "You are *not* coming with us to Belgium."

"But this is my fight, too!"

He shook his head, resolute. "You didn't start this fight, and you're not going to finish it. Right now the only thing I care about is our survival. Hell, I don't care if you ever talk to me again. I just want you to live long enough to make that decision when all of this is done."

She glanced at Ulster, looking for support. "And you're okay with this?"

Ulster nodded. "More than okay. In fact, I fully support it. Trust me, my dear, the Archives are a tad more comfortable than that vault at Sotheby's. Remember how dreadful that was? Although I admire your spunk, I think it's time for us to step aside. While the boys are in Bruges, we can make a large contribution in Küsendorf."

"Doing what?"

"Research, my dear, research! Obviously, we still need to authenticate your letter. And the puzzle box must be examined in much greater detail. Of course, there's also the matter of your family tree. I have some wonderful new software that will aid our search. Simply type in what you know, and we can follow the leaves and branches back to your roots. I promise, my dear, it will be time well spent. And it might help us understand how you're connected to Nostradamus."

65

Ostend, Belgium

(16 miles west of Bruges)

Located near the Belgian coast in the Flemish province of West Flanders, the Ostend-Bruges International Airport is a small facility that mostly handles charter and cargo flights. Because of a scarcity of passengers, the terminal's security was typically a rubber-stamp procedure. Customs officials checked passports and cargo manifests, but if everything appeared to be in order, people and crates were cleared without much hassle.

Payne and Jones weren't worried about their identifications. They had fake passports with fake names, which had been made by the Pentagon. However, they were concerned with the cargo they were bringing into the country. Before Ulster's security staff picked up Megan and Ulster and took them to the Archives, they filled a wooden crate with guns and supplies and loaded it onto the plane. The guards covered the crate in stickers that read: FRAGILE—ARTIFACTS. They also printed a fake manifest, listing a number of items that were supposedly on their way to a private collector in Bruges. Of course, none of the items were actually in the crate, but thanks to their alleged fragility, they made it through customs without a thorough inspection.

Guards were afraid of breaking priceless relics.

A cargo van and additional supplies, arranged by Ulster, were waiting for Payne and Jones when they arrived. They loaded the crate into the back, then pulled through the main gate of the terminal. It was early afternoon, and Bruges was less than thirty minutes away.

They had plenty of time to prepare for their mission.

Days in Belgium are quite short in mid-December. The sun doesn't rise until after eight thirty a.m., and it sets well before five p.m. That gave Payne and Jones more than two hours of darkness to play with. Two hours to survey Château Dubois and search for guards before Keller would be called at seven p.m. After that, they would use the element of surprise to gain the upper hand.

For two ex-MANIACs, home-field advantage made little difference.

While flying to Bruges, the duo had studied photographs of Dubois, blueprints of his house, and a topographical map of the terrain—all provided by Randy Raskin. He had even been willing to give them access to a live aerial feed from one of the military's reconnaissance satellites, but they had politely refused, not wanting to bring any unnecessary attention to their operation.

Wearing dark clothes, Payne and Jones parked the van in the nearby woods and hiked a half mile to the edge of Dubois's property. His fourteenth-century castle sat in the middle of several acres of land, most of which was overgrown with trees and brush. In the summertime, when everything was in bloom, passage would have been difficult without a machete. But in the wintry cold, the trees were bare and vegetation was at a minimum. The only thing slowing them down was the snow on the ground and their desire for stealth.

Built from red brick that had faded over the years, Château Dubois was an impressive medieval structure. Standing four stories tall with spires that climbed even higher, the peaked roof was lined with gray tiles that appeared pale green in certain light. But under the cover of darkness, the roof couldn't be seen from the ground. The castle seemed to stretch from the snow-covered lawn up into the clouds, like something out of a fairy tale.

It was unlike any building they had scouted before.

Due to the early hour, the château's security system had not been activated and wouldn't be until after ten. There were too many people (Dubois's personal chef, his butler, and his cleaning staff) working inside for alarms or motion sensors. A few armed guards patrolled the outer perimeter and another was stationed at the front gate; otherwise, Dubois had very little protection. His reputation as a cold-blooded killer was what kept rivals at bay.

Fear was a far more effective deterrent than a barbed-wire fence.

Payne and Jones crept around the castle's periphery, searching for cameras or dogs or anything that might be a threat, but the only thing they saw was the bastard who had tried to kill them. Dubois was sitting in his library, reading a book near a roaring fire. He was smaller and more civilized than Payne had imagined. For some reason, he had pictured the devil incarnate—blood dripping from his fangs, horns thrusting out of his skull. Instead, he saw a well-dressed man who resembled half the men at his charity function at the Cathedral of Learning.

Dubois looked more like a CEO than a crime lord.

However, years of training had taught Payne never to be fooled by appearances. During his time in the MANIACs, he had seen baby carriages filled with bombs and kids carrying automatic weapons. He had witnessed terrorists dressed as holy men and monks strapped with homemade explosives. Payne had even read a story about a war criminal getting arrested in Miami while wearing a bathing suit and flip-flops. The guy had slaughtered thousands of Jews in a Nazi concentration camp and had never been caught. Ironically, he got busted stealing a corned beef sandwich at a local delicatessen. Not surprisingly, the Jewish owner showed no sympathy and decided to press charges.

Simply put, there was no way in hell Dubois's fancy clothes and upper-crust ways were going to conceal the type of man he was. Nor would it prevent Payne and Jones from doing what they needed to do. The truth was they weren't there to kill Dubois in cold blood. If they had been, they could have shot him through the bay window and scurried away before they were even spotted. Instead, they were there to negotiate with Dubois. To talk some sense into him. To help him understand the error of his ways. But if he objected, and they were certain he would, they were more than willing to fight for their lives.

BY SIX FIFTY-FIVE P.M., Payne was back at the van, checking his equipment and going over last-minute details with Jones via a flesh-colored earpiece that he concealed in his ear. Each of them knew what they needed to do, and both men were confident they would survive. Otherwise, they would have come up with a better plan.

The call came at precisely seven p.m. Payne let it ring a few times before he answered Keller's phone. When he did, there was no pretending. He didn't disguise his voice or claim to be someone else. For their plan to work, Dubois needed to know whom he was dealing with and what they were capable of doing.

"Hello," Payne said.

Dubois paused for a moment. "To whom am I speaking?"

"The man you've been trying to kill."

Dubois smiled. "You'll have to be more specific."

Payne pressed on. "I take it this is Frankie Death."

"Please, call me François."

"Sure thing, Frankie."

"Ah, one of the Americans," Dubois said smugly. "As crass as I had expected."

"Crass, yet well informed. How's that book you've been reading? You seemed pretty engrossed when I was watching you in your library. That fire looked mighty toasty."

Dubois cleared his throat, slightly unnerved. "Are you watching me now? How many fingers am I holding up?"

"I'll answer your question if you can guess *which* finger I'm holding up."

"The vulgarity continues."

"What can I say? When a man tries to kill me, I get slightly pissed."

"Touché."

"So," Payne said, "what do you want? Remember, you called me."

"Actually, I rang Monsieur Keller, not you. But why quibble over details? Since you have his phone, I will assume you also possess his artifacts."

"Wow. That's pretty impressive. Are you psychic or something?"

Dubois ignored the sarcasm. "If you have the items in your possession, I would love to view them. Can I interest you in a meeting?"

"We didn't come to Bruges for Brussels sprouts."

"Shall we say my château in twenty minutes?"

"Sorry, Frankie, my snipers are getting cold. Let's make it your château in twenty seconds. In fact, I'm pulling up to your gate as we speak."

66

After receiving instructions from Dubois, the guard at the front gate didn't talk to Payne or search him for weapons. He simply opened the gate and waved him through.

Payne wasn't the least bit surprised. He had dealt with men like Dubois before. Whether it was hubris or lunacy, they falsely believed they couldn't be caught or conquered. They felt their intellect, or their strength, or their personal god would help them overcome every obstacle they encountered, and in the end, they would emerge unscathed.

Payne's goal was to make sure that didn't happen.

As he drove the van along the stone driveway, he spotted Dubois on the steps outside the main entrance to the château. Dubois was simply standing there, waiting for his arrival. He even gave Payne a friendly wave, as if they were long-lost friends who were about to catch up over cocktails. But Payne ignored him. He was far too occupied with the positioning of the van.

Driving ten feet past Dubois, he shifted into reverse, and then backed up to the bottom of the steps. Payne glanced at his side-view mirrors to make sure he was where he needed to be and saw Dubois's face bathed in the taillights. The arrogant bastard even moved a few steps closer, drawn by the objects that had been promised to him. Payne shook his head in frustration. If he had been a merciless killer, he would have tramped on the gas and hit Dubois with the van. It would have been so easy to do. There would have been a *thump*, followed by a scream. After that, Dubois would be out of their lives forever.

Unfortunately, Payne's conscience prevented him from doing it.

He was more than willing to kill, but not without provocation.

Some people might argue that Dubois *had* provoked him by sending assassins to Pittsburgh, Philadelphia, and Geneva. However, as far as Payne could tell, those men had been sent to retrieve the Nostradamus artifacts, not to kill him specifically. Obviously, they had been told to eliminate everyone who got in their way, but Payne had no proof that his life (or his friends' lives) would be in danger *after* Dubois acquired the items he wanted. In fact, if the meeting Dubois had arranged with Keller was any indication, he was prepared to purchase the artifacts for a fair price, if given the opportunity. Otherwise, Dubois would have sent a hit squad to Lausanne to kill

Keller and retrieve the puzzle box without giving him a cent.

At least, that was the way it seemed to Payne.

Before he was willing to kill a man he had never met, he needed to look him in the eye and decide whether or not they could come to an agreement. If they could, that was great. Payne and his friends could walk away feeling safe, and they would happily allow Nick Dial and his team at Interpol to build a case to put Dubois away for the rest of his life—using the gunman they had captured as a witness. On the other hand, if they couldn't come to an understanding, Payne would do whatever he needed to do to protect the people he cared about.

All he needed was five minutes alone with Dubois.

After that, he would know how this would end.

DUBOIS STUDIED Payne as he opened the van door and climbed out. The first thing he noticed was Payne's size. He was much larger than the Frenchman had expected. But that wasn't the only thing that stood out. Payne was wearing a wool cap that covered his ears, dark clothes, and mud-splattered boots. That told Dubois he had been doing *something* in the nearby field. Maybe it was advanced surveillance, or maybe he had been eliminating the château's guards, one by one.

Either way, Dubois realized Payne was a worthy adversary.

"Welcome to my home," he said in a friendly tone.

"One of many, I must admit, but certainly my favorite. Any trouble finding it?"

"No trouble at all. The satellite knew exactly where to look."

"Come now, Mr. Payne. There's no need to threaten me with snipers and satellites. By now, I am fully aware of your military background. I am also aware of your personal wealth. A man who can't be fought or bought is a rare man indeed."

"Apparently, we have that in common."

Dubois placed his hand on his heart and bowed slightly. "Finally, a kind word. Perhaps we won't be enemies after all."

"Perhaps."

"So," Dubois said, "what have you brought for me today? May I take a look?"

Payne nodded. "Of course."

Dubois opened the cargo doors and stared at a slatted wooden crate in the back of the van. Made out of pine, it was twenty-four inches long, ten inches wide, and ten inches deep. A box, wrapped in several layers of bubble wrap, sat inside the crate.

Smiling at the possibilities, Dubois noticed a plastic pouch attached to one of the front slats. He peeled it open and pulled out the shipping manifest that had been stamped at the airport. He held it up to the light, his eyes scanning the document. The puzzle box was listed first, followed by two carrying cases that contained "miscellaneous parchments."

Payne said, "I won't even pretend to be an expert like

you, but I was warned we shouldn't open this stuff in the cold. Something about permanent damage."

Dubois nodded, never taking his eyes off the crate. "That is correct. The elements have ruined their fair share of antiquities over the centuries, which is why I keep mine in an optimal environment. If I may be so bold, may I offer a temporary solution to our problem?"

"I'm listening."

"Instead of leaving the artifacts in the cold while we conduct our business in the warmth of my château, perhaps we can bring the crate with us?"

"I don't know about that."

"Obviously, we won't carry it *ourselves*. A member of my staff will do that for us."

Payne paused, pretending to give it some thought. "Fine, I'm willing to allow it under two conditions. Number one, the crate *never* leaves my sight. I go wherever it goes."

"Of course," Dubois said, "I wouldn't have it any other way. And number two?"

"We conduct our business in your library."

Dubois raised an eyebrow. "That can be arranged, but why there?"

Payne smiled. "As you know, that's one room I've already scouted."

DESPITE HIS aversion to the cold, Jones lay on a blanket in the snow, staring through the scope of an M24 sniper rifle. Dead brush and leaves concealed his position on the outer edge of Dubois's property, where he was just beyond the reach of the château's outdoor lights. An earpiece, similar to the one that Payne was wearing, allowed him to listen to Payne's conversation with Dubois. And if the situation required it, he could also speak to Payne.

Jones watched in silence as members of Dubois's staff carried the crate up the steps and into the château. As Payne and the others walked through the hallways of the massive home, they were temporarily out of view. But Payne did his best to inform Jones about the layout of the château by making casual conversation with Dubois, asking him about certain rooms and pointing out anything that had been modified from the blueprints.

Jones, who had trained at the U.S. Army Sniper School at Fort Benning, slowly inched his rifle to the right, waiting to reacquire his target through the library's window. Less than a minute later, Dubois's head was once again in his crosshairs, where it would remain at all times.

Although Jones had been an "average" sniper in the military—mostly because his appointment to the MANI-ACs had limited his advanced training—it still meant he was one of the best in the world. That's how deadly American snipers are. According to figures released by the U.S. Department of Defense, the average number of rounds fired in the Vietnam War to kill one enemy soldier with an M16 was 50,000. The average number of rounds fired by U.S. snipers to kill one enemy soldier was a staggering 1.3 rounds. That's a cost difference of

$23,000 per kill for the average soldier versus $0.17 per kill for the military sniper.

Nowadays, American weaponry is much more advanced than it had been in Vietnam, but the current figures are still shocking. According to the U.S. Army, the average soldier will hit a man-size target ten percent of the time at three hundred meters using the M16A2 rifle. Graduates of the U.S. Army Sniper School are expected to achieve ninety percent first-round hits at six hundred meters, using the M24 sniper rifle—the weapon that Ulster had acquired in Geneva for a small fortune.

To Payne and Jones, the rifle was worth every penny.

From where Jones was currently positioned, less than two hundred meters away with virtually no wind to speak of, the odds of him missing were about the same as hitting the lottery.

It *could* happen, but Payne was willing to bet his life that it wouldn't.

67

Dubois's butler placed the crate on a table in the middle of the library and then waited for further instructions.

"You may leave us," Dubois said dismissively.

"And close the door on your way out," Payne added.

Unsure of what to do, the butler looked to Dubois for permission.

"Hey," Payne said, goading his host, "I had the balls to come to Bruges. The *least* you can do is talk to me in private."

Dubois smirked at his guest and then nodded his consent. A few seconds later, the door was pulled shut with a soft *click*. The two men were finally alone, just as Payne had wanted. Knowing full well that Jones would watch his back, Payne turned away from Dubois and admired the leather-bound books that lined the shelves. Most of them had been written in French, but a few foreign titles were sprinkled in. A German book named *Arcanum* caught Payne's eye. He picked it up and thumbed through the pages.

"So," Dubois asked, "is this when you try to kill me?"

Payne laughed. "Trust me, Frankie. If I wanted you dead, you'd be dead."

"Perhaps. Of course, you realize the same applies to you."

Payne smiled and returned the book to the shelf. "Are you sure about that? It seems the first fifteen guys you sent weren't very effective."

Dubois waved off the comment. "Merely pawns in the grand scheme of things. Although not lethal, they were quite effective in some ways."

"Really? How do you figure?"

"Well, you are here with the artifacts. Ultimately, that is all I cared about."

Payne turned and looked Dubois in the eye. He needed to size him up. "I kind of figured as much. Meanwhile, my agenda is a lot less materialistic than yours. I'm here to talk about our personal safety. Are you familiar with the concept of MAD?"

Dubois furrowed his brow. "I'm afraid I am not."

"It stands for mutual assured destruction. It's a military doctrine that was developed during the Cold War. Simply put, it means when two adversaries have reached a certain level of strength—for instance, they each possess nuclear weapons—there can be no winner if they go to war. Damage would be so severe that both sides would lose, no matter what."

Dubois nodded in understanding. "This is a term I did not know, but one I shall remember. You are America, and I am France. We should not fight."

"Exactly."

"In my country, we would call this *détente*. Do you know this word?"

"Actually, I do."

Dubois smiled. "We were at war. Now we're at peace. This is reason to celebrate."

"I don't know about that."

Dubois ignored the comment. "Are you a connoisseur, Mr. Payne? My cellar is filled with some of the finest wines that money can buy—and a few that money can't. Shall I send for a bottle?"

"I appreciate the offer, but there's still business to be discussed."

"Ah, yes, the quaint American tradition of *not* mixing business with pleasure. I don't know whether to applaud or complain. Perhaps some other time then."

Payne walked along the shelves, looking at relics. "Perhaps."

Dubois watched him as he moved about the room. The entire time, he searched for weaknesses that could be exploited. "Tell me, do you have an interest in antiquities?"

"I didn't until recently. But the last few years have opened my eyes to ancient cultures. Slowly but surely, my interest is starting to grow."

"I read about your discovery in Greece. Well done."

Payne smiled. "And I heard about your obsession with Nostradamus."

"*Obsession* is too strong a word. I think *curiosity* would be sufficient."

Payne stopped and turned. "Come on, Frankie, don't downplay your fixation on my account. A man who merely has curiosity wouldn't go to such lengths to add to his collection."

"Perhaps not."

"Speaking of which, I have to admit I'm kind of disappointed. I was fully expecting to see your collection on display. That was one of the reasons I was willing to fly to Bruges. I've heard amazing things about the items you've assembled."

Dubois stared at him, trying to determine if Payne was being sarcastic. "If your interest is sincere, I will happily appease your curiosity. If not, I'd rather not waste our time."

Payne raised his right hand. "Honest, François, I'd love to see it."

A smile crossed Dubois's face. "In that case, it would be an honor."

JONES PRIDED himself on many things, and multitasking was one of them. Whether it was shaving while driving or downloading music while answering e-mail, he had the ability to do two things at once without a drop in performance. Therefore, when his phone started to vibrate in his pocket, he didn't hesitate to answer it even though he was staring through his scope at his target. He simply hit the mute button on his earpiece, which prevented Payne from hearing what he was about to say—but still allowed Jones to listen to Payne and Dubois.

"Hello," he whispered, not bothering to look at the caller ID.

"Mr. Jones, this is Butch Reed calling. Did I catch you at a bad time?"

Reed was head of security at Payne Industries. An ex-Marine who had lost a foot in the Gulf War, he had been hired by Payne's grandfather as a security guard and quickly moved up the ranks, impressing everyone with his intelligence and work ethic. Now he was in charge of all security matters, including personal protection for Payne and Jones. Whenever they were away on business or were working with the military on a classified project, Reed kept an eye on things.

"Kind of," Jones whispered. "Can I call you later?"

"Actually, sir, this can't wait. It involves your safety and potentially Mr. Payne's."

"Go on."

"I'm afraid I've got bad news, sir. Someone tried to burn down your house."

Jones blinked, suddenly distracted. "My house?"

"The blaze has been contained, but I'd estimate the damage at sixty percent. It would have been worse if not for the snow. As it melted, it helped put out the flames."

Jones took a deep breath, trying to keep his emotions in check. "Arson?"

"Yes, sir. Someone threw a Molotov cocktail through your front window, according to a neighbor. By the time the authorities arrived, the man was long gone."

Jones connected the dots in his head. To him, there was no doubt who was responsible. Just as Dial had warned, Dubois wouldn't stop. No matter what.

"Sir," Reed continued, "please tell Mr. Payne that I've tripled the guards at his home. I tried his cell phone, but it goes straight to voice mail. Have him call me if he has any questions."

"His phone is broken, but I'll tell him. You better believe I'll tell him."

Reed heard the anger in his voice. It was a tone he had never heard from Jones before and one he hoped to never hear again. "Be careful, sir."

"Fuck careful," Jones snapped as he hung up the phone.

WALKING TOWARD his fireplace, Dubois pointed to the elaborate mantel that surrounded the roaring fire. Made out of gray stone, it was intricately carved and featured knights on horseback battling dragons of all shapes and sizes. "Are you familiar with medieval architecture? Many artisans, particularly those from the lower class, had a fascination with mythical creatures. Some of their pieces I find primitive and rather distasteful, but this one I enjoy. Notice the repetition of triangles on the rim of the fireplace. It represents the teeth of the dragon."

"I like it," Payne admitted. "I've always liked dragons."

Dubois smiled. "And I've always liked fire."

"As fascinating as that might be, what does it have to do with Nostradamus?"

"Like the prophet himself, I am someone who values secrecy, which is one of the reasons I fell in love with this château. Hidden among its walls are dozens of corridors and chambers that protect my most precious possessions. Including my collection."

Dubois placed his hand on the side of the mantel and pulled a latch that had been concealed by the stonework. As if by magic, the bookcase to the left of the fireplace swung away from the wall, revealing a secret passageway that wasn't in the blueprints.

"I call this room the Dragon's Lair."

68

P ayne couldn't believe his ears. Dubois had just referred to the secret room where he kept his collection as his *lair*. It was the same term Nostradamus had used in his quatrain. He claimed the book that belonged to his heir would be *hidden in ink inside his lair*.

That couldn't be a coincidence, could it?

Even a realist like Payne had to admit too many coincidences in a row meant something else was going on, something beyond his understanding of the world. He still wasn't ready to believe that Nostradamus had foreseen all the events of the past few days, but he was no longer willing to dismiss things quite as easily.

"After you," Dubois said with a slight bow.

"Sorry," Payne said as he grabbed the box from the crate, "my parents warned me about older men and secret rooms. That's why I wasn't an altar boy."

Dubois smirked at the vulgar joke and led the way into

the hidden chamber, pausing to flip a switch just inside the entryway. Suddenly, the entire room was bathed in soft light. Three of the walls were lined with shelves filled with books about Nostradamus and other famous prophets. Some of the volumes were centuries old, and others were more recent. But Payne barely noticed them. Instead, his gaze focused on the glass display case that had been mounted along the fourth wall, directly across from the lair's entrance. He set the box on a small table in the center of the room and then moved toward the case.

"Please take a closer look," Dubois encouraged.

Payne moved forward, searching for anything that resembled the object described in the third line of the quatrain. Of all the items, the most likely candidate seemed to be a leather-bound journal displayed in the very center of the case. "What's that?" he asked.

"*That* is the crown jewel of my collection. It is the earliest known edition of *Les Prophéties*, handwritten by Nostradamus himself. The first public installment was not published until 1555, a full two years after his last entry was dated."

"Wow, that must have cost you a lot."

"Actually," Dubois said as he backed away, "it didn't cost me a cent."

"How'd you manage that?"

"Quite simply, really. I took it."

"You took it?"

Dubois pulled a pistol from the small of his back. "Allow me to demonstrate."

Payne turned around slowly. He was fully expecting to see a gun in his rival's hand. "I admire your confidence, but that's not going to happen. You know, considering the circumstances."

"The circumstances? I'm not stupid, Mr. Payne. I'm fully aware that Mr. Jones is lurking in the darkness. Why do you think I pushed for this meeting to be held inside?"

"I thought maybe you wanted to cuddle."

Dubois couldn't help but smile. "Hardly. I did it so we could have a conversation without interlopers."

"And you think you're safer in here?"

"All the windows in my château are bulletproof. They were made by the same company that outfitted the White House. Sniper fire won't even leave a mark."

Payne shrugged. "Oh well, I guess we'll have to kill you some other way."

"I guess so. In the meantime, tell me about the girl."

"Sorry, you're not her type."

Dubois ignored him. "Why is she involved in this? What's her significance?"

"She has no significance," Payne lied. "The only reason she's involved is because your men killed her neighbor."

"Her neighbor was a *thief.*"

"Coming from a thief, is that a compliment or an insult?"

Dubois smirked at the comment. "I'm getting tired of your insults."

"Then why don't you come over here and do something about it?"

"There's no need, Mr. Payne. I can silence you from here."

A moment later, Dubois lifted his gun and fired.

———

JONES WAS on the move long before he heard the gunshot in his earpiece. In fact, he had abandoned his position in the yard as soon as he got off the phone with Butch Reed.

Dubois had burned down his house. The bastard needed to pay.

While hiding his sniper rifle in the brush, Jones told Payne what had happened and told him he was on his way to the château. It was the main reason that Payne had been willing to go inside the Dragon's Lair. He knew his backup would be there soon.

But not soon enough.

THE FIRST shot hit Payne squarely in the chest, catching him by surprise and knocking him off balance. But that wasn't good enough for Dubois, who fired two more times at close range. The second shot struck Payne in his abdomen, and the third tore through his left trapezius, just missing the arteries in his neck. The bullet, after passing through skin and muscle, shattered the display case behind him and embedded itself in the stone wall.

Payne slumped to the floor, stunned. Blood leaked from his wounds as shards of broken glass fell upon him, cutting his hands and face.

Wasting no time, Dubois reached into his pocket and pulled out a *chatellerault*—an antique French switchblade with a distinctive S-shaped cross guard. With a skilled hand, Dubois flicked it open and plunged its tip into the bubble wrap that protected the package. Payne, who had been paranoid about leaving it in the library, had been kind enough to carry it inside the lair. Now the last image he would see before he bled to death would be his rival opening the box.

Dubois grinned at the thought.

And from the floor, Payne grinned as well.

The instant Dubois cracked the inner seal of the package, a large ball of flames erupted in his face, catching his hair, skin, and clothes on fire. The homemade explosive, which had been rigged by Jones in the back of the van, was their insurance policy in case something happened to them before they confronted Dubois. They figured if they were dead, it was the only way they could stop Dubois from killing Megan and Ulster.

Dubois howled in agony as his skin blistered and bubbled like cheese on a pizza. He tried in vain to smother the flames by dropping to the floor and rolling around, but all that did was spread the fire. In a flash, one of his bookcases ignited, filling the room with thick, noxious smoke that blinded Payne and made it impossible to breathe.

Alive because of his Kevlar vest, Payne reached his right arm over his head and snatched the edition of *Les Prophéties* from the shattered case. The blood from his wounds stained the book's cover as he pulled it against his chest and started crawling toward the doorway. Choking on the fumes and coughing loudly, Payne moved closer to the exit he couldn't see. It was up ahead *somewhere*—that's all he knew. And if he didn't reach it soon, he would be burned inside the Dragon's Lair.

Suddenly, from the darkness behind him, Payne felt a bony hand brushing against his lower leg. At first it felt like a dog nipping at his heel, but it quickly turned into a hound from hell as Dubois latched onto Payne's foot with all the strength he could muster. The flammable fluid that had ignited the blaze quickly spread from Dubois to Payne's clothes. Seconds later, his lower leg was engulfed in flames.

"Jon!" Jones screamed as he burst into the library.

"In here!"

Jones ran toward the sound as Payne rolled over and kicked Dubois several times, trying to free himself.

"Where are you?" Jones demanded.

"He's got my leg!"

As flames climbed the walls and ignited the ceiling above, Jones dove into the room and crawled toward the screams of his best friend. He blindly grabbed the first thing he could find, which happened to be Payne's left arm, and pulled it with all his might. The sudden force freed Payne's foot from Dubois's grasp. It also saved his life.

Lightning bolts of pain shot through his ruptured trapezius as Jones dragged him out of the lair and into the fresh air of the library. But Payne's agony paled in comparison to Dubois's as the bastard burned to a crisp alongside his prized collection.

Ironically, his search for the future had ended his own.

69

During the long drive to Küsendorf, Megan had pondered everything that had happened over the past seventy-two hours. Prior to Sunday night, she had never heard of Payne and Jones, had never been to Europe, and knew very little about Nostradamus. Now the ex-MANIACs were risking their lives to save hers, she had been smuggled to the Ulster Archives in the Swiss Alps, and she found out she might be a blood relative of the famous prophet.

Other than that, it had been an uneventful three days.

After unpacking her suitcase and showering, Megan changed into a clean pair of jeans and a sweater. She didn't know how long she would be sequestered at the Archives, but as Ulster had promised back in Geneva, her stay wouldn't be uncomfortable—not with a gourmet kitchen, a private suite, and one of the best research libraries in the world. While she was there, she fully intended to do her part, whether that was running errands, cooking meals, or researching her family tree. Obviously, she didn't have the academic background to translate ancient texts or to carbon-date the parchments, but she wasn't the type to sit around all day. Having lost her parents at such an early age, Megan had developed an extraordinary work ethic. Not only to impress the various foster families she had lived with, but to learn as much as possible before she was forced to live on her own.

With an hour to kill before dinner, she got permission from Ulster to examine the puzzle box in one of the research labs. After lining the table with a sterile sheet of plastic laminate, he placed the box on a soft cloth to protect it. Then he gave her a pair of latex gloves to reduce the fingerprints and oil residue on the wood.

"Tell me, my dear, why the sudden urgency? As I mentioned earlier, there will be plenty of time to inspect the box after dessert."

"Call me crazy," she said, "but a theory popped into my head while I was in the shower. And I didn't want to wait half the night before I tested it."

"What type of theory?"

"While turning the knobs for hot and cold water, I started thinking about the dials on the puzzle box. There are four dials in total, right?"

Ulster nodded. "And each of them has three numbers."

"Exactly! But so far we've only discovered *two* combinations. The date that Nostradamus died and the date that Louis Keller was supposed to open the box."

"July second of 1566 and December first of this year."

She smiled, glad that he was following along. "That means eight of the twelve numbers have been used in the two combinations."

He did the math in his head. "Two numbers on four dials for a total of eight."

"And unless I'm mistaken, none of the numbers were used twice. That leaves one number on each of the four dials that has *not* been used."

"Good heavens! I think you're right."

"Considering the events of the past few days, I figured it was worth checking out."

Ulster grinned and patted his stomach. "As far as I'm concerned, dinner can wait!"

"I was hoping you'd say that."

"So," he said excitedly, "do you know the combination? I'm embarrassed to admit this, but I can't remember the four unused digits."

She smiled sheepishly. "Neither could I."

"No worries, my dear, we'll simply use the process of elimination to figure it out."

Megan nodded and placed her gloved hand on the first corner. She twisted it slowly, careful not to break it. "The choices are three, seven, and twelve."

"Seven represents July, the month that Nostradamus died. And twelve represents December."

She twisted the knob to three. "That leaves March."

"Beware the ides of March," Ulster whispered.

"Pardon me?"

"Sorry, my dear, it's a line from Shakespeare. Julius Caesar was told to *beware the ides of March*. Later, he was killed on that date."

"What date is that?"

"The ides of March—or *Idus Martias* in Latin— means March fifteenth."

She ignored the Latin and focused on the second knob. "Sorry, no fifteen. Our choices are one, two, and twenty-five."

"Nostradamus died on the second, so the two has been used. And Louis opened the box on the first. That leaves twenty-five."

Megan nodded and slowly turned the dial. As she did, the numbers clicked in place in her mind. "No way!" she shrieked.

Ulster flinched in his seat. "What's wrong?"

"The date! I know what it means!"

"Really?"

"It's March 25, 1982. I'm sure of it!"

He sat there, confused, trying to figure out its significance, wondering if it was historically significant in any way. "I don't get it, my dear. What happened on that date?"

She twisted the knobs into place. "It was the day I was born."

As if on cue, the puzzle box emitted a loud *pop*. A split second later, a three-inch square was ejected from the middle of the front panel. It fell onto the soft cloth directly in front of Megan. "Holy shit!"

Ulster's eyes widened while he leaned in for a closer look.

"There's something in there," she insisted. Her voice was calm, but her heart was nearly thumping out of her chest. "I think it's a folded parchment."

"Don't touch it! Please don't touch it!"

"Why not?"

He signaled for her to wait while he lumbered toward the cabinet on the far side of the room. He threw open the doors and retrieved a pair of long tweezers. "Please use these. They'll do far less damage than your fingers."

She smiled, thrilled that he would let her do the honors. When he had yelled for her to stop, she was afraid he was going to push her aside and take over.

"Thank you," she said.

"For what?"

"For letting me do this."

Ulster patted her on the shoulder and handed her the tweezers. "Considering the date of the combination, I believe you were *destined* to do this."

She shrugged. "I guess we'll find out soon enough."

With a gentle touch, she slid the tool inside the puzzle box and clamped onto one of the folded edges of the parchment. Then, ever so carefully, she pulled it toward her until it was free from the secret compartment. "Now what?" she asked.

"Place it on the table," Ulster whispered.

Her hand trembled slightly as she turned to her left and followed his instructions. As soon as she released the parchment, she breathed a huge sigh of relief. "How was that?"

"Perfect. Like a surgeon."

"I don't know about that, but thanks. So, what do we do now?"

"Now's the fun part. We get to open it."

"With what?"

"Your hands will suffice."

"No tweezers?"

"No, my dear. Those were simply to remove the parchment from its cramped quarters. Now that it's free, I believe your gloved fingers will pose less of a threat than a sharp tool."

"You're the expert," she said as she inched her chair to the left.

Using both of her hands, she unfolded the document once, then again, and then a third time. Finally, she could see words, and dates, and a bunch of straight lines. She unfolded it a fourth time, and then a fifth. Every time she did, it grew larger before her eyes. What had once fit inside a tiny space had grown to the size of a road map.

"Lay it flat, so we can read it," he urged.

With trembling hands, Megan laid it on the table, curious to find out what had been hidden for so long, anxious to find out why she had been selected to open the box.

The answer left both of them stunned.

EPILOGUE

SUNDAY, DECEMBER 20

Pittsburgh, Pennsylvania

Payne rested comfortably in the main conference room at the Payne Industries Building. His left arm was in a sling and his right foot was in a walking boot. It protected the gauze wrapped around his minor burns. His injuries would have been far worse if not for the Kevlar vest he had been wearing under his clothes at the château. Other than a few bruises, the gunshots to his chest and stomach had merely knocked the wind out of him. Four days later, the marks were a distant memory—like all the other times he had been shot in body armor.

"You ready?" Jones asked as he grabbed the remote control. "Because the Steelers game starts in two hours. We need to leave for the stadium soon."

Payne nodded. "I'm ready."

"No more missed games. I don't care about the hole in your neck."

"It's not my neck; it's my trapezius. And I said I'm ready."

Jones grinned. "It's about time."

With a touch of a button, he turned on the video camera and monitor that had been set up on the conference table. As the screen flickered on, thoughts of the previous Sunday flashed through their minds. It was hard for them to believe only one week had passed since their last videoconference with the Ulster Archives. Back then, they were trying to decipher the mysterious letter that Ashley had brought to the Cathedral of Learning. Now they were about to find out if the Nostradamus artifacts were authentic.

Adding to their déjà vu was the image that filled their screen. Ulster was sitting at the same antique desk as the last time. On the wall behind him was the same dry erase board, covered with many of the same notes, and a silver tray filled with several colors of markers. As far as they could tell, the only major difference was the number of people on the screen. Ulster was no longer alone. Now he was accompanied by Megan, who sat in a chair to his left.

Payne smiled as soon as he saw her. Although they had spoken on the phone the night before, this was the first time he had seen her since they had parted ways in Geneva.

"Good morning," he said into the camera.

"Good morning to you, too," she replied.

"Actually," Ulster said, "it's late afternoon over here, but we appreciate the sentiment. How are you feeling, Jonathon?"

Payne gently touched his shoulder with his opposite hand. "This sling is a pain in the butt. Thankfully, I'll be free from it soon."

"Thank God for that," Jones muttered.

"Do I detect some tension?" Ulster asked.

Jones nodded. "*Lots* of tension."

"Over what?"

Jones snarled at Payne, "I saved the guy's life, and how does he repay me? He makes me his friggin' butler."

"His butler? What do you mean?"

"As you know, my place is kind of crispy right now, so I needed somewhere to stay. Jon was kind enough to offer me a room in his mansion, but he didn't tell me about the catch. I've been his manservant for the past three days." He continued his rant in a mocking tone. *"I can't butter my toast! My foot needs ointment! Give me a sponge bath! I feel dirty!"*

Payne laughed at the claims. "I ask the guy to open one jar of pickles for me, and he hasn't shut up since. If he keeps this up, I'm going to smother him in his sleep."

"I can't hold the pillow. Please stop squirming!" Jones teased.

Payne rolled his eyes at his friend. "On that note, let's talk about something factual. I was intrigued by the trust fund at Credit Suisse—the one that paid for the safe-deposit box—so I had a computer researcher at the Pentagon do some checking for me. With his hacking skills, he managed to track down the name of the company in charge of the fund. Unfortunately, it wasn't a *real* company. It was a shell company with two mailbox offices."

"What does that mean?" she asked.

"Sometimes people set up fake companies for tax purposes. In this case, the offices were nothing more than mailboxes in Paris and Tokyo."

"Tokyo?"

He nodded. "That's where your mysterious letter was mailed from. We figured that out once we had a chance to examine the stamps and the postmark. They were Japanese."

"And," Jones added, "the business address in Paris is only a few miles from the airport. Remember, that's where the phone that sent you the text message was purchased. We don't know where any of this is going to lead, but we'll keep on looking. We hate loose ends."

"Me, too," she admitted. "Will you know something before I get to Pittsburgh?"

"You're coming to Pittsburgh?"

"Didn't Jon tell you? He invited me to his house for Christmas. Just the three of us."

"Thank God!" Jones blurted. "Now *you* can be in charge of his sponge bath."

Payne glared at him. "Why do you say stuff like that?"

"Because it's funny," Jones said, grinning.

"Anyway," Payne said, "where do we stand on the carbon dating?"

Ulster rejoined the conversation. "We have conclusive data on all the documents—except, of course, for the journal you acquired in Bruges. Due to its late arrival, we are still testing it."

"What do you know so far?" Jones asked.

"The letter mailed to Megan is authentic. So is the puzzle box, and all the documents found within its walls."

"Define *authentic*," Payne said.

"Carbon dating doesn't give us an exact date, per se. It simply gives us a time window of approximately fifty years. Everything that we've tested has fallen within the same period, sometime between A.D. 1540 and 1590."

Jones nodded. "In other words, the years surrounding Nostradamus's death."

"Precisely."

"What about the handwriting?" Payne wondered.

"We flew in an expert from France, who feels the writing on all the documents is a perfect match to the Nostradamus samples that have survived over the years. While he was here, I also had him peek at the journal, and he feels it's a perfect match as well."

"So," Jones said, "what's the consensus?"

"As far as the Archives are concerned, these documents *were* written by Nostradamus."

"Awesome!"

"Even the Birthday Tree?" Payne asked.

Megan smiled at the reference. "Yes, even that."

Ever since Payne had learned of the final parchment, he had referred to the document as the Birthday Tree. The nickname stuck because it perfectly summarized its contents.

To prove he wasn't a con artist who had capitalized on ambiguous quatrains, Nostradamus had created his family tree for dozens of future generations, starting with a son from his first wife—a child that most people believed had died from the plague. According to this document, that wasn't the case. The boy had survived and had been raised by his maternal grandparents, although Nostradamus didn't explain why. But he did provide the boy's name and the date every member of his bloodline would be born. The chart started with Nostradamus at the top and ran all the way to Megan Moore, who was his closest living descendant. Using Ulster's software, she had double-checked many names and birthdates, and so far Nostradamus had been remarkably accurate.

"Any thoughts on why the tree ended with you?"

"Who knows? Maybe I'm not going to have any kids."

"Actually," Ulster suggested, "I might have another possibility."

She looked at him, surprised. "You do?"

Ulster nodded. "While examining the Bruges journal, I started to ponder the significance of line three of the final quatrain. He claimed the fortune would be *hidden in ink inside his lair.*"

"And that's where I found it," Payne assured him.

"Actually, the phrase that caught my eye was *hidden in ink*. I figured, if he wrote secret instructions in UV ink on one of the parchments, what if he did the same thing in his journal? What if line three gave us the location of the item *and* told us what to do with it?"

Payne sat up in his chair, intrigued. "Go on."

"I tested my theory a few minutes ago, just before I made this call, and it appears I was correct. The journal is filled with notes, written in UV ink."

"Are you serious? Why didn't you tell me?" Megan demanded.

"I literally just found out, my dear. I figured I'd share it with everyone at once."

"And what did it say?" Payne asked.

Ulster smiled and looked into the camera. "It appears to be a prophecy."

AUTHOR'S NOTE

For those of you who have read my other novels, I'm sure you realize that I like to tackle controversial subjects in my writing. Whether it was racism in *The Plantation*, the history of Christianity in *Sign of the Cross*, or Islamic terrorists in *Sword of God*, I'm not afraid to put my head on the proverbial chopping block. (Actually, since the chopping block *is* the punishment for many Islamic terrorists, maybe that's a poor choice of metaphor.)

Anyway, my point is this: I'm not afraid of taking chances.

During the past year, while researching Nostradamus and his prophecies, I've encountered an equal number of believers and nonbelievers. Although their positions couldn't be further apart, both groups had one trait in common: They were passionate. Many praised my choice of topics, pleased that someone was writing a thriller about Nostradamus. Meanwhile, others were less than complimentary. The terms I heard most often were "crackpot" and "charlatan." I think they were talking about Nostradamus, but maybe they were talking about me!

Either way, I knew I had chosen wisely, because everyone had an opinion.

With that in mind, I did my best to stay neutral on the topic. I presented some of the best-known stories about Nostradamus and some of the lesser-known ones. And since *The Prophecy* is a novel, I also made up a bunch of stuff—although I'll never reveal what.

Ultimately, I wasn't trying to change your opinion about Nostradamus. My only goal was to entertain.

For additional information about my writing and answers to frequently asked questions, please visit my website: chriskuzneski.com.

And now a special excerpt from
Chris Kuzneski's next exciting novel

THE
SECRET CROWN

Coming soon in hardcover from
G. P. Putnam's Sons!

PROLOGUE

JUNE 13, 1886

Lake Starnberg
Berg, Bavaria

For years he had been paid to protect the king. Now he had orders to kill him.

And it needed to be done today.

Without witnesses. Without wounds. Before he could slip away.

Tracking his target from the nearby trees, he watched Ludwig as he left the castle grounds and strolled along the shoreline. The king wore an overcoat and carried an umbrella, protection from the threatening skies that had blanketed the region for much of the day. Normally the sun wouldn't set until quarter past nine, but the approaching storm made dusk come early.

A storm that would wash away any signs of foul play.

The assassin checked his watch and noted the time. Ten minutes to seven. Dinner would be served at eight and not a moment before. If his target was late, an alarm would be sounded and a search party would be formed.

That much was certain. This was a turbulent time in Bavaria, and Ludwig was the central figure in all the drama, somehow both loved and hated at the exact same time.

Some viewed him as a hero, a brilliant visionary who could do no wrong. Others saw him as a madman, a paranoid schizophrenic who had bankrupted the royal family with his flights of fancy. The assassin realized the truth was probably somewhere in between, though he couldn't care less about politics. He was there to do a job, and he would do it without mercy.

"Go to the boathouse," he whispered to his partner. "Signal me if we're alone."

His partner nodded and then crept through the woods without making a sound. They had positioned themselves along the northeastern shore of Lake Starnberg, the fourth largest lake in the German Empire. Created by Ice Age glaciers, it extended fourteen miles from north to south and two miles from east to west. This time of year, the water was too cold for swimming, effectively trapping Ludwig along the coast with no means of escape.

Without a boat, the lake offered no sanctuary.

Without a miracle, Ludwig would be dead before dark.

The assassin smiled, confident in his ability to finish the job. In recent days Ludwig had been followed by a team of guards whose sole task was to protect him. Not only from his enemies but also himself. This night was different. Bribes had been paid and arrangements had been made that would guarantee his isolation. As expected, the lone obstacle would be Ludwig's psychiatrist, a man of advanced years who watched over his patient. The assassin would strike him first. And then he would turn his attention to Ludwig, the fabled Swan King.

The assassin glanced at the boathouse, waiting for his partner's signal. The instant he saw it, he slipped behind his two targets, effectively cutting them off from the safety of the castle grounds. He did so silently, careful not to give away his position until he was close enough to strike. In a matter of seconds, he had cut the distance to twenty feet.

Then fifteen.

Then ten.

As he narrowed the gap to five feet, his focus shifted to the makeshift weapon he held in his hand. Plucked from the nearby shore, the stone was brown and jagged and stained with mud.

A moment later, it was covered in blood.

The doctor fell at once, unconscious before he even hit the ground. His skull shattered by the blow, his ribs fractured from the fall. Yet neither injury proved fatal. Minutes would pass before the doctor would take his final breath, his lifeless body dragged into the depths of the cold lake where he would eventually drown—punishment for the role he had played in the charade.

In the meantime, the assassin had more important things to worry about. Before leaving the royal palace in Munich, he had been given an assignment unlike any other. Two tasks that he needed to complete before he returned home. Two tasks that would rescue his kingdom from financial ruin and ensure its future for decades to come. Two tasks that would not be easy.

Get Ludwig to talk, and then silence him forever.

1

PRESENT DAY
WEDNESDAY, SEPTEMBER 15

Bavarian Alps, Germany
(61 miles southwest of Munich)

Klaus Becker stood perfectly still, careful not to attract attention as he eyed his mark from his concealed perch in a nearby tree. Some less-experienced gunmen would have used military-grade optics to guarantee a kill shot from this range, but what was the challenge in that? To him, if his prey didn't have a sporting chance, Becker wanted no part of the fight.

That was the code he lived by, the one his father had taught him.

The one he hoped to teach his kids someday.

Unfortunately, that day would never come because he would soon be dead.

Unaware of his impending fate, the forty-year-old cocked his head to the side and squinted as he stared down the barrel of his rifle. Suddenly the world around him blurred and the only thing that mattered was the mammoth target that had roamed into his field of fire.

Weighing more than six hundred pounds, the Russian boar had two deadly tusks that were nearly twelve inches in length. Highly intelligent and often cantankerous, wild boars were common in central Europe, but they rarely reached this size. Only mature males in the harshest of climates ever grew so large, which was the main reason that Becker had traveled here for a few days of hunting.

He wanted his shot at some sizable game.

The snowcapped peak of Zugspitze, the highest mountain in Germany, could be seen to the west. It was part of the Bavarian Alps, which stretched across the region like a massive wall and formed a natural border with Austria to the south. The rugged peak could be climbed via several different routes from the valley below, the one that cradled the town of Grainau, but none of the trails interested Becker. As an experienced hunter, he knew Russian boars would forage for food in the thick groves below the timberline—the highest elevation where trees and vegetation are capable of growing—so he positioned himself in the middle of the forest, far from the hiking trails and far from any interlopers.

Out here, it was Becker against the boar.

Just like he had hoped for.

After taking a deep breath, Becker made a slight adjustment to his aim and then pulled his trigger. Thunder exploded from the barrel of his Mauser M98 hunting rifle as the stock recoiled against his shoulder. A split second later, the boar squealed in agony as the 9.3 x 64 mm bullet entered its left flank and burrowed deep into its lung. Remarkably, the boar remained standing. Without delay, its survival instincts kicked into flight mode. Since the gun blast had come from its left, the boar bolted quickly to its right, disappearing into the undergrowth that covered the forest floor.

"Scheiße!" Becker cursed as he jumped out of his tree stand.

To kill his prey, he would have to track it on foot.

Following the blood trail, Becker moved with alacrity. Despite their girth, boars weren't fat like domestic pigs and could run surprisingly fast—able to reach speeds of more than fifteen miles per hour. Carrying a rifle and dressed in camouflage, Becker couldn't even travel that fast on a bicycle. Still, given the amount of blood he found on the hillside, he knew this was a race he would eventually win.

With every beat of the boar's heart, it was a little closer to dying.

And Becker wanted to be the reason it did.

Five minutes later, he caught up with the wounded boar in a natural cul-de-sac, formed by the steep incline of the mountain and a pile of fallen rocks and trees. Years of experience had taught Becker about the dangers of injured animals, especially when they were trapped. He knew if they felt threatened, they would attack with every bit of strength they had left. And since Becker didn't want to get run over by a six-hundred-pound bowling ball with sharp tusks, he stopped a safe distance from his target and raised his rifle to finish the job.

"Steady," he whispered in German. "I'm not going to hurt you."

The boar snorted loudly and focused its beady eyes on Becker while a soft growl steadily grew from deep inside its throat. Sensing what was about to happen, the boar decided to get aggressive. Suddenly, without warning, it lowered its head and charged forward, reaching its top speed in only a few steps. Becker expected as much and adjusted his aim, compensating for the boar's pace and the shrinking distance to his quarry. Without flinching or jumping out of the way, Becker calmly pulled the trigger, confident that he wouldn't miss.

Fortunately for him, his aim was true.

The bullet tore through the boar's skull and plowed through its brain, killing it instantly. One moment it was charging at Becker, the next it was skidding to a halt on its belly—as if someone had turned off its power via remote control. Just to be safe, Becker fired a second shot into its brain before he approached his prey for a closer look.

Although he had seen plenty of Russian boars in hunting magazines, the pictures didn't do the animal justice. This beast was huge. Coated in thick brown fur with stiff bristles, it had a large snout, sharp tusks, and a muscular torso. Becker walked around it twice, poking it with his rifle, making sure it was truly dead. The last thing he wanted was to be gored by an animal on its deathbed. He quickly realized that wouldn't be a problem with this boar.

Finally able to relax, Becker laid his weapon off to the side and touched the boar with his bare hands. There was something about a fresh kill—when the body was still warm and the blood had not yet dried—that satisfied something deep inside Becker, a primal urge that had been embedded in his DNA by long-lost ancestors who had hunted for food, not sport. Whether it was the adrenaline rush from the chase or the power he felt when he ended a life, hunting was the only time he truly felt alive.

Ironically, it was the thing that led to his death.

The first time Becker heard the noise, he didn't know what it was. He paused for a moment, scanning the terrain, making sure that another animal hadn't smelled the blood and come looking for a meal. He knew these mountains had wolves and bears and a number of other creatures that would love to sink their teeth into a fresh chunk of meat—whether that meat came from a boar or a hunter. Either way, Becker was ready to defend his turf.

But he wasn't ready for this.

Before he could run, or jump, or react in any way, the unthinkable happened. A loud crack emerged from the ground beneath his feet and the earth suddenly opened. Becker fell first, plunging deep into the man-made cavern under the forest floor. He was followed by dirt, debris, and finally the boar. If the order had been reversed, Becker would have lived to tell the tale with nothing more than a few cuts and bruises because the massive boar would have cushioned his fall. But sometimes the universe has a wicked sense of humor, a way of correcting wrongs in the most ironic ways possible, and that's what happened in this case.

A split second after Becker hit the ground, the boar landed on top of him.

Two tusks followed by six hundred pounds of meat.

If Becker had survived his fall, his discovery would have made him a wealthy man and a hero in his native Germany. But because of his death, several more people would lose their lives as the rest of the world scrambled to discover what had been hidden in the Bavarian Alps and forgotten by time.

2

SATURDAY, SEPTEMBER 18

Pittsburgh, Pennsylvania

Thirty feet below the surface of the Ohio River, the man probed the riverbed, hoping to find the object before a lack of oxygen forced him to ascend. He had been scouring the rocks for more than four minutes, which was a remarkable length of time to be submerged without air—especially considering the adverse conditions of the waterway.

Thanks to a midweek thunderstorm that had caused minor flooding in the region, the current was unusually swift. It tugged on his shoulders like an invisible specter. To remain in place, he had to swim hard, his arms and legs pumping like pistons. Eventually, all of his movement stirred up the sediment around him, turning the bottom of the river into a murky mess.

One moment it was as clear as vodka, the next it looked like beer.

Equipped with goggles that barely helped, he probed

the silt for anything shiny. He found an empty can and a few coins but not the object he was looking for. Yet he didn't get frustrated. If anything, his lack of success sharpened his focus and made him more determined. This was a trait he had possessed since childhood, an unwavering spirit that kept him going when lesser men would quit. A quality that had lifted him to the top of his profession.

A trait that made him dangerous.

In the darkness behind him, something large brushed against his feet. He turned quickly and searched for a suspect. Weighing over twenty pounds and nearly three feet in length, the channel catfish had four pairs of barbels near its nostrils that looked like whiskers. Known for their ugliness and their indiscriminate appetite, the catfish swam next to him for several seconds before it darted away. All the while he wondered if the fish had swallowed the sunken treasure and was simply there to taunt him. During his years in the Special Forces, he had heard so many fish stories from Navy personnel that he didn't know what to believe. Even if only one percent of them were true, then anything was possible underwater.

No longer distracted by the catfish, he continued his search. From the burning in his lungs, he knew he had less than a minute before he would have to surface—and he refused to do so empty-handed. With a powerful kick, he propelled himself closer to the riverbed, careful not to scrape himself on the rocks that dotted the terrain. Then, using his boat's anchor as a starting point, he allowed the current to push him downriver for a few seconds so he could gauge its strength. Since it was strong enough to move him, a 240-pound man, there was no telling how far it might have moved the artifact. Ten feet? Twenty feet? Maybe even fifty?

Or would its size and shape prevent it from being affected at all?

From experience he knew weapons sank fairly straight, regardless of the force of the river. Drop a gun or knife in a body of water, and it would sink directly to the bottom—even in a strong current. But something this small? He had no idea where it would land or what it would do when it got there.

In the end, all he could do was guess and hope for the best.

Careful not to stir up more sediment as he coasted along, he let the river guide him, hoping it would lead him in the right direction, praying it would take him to the treasure. With every passing second, his lungs burned more and more until it felt like he had inhaled a flame.

Time was running out, and he knew it.

If he didn't give up now, he would soon be dead.

Reluctantly, he tucked his legs underneath him, ready to launch himself from the riverbed, when he felt something metallic under his foot. Without looking, he reached down and grabbed it, then propelled himself toward the world above. Time seemed to stand still as he stroked and kicked his way through the murky water, unsure where he was or how far he had to go until he reached the river's surface. The instant he did, he gasped for air, filling his lungs with breath after breath until the burning subsided. Until he knew he would survive.

Then, and only then, did he notice the world around him.

The city of Pittsburgh to his east. The football stadium to the north.

And the crowded boat that had waited for his return.

"So?" someone asked. "Did you find it?"

Too tired to speak, Jonathon Payne simply nodded and lifted the lost bottle opener over his head. The instant he did, the partygoers erupted—not only would they be able to open the remaining cases of beer, but most of them had wagered on the success of his mission.

"Shit!" shouted David Jones, who had lost big money on his best friend. Although D.J. had served with Payne in the military and knew what he was capable of, he didn't think anyone could find such a small object on his first dive into the murky river. "Hold up! Let me see it."

Payne swam slowly to the boat and handed it to Jones. "Please don't drop it again."

"What do you mean *again*? I didn't drop it the first time."

"Well, someone did, and it happened on your watch."

"My watch? Why is it *my* watch? It's *your* boat."

Payne used the dive ladder on the back of his yacht to climb out of the water. Per tradition, he threw a party on the last weekend of summer to commemorate the end of the boating season. After today, his boat would be dry-docked for the cold months ahead.

"As captain of this vessel, I'm putting you in charge of the bottle opener."

Jones handed him a towel. "And what if I decline?"

"Then you're in charge of cleanup."

"Screw that! I don't do garbage. I'll guard this opener with my life."

"Yeah." Payne grunted. "I had a feeling you'd say that."

To the outside world, the two of them didn't appear to have much in common, but that had more to do with their looks than anything else. Payne was a hulking six foot four. Muscles stacked upon muscles, his white skin littered with bullet holes and stab wounds, his brown hair perfectly disheveled. He had the look of a gridiron legend, an ex-athlete who had lived his life to the fullest but still had more worlds to conquer. Born with a silver spoon in his mouth, he decided to sharpen the handle and use it as a weapon, serving several years in the military until his grandfather died and left him controlling interest of his family's corporation.

Unfortunately, he had been craving adventure ever since.

Jones, too, was an adrenaline junkie, but he looked more like an office clerk than an officer. Known for his brain instead of his brawn, he possessed the wiry build of a track star, someone who could run a marathon without breaking a sweat but wouldn't stand out in a crowd. Although his mocha skin and soft facial features made him look delicate, Jones was lethal on the battlefield, having completed the same military training as Payne.

In fact, the two of them used to lead the MANIACs, an elite Special Forces unit composed of the top soldiers from the Marines, Army, Navy, Intelligence, Air Force, and Coast Guard. Whether it was personnel recovery, unconventional warfare, or counterguerrilla sabotage, the MANIACs were the best of the best. The boogeymen no one talked about. The government's secret weapon. And even though they had retired a few years earlier, the duo was still deadly.

"By the way," Jones said, "I heard your phone ringing when you were underwater. What a *fabulous* ringtone. Is that a Menudo song?"

Payne growled and shook his head in frustration. A few weeks earlier, someone had figured out a way to change the ringtone on Payne's phone through a wireless connection. No matter what Payne did to stop it—including purchasing a new phone and even changing his number—the culprit kept uploading the most embarrassing ringtones possible. Apparently the latest was a song from Menudo, the Puerto Rican boy band that had launched many pop stars.

"Did you answer it?" Payne asked, confident that Jones was guilty.

Jones laughed. "Of course not. I'd *never* touch your phone."

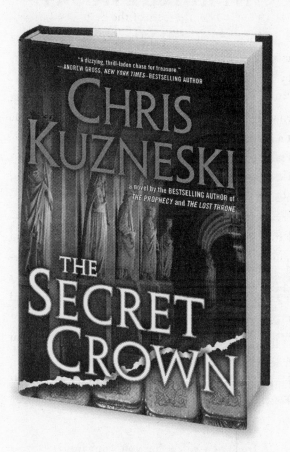

Chris Kuzneski

THE
LOST THRONE

Carved into the towering cliffs of central Greece, the Monastery of the Holy Trinity is all but inaccessible. Its sacred brotherhood has protected its secret for centuries.

In the dead of night, the monastery's sanctity is shattered by an elite group of warriors carrying ancient weapons. One by one, they behead the monks and hurl the bodies from the cliff top to the rocks below. The holy men take their secret to their graves.

Halfway across Europe, Richard Byrd has uncovered the location of a magnificent treasure, but there are those who will stop at nothing to prevent its discovery.

Hoping to save himself, Byrd contacts Jonathon Payne and David Jones and begs for their help. The duo rush to Saint Petersburg, Russia, and quickly find themselves caught in an adventure that will change their lives forever.

"A fresh new voice that you won't forget."
—W.E.B. Griffin, *New York Times* bestselling author

penguin.com

FROM *NEW YORK TIMES* BESTSELLING AUTHOR

CHRIS KUZNESKI

SWORD OF GOD

"Kuzneski's writing has the same kind of raw
power as the early Stephen King."
—James Patterson

In a secret bunker, one of the world's most dangerous terrorists is under interrogation—until he is rescued, and his captors are slaughtered.

Ex-MANIAC honcho Jonathan Payne vows revenge—but there is more to the bloody atrocity than terrorist reprisal. There is a plot in motion that, if successful, will burn the world in the fires of holy war.

FROM *NEW YORK TIMES* BESTSELLING AUTHOR

Chris Kuzneski

SIGN OF THE CROSS

Three crucifixions on three different continents.
A secret that could destroy the faith of billions.

On a Danish shore, a Vatican priest is found—
hanging on a cross. Within days, the same crime
is repeated…this time in Asia and Africa. Meanwhile, deep in the legendary Catacombs near
Orvieto, Italy, an archaeologist unearths a scroll
dating back two thousand years, revealing secrets
that could rock the foundations of Christianity. Its
discovery makes him the most wanted criminal in
all of Europe. But his most dangerous enemies op-
erate outside the law of man…

penguin.com